JAAN KROSS

A PEOPLE WITHOUT A PAST

VOLUME TWO *of*

BETWEEN THREE PLAGUES

THE STORY OF BALTHASAR RUSSOW

Translated from the Estonian by
Merike Lepasaar Beecher

MACLEHOSE PRESS
QUERCUS · LONDON

First published in the Estonian language as *Kolme katku vahel* by
Eesti Raamat, Tallinn, Estonia in 1970–80
First published in Great Britain in 2017 by MacLehose Press
This paperback edition published in 2018 by

MacLehose Press
An imprint of Quercus Publishing Ltd
Carmelite House
50 Victoria Embankment
London EC4Y 0DZ

An Hachette UK company

Copyright © Heirs of Jaan Kross
English translation copyright © 2016 by Merike Lepasaar Beecher
Copyedited by Rukun Advani · Map © Emily Faccini

The translator wishes to acknowledge the generous support received from the
Cultural Endowment of Estonia and its Traducta translation grant programme.

The moral right of Jaan Kross to be
identified as the author of this work has been
asserted in accordance with the Copyright,
Designs and Patents Act, 1988.

Merike Lepasaar Beecher asserts her moral right to be identified as
the translator of the work.

All rights reserved. No part of this publication
may be reproduced or transmitted in any form
or by any means, electronic or mechanical,
including photocopy, recording, or any
information storage and retrieval system,
without permission in writing from the publisher.

A CIP catalogue record for this book is available
from the British Library.

ISBN (MMP) 978 1 78429 954 5
ISBN (Ebook) 978 1 78429 955 2

This book is a work of fiction. Names, characters,
businesses, organisations, places and events are
either the product of the author's imagination
or are used fictitiously. Any resemblance to
actual persons, living or dead, events or
locales is entirely coincidental.

10 9 8 7 6 5 4 3 2 1

Designed and typeset in Cycles by Libanus Press
Printed and bound in Great Britain by Clays Ltd, St Ives plc

CONTENTS

ÅLAND

50 MILES

SWEDEN

STOCKHOLM

TALLINN

1	BISHOP'S HOUSE & OLD MARKET	8	APOTHECARY
2	ST NICHOLAS' CHURCH	9	DOMINICAN MONASTERY
3	DOME CHURCH	10	VIRU GATE
4	TOOMPEA CASTLE	11	TOWN HALL
5	TALL HERMANN	12	NUN'S GATE
6	ST OLAF'S CHURCH	13	GREAT GUILD
7	HOLY GHOST CHURCH	14	GREAT COAST GATE

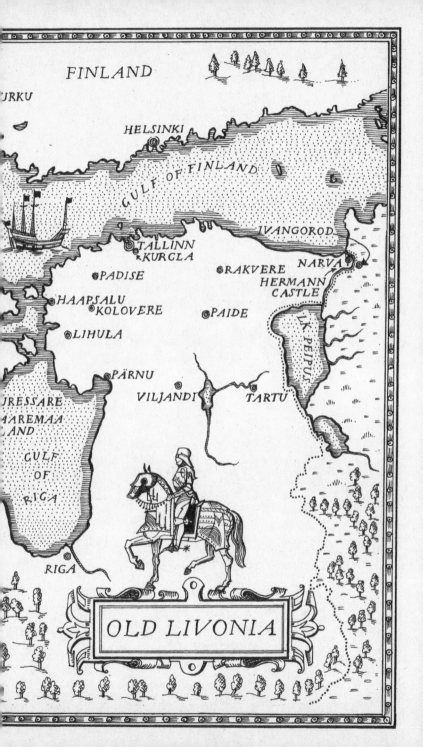

FINLAND

URKU

HELSINKI

GULF OF FINLAND

IVANGOROD

TALLINN
KURGLA

RAKVERE
NARVA
HERMANN
CASTLE

PADISE

HAAPSALU
KOLOVERE

PAIDE

LIHULA

LK. PEIPUS

PÄRNU

VILJANDI

TARTU

JRESSARE
AAREMAA
AND

GULF
OF
RIGA

RIGA

OLD LIVONIA

TRANSLATOR'S PREFACE

Between Three Plagues: The Story of Balthasar Russow was published between 1970 and 1980 in Estonia, in four volumes. In this translation, titles have been given to each volume: Volume I, *The Ropewalker*, includes Jaan Kross' first two volumes. Volume II is *A People without a Past*, and Volume III, *A Book of Falsehoods*.

Kross' story of Balthasar Russow (c. 1536–1600) is not only the life story of the man, but an account of his writing the *Chronicle of Livonia* (published in 1578 with a later edition in 1584). The *Chronicle* recounts the history of Livonia from the thirteenth through most of the sixteenth century, focusing on the period to which Russow himself was witness: the years leading up to and including the Livonian Wars (1558–83).

Balthasar comes from peasant stock, in a strictly stratified society dominated by German manor lords in the countryside and German nobles and gentry in town. They are largely descendants of the Germanic Crusaders who conquered the territory of Old Livonia in the early thirteenth century.* The Town Council is exclusively German. Germans dominate the skilled crafts as well as the professions in Tallinn, barring access to those of peasant background. They refer to the peasants as "bumpkins" and "yokels", and to town dwellers of peasant extraction as "non-Germans" or as "Greys". (Grey is the color of their home-spun clothing.) Opportunities for the non-Germans are limited. But Balthasar is ambitious. He grows up in the fishing village of Kalamaja, outside the walls of Tallinn. His father, Siimon Rissa, is a wagoner, hauling goods and peoples' belongings across Livonia. Siimon is able and willing to pay for his son's education at the town school. Bal is eager to learn, to acquire an education and gain a position in a world more exalted than that of his rural forebears and relatives. At the same time, he sees them as part of himself.

* In 1207, when the indigenous people of Old Livonia had been conquered and converted, the land was named *Terra Mariana*, in honor of the Virgin Mary. It was known by that name until 1561. (The name "Mary's Land" is used in the novel on occasion.)

The title of this volume, *A People without a Past*, was suggested by a few lines in the first chapter. As Balthasar is about to deliver his first sermon at Holy Ghost Church, he muses that he wants "to speak about the signs of God's justice in the fate of this wretched land where nothing is remembered". And when he looks down over the congregation, he realises what his mission in life is to be: "In this land where nothing is remembered, I should start writing down the things that have happened here, so that people will start to remember." A people without memory is a people without a past – a people without an identity. Already in *The Ropewalker* there are several intimations of the chronicler-to-be. Balthasar makes notes of current events and dates them, laughing at himself: As if I were about to start writing a chronicle! As a student in Stettin, he writes about Pomerania, imitating Julius Caesar's opening lines to his commentaries on the Gallic Wars. But the full story of the writing of the *Chronicle* is told in this volume: Balthasar's purpose in undertaking it, his doubts and apprehensions about what to include and omit, his efforts to collect information, and the attempts of the worthies on Toompea Hill to thwart its delivery to the printer.

There are several defining events in *The Ropewalker* that are recalled in this second volume. One is the opening scene in which Italian acrobats, visiting Tallinn in 1547, perform spellbinding feats of skill and daring on a rope high above the walls of the town. It is an event that remains in Balthasar's mind and memory all his life. Another defining experience is his time studying in Stettin, where he learns about the world beyond Livonia and becomes an educated man. His uncle clearly expects that it has created a rift between them. When Bal appears in Kurgla at the time of the peasant uprising he finds the villagers preparing to join the rebellion. Why, one might ask, is Balthasar drawn into the conflict instead of returning to Stettin to continue his studies as he had planned? Perhaps, in part, to refute his uncle's peremptory remark: "Of course, the peasant uprising is not your concern." Bal was not intending to join the peasants but once the challenge is uttered he realises that it *is* his concern, and he takes up their cause as his own. He affirms his loyalty to his kin and acknowledges his own peasant roots, but his travels and his education have revealed to him a wider world, one that his kin will never know. What he is determined to give to them and all their kind, with his chronicle, is their history – their past – and thereby an identity.

PART ONE

PART ONE

CHAPTER ONE,

in which a young man demonstrates that he has outgrown his immature ways and attitudes and indeed become a man, for he takes the time to ponder, even in the course of his daily duties and many obligations, the question of how he arrived at the position he holds, something that still causes him to marvel, which perhaps shows that his maturity does not yet extend much below the surface.

The house was without a doubt needlessly large and uncomfortably empty – this house of the pastor of Holy Ghost Church, here in the eastern part of the courtyard, between the school, the Almshouse and the back wall of the Apothecary. Its heavy grey limestone walls were crumbling, and its low windows in their lead casings peered across the small ancient graveyard at the high, stone-framed windows of the church, as if intent on staring down a rival.

Built at the same time as the church, the house was now nearly two hundred and fifty years old. The master-builder must have known, therefore, that he was not constructing just another residence and storehouse for some merchant, but a dwelling for the pastor of the church attended by both Town Council members and town Greys – someone who would require a home where he could also carry out his pastoral duties. And yet, the master-builder had not taken the trouble to draw up a specific plan for its layout or its rooms, and the house was built according to the same design as most merchants' and council-men's houses in Tallinn. Which is not to say that it was on a par with the finest of these dwellings, for the congregation of Holy Ghost

Church had, from the beginning, consisted primarily of non-Germans. For curious reasons now long forgotten, the church also fulfilled the functions of a chapel for the Town Council. Consequently the pastor's house was not at all inferior to the homes of, let us say, some of the less affluent merchants of the Great Guild.

Until the Great Cleansing of the Faith, many of the pastors of Holy Ghost Church (Johann of Gotland and several others after him) had taken it upon themselves when the situation required – and, as old records showed, sometimes even when it did not – to assume an owner's prerogative when making repairs. If we were to compare a house to a ship – for what is a house if not a cog or carrack or caravel, albeit made of stone, providing shelter to mortals on the unprotected seas of Time as they sail through fierce winds whipped up by the Evil One and past reefs strewn about in the sea by his henchmen, towards the shores of their Heavenly Father? In effect, if indeed we should wish to compare a house to a ship, we could say that this home of the head pastor of Holy Ghost Church had sailed through the time of the Great Cleansing into the days of our pure faith like a ship that had had the good fortune to bring both its stern cabin and its figurehead unscathed through terrible turbulence. If one had to acknowledge now, as we have done, that the house was beginning to deteriorate, it was through no fault of its occupants. For as the old men of the Almshouse – toothless, yet with plenty of bite to their remarks – observed at those moments on All Souls' Day when their allotted portion of ale had sufficiently loosened their tongues, the rear courtyard of their own Holy Ghost Church was only one of many places that provided evidence of a situation not to be denied: that is, that ever since the doctrine formerly promulgated within the houses of God had been cleansed, those houses themselves (and their outbuildings, which we are actually talking about here) had been neglected, some even falling into disrepair and decay. Not even Erik of Sweden had managed to improve matters, though he had been ruling the land – at least Tallinn, if not all of Livonia – for nearly five years. Of course, doctrine was what mattered most, not stone or plaster or paint. That went without saying. And religious doctrine was now so purified in Livonia that no other believers – not Anabaptists or Mennonites, not Water-carriers or Dung-carts or Zionists, or whoever they all were in Germany – could pollute this land. At times it also seemed to Bal that, leaving aside what had transpired with purifying the church of its "sinful pomp and splendour", the parsonages were simply not being maintained as they had been in the past. Simplicity in itself, of course, was pleasing to God . . . But then again – perhaps things were not quite like that, after all. Or was it that he just saw things differently now that the matter affected him personally – now that he was no longer the wilful offspring of a Kalamaja wagoner, nor a brash upper-level student at Tallinn's Trivium School, nor a lodger hungry for bread and knowledge, living with a poor assistant pastor? He was not even the deacon of this same Holy Ghost Church any longer, as he had been the past two years. Three weeks ago he had been ordained its pastor and presented to the congregation as "Pastor Balthasar Russow" – or, as he had heard someone say less formally, but most respectfully, "our Superior, Balthasar". . . unless that was merely an effort to curry favour, a mode of flattery which is sometimes difficult to distinguish from honest talk.

So that when our Superior Balthasar (*Hm!*) now walked between the stone slabs in the graveyard towards his door (*I must clean the dead leaves and splattered mud off these stones – or rather, I must have them cleaned . . .*) he was quite content with his new home, and yet somewhat dissatisfied. He considered with satisfaction the bold height of the gable: its grey peak, rising above the deep-blue shadow cast by the church roof, was bright with sunlight as far as the pulley beam (at least now, at midday). He was pleased with the twenty-four small glass panes in the great-room window with its thick iron bars that were visible from the courtyard – as though this were a storeroom for foreign treasures of the kind displayed in the shops of the town merchants. Pleased, too, with the solid fir door in its arched limestone frame, as he reached beneath his cape to pull out a heavy key from the pocket of his doublet. But he was not at all pleased to see that a number of moss-covered tiles had slipped out of place on the north side of the roof, letting the September rains of last week fall straight through into the attic. Nor was he pleased with the sadly neglected walls of the stables and barn. Nor with the worn yellow paint on the front door, nor the way in which the stucco had flaked off the walls in unsightly patches, as though the house were afflicted with eczema. Not at all pleased . . . Indeed, it seemed there was so much repair and rebuilding to be done here that he had no idea how, in these confoundedly lean times, he was to find the means for it all . . . It would not do to ask the gentlemen of the Church Treasury for more than a very modest sum now that he himself was at the head of its governing board. But the pitiful sum of fifty marks, by which his salary was to increase in his new capacity as Head Pastor, was next to nothing in the context of today's exorbitant prices, and especially if one needed to build or repair. And, in fact, there was the matter of his entire yearly income of four hundred marks, which was worth no more than seventy-three or four thalers! And what could a man possibly build with that when a mason charged a thaler for a threshold alone!? Or when a dram of communion wine cost a whole farthing . . .

He was about to thrust the two-pound key into the keyhole when it occurred to him that he could just use the knocker instead – *knock-knock-knock* – and the door would immediately be opened. For inside there was a maidservant, Barbara, who had come with the house. She had served the departed Herr Schinckel before him, and rumour had it that she was the widow of a mercenary soldier in the service of the town, killed fifteen years ago in some skirmish or other, and thus she had become Schinckel's housemaid while still a young girl – and everyone knew what else she had become as well . . . Now known as *Barba*,* she was a large-boned woman, with a smooth face and lively eyes. On Saturdays she curled her ash-blond hair with a curling iron, and in the process filled the entire house with the smell of scorched hair, all the way up to the attic. Her breathing was often so pronounced that her high, pointed breasts heaved and fell visibly under her white linen apron. She was both inquisitive and garrulous, though in this regard (apparently thanks to Herr Schinckel's instruction) she knew more or less where to draw the line. One thing was certain: she knew all the gossip in town.

Balthasar refrained from using the knocker and opened the door with his key. Perhaps it was a penalty he imposed on himself, because, as it suddenly struck him, he had been more aware than he should have been of the rise and fall of the maidservant's breasts . . . The key made a grinding sound in the lock. He laid his cloak over the outstretched arm of the girl who had hurried to receive it – he would have preferred that the girl not be at home just then . . .

She said: "Twice, there were those looking for the Pastor."

"Who?"

"The man . . . um . . . it was the man the Pastor was going to hire as the new bell-ringer, Märten . . . or something . . ."

"Ah. What did he say?"

"He said he'd come back this evening."

"Hm. And who else?"

"There was a messenger from the furrier. The Pastor's coat is ready."

"Already . . . ? Fine."

He motioned with his chin for the girl to go back to the hearth in the kitchen and remained standing, straddle-legged, in the middle of his great-room.

* Later referred to as Barber.

Yes. The room was in fact quite bare. It was a good thing that the congregation had put some benches along the walls, else the room would have been completely barren. His own things could not have been put in here anyway, since the great-room was being used for confirmation classes. In any case, abundance of possessions was scarcely his problem – what did he even own that he could have brought here from his deacon's apartment? A few chests with clothing and books. A bed. A lectern. Three stools. A few plates and bowls. That was all. He had even been obliged to sell the silver inherited from his father in order to pay his debts to Herr Sum and others. Yet, empty though it was, the room was beautiful – with its smooth and not too scuffed limestone floor, its clean white walls, its broad ash-wood stairway, its white log ceiling decorated with painted pink blooms and green foliage. Not inferior at all to the great-room of Rector Wolff, which he had considered very fine indeed. And not smaller either, even though the northern third of the room had been walled off long ago for use as the sacristy – for which the church had, oddly enough, not found space within its own walls. A separate door led into the sacristy from the courtyard. Another provided access to it from the great-room.

Stepping to the door of the sacristy, Balthasar looked to left and right. It too was fairly bare, but for a few pieces of furniture donated by members of the congregation. A lectern. Next to it, a window framing a view of the north-east corner of the church and the *köster's* house and the red roof of the girls' school in the autumn sun, which sent transparent, iridescent beams of light through the window and across the limestone floor. On the lectern, the parish register with its brass corners. (An interesting book to leaf through, comparing the handwriting of Böckhold and Wanradt and Koell and Killonius, the crabbed script of one and the flourishes of another . . . Fifty years of the christenings and weddings, births and deaths of the town Greys.) Behind a small iron door in the left wall was a vault containing the congregation's money – a paltry sum, to be sure – and important papers. He then turned to examine the great-room. It was about the size of a small wedding hall, if one saw the sacristy as part of it – and the staircase, rising wide and grand and straight up to a sudden, bold curve, which seemed to be all but calling to him, summoning him to ascend to the small room next to his bedchamber, which he was planning to set up as a proper writing room.

All said and done, and notwithstanding its several warts and blemishes, he found this an unexpectedly impressive and stately house, and a sense of well-being enveloped him like a light, warm, woollen garment, though the chill wind of incredulity managed to penetrate it from time to time, for the garment was not all that thick . . . But then even the wind was not exceedingly icy, and it blew in gusts that were becoming ever less frequent . . .

After living three weeks in the house, Balthasar did not yet feel *entirely* at home. But he was wholly content with his own rise in position and status over the course of the last three years, with the exception, perhaps, of what had happened at the beginning, upon his return from Bremen, when he had disembarked in the harbour in Tallinn and set out for Kalamaja with his bundle and chest. It reminded him of the way he had left this homeland harbour five years earlier. For he had no more possessions upon his return than he had had at his departure. Just the reverse: in that early-dawn hour when he had stolen aboard the *Dolphin* at a pier wet and slippery with seawater, to set out on his distant journey, he had at least had two heavy bags of bread with him. Upon his return, not even one. (All he had brought back was Märten's carving, mainly because something had held him back every time he was on the verge of giving it away or leaving it behind.) When he left, he had had a hundred and sixty silver marks in his purse. When he returned, he was two hundred and twenty-eight marks in debt – he owed Kimmelpenning a hundred marks and Herr

Sum a hundred and twenty-eight. But of course he had an inheritance awaiting him in Tallinn. He knew that once he had paid off his debts he would still have about fifteen marks jingling in his pocket. In addition, he was now in possession of an education . . . Even so, the most he could hope for was a position as deacon in some dilapidated church in an outlying northern village, most of whose inhabitants had probably fled into the woods. He could not hope for a post as pastor, even though the peaked roofs of his beloved Tallinn, crowded inside their stone-wall enclosure, looked rather modest and unassuming compared to the rows of grand residences in Bremen with their several storeys and verandas, reflected in the river below for a distance of half a league. His prospects seemed still less promising when he noted that under the rule of King Erik the town had lost the last remaining traces of its faded prosperity. As he trudged from the harbour towards Kalamaja, peering out from behind the chest he was carrying on his shoulder, Balthasar saw that Herr Horn had still not managed to repair the bites his cannonballs had taken out of the walls of Toompea. And saw that the Poxhouse at the Great Coast Gate was in ruins, and that the soldiers of His Majesty Erik, King of Sweden, Duke of Estonia, *et cetera*, had not received their wages for nearly half a year – judging by the faces and attire of those that were unloading barrels of some kind off a Swedish carrack onto the pier.

But Balthasar had barely a day or two to rest under Annika's care at Kalamaja. She had endless questions, of course, which was not surprising at all, considering his five-year absence and everything he had seen – distant towns and countries and men and schools with exotic, unfamiliar names. She was eager to hear from him about everything. And then Balthasar had to answer one particular question as well. Judging by the tone of voice in which she posed it, it was to her the most important one – or so it seemed to Balthasar.

They were sitting together in the old, low-ceilinged chamber where

Balthasar had lived for most of his boyhood years. In the course of the first day, half the night, and the following morning they had each asked and answered countless questions, so that, listening to her brother's vivid descriptions, Annika began to feel she could actually see the scenes he described, as if she herself had returned from wandering in those distant lands. And Balthasar began to feel as though here he might soon take the reins of his life in hand again. For it appeared that not very much had changed after all, even though his father was dead and his cargo-transport business had been terminated. And Kimmelpenning was dead, too. And Meus. And old Truuta. And the Doctor and his wife had moved away to Mitau a year ago (*Really!*) for Herr Kettler had in the meantime become Duke of Kurland under the Polish king (*Oh yes. That I know.*) and living under the Swede had become too risky for the Doctor. Incidentally, it was said that Kettler had once locked him up. Mitau of course suspected him of maintaining contact with Stockholm. And yet, after everything . . . these old log walls, these smells of smoke and soot and bread and tar and leather, these low ceilings. My God, those three knots in the half-hewn logs above his plank bed were still there! Those knots in the wood that had always become two eyes and a mouth when he had lain there as a boy, staring up at the ceiling in the darkening hours – the eyes and mouth of a household spirit, or an angel, or his Kurgla grandfather, or an earth-god, or God in Heaven. Together all these things exuded some kind of – oh, Balthasar knew it was childish, but still – a surprising sense of safety and security. As did his "big sister", already a woman of thirty-four or five, redolent of resin soap, and even in her plain grey dress – plain as the attire of the Beguines – she was a beautiful and brave and self-possessed widow, a genteel lady (for how else would one speak of a pastor's widow but as a lady?). Balthasar did not yet dare enquire about her plans for the future, or whether there might be a prospective husband on the horizon . . . And then Annika asked the question:

"Bal, you didn't get the letter I sent to Stettin, in which I told you about father's death, did you?"

"No."

"But the one I sent to Bremen, did you get that one?"

"Yes, as I told you."

"Yes . . . But tell me . . . what I wrote to you about Herr Vegesack . . . the story he told me on his deathbed – is it true?"

Instead of answering, Balthasar asked: "Has anyone else here besides Vegesack said anything of the kind?"

"No. I know that for certain. I committed everything he told me to memory, in detail. I never heard anyone else mention you. Only I do remember that the day the peasant leaders were brought from Kolovere to Tallinn and taken to Jerusalem Hill to be broken on the wheel (there were eleven men), that same day Father came to town and stopped in to see me, and he mentioned in passing that he wondered where you might be. I said no doubt you were in Germany. He agreed: no doubt that was where you were. So – you were not here at that time?"

Balthasar knew he had to give an answer that he could stand by. Had Annika broached the subject even a minute earlier, the heady joy of homecoming, in which he was still afloat, would have induced him to say too much . . . But now, just a split second after learning that Siimon too had held his tongue, Balthasar felt that he had the right to keep silent as well. Without having to chastise himself for keeping secrets. For *knowing* does not necessarily contribute to one's peace of mind. Neither for the one who knows the secret, nor for the one who knows that his secret is known.

"You're asking whether I was here . . . ?"

Balthasar looked his sister in the eye. Maybe it was purposely such a long look. Purposely, so that his sister, if she were astute enough, could interpret his answer this way or that.

"No."

"Aha," said Annika, with a kind of shameless and familiar and therefore doubly irritating casualness. "So now I know."

"Know what?"

"Well, that the answer is – No."

They spoke no more about it. When would they have had the opportunity anyway? For Balthasar had to hurry to town to notify the Council of Clergy. He wanted to take care of this right away, so that the waiting period of one or two months, over which the decision concerning his assignment to a pulpit would be made, could begin as soon as possible. He had paid the necessary visit to the secretary of the council at the sacristy of St Olaf's Church, Meus' familiar old sacristy, after which he would have to wait only one more week. In the meantime, Herr Balder had snared him into joining the new schoolboys, all complete strangers to him, in slogging through a performance of the *Trinummus* by Plautus, with Balthasar in the role of Megaronides. He also served as assistant to the rather lazy Herr Balder in the staging of the production. The next day, after the performance at the Town Hall, he was summoned to see Herr von Geldern – in such short order, it seems, because Herr von Geldern had deigned to attend the performance.

Balthasar did not think it likely that a conversation with this gentleman would be especially difficult. To be sure, Herr von Geldern's star had risen with meteoric speed in the intervening years. At present he was neither more nor less than the superintendent of the entire Swedish territory of Estonia. And even though the boundaries of *his* territory were vague and tended to change daily, Herr von Geldern was indisputably the most powerful individual in the local church, *de facto episcopus**, an honour bestowed by King Erik himself. From what Balthasar could remember of a brief encounter with the man at the home of Annika and Meus, he was an affable enough gentleman –

* De facto bishop (Latin).

23

especially to those who paid sufficient heed to his stature. It was no sin, after all, that Balthasar still owed a hundred marks to the departed Kimmelpenning's estate. Had a novice preacher ever returned home free of debt after his studies in Germany, he wondered. Besides, no-one knew a thing about his debt to Kimmelpenning. Nor about his debt to Herr Sum. True, Rector Wolff may have sent a letter of complaint to the Town Council about him before receiving the money from Herr Sum – if that were the case, Herr von Geldern would know about the debts. But unpleasant though they were, these were old matters, after all, by now long settled. Herr von Geldern could know nothing about the rest . . . Nothing about all the times that the Devil had lured the young student from the path of virtue into the thickets and swamps of vice (as the Horned One is known to do with students). Nor could Herr Geldern know just how far off the path Balthasar had swerved in his student days and what kind of unanticipated detours he had taken (as one, who was by now lying under the sod, had noted) . . . it would be sensible, in any event, to keep eyes and ears open. For Balthasar could hardly hope that the Lord God would repeat the miracle He had once before performed for him when hope and fear hung in the balance – the time he had been summoned to Rector Wolff, expecting to be punished for his foul acts, and instead, lo and behold, became the rector's young friend.

He could scarcely hope for that . . . And yet, God had a very similar outcome in store for him on this occasion. Possibly one even more curious.

Herr Johann Robert von Geldern received Balthasar in the same large parsonage of St Olaf's Church, on Lai Street, where he had his residence and saw his parishioners, and which had now been fitted out as the seat of his superintendency as well. Unlike the way men of rank and status often treated their inferiors, Herr Geldern did not keep Balthasar waiting before acknowledging him. He set his goose-quill down on the writing desk as soon as Balthasar entered and turned towards him in a friendly manner.

Yes, he was a little older and greyer. But he was still the same agreeable gentleman that Balthasar had met at the home of Annika and Meus, big-boned and grey-eyed, wearing a splendid cloak trimmed with mink, for his study, on account of its high vaulted ceiling and thick walls, was quite cold. Nor did he need to rummage around in his memory to recall if he had ever met Balthasar before yesterday; he recognised him right away and blessed him, making the sign of the cross over him with the astonishing hauteur and facility with which high officials execute such ritual gestures.

"Yes, I remember you. From our meeting at the home of our young friend Frolink, whom God took from us much too soon. What a fine, full-flavoured plum wine he served us. Do you remember? The Doctor and Frau Katharina were in Finland at the time . . ."

Herr Geldern deigned to converse most affably with Balthasar. True enough. But he had not merely grown slightly greyer, he had also become a little more self-important, considerably more self-important, one might say. For in the corner of his ever-judging and evaluating eye, there seemed to be a glint from time to time of what could only be disdain – *So, this is the next yokel who intends to lay claim to our pulpit . . .* – or something to that effect. And his voice, off and on, was tinged with irony. It was the kind of hearty pretence to friendship that prominent older men enjoyed using with much younger ones – it was not pleasant. God knows what experience Balthasar was drawing upon, but his view was that they mostly played this kind of game when their intentions were not the best.

"Well, well, so now you are back in your homeland. Yes indeed. What you said about Bremen was very interesting. By the way, with respect to religious strife, we are at peace here, thank God. Even though the war is not about to come to an end. Of course, we now have a stable power in the land. But even quite recently the wretched state of our constantly shifting hopes and fears drove even some of our brightest men to act like fools. I'm thinking of our friend the Doctor. At present he is serving Kettler and the King of Poland. Did you know that? It is, of course, no fault of yours. You were already in Germany at the time. I know. And his poor little wife is not at fault either. Of course not . . . So, now you are back then, and we have to set you up in a pulpit. Well, you can no doubt imagine the state of our Christian church these days in the counties of Harju and Järva. There is no shortage of positions . . . more than half the pulpits are empty. But more than half the congregations no longer exist either. Because all of them –Moscow and Poland and Denmark, the bands of Tatars, the manormen, and all kinds of looters and pillagers – they're all out for themselves. So if our Swedish Majesty's army is not nearby to keep peace and order, one could say that as soon as the fires in a village die out, smoke begins to rise from the manor. And it's the same with the churches. Some are in ruins from the war, others from decay. Not to mention the church estates. So, in conclusion . . ."

Balthasar knew just what Geldern would say next: He would say, in conclusion, that though he had nothing splendid to offer him, it might be worth his while, as a young man setting out to plant his first tree in the Lord's vineyard, to bear in mind what Jehovah said to his fore-fathers: "In the sweat of your brow shall you eat bread." And Geldern would probably add – for good reason, given the current state of things (such elderly and respectable men always spoke for good reason, even when there was only a grain of truth in what they were saying, the Devil take them!) – Bal could almost hear him say it: In the sweat of your face, by the sweat of your efforts, in preparation for the possibility that your own blood will flow, if the Lord God has so determined . . .

But instead, Herr Geldern said: "So, it is truly the Almighty's own hand that intervened, just last month, to arrange things in such a way

26

as to enable us to offer you a position as second deacon, alongside Bushauer."

Balthasar thought quickly. It was well known that among Livonian pastors there were several bearing the same family name, harking back to those distant days when a parish was akin to a gold mine, so that the first man in the family to attain a pastorate immediately summoned his even minimally qualified brothers and cousins to follow him, manoeuvering his sons into good positions, too, as early as possible. Only in rare cases did the names actually reflect a true familial calling . . . But Bushauer . . . Bushauer . . . ? Balthasar could think of only one man by that name: five years ago he had been deacon at Holy Ghost Church, a small man, like a little loaf of well-risen barley bread, a somewhat simple and silly fellow. But in what other country parish was there a Bushauer? Was it in Hageri? At least that wasn't an utterly godforsaken outpost . . . even though the church had apparently burned down. No, there was another, Bu . . . Bü . . . Bunemann . . . in Ambla? Well, Ambla would do . . . though the area had been plundered. But wait, the deacon there was . . . who was it? . . . yes: Buddenbrock!

"That would be – for which church, your Honour?"

"For Holy Ghost."

"Which Holy Ghost?"

"The only Holy Ghost Church in the entire bishopric is the one in Tallinn. And that is the one I have in mind. *Ha-ha-ha-ha*! And just where else would I put a man like you?"

On Friday afternoon of the same week in which Balthasar was to deliver his first sermon at Holy Ghost, he was summoned to the Kõismäe Hill district to serve Communion to a sick parishioner. In fact, it was Pastor Schinckel who had been summoned. But Schinckel had the fever with which he was often lately afflicted, and did not even know if he would manage to make his way across the cemetery to the church the following morning to hear Balthasar's sermon. Bushauer, meanwhile, had badly twisted his ankle in a fall on the slippery streets after the winter's first frost. So that it was Balthasar who went to serve Communion. On his way home in the bitter cold, he sought shelter in the Grey Seal tavern near the harbour, from the icy north wind that blew right through his light dogskin doublet. He sat down amid the hum of talk, in front of the hearth. When he had drunk half his beaker of wine, he heard the strains of a drunken song – the buzzing pub had quietened to listen to it.

Balthasar recognised the singer immediately, the grey-stubbled, one-legged beggar who had managed to get hold of – the devil knows where – a kind of cymbal. It was none other than Lunt-Laos, that harbour vagrant and Almshouse inmate, the former rope-maker. As shipping in Tallinn declined, Lunt-Laos had sunk ever deeper into drink. And then about five or six years ago, when the Muscovite tried to take the town, he had joined the townsmen in fighting off the enemy in the Sandhills, where he was hit by a bullet from an arquebus and lost his right leg – he was lucky to have survived. Now he stumbled about in the harbour and at the market and begged in the taverns, and, swigging beer, bragged about his glory days as a craftsman: the time, for example, when he was charged with making a rope for those Italian skywalkers – the world's longest magic rope, the rope of all ropes – for no other rope-master could promise to twist that rope as quickly as he. When Laos was fortunate enough to get a little more to drink, he sang to the tavern guests, either his own songs or those he had picked up in other pubs, droning and ambiguously worded ditties that could be bitingly sarcastic. He had on occasion been put into the stocks in the tower behind the transport yard, on account of his vulgar songs. But since it seemed somewhat grotesque to lock such an old, one-legged derelict with a crutch, in the stocks – and since no-one could fully remember the words to his songs after the fact, not even Lunt-Laos himself, the bailiff had always released him, cursing: "If you, you infernal blackguard, have sunk so low as to become a beggar, abandoning the honest work of a rope-maker, you had best abandon your old trade completely! Or else I'll have you twist a rope for your own scrawny neck!" At the moment, Laos was intoning a song that Balthasar recognised immediately, and he set his half-empty beaker down on the table and listened. But this was a song that would not have offended anyone in the Tallinn of King Erik.

> Ordermaster in Livonia was I.
> My name is known in places far and nigh.
> I am Lord Kettler. Everybody knows me,
> Most of all the girls, the pretty ones, especially.
> My sweet whispered words went to their head
> And softened them up . . . and they came to my bed.
> I've been fined and whipped – Heaven's made me pay.
> In thicket and swamp I hide to this day.

Yes, there were a couple of lines here that Herr Antonius had not sung to Balthasar that time. But then followed some completely unfamiliar, surprising new verses:

> A doctor was living in Tallinn town,
> Held by two lords in high renown.
> Half his money he received from me
> And half came from the Swedes, you see.
> He rolled up his sleeves to doctor me,
> And who knows what he rubbed on me . . .
> I threw him in gaol with the help of my men,
> And his loving wife approached me then.
> She hastened to me, knowing no shame,
> And shot that red arrow, without shame,
> That between her snow-white thighs she kept
> When I with her in Riga slept.

At this point the bearded seamen and the barge-workers and even some snobbish Blackheads, who had come into the pub to get warm, howled and guffawed so heartily that Laos paused to empty his beer mug and pushed it towards them for a refill, before continuing:

Then I set the husband free,
In return for his wife's generosity.
I gave him estates – I cared for him well –
Along with serfs whom he could sell.
Let merciful God recall this good deed
At this poor sinner's last hour of need.

The new wave of jeering laughter did not match what had preceded, but it overwhelmed Balthasar nonetheless. As did the din of the revellers, which rose again once the laughter had subsided. Balthasar gulped down his wine and slammed the door of the Grey Seal behind him. There was nothing in the song he did not already know. He knew Katharina had lain with Kettler too . . . and whether it was only in Tallinn or in Riga, as well, didn't really matter . . . Even so, it was one thing to know it, and confoundedly another to hear a song about it, in a place like this. To hear it all rehashed amidst the jeers and the guffaws . . . *Ooh!* Balthasar rushed headlong towards the Great Coast Gate and felt the bitter wine and a burning shame rise in one hot surge to his heart, even as the piercing, icy, north-east wind lashed his back. The swords of shame and rage clashed against each other inside him . . . He reached the shelter of the Great Coast Gate. He was sweaty and he was cold. Or had he contracted Herr Schinckel's malady?

No. He did not have a fever. But the strangely coinciding sensations of hot and cold did not abate. At least not by the time of his inaugural sermon on Saturday morning. Later, both the sermon and the day itself were only a hazy, superficial memory. It had not gone as anticipated, had not been nearly as memorable as that occasion, long ago, when he had had his first intimation of the marvel of words, of their power to touch hearts and move people – that unforgettable moment next to his grandfather's coffin in the back chamber at Kurgla.

The severe frost of that candle-month* in 1563 arrived without warning, and the church was cold through and through. Just like a misty ice cave, thought Balthasar as he entered the church by way of the small north-east door and started towards the pulpit. Foggy, from the breaths of the assembled townspeople in their jackets and jerkins, shawls and sheepskin coats, a grey mass, the colour of weather-beaten boats. Oh, he should have been concentrating on the Scriptures, on the passages which formed the basis of his sermon, the twelfth verse of David's Psalm 88, which he had translated himself from Doctor Luther's Bible: "Will they know Your wonders in the dark, and Your righteousness in a land of forgetfulness?" He had wanted to talk of the miracle that God had wrought – in protecting and punishing – but finally in protecting this town. He had wanted to feel in himself God's miraculous intervention, in that he, Bal, son of Siimon Rissa, was speaking to them from the pulpit of Holy Ghost Church ... Yes, he had wanted to speak about signs of God's justice in the fate of even this wretched land where nothing was remembered . . . But instead, he was thinking as he climbed the steps to the pulpit, that the people murmuring and wheezing down there sounded like a snowstorm blowing over the frozen gulf, and the stairs were creaking in the cold almost like the fence posts at Kalamaja on a morning of a bitterly cold frost. There was Traani-Andres, over there, with his yellowed face and grey beard, next to his lively wife Krõõt and son Päärn, nearly a man already. And there were Taavet and Käsper, who used to work for Father on his cargo wagons, and dozens of familiar faces from Kalamaja . . . hundreds of faces. In this land where nothing is

* February.

31

remembered, he thought, I should start writing down the things that have happened here, so that people will begin to remember (but vulgar songs in taverns should be prohibited!). Later, when he knelt in the pulpit and straightened up again and was about to speak, he felt a throbbing shame because of that one indecent song, as though yellow polecats were racing over his chilled body, and his mouth was stiff with the cold. He knew that whatever he did manage to say would not reach those grey, bundled forms, but would hang in the frigid air between him and them, suspended above the mist of their exhaled breaths.

And so it was that the lewd song about Katharina remained oddly associated in his mind and memory with his inaugural sermon. But in the flurry of the first months at his post, when he was not only pulling his own wagon but that of Schinckel and Bushauer as well, he scarcely had time to ponder the surprising ease with which he had acquired his position. To tell the truth, it was still not clear to him which was the more remarkable – the way he had become a deacon at the venerable Holy Ghost Church of Tallinn, or that which happened a few months later.

On a windy spring morning of that year, 1563, he was urgently summoned by the Superintendent's scribe to a meeting of the Church Treasury at the Great Guild. The devil only knew what it could be about. Discussions at those meetings usually included all possible church matters relating to salaries, living quarters, repair work, the upkeep of church buildings, and the oversight and financing of church lands. Balthasar arrived late; he had barely managed to seat himself at one end of a bench when a dozen pastors and church elders, nearly all of whom he knew, at least by sight, entered the small guildhall with Herr Geldern at their head and sat down in the carved seats along the walls. As he passed Balthasar, Herr Geldern whispered through a cloud of musk:

"Balthasar, do not say no, when I say yes!"

Herr Geldern asked Pastor Tegelmeister of St Nicholas' Church to say the opening prayer. He would not burden himself with that task. After that the assembly sang "A mighty fortress is our God" in smooth, practised voices, but with a kind of professional passivity, because they were amongst themselves here, after all, so there was no need to summon particular feeling or enthusiasm. Then Herr Geldern spoke:

"With the help of God, our Church Treasury has for a long time been that little boat of reeds in which the money matters of the Christian church in Tallinn have been floating like the child Moses, unharmed and healthy, along the crocodile-infested river of time. But old men grow weary, not only at the helm of large ships, but also at the helm of our Treasury. Therefore, we would like to grant our brother, Herr Lambert, the relief that he has requested of us: that is, to be freed of his responsibilities as manager of our financial affairs, in order that in the remaining years that Our Lord grants him, he might devote himself to the care of his congregation. For he is carrying seventy years and more on his back, and his eyes can no longer distinguish a shilling from a farthing, which in itself is a small matter, but it might eventually lead to the kind of confusion in our accounts that those who wish us ill could use to damage our good name. So let him minister solely to his congregation from now on. It is not our fleshly eye but our spiritual eye which distinguishes the seed of God from that of the Devil, and we are confident that he can manage that quite well."

It was clear that Herr Lambert's situation had been settled beforehand. There was not a murmur of protest among the lords of the Treasury. There was but the sound of sand peppering the red–blue–yellow panes of the guildhall windows – the whirling winds had been gaining force – and the voice of Pastor Harpe of St Olaf's, intoning an amen in support of Herr Geldern's comments. Whereupon Herr Lambert laboured to his feet and cleared his throat. He screwed up his eyes as he pulled the seal and key of the Treasury out of his pocket and laid them down on the little table next to Herr Geldern's chair.

Then he bowed, partly sideways, partly with his backside towards the assembly, and said:

"I humbly thank Our Lord and my esteemed colleagues for the help that He and they have afforded me until now."

And then, shuffling slightly, yet moving quite nimbly, he stepped towards Balthasar and took a seat next to him.

In effect, as to the gratitude to God and colleagues that Herr Lambert expressed – there were grounds for it. For Balthasar had heard that the confusion created under Lambert's aegis in the Treasury was so great that it could have occurred only under an eye that not only saw no difference between a shilling and a farthing, but could not distinguish between a silver thaler and a black bull, either. Herr Geldern continued:

"And thus we need a new man to replace Herr Lambert for the next three years. As we all well know, the supervision of the Church Treasury is not an easy matter; it demands an enormous amount of time and exactitude. And thus I believe that we should not ask one of our elder and more distinguished members to shoulder that task, for their responsibilities to their congregations already represent a formidable burden – and the greater their dedication, the greater that burden. We will choose a young man to head the Treasury. One who has so far shown himself in a good light and who aspires to even greater recognition. We will keep our eyes on his hands without embarrassment, and stand behind him with both our blessings and our horsewhip. I believe that our young friend Balthasar Russow is the best man for the job, and for this reason I have summoned him to appear here before us."

Perhaps, when Herr Geldern spoke of finding a *new* man for the job, Balthasar had an inkling for just an instant of what was about to come. Who knows. Be that as it may, his surprise now was so great that it was several moments before he became aware of the buzz and murmur that rose from the gathering. He had no idea how business was handled at such a meeting or how likely it was that Herr Geldern's extraordinary proposition would be approved. When the murmur subsided and no objections were voiced, he realised that they were in agreement with Herr Geldern because of the rumours about him. Rumours about his close contacts with certain highly placed men in Stockholm. Certain lords close to King Erik himself. That was why they were swallowing his outlandish proposition. But Balthasar did not have the chance to ask himself why Herr Geldern was doing what he was doing, because someone coughed – ah, it was the ever-irascible, ever-sickly Herr Tegelmeister, Head Pastor of St Nicholas' Church and former director of the Trivium School, where Balthasar had been a student not so very long ago – it was he who had coughed, though quite respectfully, and now he spoke:

"Our esteemed Herr Superintendent's choice is a very good one. But should we not give the man who has been chosen more time to attain a level of maturity and competence in these affairs? I am raising the question, merely – well – in the interests of protecting him, if I may put it that way. And naturally, in our own interests as well. And thus I wonder – were it not even better to appoint someone to oversee our financial affairs, whose personal wealth provides evidence of his ability to manage property and money, in order to prevent another slide into a situation where the Treasury's money might get mixed up with the treasurer's . . ."

Herr Geldern interrupted him with a smile: "My dear Tegelmeister—" And it was clear to Balthasar that the cordial tone was intended to convey a message: Stop your quibbling! "My dear Tegelmeister, the best man for this job is one who has nothing himself that might possibly become mixed up with the Treasury's funds. Thus, if he suddenly acquires something beyond his means, it will be immediately apparent, and we can demand to know where he got it!" He turned to Bal: "Is Balthasar Russow prepared to assume responsibility for the Church Treasury if we lay this burden upon him?"

35

Balthasar stood up to reply. He had, despite his own circumspect stance, recovered remarkably from his initial astonishment.

The Treasury's affairs were without question exceedingly complex. He would have to manage thirty or forty thousand marks in mortgages on fifty town houses. Interest. Leases. The Almshouse settlements with their incomes and expenses. The salaries of pastors, deacons, cantors, *kösters*, bell-ringers, and servants of the church. Apartments. Renovations. He would have to see to it that all payments were deposited and nothing overlooked and that everyone received his due . . . An overwhelming job . . . But if he managed – Good God, how could he handle it? – someone who had never managed more than a mark a week? – But if he did manage it, he would be next in line behind Herr Geldern . . . If . . . But if the others trusted him, and since Herr Geldern apparently trusted him (but why? – no doubt, because of his deep insight into human nature, why else . . .), why should he then doubt himself . . . ?

He heard, on the other side of the wall, the footfalls of market goers on the cobblestones, heard the wind whip up an armful of trash on Saiakang Way and toss it against the high red–blue–yellow panes of the guildhall window . . . And he said, almost angrily:

"My lords. You decide this matter." (In point of fact, that's the way matters actually stood. The decision was theirs, not Herr Geldern's.) "It is up to you. I have just one thing to say. There is perhaps not even one among you less suited for this position than I." (The "perhaps" rendered the statement more or less true. At least he did not have to be embarrassed by his words. For all the men here had been serving much longer than he – be it in the Town Council or the church.) "But there is no-one among you who would put greater effort into the job if it were assigned to him."

He sat down. Though he dropped into his seat rather abruptly, he felt, even before his behind touched the bench, a little ashamed of his answer, notwithstanding that some of the lords nodded and murmured approvingly at his words. He felt that the way he had composed his response, uttering first the *con* and then the *pro*, and not vice versa, showed very clearly that he actually desired this most burdensome position. Naturally, it was not because of his reply, but because of Herr Geldern that the members of Tallinn's Church Treasury approved Balthasar as its manager that very morning.

After that it did not especially surprise him when, upon the death of Herr Schinckel, it was he, Balthasar, who was elevated to the position of Pastor at Holy Ghost, and not little Bushauer, his fellow deacon, who had faithfully toiled at his post for nine years. No, all this did not surprise him much anymore. For just how much does it take to convince a young man of his own mettle? No, no – not his mettle as measured according to God's standards, but as compared to those around him and next to him on life's path. Especially since he had already found, in the course of his life, some evidence of his abilities – on the shore at Kalamaja, for example, prising rocks out of his father's cabbage patch, and in his first year at the Trivium School, and even up in St Olaf's steeple that time . . . So why should he have any doubt at all about his qualifications for filling Herr Schinckel's position? He had certificates from several institutions of higher learning. Rector Wolff, too, had finally sent him the one from Stettin. Moreover, he had a genuine whiff of Wittenberg about him! He had not had time to become a Master. But what he had attained was more than sufficient to qualify him to be Herr Schinckel's successor. And the Superintendent respected him (a Wittenberg man himself, after all!) though at times Balthasar was not entirely convinced of his respect. There was that occasion, for example, when, after a regular meeting of the Council of Clergy, Herr Geldern had stopped in front of him with a seemingly friendly, though somewhat barbed, remark:

"Well, and how have we, poor sinners – *ha-ha-ha* – how have we lately taken care to ensure that the Lord God *have* something for which to grant us forgiveness . . . ?" There was a kind of mockery in this that puzzled Balthasar, and he was at a loss as to how to respond.

Yet he knew that Herr Geldern had spoken well of him on numerous occasions – among other things, about his efforts with respect to the affairs of the Church Treasury, which began to function smoothly as a result of his hard work. Herr Geldern had especially hailed Balthasar's ability to minister to the congregation of Greys – childlike, coarse, stubborn as they were. To be sure, this praise could be interpreted this way or that . . . But in any event, Balthasar spoke to the Greys in their own tongue better than any other preacher in Tallinn. Better than Harder, who had largely forgotten his parents' tongue and could manage but a mangled, broken speech – which he nevertheless seemed to take pride in. And also better than Mõnnick and Bushauer, and even better than the pastor of the Almshouse Church, Jürgen Kur, a native of Patika, who had maintained his rough country-speech despite his university studies in Rostock, and who spoke it with great gusto, not only in the pulpit, but on the street and at the market as well. But compared to any of the others, Balthasar knew the language better and more extensively than they did. He knew all its words and idioms, their direct and suggestive and figurative meanings, its curses and insults and, in addition to all that, the yarns that were spun into song. Yes. And he took special pleasure in trying out the words with his tongue and then shaping them against the roof of his mouth to make them clear and solid, and then – *whoosh!* – letting them take flight, or – *boom!* – tossing them out into the congregation. And he had noticed that his flock enjoyed it too, even though he took them to task much more sternly for their indifference and lethargy, their cheating and stinginess, their backbiting and complaining, and a thousand other failings than the departed Schinckel, with his halting, mincing words, ever had.

Furthermore, his interactions with his congregation involved more than admonishing them to mend their ways. There were occasions when the shepherd and his flock shared a deep sorrow or great joy such that the distance between them seemed to dissolve entirely, causing him considerable unease. He was, after all, a learned man, educated in German schools, in effect a Herr (not, of course, like Harder and others who outdid the Germans at being German), but he too was nevertheless a Herr! The country folk from the outskirts – from the villages of Kõismäe and Pleekmäe and Kalamaja and Härmapõllu – and the town's domestics and hirelings living in servants' quarters and hovels, should not so publicly have overlooked that . . . Or, God knows whether they should have overlooked it or paid heed to it . . . It would have pleased him most had they not so openly forgotten his status but had behaved towards him as they generally did with any man of standing. Yet at the same time he wished that he might feel – granted, not all the time, which would perhaps become burdensome, but now and again, at moments when the heart needed it – that in these low dwellings, in these sooty corners behind the pigs'-bladder windows, by the light of a splint-flame or oil lamp, at wedding or funeral feasts, at cradles and graves, at the cry that accompanied the entrance into this life or the departure from it, and in life's everyday trials and triumphs – that he were thought of not *only* as a Herr, but also as one of them . . .

In fact, that is the way the general attitude towards him was taking shape. And so he did not have much cause to wonder about his advancement. But this house, in which his reasonably explicable success suddenly became visible and concrete – as he looked from the threshold of his sacristy to left and right, around and above him, at the solid white walls half a fathom thick, at the vaulted ceilings and the stairs – this house still surprised him. Which is not to say that he felt out of place in it, exactly . . . But he had undertaken at least one activity to justify this very large room: he was giving singing lessons here to the schoolboys of Holy Ghost Church. The departed Beseler had begun this instruction a dozen years earlier, but it was abandoned by his successor, Schinckel. Beseler was a conscientious and hard-working soul who had translated the Gospels into the local tongue – a text still used by the congregation of Holy Ghost. He had planned to publish a hymn book as well – had a manuscript half-finished when the plague took him to his Maker in the year '54, just as had happened years earlier with Susi-Hans, whose hymn translations made up the bulk of Beseler's manuscript. So now Balthasar, following Beseler's example, herded the older boys of the Holy Ghost School into his great-room every Tuesday and Friday afternoon. The benches stacked along the sides of the room were set up in rows. And two dozen young scamps, fledglings and whelps in grey jerkins, with close-cropped hair and bright eyes – the ones whom God had blessed with even the most minimal singing voice – clattered into their seats. *Köster* Caur, whose eyes, blue and bleary, evoked the mask of tragedy and whose greasy white beard resembled a chicken's rump, sat at the little positive organ borrowed from the storeroom of St Nicholas' Church. To Balthasar it seemed as if he were seeing two dozen replicas of his younger self, as he stood in front of these boys, from whom he caught whiffs of sweat and mud, boot polish and oatmeal porridge. He took Beseler's old manuscript out of the drawer in the pulpit and began:

"Boys! I say, and I will repeat: You are the ones who must lead the congregation in song! They have to learn from you, so that no-one listening to the singing need be pained, and so that, in time, their singing will bring joy both to their fellow man and to God. Repeat after me:

O God grant that here and now
A time of peace may reign!
What rod and staff can comfort us
And keep us safe from harm,
But Yours alone, O Lord?!"

40

The boys repeated the words as well as they could, two, three, four times, and as Caur warmed up the organ, which at first wheezed and then blared, and the bright young voices rose to follow the music, Balthasar listened. How beautifully Susi-Hans had managed to fit his words to this little song of Doctor Luther's, the words and melody coming together in a way simply not to be found elsewhere in country-tongue, though in German the verses of Waldis of Riga or Sachs of Nüremberg also demonstrated similar felicitous phrasing. And among church hymns, there were only Luther's own masterful verses . . . Why was it that the Lord God sometimes summoned to Him the brightest head before it could complete what it had begun for His glory, before it could begin to spread its light into the darkness . . . ? He could remember old Siimon talking about Susi-Hans. In school and in church, people even today were talking about his remarkable intelligence. Lying on his deathbed, in the grip of the plague, he had had sufficient strength and clarity of mind to stipulate that the farthings he had inherited from his fishmonger father for his education not be merely distributed among relatives. They were to support his mother until her death, and most of the money was to go to the Town Council for the education of a young man who would undertake to finish the work that he, Hans, had begun, for sooner or later one such was bound to come along . . . And the words of Susi-Hans, the words of his verses, were to this day the riverbank of purity and clarity that the congregation, following the lead of the boys' choir, strove with such uneven results to reach. But at the time of his death, Hans was only twenty years old . . . Thinking about that made this great-room of the pastor's house seem even more unjustifiably grand than it perhaps really was . . .

"Barber!"

This was the slightly gruff, curt name commonly used in these parts for women of the lower classes who had been named for St Barbara. This was not the case for noblewomen such as Barbara Tisenhusen from Rannu, the unfortunate woman about whom Balthasar had heard so much talk during his own schooldays, before the start of the war and all the unrest that followed.

"Barber – you may bring the food to the table!"

"It's already on the table, Pastor."

Balthasar stepped into the great-room. Right. The little round table had been placed under the window, bright with its twenty-four opalescent panes. Upon the table a pewter tray of steaming meat made his mouth water, and next to it was a tankard for beer, fashioned of alternating strips of light and dark juniper wood that Uncle Jakob had brought from Kurgla. Barber had wanted to substitute a German beer stein for it, but Balthasar instructed her to carry on using the one made of juniper. It imparted a most pleasing, bitter smell to each sip of beer. So the table was set. A dogskin was spread out on the stone window seat, as it had been every day in recent weeks.

"Sit down and eat with me."

This suggestion was so unexpected (yet perhaps secretly hoped for) that Barber's quick, grey eyes rounded in surprise.

"I . . . I've already eaten . . . You were so late . . . but, well, of course . . . thank you – I—"

"Come, come. And bring two beakers. Two of the larger ones. Fill them with red wine. You know, from the cask in the sacristy."

It was the same wine he served at Communion, and he had already drunk a goblet of it himself. (For it is said that one should not muzzle the ox that threshes the grain.) And he still owed Timmermann for twenty measures.

Barber returned to the table with the wine beakers. She had dried her face, damp from the heat of the hearth, and combed her ash-blonde hair. Her calm, somewhat expressionless features were flushed, and she tried to keep her eyes downcast – but darted a quick glance at Balthasar, in spite of herself.

"Sit down."

Barber put the beakers down and took a seat on the dogskin. Balthasar realised only now that he had expected her to bring a stool for herself. The dogskin was not from a particularly large beast, and Barber's backside was not especially small, so that Balthasar had either to sit partly on the cold stone or quite close to his housekeeper. Alright, alright. He sat partly on the stone and folded his hands. "Bless, O Lord, this our meal." He did not audibly speak the words of the prayer. Maybe he didn't even articulate them in his thoughts. For he did not like what he intended to do. But Barber's sitting down on the dogskin spurred him on. Yes, that which restrained him in effect spurred him on . . . The fact that Barber so obviously looked at him as if she herself were the widow of a master craftsman – a widow with house and work room, be it forge or tannery or what-have-you, with all its tools and stores of materials and even its customers – a widow unattached now and available, and as if Balthasar were but a journeyman to her departed husband, a journeyman who had risen to master-status and moved into the house but had not yet managed to fulfill *all* the obligations due the master's widow. Whether by way of a trip to the altar or otherwise, that in itself was of little import. Honest artisan-widows through the generations had managed this by means of a respectable marriage ceremony, to be sure, but she – Oh Lord, she, the forgotten Klaus Schreilaut's Barber, the departed Herr Schinckel's Barber – would, in the case of this strapping young man, place her trust in God's mercy even without benefit of the sacrament . . . And there was no reason that this village wagoner's son, which he was, after all, should spurn her.

"Well, let's drink. To warm ourselves. This house is so cold."

They emptied their beakers halfway. Balthasar gave Barber a piece of roast pork and picked up a good-sized chunk himself. This was not Dr Friesner's upper-class table and they made no attempt to use those awkward pronged utensils.

Balthasar could feel the wine spreading through his limbs, as his body, shivering with cold, and his thoughts, shuddering with aversion to this woman, grew warm. He said:

"Well Barber, tell me: what's the news in town? And what are people saying about the pastors?"

This was the first time the new pastor had turned to Barber in this way over the three weeks he had been living in the house, his first personal words to her. Barber realised suddenly that there was an opening in the impenetrable wall around this man. The door had opened a crack . . . Why should she not hasten in with quick step and willingly? The news? Heavens . . . there was nothing in particular to report . . . People always talked about the lives of the pastors, of course, and their doings . . . in whispers naturally, as always with the gentry . . . But the stories did indeed reach her ears, being *one of them*, after all . . . not the pastors' wives, but their housekeepers and serving girls and even some of the assistant-pastors' wives and those of the cantors and bell-ringers, naturally, so that . . .

Balthasar would like to ask her outright to tell him what people in town think of the fact that he has taken Schinckel's place. But he thinks it best not to start with himself. He decides to use a side-door. (With no idea of just how close he is about to get to the flaming hearth which will make his face burn . . .) He has noticed that the housemaid at Herr Geldern's – Greta, fortyish, talkative – is Barber's friend and kinswoman. He touches his cup to Barber's and asks:

"And how are things in our new bishop's house?"

For six months ago, Herr Geldern was officially pronounced bishop, having been duly elevated to this honoured status by means of all ecclesiastical ceremonies and royal edicts. Barber takes a large swallow of wine and draws a deep breath of relief that he has posed a question that she can answer at length. She shifts in her seat, moving (perhaps unawares) a bit closer to her employer. And he (very aware) stays where he is, noting her damnably pointed breasts.

Barber says: "Aye, the bishop's house is full of happiness and joy now . . . for the third year already . . ."

"But it hasn't even been a year yet . . ."

"No, I'm not talking about that. The mitre on Herr Robert's head – that's another matter . . . that's such a big thing that – well, as if I didn't know about these things . . . being that if God hadn't called my Herr Schinckel to him, he might've—" (This of course reveals Barber's ignorance . . . the very fact that she can talk seriously about Schinckel's prospects . . . it's laughable . . . in Tallinn no pastor of a Grey congregation would be elevated to bishop . . . and she actually thinks Balthasar wouldn't know any better . . .) ". . . If indeed God had not called him away. But I was going to talk about something else – about the fact that now, after a long time, there is peace and sunshine in our bishop's house. After several years of stormy and cloudy weather. As it always is with married folk – no matter who they are, whether a bishop and his wife or a simple pastor and his, or some rude mercenary and his young wife – when the millstone which the husband has rolled onto his wife's heart is rolled away. Whether by God, making use of a chance event, or by the husband himself, which can also happen from time to time . . ."

"I don't understand what you are talking about."

"I am talking about the fact that for a long time a heavy burden weighed on the heart of our bishop's wife. Rolled there by the bishop. Or let's say – the Devil. As one might put it, just between us. And in any case, this discussion here – as the Pastor of course understands – is just like one in a confessional. Yes. When the lady of the house carries a burden of some kind on her heart, then there is no sunshine in the house and it is gloomy and cold and everyone's mood is dark. But when the weight is rolled off or the cloud is blown away, the sun comes out and shines on the inhabitants of the house in such a way that . . ."

Barber had nearly emptied her beaker and in the meantime they had also drunk beer with the meat and bread. So that several times already the housekeeper had looked straight at the master of the house with her slightly bulging grey eyes – perhaps to indicate to Balthasar the possibilities of sunshine in this very house. But the master of the house asked:

"What cloud and millstone are you going on about?"

"Why, it's about the stone that was lifted from Frau Geldern's heart, of course, when the Doctor and his wife moved away from Tallinn to live with Kettler!"

"Why did that matter to her?"

"Good Lord, that Katharina, that wicked witch, had wrapped our bishop so around her little finger that . . . Exactly the way they say that things were, or even worse than they were, in the dark days of the popes, with all those wenches and harlots and paramours of the bishops . . ."

"Katharina, the Doctor's wife . . . with Herr Geldern?!"

"Oh yes. There's no way the Pastor would know. The Pastor was already in Germany. And it was not talked about outside the Gelderns' house. But I knew about it from Greta long ago. And the clouds are not completely gone even today, I take it. Just last year, she was deeply troubled when Herr Robert went on a visitation to his churches in Harjumaa and when it was later revealed that he had galloped off to Pärnu for three days – just a week before the Poles took it over from the Swedes."

"And why was the bishop's wife concerned about *that*?"

"Well, Frau Friesner was supposed to have arrived in Pärnu from Mitau at just the same time."

"Last year . . . ?"

"Last year – yes. But these were merely passing worries for her. The kind that wives of great lords always have to bear. And the shrewd ones are shrewd enough not to make a noise about it. And our bishop's wife apparently also said: 'My old man is making a fool of himself with this witch and risking his life, galloping through battle areas and

46

rioting marauders, into towns besieged by the enemy, and here he is elevating into pulpits those who formerly bedded that witch . . . But I thank God that that witch has at least gone away from here.'"

Elevating into pulpits those who formerly bedded that witch . . . *Hm* . . . This was naturally somewhat unpleasant to hear. A blow to one's honour . . . And to hear, once again . . . mention of her lovers . . . Balthasar, with God's help, had put the whole affair behind him. Quite some time ago, in fact. But it would be interesting to know who . . .

"And whom did the bishop's wife . . ." (suddenly, Balthasar's voice became oddly hollow, and he lost the end of his question, so that he had to make an effort to rephrase it) " . . . mean . . . by . . . her . . . former . . . lovers?"

For even in mid-sentence he was overcome with shame at his ignorance, yet the shame dissolved, became inconsequential, for it was followed by the dismay of realisation. The dismay of certainty.

But no! But no! But no!

But it was, in any event, the dismay of possibility . . .

He put down his wine beaker and stared at the greyish wall that had once been a white wall. So here was the reason for Herr Geldern's unexpected kindness and the reason behind Balthasar's unaccountable advancement! Not his own merits, after all!

He did not really hear what Barber was saying, her voice coming from somewhere distant . . .

"You're asking who it was that she was referring to? By God, I don't know. In this town alone there are over twenty men in different pulpits, and then you add the ones in the countryside. And I'm not sure even Greta knows. But if the Pastor wishes, I can find out tomorrow."

Balthasar murmured: "That won't be necessary. Not necessary at all." And he realised just how impossible, how utterly impossible it was to brush off Barber's story as the mere gossip of women chattering around a soup kettle or washtub. On account of one particular memory

47

that now flashed before his eyes. It was the expression he had once seen on Frau Geldern's face. A momentary expression. It was on the one and only occasion, six or seven years ago (Lord, how long ago!), when the Gelderns had come to visit Meus and Annika at the Doctor's house. Herr Geldern had been complaining about a pain in his back, and when he heard that the Doctor was not in Tallinn at all but in Finland, he asked: "And what about his beautiful wife Katharina, is she with him, lost like a pearl in a haystack?" That was the moment when the curious expression had slipped over Frau Geldern's face, the pained, angry look of a jealous woman.

Which meant it was all true. And he himself was enjoying the honour of his current post not because of his own competence and effort, but rather because... Oh God, had he really been foolish enough to consider his elevation to a respected position as evidence of a miracle performed by God, a miracle he had earned by his keen intelligence and indefatigable hard work? And now it was revealed that it was in fact a gift from Satan – a reward for his lechery.

He pushed the table back with such force that one of its legs, catching between the stone floor tiles, cracked.

"Enough!"

He did not want to meet Barber's eyes, round with surprise. He wanted to look away, but, on purpose, glared into her face instead. He stood up. He felt as though he had dirtied his clothes with something indecent. As though he should tear them off and cast them into the fire. And as though he absolutely had to do something, go somewhere, undertake something. And free himself from his housekeeper's glance. He muttered:

"Clear the table. I'm going to the furrier's."

He noticed, only when he was halfway down Apteegi Street, that he was bareheaded and coatless, wearing only his doublet, and that he had forgotten to take along money to pay for his coat. If, that is, he were to go to the furrier's at all, which seemed suddenly of too little consequence to make him return home for the money. At the moment he could bring himself to do nothing but continue on his way, straight ahead, without arriving anywhere too soon. Furthermore, he would have had to take the it from the church's strong-box, for he barely had a mark and a half to his name, and the coat – though a fairly inexpensive one of simple Göttingen wool lined with the cheapest red-brown calfskin – still cost twenty marks.

He stomped down Apteegi Street with a hurried and heavy tread, hands behind his back, teeth clenched, eyes half closed. Reaching Munkade Street, he burst into the abbey courtyard and clomped noisily through the squealing throng of boys batting at a rag ball and making the mud fly. Perhaps he was thinking to himself that twenty years were as nothing in God's eyes. He acknowledged some of those who greeted him, by raising his chin, but did not respond to many others, for he did not notice them. He turned into Müürivahe, behind the abbey, and marched on vaguely towards Bremen Tower. It was not anger that was driving him on. It was the despair of not being able to get out of his own skin. He realised: there were people who knew, maybe everyone knew – of course, everyone knew that Balthasar Russow had become the pastor of Holy Ghost Church because Frau Friesner had . . . favoured him . . . her act of charity – yes, as an act of charity – *oooh!* – the charity of the very woman who was the subject of shameless songs sung in the taverns of Tallinn . . . And this was inside him, it was all around him. He could not get it out of himself nor get himself out of it. On his right, rising up out of mounds of mud and rubbish was the town wall – wall, wall, wall, wall . . . Maybe, looking at the severe, dark-grey, fifteen-cubit-high wall, he even felt a sense of satisfaction at the sight of something so clearly insurmountable . . . But then he came to the cobblestone street descending to the Small Coast Gate, and the inner-gate towers and the arched gate itself and beyond it. Here he saw, squeezed between the protective walls, the long, narrow, grey enclosure with the outer gate at one end, and beyond it a flash of the autumn green of cabbage plots on the other side of the moat. Balthasar did not go out of the gate but trudged on past it and along Müürivahe Street towards Hattorp Tower. Perhaps his spirit rebelled at the very sight of the gate, for its presence there was at odds with the intensity of his despair.

He rushed past people coming towards him, without noticing them. For the twentieth time he thought: And so my advancement and my position are forever linked with that harlot's skirts . . . He did not even notice the smells emanating from the houses and the archways, the way he usually did – the smells of juniper and aspen shavings from the coopers' workshops, the odour of tannin from the leatherworks, the acrid clouds of coal dust and iron filings from the smithies . . . He thought: I'm afraid that harlot's carnation scent will forever be in my nostrils, no matter how much I blow my nose and sneeze . . .

When he turned left at Herr Brockhusen's houses to trudge up to Sand Hill, intending to keep to the backs of the buildings in order to arrive at St Olaf's Church, the gates at the old Russian covered market to his right were suddenly pushed open and, about fifty paces ahead of him, a motley crew of a hundred mercenary soldiers poured out onto the street. Right, the covered market now housed the Swedish garrison, as mandated by the Town Council, which had even given permission for stoves to be built into the ramshackle merchants' houses. It was necessary to concede this to the Swedes – they ruled the land, after all. It had been denied to the Muscovites – mere visitors – for fear that if allowed to build stoves for themselves they would settle here, whereas if denied, they would scurry back home every winter to the warmth of their own stoves. The whooping and laughing and yawning herd spreading out into the street up ahead irritated Balthasar a little. He slowed his pace to give the company time to start moving.

He thought: So this unruly cohort snatched from the taverns of Stockholm constitutes a quarter of old Herr Horn's forces, which are supposed to ensure us a more secure era in Livonia? But there has never been an era as insecure and tottering as the current one . . . King Erik is waging war against the Danes and Poles and the Muscovite, all at the same time, and the local fortified castles have been changing hands for many a year . . . And most bizarre of all – Duke Johan, Herr Horn's duke, Balthasar's duke, as it were, is locked up in Gripsholm Castle, a prisoner of his brother Erik . . . Bal paused for a moment, recognising on the breeze the odour of horses from Brockhusen's stables – a sweet smell from his childhood, reminiscent partly of home, partly of Kalamaja, partly of his father's work clothes . . . He thought: But if there is in me even a kernel of that temperament and spirit that I have dared to believe in, will it now abandon me . . . simply because Katharina spoke to Geldern on my behalf? . . . The company ahead of him shambled up the hill in disarray, with its captain and provost and unit leaders, and he followed. And what did the gossipy blather of old women matter? No! It mattered not one whit to him what someone somewhere might have said! Whatever truth there might be in it . . . Nothing inside him would disappear because of it – if it was truly there. And he would show them . . . He quickened his step, for he could no longer tolerate the ambling pace of the soldiers. He would show them yet, by God . . . He caught up with the company and started to push his way past them. It was not dangerous, of course, for a man in broad daylight on a city street . . . Threadbare peasant jerkins. Multicoloured rags like jesters' costumes . . . Snatches of talk mingling with the smells of onion soup and beer:

"Five thalers and a new linen shirt – all lost up the arse of a card game . . ."

"But a wench like the one in the backroom of the Green Frog . . . ahhh . . ."

"Here or in Germany or Finland or Ingria – it's all the same, no matter what flesh you're thrashin' . . ."

Flat peasant faces. Ash-blond brows. Pale new beards sprouting. Jutting chins, upturned moustaches, the faces of brawlers looking for a fight. Clever, dull, arrogant, mocking eyes. Scars, both old and fresh, criss-crossing tanned cheekbones, scars received the devil knows where – in Bleking, Småland, on ships at Lübeck, on the Danish islands, on Gottland, in Ingria, Haapsalu, Pärnu, near Paide, or in hand-to-hand skirmishes right under the gates of Tallinn . . . Balthasar pressed on between the soldiers, who made way for him more or less politely. He thought: I do possess after all – yes, I do – the wherewithal to prove to myself and others . . . if I just apply myself, as I plan to . . . if God will help me . . . He continued at an ever-quickening pace through the shadows cast by the plumed hats, through the tramping of boots and the smells of boot polish and sweat. Someone recognised him. Someone grunted: "Hoho . . . Herr Pastor is flying by like a bullet . . ." And another voice added: "As if he were trying to squeeze in a quick little visit to the bell-ringer's wife before delivering his sermon to us – ha-ha-ha-ha . . ."

Balthasar realised that, unarmed as they were, the men were heading for the old convent church, which had now been handed over to them as the garrison church. He thought: Go on, go on. And listen to the sermon. Pray. Cleanse your souls. Every one of the likes of you has filth in his soul . . . For just an instant he felt his own purity, his superiority, to this coarse crowd – and then, a pang of shame . . . But he suppressed it – it was not appropriate just then . . . With slightly intoxicated pleasure he thought (who knows where it suddenly came from): Yes it was all in him and around him . . . these men, their faces, acts, words, smells . . . and those of all the other troops that walked the ground in this land . . . and their captains and field marshals and dukes and kings . . . and this town, whose walls echoed with the stomping of their boots . . . and the people of this town, its burghers and Greys, its men and women, the lives of all of them – and the countryside around this town all the way to the horizon and beyond the horizon . . . inside him and around him . . . not cadged for him by Katharina but granted to him by God . . . He managed to get past a large, bald provost, and found himself next to a captain wearing a plumed hat. He glanced at the young face with its sparse reddish moustache. He had seen the man before, but where? When? Once past the company of men, he came out onto the open street. Behind him he heard the soldiers turn into the convent courtyard. Hurrying on towards Nunna Tower, he suddenly remembered: that captain with the red moustache was none other than Ensign Boije, whom he had met eight years ago in Turku, in the waiting room of the duke . . . *Hm* . . . Herr Horn had apparently eluded the suspicions of King Erik only as a result of his extraordinarily adroit maneouvring. He had of course been very close to the duke, who was now considered a traitor to the state. Many of his retinue were now shorter by a head – even those of lesser status, and some had experienced the anger of the king in other ways. Like this fellow here, apparently, who had been an ensign at twenty and now at twenty-eight was just a captain, while others in that time had been elevated to field marshals . . . What remarkable, memorable stories there were in this land where nothing was remembered . . . He raced along Mäealuse Street, towards the gate at Pikk Jalg, sensing, rather than thinking: All of this is in me, and from time to time I feel like an overladen wine press and realise that I just have to start pressing it out – "Why – hello Herr Balthasar! Master! Herr Balthasar has come for his coat!"

Only at that moment did Balthasar realise that he had in fact marched into Master-Furrier Gandersen's workshop, where the furrier and two journeymen were hard at work.

Master Gandersen was straddling a long bench under the open window, his stomach pressed against a vertical post rising from the bench, with a two-cubit-long scraper attached to it, rounded at the front like the prow of a cog. He was working on a beautiful grey-brown badger hide. *Swish-scrape, swish-scrape*, he pulled it from one side and then the other, back and forth across the rough paunch of the scraper, so that the afternoon light coming from the window shimmered in the sour-smelling cloud of tannin. Master Gandersen's journeymen were greasing fox pelts at a table under the stairs leading to the great-room. The snub-nosed Peeter was the one who had hailed Balthasar upon his arrival. Outside, visible through the open window, four apprentices were at work in the middle of the yard, between the house and the barn at the base of the knoll. Using narrow staves they were pounding the pelts stretched out on wooden blocks – pelts of wolves or dogs or who knows what creatures, beating the dirt out of them. *Whack! Whack! Whack! Whack!* With each whack what looked like a fine dusting of snow rose into the air.

Master Gandersen got off his workbench nimbly enough, considering his years, and stepped forward to greet Balthasar – he could hardly have done otherwise, for even though Balthasar was of peasant stock, he was a clergyman. And the master craftsman did not overlook the necessary courtesy due a cleric, no matter that he himself was distinguished, prosperous and possessed of the dignity of age. Moreover, Master Furrier Gandersen of the shop behind Rataskaevu Street – a German who had long been a citizen of the town, a man of fifty with slightly slanting black eyes and a dour Tatar face – was not by nature arrogant or haughty. He knew his place: his wealth and prominence put him roughly in a middle position among the town's master craftsmen, or perhaps slightly above middle, but not by much. His polite haste was precisely suited to a sensible master artisan's encounter with a client such as this. He told Peeter to clean his hands of grease immediately and to bring the Pastor's coat, and at the same time he exchanged a few suitable observations with him about the way September this year was as unpredictable as April . . . And only when Balthasar was standing in the middle of the workshop in his new fur-lined coat, surrounded by cloud shadows and various floating hairs and dust particles and by brown and reddish and yellow and grey animal skins, and when the master and his journeymen stepped back ceremoniously, and the apprentices who had entered the room clicked their tongues as if to say, Just look at how fine a piece and how well, with God's help, it has turned out – only then did Balthasar recall that he had no money with him . . . He pursed his lips and calculated quickly how he might handle the situation respectably. Yes, in the name of decorum there was nothing left but to borrow the money from church funds . . . He said:

"Someone should come with me, to whom I can hand over the payment."

"Peeter would be accompanying you in any event," said Master Gandersen. "Herr Pastor should not have to carry his coat himself, after all."

"No, no, there's no need of that . . . I'll just leave it on," muttered Balthasar, and only too late realised, first, that his modesty was misplaced, inappropriate to his status (he still did not know how to be who he was!), and second, that the master might view it as an attempt to postpone payment. But instead of choosing a new track, he continued on the same one. "The weather's cold, after all. That's why I came wearing only a doublet."

"As Herr Pastor wishes," the master agreed, "and there's no hurry whatsoever with the payment . . . None at all . . . It's not as though we were dealing with some who-knows-who . . ."

Just then Balthasar heard someone coming *tap-tap-tap* down the stairs in back of him and a pleasant, soft voice said: "Father, I'm going to Pikk Street to see Birgit. Send someone to fetch me at ten o'clock."

"Listen, Elsbet," said Master Gandersen, "since you're going in that direction, go along with Herr Balthasar. He'll give you the twenty marks."

So, he's in a hurry for the money after all, it seems, and he does think I'm some who-knows-who. Balthasar turned to look at the daughter (Elsbet, was it?), seeing her pause, half in a shaft of sunlight and half in shadow at the turn in the stairs. Oh, wasn't she the image of her father (such daughters were said to be happy), surprisingly like her father, but nevertheless quite different. She had unusual eyes too, but not as slanted, and not black, but a transparent grey-green and oddly elongated – such eyes must be the eyes described as – he could not recall where, but possibly in Ovid – as *oculi amygdalae*.[*]

Elsbet was wearing a filmy green shawl of Eastern silk over her head and a fine, dark green wool cloak, trimmed in red-brown mink – a furrier's daughter after all – and at the moment, her soft, well-defined mouth was slightly open in fleeting embarrassment. Balthasar said:

"It would please me if the young lady would help relieve me of my debt for the coat." He opened the front of the coat and stuck his hand inside so that he could run it along the wonderfully silky calfskin lining. "Well then, let's go. Your father has made me such a warm coat that I am beginning to feel quite hot."

"Fine," said Elsbet, "I'll get my purse from the chamber. Twenty marks is a lot of silver."

She hurried up the stairs, holding up the hem of her cloak. And Balthasar thought: *Hmm* . . . Master Gandersen would not have asked his lovely sixteen- or seventeen-year-old daughter to accompany some mercenary ensign or a brother from the Blackheads or a craftsman's apprentice. But he trusts her with a clergyman . . . We will not betray that trust, of course . . . And the old man's obvious *sumptio*,[†] which could actually be called *confisus*,[‡] is normal, after all, and pleasing, but still . . . Elsbet came down the stairs, shoes tapping, and Balthasar

[*] Almond-shaped eyes (Latin).
[†] Assumption (Latin).
[‡] Confidence (Latin).

took leave of those in the workshop: "Farewell and God be with you."

They stepped out into the afternoon light of the street, into the sounds of the creaking well-wheel at the crossing, of pails clanging in the wind, of water sloshing, and of voices at the well. Balthasar felt overly warm in his coat. He asked Elsbet to wait a moment, crossed the wet cobblestones to the well, where he borrowed someone's mug, dipped it into the nearest pail and drank – one gulp, two, three, four, looking at Elsbet over the rim of the mug. It seemed to him that there was a light blush on the girl's dusky cheek. Her hair – the wind blew the shawl to the back of her neck and she loosened the knot and tied it back under her chin – and, yes, her hair, touched by the late-afternoon autumn sun falling just then between the houses near Kiek in der Kök Tower, looked like the crown of a willow tree in the wind – the leaves, dark on one side and light on the other, so that it was not possible to determine their true colour. . . Balthasar gulped down his ninth, tenth, eleventh draught. Yes indeed, Elsbet Gandersen was a truly pretty girl. He swallowed his twelfth mouthful of the clear, refreshing water, as though he needed it for casting some kind of magic spell . . . But when they continued on their way together, Balthasar admitted to himself that this borrowing from the church's coffers went against his grain, at least a little. His discomfiture clashed with his pleasure at walking with Elsbet beside him, and the confusion of feelings disconcerted him more than he would have wished. So that they had already arrived at Town Hall Square when he thought to ask her:

"Has Fräulein Elsbet perhaps had occasion for some book-learning too?" And immediately thought: Well, she'll probably forgive a clergyman for posing such a question. Hopefully. But to tell the truth, it would have been hard to come up with a more stupid question – the first question to a beautiful young girl . . . But Elsbet answered politely:

"Agnes taught me to read. She is three years older than I."

"Your sister?"

"Yes. And father had me study with the nuns for four winters."

"Indeed . . ." said Balthasar approvingly. Why, this was a girl with whom he could discuss any number of things! But he asked, in order to better the impression his first question might have left:

"And what do you like best – Terence, or housekeeping, or dancing?"

And again the girl responded with aplomb:

"Girls are not given Terence to read. And when you're dancing, dancing is the best thing to be doing. And the same with housekeeping. We are used to doing housework at our house. Our dear Maijke could not manage it on her own. We have a big household and animals as well . . ."

"Who is this Maijke of yours?"

"The housekeeper and head of the household . . . Our mother died a long time ago. So long ago that I don't even remember her . . ."

They had turned in at the cemetery and arrived at the entrance to the pastor's house. Balthasar turned the key and opened the door. He said – so long after the fact that his statement seemed to hang suspended in the air above the door:

"The same with my mother."

They entered the great-room. There was no way for Elsbet to know that the wall-recess in the sacristy, from which Balthasar intended to take the necessary twenty marks, held the congregation's money. Still, Balthasar did not want to take it out in her presence.

"Please wait here for a moment—"

He looked around to see where Elsbet might take a seat. The wooden benches used for the congregation were ranged against one wall, but they were fairly dusty. Barber had cleared the table and pushed it into the corner. But the dogskin was still spread out on the window seat. Balthasar took Elsbet by the hand and led her to the seat. It wasn't absolutely necessary, of course, to take her hand, but it was a fairly common gesture for a cleric. The girl's hand in his large paw, full of life and energy, delighted him, and its surprising smallness made him chuckle. And for one so practised at housekeeping, it was as soft as the hand of a manor lord's daughter . . .

"Here."

Elsbet sat down on the dogskin and waited until the pastor brought the twenty marks from the sacristy. To tell the truth, Balthasar did not notice any reluctance in his hands as he counted them out.

"Here you are. And thank your father for the fine coat. We shall meet again, God willing."

He saw her out, locked the door and stood for a moment in the middle of the room trying to recall something. A long moment. Right – *that's* what he had planned to do.

He bounded up the great-room staircase, taking three steps at a time, and entered his small study. It was a square cell of a room with rough white walls, two cubits thick, and a window that looked down into the Almshouse courtyard and the backyards of the houses on Munkade Street. There were no furnishings here other than an old lectern, its surface dried and cracked, set in the right-hand corner under the window, and a three-legged stool across from it on the uneven floor. And one other thing, which could hardly be considered a household appointment: in the wall above the lectern, an iron door a square foot in size, spattered with the whitewash recently applied to the walls. Balthasar did not know what Herr Schinckel had kept behind that door. (Maybe the congregation's money . . . so that it would not be as easily accessible as downstairs . . .) In any case, Balthasar had something else stored in it. Something that actually was not anything yet. But which, he suddenly felt today, had to become something . . . He fished out the little key on the string around his neck and opened the iron door. He had considered his written notes at least important enough not to be left lying about on the lectern or anywhere else. And even if they were not of great importance (for he had felt it was bizarre and somewhat amusing that he was wasting his time on them), at least they might seem suspicious – even dangerous – should Barber or someone else chance to come upon them. He set a package of paper on the corner of the lectern, containing a few dozen, perhaps even a hundred, small greyish sheets with rough edges. Lifting off the first three or four sheets, he arranged them in sequence, one after the other. With a sense of recognition and estrangement, with pleasure and misgiving, he read his own large, scribbled handwriting:

(Things I heard from my father, which he most likely had seen with his own eyes):

In the year 1536, at Candlemas, Master Brueggenei trotted into Tallinn in full regalia, for its citizens were to swear fealty to him. But as he was being feted at the Town Hall, there very nearly came to pass a great mischance between the nobles and the citizens. For a certain nobleman and a merchant's journeyman decided to hold a joust in honour of the Master. But when the journeyman unseated the nobleman from his horse, the other nobles became incensed that such a one should seek the prize for himself in the presence of the prince and other estates. And they raised their voices in unrestrained, ill-tempered protest – and there arose between the nobles and citizens and their supporters such wrangling and grappling that swords were drawn and a terrible roar was heard. With gesture and word the Master urged calm from the window above in the Town Hall, and he threw his hat from his head and bread from the table down among the rioters to quiet them, but to no avail. Then the guild houses and ale halls were quickly closed, that those inside might not get out to add to the clamour and disorder. Until finally calm was restored by the Burgomaster, the esteemed Thomas Vegesack . . .

(Things the entire town knows, about which I heard in more detail from my sister Annika and old Traani-Andres):

In December of 1565 Christoffer, Margrave of Baden, came with his wife Cecilia, sister of the Swedish King Erik and of Duke Johan, from Stockholm to Tallinn. The ship arrived just before evening, and darkness had fallen by the time they disembarked, and so they came to shore where God led them. And He sent them to the landing place at the back of Traani-Andres' cabbage patch, so that they and their retinue arrived at Andres' and Krõõt's hut and let themselves be offered lodging under their roof for the night. Krõõt had run to Annika, knees trembling, and begged her to invite these high personages to her home, for Annika's house was more presentable and she herself quite the lady. But Annika had declared she would not act contrary to God's will nor create difficulties for the lords or for herself . . . (That does not really surprise me exceedingly, given what I know of my sister . . .)

(Things I have heard whispered by those well informed):

That Duke Johan has become a traitor to his fatherland because of his love for his wife, sister to Sigismund, the King of Poland, to whom he loaned a hundred and twenty thousand thalers in the name of his wife's beautiful eyes, at the same time that his own brother was about to wage war against his wife's brother.

Balthasar turned towards the window and looked out. He gazed at the black-bellied autumn clouds, reddening now in the evening sun, as though clad in armour reflecting the flames of nearby bonfires. They drifted above the rooftops, one after the other, from north to south, reminding him of something he had not yet put on paper:

Before Duke Johan was sent to Stockholm and before he was sentenced to death by the Diet (so that King Erik might then grant his brother clemency with a sentence of life imprisonment), he had been imprisoned in his castle at Turku . . . Good Lord, maybe in the same room – of course it was in the same room – where Balthasar had seen him eight years before . . . And when the Duke had been transferred with his bride to Sweden, Erik's officials found many portraits of his beautiful Catharina on the walls (no, no, not of Frau Friesner, but of the Duchess, his Jagiellon), portraits painted by the Duke himself . . . Interesting . . . what did the woman look like, whose face the Duke had painted on his walls and about whom his brother, the king, was reported to have said: You deserve the sword because of this woman, because for her you have repudiated the faith and the kingdom and the blood of your father, you traitor!

Balthasar turned his back to the window and stared at the white wall of his writing room. Holding a coarse grey sheet of paper he mused, apprehensively and hopefully: could he really manage, eventually, to put something together from the scattered notes that he had begun to compile about events in this land (as though he didn't have enough to take care of and attend to) something that, with God's help, might have a face and hands and feet, and the breath of life and the spirit of truth in it?

And just then it seemed to him that if he strained his eyes, he would see something on his whitewashed wall, an answer to his question . . . But if he saw anything at all on the rough white surface, it was a momentary glimpse of a face – the furrier's daughter's face, Elsbet's face, her mouth, slightly open in surprise, her almond-shaped, grey-green eyes, transparent, yet so very dark.

CHAPTER TWO,

in which punishments that are no doubt deserved begin to descend upon a town before the cock has crowed twice, and a man of pique and stubbornness (which, if it is not forgotten, may be considered grand someday) and with a heart full of trepidation (about which nothing may ever become known) strives to forge ahead in unpredictable and tumultuous times.

Early in the morning on the nineteenth day of the month-of-rye[*] in the year 1570, a strong and oddly steady north-west wind began blowing through Tallinn. It rose from a reddish haze on the horizon and gusted across the surging blue-black sea, bearing a mass of sultry air to the shores of Kalamaja.

The sea rose high with the wind; tall, flattened grasses trembled low to the ground; lengths of netting flapped on drying-frames. The door of Vuurman-Ants'[†] breezeway blew in and out, its hinges creaking. But the hoarse snatches of song sounding from nearly twenty throats – ". . . and now again a little lamb . . . stands beneath the cro-o-o-oss . . ." – drowned out the creaking entirely.

The nearly twenty people crowded into Vuurman-Ants' low-ceilinged chamber almost filled the small, shadowy room. Their song rose on grey stubby wings, fluttered briefly against the sooty ceiling, grew weak and irregular, and expired. Liberated from the effort of singing, the tense faces of the fishermen and wagon-drivers, the boatmen

[*] August.
[†] Ants the carter.

and dock workers and their wives relaxed and softened. Piret, wife of Vuurman-Ants, made her way between the christening guests, infant in her arms, and set the wailing bundle, now officially received into the Christian community, into his hanging cradle. Vuurman-Ants, a bit self-conscious, mumbled a few words befitting the occasion:

"I would now like to invite our Herr Pastor to be first at our humble table . . . Ahem . . . The times being difficult . . ."

People parted to let Balthasar through. He approached the table, deep in thought. Of course, the times were more than difficult. They were grievous. Such deplorable incongruities! The worse conditions became, the more the fashion grew of extravagant family banquets. Not just in the German burgher families, but in the homes of the Greys as well. The Town Council had just recently – how long ago was it . . . a year or so ago – enjoined people to limit the excesses of their wedding celebrations. But did anyone pay heed? No orders or prohibitions had been declared against such profligacy at christenings. Oh well, just how extravagant was this table display anyhow? A few big wooden trays of boiled pork shoulder, a clay bowl of fire-roasted pike, a few stacks of nicely browned barley griddle-bread, and a fizzing keg of ale in the corner . . . It made his mouth water and throat feel parched, for he had not eaten a crumb since the morning. All the same, he had meticulously carried out the duties required of him: he had sprinkled holy water on the downy head of the little fellow and christened him Mats, as his parents wished; he had made the sign of the cross over his face; he had admonished the parents and godparents to raise the child as a good Christian. Nevertheless, it all seemed implausible to Balthasar – the hushed, shadowy room, the waiting dining table under the greyish light from two tiny windows, the silent circle of deferential faces, the faint whimpering of an infant somewhere in the background – implausible, upon this low, bare ridge of shore, on a sea baring its teeth below the walls of a town paralysed by fear. Only two days before, marauding bands of Russians and manormen had absconded with four hundred head of cattle outside the town gates. And then there were the rumours that had been haunting everyday life in town for weeks now, both in dreams and by daylight: rumours that Magnus, the one-eyed Dane, had not only been declared King of Livonia by the Grand Duke, but that the duke had offered his own sister as wife to the callow youth, and that now this king was approaching with a sizeable army, though no-one knew where he was coming from – from Rakvere or Narva or Novgorod or Pskov or Põltsamaa. In any event, his was said to be a huge army made up of Germans and Russians and Tatars, coming to occupy the town of Tallinn and to inflict gruesome punishment on it for its recalcitrance . . .

"Would the Herr Pastor, please, take a seat at our table now," repeated Ants' wife Piret, and Balthasar started, suddenly recalling everything he had planned to get done that day – and all the *other* things he had determined to do as well.

He swallowed as he replied: "My dear parishioners, unfortunately I do not have the time. But I will take a little ale"– he turned towards his host – "while you fetch my payment."

The host filled a large mug from the keg. The hostess said: "Another one for the bell-ringer." As they were draining their mugs of ale – Balthasar standing by the table, and Märten at a little distance from it – their host counted out five farthings for the Pastor, thinking what an odd fellow this pastor was, wouldn't even allow himself time to sit down.

"God bless your meal. Even when I am not here, Christ is among you if you will receive Him. And take care that the men not get too far into their cups. And that you all come to Communion more often."

Balthasar walked through the crowd and towards the door, Ants and Märten following. He paused for a moment in front of the cradle, next to the young mother, who was changing the little one's nappy, and he could not resist the temptation to give the velvety little buttocks a light tap with his finger.

At the door to the storm porch Ants counted out the five farthings into Balthasar's hand.

"Really? Only five?"

"And how much should it be?"

"From you – eight."

"Why so much? Kuslapuu-Toomas paid only five!"

"And how many horses do you have?"

"Four . . ."

"Well now, Toomas has two. So I should, by rights, charge you ten."

Balthasar pulled his worn, goatskin money pouch out of his pocket (it was empty) and waited while Ants, muttering, counted out three more farthings into his palm.

The pastor and the bell-ringer now turned hurriedly out of Ants' wattle gate and set out for the town walls, following the uneven path along the top of the slope. Balthasar, his coat open and flapping in the wind, went on ahead, with Märten following ten paces behind, the chest with the baptismal implements hanging from a strap over his shoulder. They had walked another fifty paces when, at a bend in the road, Balthasar turned to look back. From this high vantage point he could clearly see Siimon's old house. It was to the right, the last house on Hundimäe Point, facing the sea. In the hazy, red-gold sunlight, it looked grey and low-slung, and as though the blue-black sea would wash right over its squat roof. Balthasar had had nothing to do with the old house since Annika sold it in 1567, when she married and went to live up on Toompea. Now, as he drew nearer, the chest swinging from Märten's shoulder blocked Balthasar's view of the house . . . Lord, and here he was, the very same Märten Bergkam, pale hair upright on his head, his chin pointed and downy, his pale-blue eyes deep-set in

66

his narrow, peeling, tanned face. Lord knows how he got so much sun in those twilit spaces in the tower among the bellropes, as though he were still the lookout on Herr Bushmann's *Minerva*, sailing the seas beyond the islands . . . the same Märten, his features even sharper, and resembling his birch carving more than ever. He looked as he had in fact *sometimes* looked in the old days. Like that morning that never was, of leaf-fall day,* when the blood-sprinkled birchwood underbrush had swallowed him up for several years . . . But *now* his expression was brooding and anxious, presumably because he was older . . . by how many years ? . . . Heavens! – ten years.

"Bal, hold on a minute . . . You were already at Vuurman's place when I arrived, so I didn't get a chance to tell you. I went by the Apothecary. Herr Dyck said he had been summoned to the Town Hall to deliver some calming-drops to Herr Boissmann . . ."

"What for?"

"They've heard that Magnus is on his way here."

"Really! That means – hm . . ."

"And he apparently has sent the Town Council some kind of letter . . ."

"You mean Magnus?"

"Yes."

At that they quickened their pace. Men caulking boats on the gravelly beach below looked up from tar pots and caulking-irons to follow the progress of the two, and no doubt found reason to mutter: That boy of Rissa-Siimon's rushes about hither and yon as if he always had seven tots to christen! The women under the drying racks, cleaning dried mud from nets – their hair and kerchiefs, shawls and skirts quivering in the wind – brushed away hair from their eyes with the backs of their wrists, thus concealing the knowing smiles on their lips. They huddled together and no doubt whispered God-knows-what. But of

* October 14.

course, we know what: Such a fine and vigorous man, no milk-moustache, not he, not for some time now . . . and he should be earning a goodly sum . . . but hasn't had the sense to find himself a wife yet . . . they say he goes to Kruvel's sauna to canoodle with the sauna maids there . . . Seems 'tisn't all that easy for a man like him to find a woman . . . 'cause the true-born gentry can easily refuse to give him their daughters, no matter that he's a churchman an' all . . . 'cause, of course, his roots are right here. Right here in Kalamaja, stuck firm in the beach gravel, and it looks like he's not all that keen to pull them up either . . . But it wouldn't do for him to pick a village girl from amongst the Greys . . . even though there was that young fellow, just startin' out to be a pastor, true-born German he was, who held as yon boy's sister was good enough . . .

The faint roar of the sea, high and white with cresting waves, floated over the huts and cabbage plots. Village children with grimy faces scurried across the road in front of them and peered out from their front gates. Dogs ran barking along the fences beside the walkers. Shreds of oakum, blowing from the boat-repair sites, rolled along the ground like foam, and the steady, sultry, feverish, woolly wind blew at the backs of the two men heading towards town.

They were already inside the Nunnavärav Gate and had walked along the base of the hill to the Pikk Jalg Gate, when Märten asked:

"Listen, who's the swell who was glaring at you like that?"

Märten was not surprised when Balthasar responded as though – how to put it – as though he were returning to the present from some faraway place. For he knew from their boyhood that when Bal was focused on what was around him, he took in more than anyone else. But when he was lost in his own thoughts, he seemed to be blind to his surroundings.

"What swell?"

Balthasar looked towards the right, past the haberdashery shops, and saw, on the cobblestone street in front of the Pikk Jalg Gate, three men on well-fed, restless horses, waiting to be let in. Oh yes, the gate had been kept locked day and night for the last two or three months. Ever since that bloody fracas instigated by Klaus Kursell and his armed band of men – until the day at the beginning of St John's month* when his head, along with those of his closest comrades rolled on the cobblestones of the castle courtyard . . . And now anyone who wanted to ride horseback up to Toompea had to wait for the guard to come and look him over before the heavy, riveted oak-plank gate was raised.

"The one in the middle, on the black horse."

"Oh, that's Tõnis Maidel. The Lord of Maidel Manor at Hageri. Just recently returned from serving under the Polish king. Now, of course, he's a big supporter of the Swedes."

"Just returned . . . well of course," remarked Märten disdainfully. He would have punctuated his comment with a shot of spittle had he been able to find a space between his annoyingly even teeth.

Balthasar added: "They say he's taken possession of the house he inherited from his father, behind the Dome Church.† Heh, heh . . . another time, when I have more time, I'll tell you the story. He's a crafty fellow . . . But right now" – they had arrived at Town Hall Square, at the back of the new public scales – "I have to step in to see the town fathers."

He paused under the pillory, a bit embarrassed, as he rummaged in his pockets. "Here, take this!" He had managed to extract a christening-farthing from the depths of his pocket and handed it to Märten. "Go get yourself a drink at Dyck's and talk awhile. Come home in two hours and remind me that it's time."

Balthasar crossed the windy square towards the Town Hall arcade. The market sweepers had already begun sweeping the pavement in

* June.
† Also referred to as St Mary's Cathedral.

front of the vestry. Dust clouds rose from their brooms, mingling with the trash swirling in the wind. In front of the Town Hall, the refuse had been swept into four large piles, but the more distant areas of the square were still littered with the remains of the market day. Had someone been watching the many feet that cross such befouled market places, he might, taking note of Balthasar's clumsy boots and quick stride, have smiled. For the way in which this man negotiated horse-piles and cowpats and dog turds without troubling to jump over them, but also without stepping into them, and the way he proceeded – veering a bit off course from time to time but never losing sight of his goal, the arched door of the Town Hall – showed that this trek probably represented something to him for which there was no word in his day, not in Greek or Latin or German, nor in his native tongue . . . (A word for it would not be devised until two hundred years later: the word *sport*.)

The Town Council meeting was in recess and most of the members had gone home for the midday meal. But Balthasar found Councilman Johann Boissmann at the back of the Treasury Chamber with a few colleagues.

Well, Herr Boissmann had changed almost beyond recognition from what he had looked like on Bal's graduation day in St Nicholas' Church, not to mention what he was like on that day – the day that was more like a dream than any dream, the time-that-never-was – when Balthasar had stood in the Council Hall next door, pretending to be a spokesman of the peasant king (*pretending* to be a spokesman – *serving* as a spokesman – pretending – serving – in a dream – in reality . . .). The flamboyant middle-aged lord had grown old and become dignified, the greenish bags under his narrow grey eyes even darker today than usual.

The councilmen shook hands with Balthasar. Herr Sandstede, that grey-haired, rude, aggressive lord who now replaced Herr Clodt as representative of the town, and who was sent abroad everywhere on its behalf – though he was reputed to be more skilful at wielding a sword than at weighing his words – remarked:

"Well then, Herr Balthasar, I suppose you've heard that Magnus will soon be at our walls?"

Over the past several years Balthasar had had numerous talks with councilmen – God knows, even with men of higher rank than Tallinn's burgomasters and council members. For men like Horn and Tot and other royal military commanders and vicegerents certainly thought their status higher than that of the town fathers, though most made no obvious display of it. Balthasar had met and conversed with them all, yes, but he had not yet overcome a childish temptation: the desire to *show* them, when the opportunity arose, that he was already aware of whatever it was they deigned to tell him – to demonstrate, for example, that some news or other with which they wished to astonish him was not news to him at all, and moreover, of no great moment. The devil knows, maybe this temptation arose less from youthful hubris than from his residual sense of inferiority, as a Kalamaja boy in the presence of the well-born. In any event, he now rested his palm on the broad stone windowsill of the Treasury Chamber and said coolly:

"They've been saying that about Magnus for some time now."

"No, no! It's a serious matter now," insisted Herr Schleyer, head of the town militia, a man with a magnificent moustache and a habit of blinking. "The day before yesterday, Magnus summoned his nobles to assemble under their flags in Põltsamaa."

"Well then," said Balthasar, "our fate is in God's hands."

"And in our own," said Herr Schleyer.

"Which is often one and the same," said Balthasar, leaning towards Herr Johann Boissmann's hairy ear. "I'd like a word with you."

They stepped into the empty Council Hall next door, but when Herr Boissmann paused on the threshold, Balthasar nudged him onward – perhaps from distaste for the picture of Tallinn in flames, under which

Herr Boissmann had stopped, but also from wariness at the proximity of the open Treasury Chamber door. They looked into the Citizens' Hall – a large hall, nearly ten cubits high, empty at this dinner hour. Shimmering swords of light, entering through ten high, iridescent windows on three sides of the room, crossed on the oaken floor between the pillars. Balthasar left Herr Boissmann standing on the swords of light and went to close the door. On his way back he fleetingly recalled hearing someone mention calming-drops for Herr Boissmann – but there was no time now to pursue the thought.

He said – without an *introductio*, as was his habit on occasions such as this, when he did not venture to insist, but could not bring himself to plead:

"Herr Boissmann, I need to see Magnus' letter."

Herr Boissmann's heavy chin tightened. "His letter . . . ? No-o-o . . . Herr Balthasar . . . I could in no way get that for you—"

"You couldn't? And why not?"

Herr Boissmann had never demurred before. True, Balthasar had not often requested official letters. But still, it *was* Herr Boissmann to whom Balthasar had revealed his project a year ago. It had come about by chance, actually, as is usually the case with such confidences. After several encounters, superficial though they were, at the home of the Holthusens or the Korbmachers or the devil knows whose christening or wedding, he had gradually developed a certain trust in this council-man . . . Yet Balthasar had taken the decisive step almost by chance . . . It had happened last year, on that terrible Sunday, the tenth of June. On the previous day, a foggy Saturday morning, the Danish pirate fleet had approached the sea lanes and then invaded the harbour and hauled a dozen ships out to sea. All day Sunday, from dawn to dusk, there was a frightful exchange of cannon fire between the ships and the town, a dozen of the biggest cannons having been dragged onto the bulwark at the Rose Garden and aimed at the sea. That evening at sunset, when

Balthasar had climbed to the top of the wall of the Rose Garden to take a look with his own eyes at the condition of the ships and the situation in general, he found Herr Boissmann there, taking a look as well . . .

They had stood side by side on the low wall next to the cannons and looked out over the misty lilac sea in the July night. Neither Admiral Munck's warship nor the vessels seized from the harbour were visible in the fog. Not a single light flickered at sea, not a single cannon roared. Groups of curious townspeople moved in the dark, between the bushes and the town wall, and the gunners nearby spat out the taste of gunpowder from their sooty moustaches. From time to time they shouted at the strollers to be quiet and to help them listen for sounds of creaking oarlocks from the sea, which would mean that the Danes were trying to put men ashore under cover of darkness, to rob and plunder. But they heard nothing at all other than the lapping of waves against the pilings in the harbour, now bereft of ships. Not even the gaping holes that the iron cannonballs of the Danes had smashed into the seaside wall of St Olaf's tower were visible in the dark. But when they got down from the wall and rested on the smooth surface of the big bronze cannon, to look at the sea just a little longer, Balthasar felt the heat of the cannon through his trousers. And it was then, as he passed his hand over its warm bronze back – the cannoneers had just left – that he abruptly asked: Did Herr Boissmann not think that . . . that the things that happened in an old and mighty town like Tallinn, a pitiable town long tried by fate though beloved of God – did he not think that these things, in such a town, and in this land, should be written down?

And when, without further hesitation, the councilman replied enthusiastically and in complete agreement: "But of course . . . Naturally . . . Without a doubt . . ." Balthasar confessed that he had for some time been occupying himself with this task, a little at a time. The councilman immediately expressed interest in the details of Balthasar's endeavour. And as they groped their way back to town along Pikk Street – in the dense twilight, townspeople walking about, curious about the day's battles, fell into step with them here and there, and a couple of divisions of militiamen, heading for the Rose Garden and the Parrot Garden for a changing of the guard, came towards them without torches, as per orders, the tramp of their boots echoing in the dark streets – Balthasar told Herr Boissmann that uppermost in his mind, as he wrote, was fidelity to the *unadorned truth*. Not the interests of the supporters of the Order or of Poland or Denmark or Sweden. Nor, of course, of the various views of the nobles on the affairs of the fatherland. Not even the day-to-day opinions of any of the town fathers. Only the *naked truth itself*. The councilman responded that indeed, that was the way, the only way, to accomplish such a task. He added, incidentally – and this emboldened Balthasar to take the next step, for they had reached Holy Ghost by then and the sight of the walls of his own church infused him with courage – yes, the councilman added that Balthasar seemed to him to be particularly well suited for this work: indeed, the man best suited for such an undertaking in all of Tallinn. First of all, because of his position as Pastor, whereby he had a closer relationship to Our Lord, the highest arbiter of Truth in Heaven and Earth, than a writer holding any other kind of position; second, because of his lush and lively use of language, for which he was known all over town, and which no doubt would flow from his pen as freely as from his mouth. This was what everyone was apparently saying about the Pastor's sermons, even though Herr Boissmann himself had not attended services in country-tongue at Holy Ghost Church. And third, because of his origins: as one who had come from the town's common people, Balthasar was free of the kind of arrogance of rank and social standing that would cloud the truth-seeker's vision. (Which might lead one to conclude that Herr Boissmann's own views – those of one hailing from a long line of councilmen – were unavoidably circumscribed by the arrogance of status . . .) Balthasar stopped directly in front of his

74

own church door, under the big clock from Lübeck – the nights were already so dark that its gilt hands could not be seen – and said:

"But in order that I might record the truth without errors, I need to be able to take a look, from time to time, at the more important correspondence of the council."

"Y-e-e-e-s. That is understandable," said the councilman – and then, without prompting, took the final step, the most dangerous step, adding, "and you would like me to be of assistance to you in this?"

"Exactly."

The soldiers' footfalls had grown faint as they marched towards the Coast Gate. From the Town Hall came the sound of another group of soldiers approaching. And as Balthasar listened, waiting, he tasted gunpowder in his mouth.

"Y-e-e-e-s . . ." said the councilman, "I think that, for the sake of the honour and good name of our town, I have to do it. On condition that we both consider this . . . *ahem* . . . akin to a confessional secret. For not everyone among our councilmen . . ."

"That's exactly what I wanted to ask of you."

On the basis of this agreement, Herr Boissmann, on three or four occasions in the course of the previous year, had shown Balthasar important council letters. Recently, Balthasar had been able to copy, word for word, what his old acquaintance Herr Kruse had written about the discussions in Rakvere in St George's Month,* between the Muscovite delegates and Tallinn. But now? Today? At this moment?

At this moment Herr Boissmann took two firm steps through the beams of light in the Citizens' Hall, stopping directly in front of Balthasar:

"*Lieber Rüssow, ick sak Ihnen . . .*" and then, in mid-sentence, he switched to country-tongue, and Balthasar was not sure whether this was an insolent rebuff (which would have been entirely in keeping

* April.

75

with custom here), or perhaps an unusual expression of intimacy, as seemed to be the case, judging by his tone of voice: "*Lieber Rüssow, ick sak* – parastaegu äi ole mängiaeg†.*"

"Really? Have we two been playing games until now? Is that what you think?"

Herr Boissmann looked down at the floor and then at Balthasar, pushing out his lower lip:

"Well, in any event, it's bound to come out. In any event, everyone will know . . . And a man like you, even before others—"

"Know what?"

Herr Boissmann's voice sounded as though his mouth were full of rusty iron:

"You heard it: the news – Magnus will be here tomorrow or the day after."

"Well, all the more . . . in my view . . ." Balthasar wanted to continue.

"But my son, Heinrich . . . " and here the mouthful of iron seemed to dissolve, and the man finished his thought with what was almost a howl, "is one of Magnus' top men!"

"Ah . . ." said Balthasar, "I've heard rumours to that effect."

"Already? Well then. Then you can understand for yourself that *now* we can no longer go on as before."

"Why not?"

Of course, Balthasar apprehended vaguely, and yet clearly enough, the roots and veins and threads of Herr Boissmann's sudden refusal – how it stemmed from his son's traitorous act and his own strange position. But he suppressed his desire to understand. Maybe because to understand would have meant to recognise, in some way, a connection between Heinrich Boissmann's treachery and the elder Boiss-

---

* Dear Russow, I say (Middle Low German).

† This is not a time for games (Estonian).

mann's deeds, and that meant his own deeds as well . . . *Absurdissime*[*]! He suppressed the thought before he had a chance to think it through clearly, and continued:

"No, I do not understand at all. I think that the more difficult your son's escapade has made it for us to understand the truth of this town's history and our past, the more incumbent it is upon you, thinking of present and future generations—".

"*Hören Sie!*[†] I know myself what I must and what I must not do! And I advise you to give this thing up. Throw your papers into the fire. The town must be united now! Not chasing after some kind of truth about past events!"

Though Herr Boissmann was speaking in German again, his manner was so fraught that anyone thin-skinned would have taken his words as a tongue-lashing. And God help us, maybe our skins will always feel a little sensitive, given the many amongst us whose skin – and souls, as well, of course – have been lashed by all kinds of whips, even if we, personally have not felt their sting . . . Balthasar spoke, and a pair of sensitive scales inside him moved (the kind used by Herr Dyck to weigh ground-up rubies and sharks' teeth in his Apothecary) as he strove for a precise counterbalance to the councilman's words. He said:

"In a case such as this, I of course know too, and even without your friendly advice, what I must and must not do. And, unfortunately, I cannot thank you for anything more than what you have done on my behalf."

He whirled around and marched out of the Citizens' Hall, his short black coat swinging and his comically thick shock of russet hair glinting. Many would have thought his *tramp-tramp-tramp* was the imperious exit of a mercenary captain rather than of the peasant-pastor of Holy Ghost Church.

* The height of absurdity (Latin).
† Listen! (German).

But just *what* he could now do was not at all as clear to him as he had declared. No, among the councilmen there was no-one to whom he could turn in place of Herr Boissmann. He summoned up each face in turn – Hünerjäger, Sandstede, Luttern, Schröder, Klüting . . . stiff, haughty, arrogant. To be sure, they could be convivial at times with a wine glass in hand, but at this time of widespread fear their faces were forbidding . . . It was possible, of course, that after a little research and preparation he could approach someone like Burgomaster Korbmach . . . But Balthasar needed Magnus' letter in a hurry, immediately . . . Yet, why was it so urgent? . . . It was foolish, of course . . . He went down the stairs and walked up and down between the pillars of the arcade with the angry determination of a battering ram, trying to find a way out . . . He saw three captains of the town militia ride up to the Town Hall door and dismount with more urgency than usual. He saw Councilman Winter, the man in charge of the municipal artillery yard, hurrying across the square, dodging the whirling refuse and still chewing the last of his midday meal. The council was about to reconvene for a discussion of war news.

Balthasar walked under the arcade and realised the sheer foolishness of having put an obstacle in his own path as he had done. God knows why. At the very moment when Herr Boissmann had rebuffed him. As people do at such times, to tease themselves – or to goad themselves on? He had formulated a kind of quid pro quo: if he did not get that letter immediately, there was no point in going to see old Gandersen . . . Because if he did not manage to make a copy of it, Gandersen would not give him Elsbet's hand. Each day for the past three days, Balthasar had vowed that he would that very evening go and ask for her hand . . . Foolishness . . . Of course. No, no, now was not the time to conjure up Elsbet's eyes and arms and hair and fragrance! . . . But in any event, he had to find a way to get those letters . . . Or could he really abandon all his work . . . ? Throw his papers into the fire? In the name of solidarity with the town? (Oh, so the truth about things that have happened would be "divisive"? Ah, so truth is the half-brother of betrayal . . . ?) Well – just then Balthasar saw someone coming from the direction of the Apothecary, past the small-wares shops, towards the Town Hall, carefully steering a middle course between the manure mounds, a slowly moving but nonetheless spry little man. Balthasar turned and went towards him along the length of the arcade, went at an even slower pace than the man's.

For an instant the man was hidden behind one of the columns of the arcade, but he came into view again at the next arch, and at the second, third, fourth – ever closer, and each time, a bit larger. Somewhere in the lowest layer of his mind Balthasar was thinking: When we finally meet at the corner, he'll have grown into a giant . . . But no. When they finally met beyond the eighth arch under the Town Hall tower, at the edge of the Old Market in front of the gatekeeper's house, the man was not a giant but merely that same little Herr Johann Topff with the grey-cat face – the very same man that Balthasar had first seen at close range at the Doctor's table, where they had had the honour to be seated along with the Herr Coadjutor (*Hmm*), on the evening of Balthasar's fateful decision . . . the very same fellow he had seen on several occasions over several years, ambling about town and near the Town Hall and inside the hall itself. The very same. In the meantime, the coadjutor had become a duke, but Herr Topff had merely risen from the position of clerk of the lower court to that of scribe for the town syndic. This had occurred when Herr Clodt had finally left Tallinn and gone over to Sigismund (rumour had it that the Pole had even conferred nobility on him), and when Herr Dellinkhusen, the withered pumpkin, had been summoned to become the town syndic. The very same Topff of the grey-cat face and soft tread and slightly wobbly head, whom Balthasar knew to be one of the less prominent officials of the Town Hall, but a congregant at its chapel, and thereby also one of

79

Balthasar's parishioners . . . Balthasar recalled something else, too, from long ago . . . Here he was, that very same Herr Topff . . .

"Good day to you, in the name of God, Herr Balthasar!"

"*Salve, salve*. I was just on my way to see you."

"Really . . . ? Then do please come to my den."

"*Hmm* – I'll be there in a quarter of an hour."

"Ah, so. Well, please do come . . ."

Balthasar hurried across the square to Saiakang Way, turned the corner at the Apothecary, nodded to Herr Dyck at the window of his laboratory, strode across the cemetery, and was home. Entering the sacristy he pulled out a key to the familiar iron door of the wall-recess and put fifty marks in silver into his pocket. Ten minutes later he entered the cellar door across from the town stables, descended to the storehouse under the Town Hall, and from there climbed the stairs built into the thickness of the stone wall, to Johann Topff's door, behind the Treasury Chamber.

Knock-knock-knock.

"Yes – yes . . ."

An ink-spattered lectern, a few stools, a simple pine bookcase containing rolls of documents, a few riveted chests for more important papers. An oppressively low, vaulted ceiling, no longer white.

"Do take a seat, Herr Pastor. What can I do for you?"

True: even Herr Topff's voice reminded one of a grey cat.

"Umm . . . Our former vicegerent, Herr Horn, used to begin like this: 'I am a man of war and will get straight to the point.' In fact, I am no man of war – quite the contrary. But I too will get straight to the point."

Herr Topff was sitting on a stool across from Balthasar, hands folded in his lap. He pursed his small mouth inside his grey beard, to wait, somewhat warily, for what Balthasar had to say. When Balthasar paused to gather momentum – a pause which might well have appeared to be for rhetorical effect – Herr Topff's ink-stained right thumb began to twirl nervously around his very clean left thumb.

Balthasar spoke: "Herr Topff, I would like to make a little pact with you."

But, oh God . . . this kind of thing has occurred in the world so often that yet another examination of how a man who has once ventured onto a slippery slope is nudged onto another can hardly be of interest to anyone. Except perhaps to those curious about the *particularities* of a situation, or in how *given* men at *given* times and in *given* places behave: for example, the two men in the scribe's chamber at the Town Treasury, on the nineteenth day of the month-of-rye, *Anno Domini** 1570 . . . How one man convinces himself, first of all, that the collegium or the *sodalitas*,† or whatever one calls it, which he has been serving and which he has sworn to serve loyally (a municipal office, after all), is not intrinsically superior to that other institution, an honourable member of which is now proposing – and for a nice sum, furthermore, of thirty or forty marks . . . What is it that he is proposing? He is asking him to *choose* which of the two is superior, the one or the other: in other words, the town and its merchants, who trade in leather and salt and oil and grain, or, perhaps after all, the shepherds of our souls, meaning the holy ministry of all our pastors from Tallinn and Stockholm and all the way to Wittenberg . . . Particularities . . . How the one man *convinces himself* that the silver he is promised for making the right choice is of no consequence whatsoever given that it *is* the right choice . . . How that same man thinks to himself that this Council of Clergy no longer possesses, in this present time of our reformed faith, the secret power it once had in the dark days of the popes . . . But even today, even now, it is true *sodalitas* since it is closest to God . . . And how the man, though pleased with himself for deciding to agree, still

* Year of Our Lord (Latin).
† Brotherhood (Latin).

pretends to object . . . Because the other one, the man of the Council of Clergy, that confounded yokel with his wooden expression, looks as if he actually expects a certain resistance . . . Particularities . . . How the other man then hints (a hint which is immediately grasped) that town and this Council are, in their ultimate goals, one and the same, and that this matter should not become a cause of concern for Herr Topff, especially as it is in the hands of his own pastor . . . And the way this bumpkin, stubborn as a tree stump, though not recognising (or not wishing to recognise) the scribe's *show* of resistance, reveals his hand – oh no, he does not lay his cards out on the table, he offers but a brief glimpse of an earlier, fateful decision (perhaps, in order to confound him . . .):

"Well, you have done this before, after all. And not exactly for the most distinguished lords and authorities . . ."

Good Lord, devils like him really know everything! "H-h-h-how . . . ? For who-whom then?"

"Not just for crowned heads, but for the rebellious peasants as well. Don't you remember? *Anno LX*? So – there's nothing now to prevent our agreement at all. On the contrary, there's everything to support it."

Particularities . . . How the one man immediately recognises this as a reminder that what a man does for a servant of the Lord's he also does for – and so forth, and in return some sins will be forgiven at the Last Judgment, if not before . . . Particularities . . . How the other man, as he heads for home across the clean-swept market square (as clean as it is possible to sweep it), a copy of Magnus' letter under his arm, alternately revels in a sense of triumph and suffers a sense of unease . . . Without being entirely aware that his discomfort is nothing but a secret desire to wash his hands with strong resin soap . . . the very hands he would rub together with glee, were he not concerned about crushing the parchment under his coat . . . How he overcomes

82

his unease rather quickly, apparently blindly accepting as truth what some Spaniard is said to have uttered twenty years earlier, though he knows nothing about this man: *finis sanctificat media . . .** And how he now rejoices: I got it in the end! . . . and I persuaded him to agree to more in the future . . . Rejoices, in the benighted belief that he knows how highly the world will value his work tomorrow, or even beyond tomorrow . . . in the blind faith that if someone today or tomorrow finds a kernel of truth in his writings, it will be the result of his own great effort, and not a matter of luck . . .

Balthasar locked himself into his writing room, turned over his hourglass, rolled out Herr Topff's copy of the letter and, as the sand trickled down in a barely audible sigh, began to read:

We, Magnus, by the Grace of God, King of Livonia, Lord of the territories of Estonia and Latvia, Heir to Norway, Duke of Schleswig, Holstein, Stormarn and Dithmarschen, Count of Oldenburg and Delmenhorst, hereby proclaim to all the inhabitants of Reval,† who seek the benefits and advantages of all Christian peoples and good fortune and freedom and true weal for oppressed and imperiled Livonia, and who wish to spare themselves and their descendants eternal ruin, misfortune, misery and devastation and much shedding of innocent blood:

Since this sorrowful and afflicted land of Livonia has been woefully ravaged and devastated by many nations, and its wretched inhabitants have cried out to the Almighty, beseeching Him with sighs and groans to grant them a German Christian Sovereign, so too have we cried out from the beginning of our reign, with all our heart, for God's mercy and His guidance to help us find the means and ways to restore these wretched lands

---

* The ends justify the means (Latin).
† German name for Tallinn.

to their former prosperity, and we have attempted and embarked upon a great many measures, but God has not willed that we find a remedy in the course of these many years, until at last the Emperor, the Grand Duke and Sovereign of all the Russians, has graciously proclaimed in documents written and sealed, as well as by the customary kissing of the Crucifix, as willed by God in His inscrutable wisdom, to install us as King over all of Livonia, which pledge His Imperial Majesty has stated publicly, proclaiming the wish of the Grand Duke to convey to us the whole of Livonia, either by means of force or through negotiation, as He likewise intends to align with the Holy Roman Empire against the Turks and all foes of Christendom. Thus, no sovereign is to hold sway over Livonia save for us and our heirs or, absent such, the Crown of Denmark or Holstein, in perpetuity. Nor shall any Russian have authority to rule over Livonia, save that the Emperor and Grand Duke shall be called the Lord Protector of Livonia, in confirmation of which he has kissed the cross, swearing by his imperial kingdom and his imperial person. In return, it is fitting that we offer the Emperor and Grand Duke some modest and humble token of Our gratitude as it has been recorded and sealed with a kiss upon the Crucifix: for this purpose the Emperor and Grand Duke has sent us ahead with this present army to drive the Swedish enemy from Livonia.

If the town of Reval will now submit peaceably to us and our heirs, or, in the case of the lack of the latter, to the Crown of Denmark or Holstein, as we have previously requested of the Council, not only shall it regain its former privileges, but it shall also be granted, on land and on water and also in other places, grand, profitable and enduring benefits and privileges in abundance . . .

Yes indeed ... In all this *eloquentia* the pearly froth of Herr Schröpfer, Magnus' head counsellor, was clearly evident. "On land and on water and also in other places ..." What other places? In the clouds, in mirages, in fantasy ... *Ha-ha-ha* ... But first of all Balthasar wanted to copy it. He did not plan to comment on it, at least not today. For today he was in such a confounded hurry ...

Balthasar read and wrote by turns, the trickle of sand in the hour-glass a faintly perceptible whisper as he read. And as he wrote, the scratching of his pen and creaking of his old lectern, its surface dry and cracked, were the only sounds of time passing.

> In the event, however, that Reval should desire destruction, decay, doom, ruin, bloodshed and mayhem, let it be forewarned that the Emperor and Grand Duke will employ all imperial might and force to devastate and strip it bare and subject it to eternal submission and subservience ...
>
> But with respect to the stories that mendacious spirits have bruited about, that this war is being waged for the benefit of the Grand Duke, this is the talk of rogues and is falsehood and deceit, against which We issue a Christian warning to the people of Reval, and the liars will soon pay for it with their blood. And should all Our Christian warnings be in vain, We declare Ourselves blameless, before merciful God and all Christendom, in the calamities and misfortunes to come ...
>
> Thus ... if you come into Our embrace We will love you more than Ourselves. If you do not, We will push you face down into the dirt and strip you naked. But those who dare to lie, saying We are doing it for Our own benefit, will have their shameless heads chopped off ... As always and ever.

Balthasar finished copying this instructive document even before Märten returned from the Apothecary, the chest with the baptismal implements still slung over his shoulder. But Märten also smelled lightly of *klarett* and brought the latest news he had overheard at the Apothecary, news related by none other than a captain of horsemen who had escaped from the bishop's manor at Kiviloo. He had fallen from his horse along the way and had come to see Herr Dyck, to drink a brew of steeped snake-ash for his contusions.

Magnus had apparently left Põltsamaa three days ago and marched towards the north, and on the Narva Road had joined with the forces coming from Rakvere. At the moment, he was evidently camped near Kiviloo – with roughly twenty-five thousand men, including Russians, Tatars, Mordovians. A handful of Danes too. And, *nota bene,*[*] a good several thousand Livonian Germans.

Balthasar rubbed his square chin . . . yes, Magnus did hold an inexplicably great attraction for many of the local lords . . . rubbing his chin he realised that with all the rushing about earlier in the day, he had grown quite a rough stubble and that he should definitely run a shaving knife around the edges before appearing at the door of his bride and future father-in-law. But still – in what did Magnus' attraction lie? This mere whelp with royal blood in his veins . . . But wait – he had to be at least thirty by now, and how long is a young man a whelp . . . ?! He was a king without a kingdom, about whom there were God-only-knows how many stories circulating in the markets and taverns and in most council chambers and even in the pulpits. Stories that he was born with one eye and a goat's hoof . . . and was of such indeterminate gender that he was neither man nor woman, although the Grand Duke had offered him his niece Eufemia in marriage . . . ! Yes, Magnus had an uncanny magnetism . . . But then he was a *Christian German* ruler, after all . . . And rumour had it that even the Holy Roman Emperor supported him, to an extent . . . And that the Grand Duke, by way of Magnus, would bring peace to all of Livonia for ever and ever . . .

[*] Note well (Latin).

If only it did not turn out to be the kind of peace that immediately prevails between fisherman and fish as soon as the fish has swallowed the bait . . . ? Still, Magnus' camp did not include only that unctuous Schröpfer, and not only our old familiar Herr Kruse and that fellow Taube, who, ever since the negotiations at Rakvere were always mentioned in one breath, and not only Herr Heinrich Boissmann . . . For among the company captains and troop commanders of various rank, there were several noblemen from distinguished Livonian families, such as Reinhold Rosen from Rannu and Johann Maidel from Volluste . . . Given the perspicacity of these men (just because they possessed the doubtful integrity of mercenary soldiers, they were not blind!), the attraction that Magnus exerted had to be, clearly and incontestably, that of the Grand Duke himself . . . That same Grand Duke whose deeds were recounted in the most terrible stories (so terrible that for some years he had been dubbed the "Terrible" by his own people). Among those various tales of horror there was one in particular that made Balthasar shudder. We usually consider those things most significant which, in a good sense or bad, involve ourselves or someone we know. It was a story about the former *voevoda** of Narva, Aleksei Basmanov and his son, Fjodor. The fate of these men, whom Bal had met either in his past or in a dream, haunted him whenever he recalled it, whether awake or asleep . . . The Grand Duke had ordered that these two most loyal servants be arrested – on account of his uta, the Persson of Muscovy, and his despicable back-biting, snooping and slander – on suspicion that father and son were involved with the Greater Novgorod conspiracy. By which Novgorod would purportedly attempt to secede from Moscow and regain its former independence and glory. And the Grand Duke had had the elder Basmanov gruesomely tortured – that same black-eyed man whom Balthasar had met at Melchoir Krumhusen's house and later at

* Governor, military commander (Russian).

87

the banquet in Hermannstadt, and whom he had heard say in a voice that had made shivers run down his spine: "As a soldier I want to be wherever I can be of most use to my Gracious Emperor." And: "To me what matters is only that which serves our Gracious Emperor . . ." And then the Grand Duke had threatened the young Fjodor Basmanov with grisly tortures and demanded, as a sign of loyalty, that the son kill his own father before the Grand Duke's eyes, and, they said, he put a knife into the son's hand . . . And that black-eyed young man, who bore so portentous a resemblance to his father, the musician son who had sung and danced and played at all the Grand Duke's festivities, had become limp as a rag, the cowardly wretch, and obeyed the appalling command . . . And the Grand Duke had looked on with vile pleasure, enjoying not just that one scene but hundreds of other horrors like it . . . People said – but by God, people also said that King Magnus had only one eye and a goat's hoof . . . And people talked about (what does it mean, *people talked about*, when everyone, everywhere, *knew?!*) the things that happened in Stockholm and Uppsala in King Erik's day, at the satanic instigation of Jöran Persson, the Swedish Malyuta . . . The imprisonment of Prince Johan and the murder of dozens of the most prominent nobles . . . And then again the imprisonment of King Erik at the hands of Prince Johan, our present merciful King Johan III . . . My God – it was as though this world were no longer God's but belonged, in fact, to his Great Adversary, who, smirking, twisted and contorted all things, who spat at honour and honed a murderer's dagger on the whetstone of fidelity . . . and upon the blue flame of suspicion and mistrust distilled brotherly love into an undetected, odourless, tasteless poison . . . No-no-no – don't think of that now . . . (not now – nor another time – especially not *today*, but *when*, then? I don't know. Some other time. But definitely not now!) For now I am going to carry out that which will to a great extent determine the future. Yes, to a great extent. I'm not saying entirely . . . Oh, maybe today, at least today, I should say entirely and completely. All my earthly joy! As much as a mortal man can expect, as much as he dares ask of the Lord for himself . . .

Balthasar turned away from the lectern, folded his arms across his chest and paced back and forth on the scuffed, uneven floorboards of the barren chamber.

Let us just simply say, to a great extent . . . Let us say: Lord, let this thing come to pass . . . This talk with You is so straightforward, surely it can be conducted while I pace, arms folded . . . Because at a time like this, You do not require genuflection or folded hands . . . Lord, let me bring this thing to pass . . . Though I ought perhaps to think that You intend, by means of today's fresh news about the war, to influence me to postpone it . . . But look, Elsbet has been preparing her father for this day since last week. And old Gandersen would have done his calculations before the arrival of the news. I cannot hope, of course, that he has not yet heard of Magnus' coming. He most certainly has. And I have to overcome his reluctance with regard to the news. And I can! I can! Today, absolutely – when You have shown me that I can rely on You, for when You let Herr Boissmann remove his shoulder that had supported my plan and everything seemed about to collapse, You set another man, and it seems to me an even more suitable man, on my path . . .

"Märten!"

Balthasar had already, with a brisk stride, descended the stairs and was about to step outside when Märten appeared from somewhere inside the house.

"I'm on my way. You know where. So – hold your thumb for me."

"Now, now – there's nothing to . . ."

Balthasar stopped on his new stone threshold (a whole thaler, it had cost) and turned around:

"*Hmm.* Tell me the truth: you don't like the idea of my marrying Elsbet Gandersen, do you?"

Märten looked at his employer – his old friend. His keen eyes under their light, bristly brows appeared to recognise the sincerity of the question. Märten had just come from clearing weeds from the gravel along the walls. And now he raised his right hand, gripping a hoe, and bent his wrist to rub at the stubble on his chin, and for a moment it looked as though he were trying to keep his jaws clamped shut.

"*Hmm* . . ." (as though he were echoing Balthasar's opening "*hmm*") "Yes . . . I do . . ."

"But . . . ?"

"But if you want to know – that's the confounded problem!" Märten's words were more agitated than one could have anticipated. He sounded almost angry.

Balthasar raised his eyebrows.

"Just a minute, I don't understand. You mean you don't like the fact that you like it? Is that it?"

"You really are one damnably bright fellow. That's it. Exactly."

Märten was smiling that elusive, knowing smile that Balthasar, to this day, could not quite decipher: was he being complimented or mocked? He sensed vaguely that he was just about to ask – whether this fellow, this bell-ringer, this knave, this old friend was not presuming a bit much with regard to his employer. But before he actually formulated the question, as soon as he began to sense it taking shape, he felt ashamed, and suppressed it. He asked guardedly, though his voice was ardent and deep with relief that he could keep faith with his friend:

"Tell me outright what you like and what you don't like."

"What I like is that you're taking a definite step. How long can you be going on like this, with all kinds of doxies . . . What's permissible for a bell-ringer is not appropriate for a pastor. And you've been eyeing this girl for three years already. And the same goes for her. Or maybe even longer."

"But what's wrong then?"

"What's wrong is that I don't know any girl who'd be *more* suitable for you."

"You think that the one I'm about to marry should be *more* suitable?"

"I don't know. But I'm asking: Why this one? Eh? She's a pretty girl. Sure. But not a town beauty. Wealthy. True enough. But not the wealthiest in town. Not at all. There are a hundred or two hundred girls like her in Tallinn."

"Do you see what you're saying? You just said you didn't know a single one who'd be better suited for me. And now all at once there are two hundred of them?"

"You know very well what I mean. They would all suit you just as well as she does. So why this one in particular?"

"Because I love her."

"*Hmmm . . .*"

"And she loves me too. And those other two hundred don't know me at all."

"*Hmmm . . .*"

"And why do you think it should be someone else? And what kind of girl then?"

Balthasar felt, of course, that there was no point to his questions. Because Märten's replies would by no means change his mind. It would be absurd even to think that. But every young man – and every man is young when he goes courting, even a world wanderer like this one, nearly thirty-five years old – is interested in an old friend's opinions, unless he is a saint and free of all vanity. No matter that his friend is his subordinate in status and occupation and thus at times withdraws beyond reach, and, in this unacknowledged but undeniable distancing, at times awakens in him something like guilt, something like a sense of betrayal. Even so, his opinions were of interest – some, because it was pleasant to be in agreement, and others, because in justifying oneself one could argue them into silence . . .

"What kind of girl? *Humph*. If you want to know – either of two—"

"Well?"

"Some village beauty from Kurgla. Someone like that Epp once was. Or Fräulein von Geldern."

Balthasar was silent for a moment upon hearing Epp's name. Surprised at hearing it. And even more surprised that he had somehow anticipated it, startled and pleased, thinking, now he'll say it . . . As on other occasions, too, he had anticipated the wild turns of Märten's thoughts.

"Which Fräulein von Geldern?"

"Any one of our bishop's daughters. How should I know which one?"

"You old fool . . . what are you getting at?"

"I'm saying that you should choose a wife either from the place you're from or the place you're going. Not from somewhere in between . . ."

"*Ha-ha-ha-ha-haa.* As I said, you're an old fool. I'm going now. Set out some pens and candles and scissors for me. And a small keg of wine, too. If I manage to do a good amount of work this evening, we'll have little drink before going to bed."

At the cemetery gate on Saiakang Way, Balthasar was stopped:

"Herr Pastor, sir, we want to ask your permission . . ."

Balthasar recognised them even before they had opened their mouths. They were Matman, the churchwarden, and three church elders from the village of Kalamaja, faded hats in hand, apprehension and distress on their sun-browned faces. "We need your permission – you see, our wagon train is there – round the corner, in front of the church – forty-three wagons – with the grain and flour of the people of Kalamaja—"

"And what permission do you need then?"

"Well, what the people want above all is to stay put in Kalamaja. And if necessary, they'll make it to the shelter of the town walls in a half hour. But they can't haul all their foodstuffs in that time. So . . ."

what we're asking is permission to haul our sacks onto the vaulted arches of Holy Ghost Church."

Standing there, in narrow Saiakang Way, they all looked up at the needle-like church steeple, at the winch beams with pulley blocks protruding from either side. Matman said:

"In case our Herr Pastor doesn't know it, Kalamaja folk have for generations stored their grain on the vaulted arches of Holy Ghost in times of war. There's no other place . . ."

Balthasar grunted:

"What do you mean – *in case our pastor doesn't know it?* Just where do you think your pastor comes from?!"

Balthasar knew that there would be more than enough trouble and inconvenience with these villagers' stores of grain and flour in the event of a blockade. But they had always been granted permission, and he, of all people, had to grant it to them now. And furthermore, he was now in a great hurry . . . He said:

"God be with you. The keys are with the bell-ringer. Tell him you have my permission."

Balthasar strode out onto Pikk Street to take a look at the grain wagons in front of the church. True enough, forty-three loads, but actually there was considerably more cargo here than he had imagined, for the loads were piled onto rather large covered wagons. And in addition to the sacks of grain, all the better household goods of the entire village had been piled on as well. So be it. The vaulted arches of the church would manage to support it all. The wagon-drivers raised their hats in greeting to Balthasar.

"Good day, men! Matman and the elders are fetching the keys. The bell-ringer will receive you. Hoist it all up. Else you'll lose your belongings for sure if Magnus arrives at the town walls by tomorrow. But see to it that you make a note of everything. So there aren't arguments later."

He waved to the men on the wagons and headed towards Rataskaevu

Street. The gilded hands of the large clock on the wall of Holy Ghost Chuch indicated that he was already a quarter of an hour late.

When he got to the corner of Rataskaevu Street, he saw two long siege-culverins on wooden-wheeled carts, each drawn by four horses, rumbling down through the Pikk Jalg Gate. And then, to the loud crack of whips, the cannons were turned towards Town Hall Square.

"What are you doing, dragging these monsters here?" asked Balthasar of the officer in charge of the troops accompanying the siege-culverins.

"They were requested by Herr Winter, from the captain of the castle guards. For the rondel at Karja Gate. They're supposed to be set up there by tomorrow morning."

"So it's tomorrow – that it's going to start?"

"So it seems."

Balthasar continued on his way. He had to hurry. There might already be an order from the Council of Clergy at home, directing him to hold a prayer service in the evening if the enemy was expected by the following day. Pressing on, he squeezed his eyes shut. He heard the whips cracking in Väike-Rataskaevu Street, the mercenaries cursing and the sling-carts creaking as they rumbled along. He saw, in the brown darkness under his closed lids, the sweaty faces of the Kalamaja wagon-drivers in front of the church with their loaded wagons. And he sensed, above and behind everything, like a slow, dark wave rolling closer, its crest foaming with pikes and crossbows and pennants, sparkling here and there with the glint of helmets, that same army of King Magnus approaching with a roar as yet barely audible – with its stench of skin and sweat and horses and gunpowder – no doubt already on its way in clouds of dust, from Kiviloo to Tallinn . . .

Twenty paces from the Gandersens' house Balthasar stopped and drew a deep breath. *Think about Elsbet, Elsbet, Elsbet and not about all the rest . . . not now . . .* And he recalled a whimsical moment from a year ago.

He had been hurrying home along Harju Street, in high spirits after an official pastoral visit, and Elsbet had been coming up Kuninga Street from the direction of the Old Market with a basket full of foodstuffs. She had already nodded a brisk greeting to Balthasar from a distance, as was only proper and fitting for a young girl in an encounter with a pastor. If both had continued straight on, they would have passed each other at the corner of Lytke's smithy, at a distance of ten paces. But then and there Balthasar, for no good reason, had stopped and approached Elsbet and put his hand on her shoulder and in broad daylight, in the middle of the bustling street, to the sound of the clinking and clanking from the smithy, had said:

"Elsbet Gandersen, I think you are the prettiest girl in town."

Good Lord, this certainly was not proper of a pastor no longer very young. Especially since the pastor himself did not entirely mean what he said. Perhaps the words slipped out on account of the beautiful spring morning – they were in fact not at all appropriate – a thoughtless scholar's indiscretion, an irresponsible attempt to toss out a line to ensnare an innocent girl's thoughts . . .

The innocent girl blushed at his words and lowered her innocent eyes. But then decorously raised them again, beautiful, deep, dark-grey eyes, sparkling with glints of light, and looked straight at the pastor and said quietly, in a manner entirely seemly and becoming – it was impossible to detect in the timbre of her voice the degree to which she might have felt either offended or pleased

"Herr Balthasar . . . I am astonished . . ."

A week later, at the wedding of Master Cooper-Falck, Balthasar had met Elsbet again. And when the goblets had been filled several times with red wine and the musicians had played several pieces, he had leaned towards her ear and asked:

"Does Fräulein Elsbet remember what I confessed to her at the corner of St Nicholas' Street last Saturday?"

At that Elsbet had looked him straight in the eye by the light of many, many wedding candles, and her unusually full lips – at times sad-cool, at times childlike-warm – widened into an enigmatic smile. She shook her head, and as she turned away, the ringlets on her neck tickled Balthasar's nose . . . He felt the sensation of the contact spread from his nose through his entire body, and he laughed with pleasure to realise that he was already on this girl's leash.

And it made him want to laugh even now, even as he entered the Gandersens' great-room and workshop, the apprentices and journeymen greeting him hurriedly as he went up the stairs . . . The realisation that he, yes, was on this girl's leash, and he knew it and considered it a good thing and in some way he was actually free, not on a leash at all.

He went up the stairs where he had first laid eyes on Elsbet and he felt that he could by rights whistle . . . But then he stopped halfway up and called down into the cloud of powdered starch and hairs and sunlight suspended in Gandersen's workshop:

"Peeter!"

When the younger journeyman came to the stairs, Balthasar leaned over the thick ash banister rubbed smooth by the hands of many generations of this family, who were mostly strangers to him.

"Listen, do you know how to write? A little? Fine. I'd like you to write down for me, by tomorrow, the names of all the pelts that the people of this land and the furriers wear. Whether it's fox, weasel, calf, dog, or whatever. And next to each pelt, write down the price. So that I can compare them according to their cost and quality. Here—"

He shook out of his money pouch onto Peeter's palm the seven farthings he had received at the christening, and then bounded up the stairs, taking the last steps three at a time.

CHAPTER THREE,

in which a man recollects the early success of his sweet designs and the way they later ran aground (for the moment and place are, in spite of everything, ideally suited for such reminiscences); thereafter, however, he is knocked off his feet by a great gust and cast into a terrible river of travail, which our merciful God, who must often appear to mere mortals as an unmerciful God, decides to loose upon this unfortunate town – as though the fearsome enemy at the town walls were not punishment enough.

"Elsbet – tomorrow was to have been our wedding day . . ."

Balthasar had just freed Elsbet's warm mouth, tasting faintly of poppy seeds, from his long kiss, a most passionate kiss for a man of his age. He gazed for a moment at her deeply flushed face, then looked out of the small window in the thick wall of her chamber.

The afternoon was darkening. Through the windowpanes, he saw, as if through congealed yellow-grey rain, the slant of St Nicholas' snowy roof above the courtyard wall and Rataskaevu Street. When he listened attentively, he heard the relentless booming of cannons. He had become accustomed to the sound – it no longer disturbed him. Although muffled by rooftops and walls, the repeated rumbling clearly came from the north-east. Since that morning, Muscovite guns had been firing upon the town from the old Copper Mill on Lasnamäe Hill – as they had been doing almost every other day for the past three months, and daily over the past three weeks. A few heartbeats later there was a short, dull thud, from somewhere difficult to determine – possibly near the New Almshouse. Elsbet, who had become rigid and still in

97

Balthasar's arms after the initial barrage of cannon-fire, flinched and then relaxed almost immediately (as one counting heartbeats after a flash of lightning relaxes when the thunder finally roars), even though this time the stone cannonball had landed somewhere fairly close by . . .

"Father cannot manage it now . . . not during the siege . . ."

It was an excuse for a senseless postponement, a delay determined by God, but senseless nonetheless. And in order that this unusual man – this singularly rough-hewn and sensitive man about whom hung the whiff of wool and horse stalls and grain (but also of oak-bark ink and paraffin and sealing wax) – in order that he not perceive the postponement as a rebuff nor begin to imagine that his bride was content with the delay, she tightened her hands around his stiff neck and drew his eyes to her own marvellously luminous eyes.

"You understand, don't you?"

Of course Balthasar understood. He was not the only prospective bridegroom in Tallinn whose wedding had been indefinitely postponed because of the enemy's prolonged presence at the town walls. In his parish alone there were four others in a similar situation. However, this particular consequence of the siege did not seem to trouble his father-in-law much. Balthasar could sense with his skin that Elsbet loved him and was worried and embarrassed by their present peculiar situation, but old Gandersen seemed almost to relish the delay. Balthasar remembered precisely all the details of the fateful conversation with the old man three months ago, on the nineteenth day of the month-of-rye.

"*Herein*,"[*] sounds the response to his knock from behind the dusty door of the furrier's chamber in the back wall of the great-room.

"*Guten Tag, Meister.*"[†]

"*Tag, Herr Pastor.*"

Suspended under the low vaulted ceiling, from ropes stretched

* Come in (German).
† Good day, Master (German).

between the limestone walls, hang the pelts of dogs, weasels and other animals in surprisingly long, tubular shapes, all somewhat comical, alive and pitiable. Like pelts in general: dead things that have not been permitted to die completely.

The old man is sitting in the middle of the room at a long worktable a fathom in length, its surface rough and scarred. He is stroking a thick red fox skin with its paws splayed in front of him.

"What's the fur on the foxes like at present?"

"It's thin, sparse. Sign of starvation. What has our Herr Pastor heard about Magnus' army?"

"He is expected to arrive by tomorrow morning. Which is why I hurried to get here right away."

This is not entirely true. Although he is well aware that the matter he is pursuing will be easy to dismiss as inopportune at a time when enemy forces threaten the town, he has taken it into that round head of his that he absolutely must settle things with the old man this very day. Elsbet, it seems, has prepared her father, or the old man would not immediately have mentioned starvation. And note, he does not even bother to ask just why the Pastor is in such a hurry . . .

No. He wants to let this annoyingly hot-headed young man just stand there at the massive worktable, to keep him impaled as long as possible on the lance of his impenetrable silence. Balthasar has understood for some time what Gandersen thinks of him: God knows, even though this Balthasar is by profession a servant of God and thus, *formaliter,*[*] on a par with men of the highest standing in town, and even though he is everywhere addressed as "Herr" (a title for clergy and councilmen, but not commonly conferred even upon the prominent merchants of the Great Guild) – in spite of all this, he is not a man Gandersen approves of at the moment. Since all this is thoroughly clear to Balthasar, he does not permit the silence between them to last longer than two heartbeats.

* Formally (Latin).

"Master Gandersen, I would like to ask for your daughter Elsbet's hand in marriage."

There it is. But Elsbet is the old widower's youngest, the last one still in the nest. He has been without Agnes since the previous year. She is in the arms of the baker Horstmann. And now Elsbet has taken this bumpkin pastor into her beautiful, foolish head. As though there were not hundreds of upstanding young German men in town. But there's no help for it: he knows full well how stubborn his daughter is. He cannot blame her for it either, for there is no denying she has inherited the trait from him . . . still, will this marriage not bring peasant blood into the Gandersen household and family . . . ?! What Agnes did was bad enough – though in her case the peasant connection was distant, nowhere as bad as Elsbet's intent . . . Yes, it had made the old man sick at heart when Agnes inherited a place alongside her Horstmann at the hearth and in the bed of a woman of peasant stock – Horstmann's deceased first wife, Eebo. And when that tippler of a baker has drunk himself silly on All Souls' Day ale, he gets maudlin and belligerent and sings praises of his first wife in front of all the household, proclaiming she was quicker and prettier than Agnes . . . An outrage! And now? Elsbet's decision can of course be viewed in two ways. Either Elsbet wants to start making yokel grandchildren for the esteemed German Master Furrier . . . *Blast it!* Or she wants to boost her old father up, make him a kinsman of the Wittenberg-educated, learned worthies of the Council of Clergy . . . *Hm* . . . one can see it either way – but what's to be done except to go on postponing it . . . ?

"Take a seat."

Balthasar pulls a three-legged stool from under the table and sits down; he does so with a familiarity that Gandersen does not quite approve of. Balthasar senses his disapproval with the hairs of his eyebrows. Gandersen continues to stroke the fox pelt.

"I won't deny it – Elsbet has spoken to me. *But* . . ." His hand, with its fingertips stained brown with tannin, pauses at the fox's tail. His slanted black eyes dart a quick look at Balthasar as he continues: "But I would not have expected, at this most difficult time for the city, at this fateful moment, that a man of the cloth would pursue the matter of getting himself a wife."

Ooh . . . not mincing matters and telling a clergyman that he does not know what is meet and proper . . . No matter:

"It would indeed not be proper if the taking of a wife were simply a St Catherine's Day* prank. But that is not the case for a serious man. For a serious man, this fateful moment – as the Master so well put it – is more decisive than the siege is for the city. For how many times in a lifetime does a man take a wife? Once! And should God call her away from his side, then perhaps a second or even third time. But no more. And how many times over their life are cities besieged? Dozens of times!"

A man like this is never at a loss for words. That is clear. They flow from him like lengths of broadcloth whooshing and swishing from a woollen mill . . . Well, the Master Furrier is no laggard either when it comes to turning a phrase . . .

"Just how does the Pastor imagine this affair? In such times as these?"

"If the Master, as I dare hope, does not refuse me his daughter, the matter would be *principaliter*† settled. We would discuss the dowry. As for the wedding itself – we would of course postpone it until such time as no siege appears imminent, or until the siege is ended."

"The siege ended? . . . But Magnus is said to have twenty-five thousand men! If Magnus conquers the town, what then?"

Gandersen is worried about the fate of the town. He wishes that this man with his peasant–yokel hide – an educated man, after all –

* November 25.
† Basically, principally (Latin).

would calm his anxieties by saying his worries were entirely baseless, for Magnus, even if he proved mad enough to try, would only bloody his own head running against the town's walls and towers. It would have been pleasant for Gandersen to hear such reassurance and respond: It's just words, just words, Herr Pastor. They said Magnus was coming from the Grand Duke with cannon of unprecedented power. So that we don't know in advance what to expect. Not a thing. Maybe he'll take the town after all. And *then* what?

But the obstinate boor offers no consolation to the worried burgher. Instead, he says, with insolent equanimity:

"In that case too, the siege will be over."

"But in that case, will we still be alive?"

"If we're no longer alive, we'll no longer need anything. But if, God willing, we live through this – does Master Gandersen believe we will no longer need calfskin coats? That we will no longer want to marry?"

"Listen, let us discuss it when the siege is over . . ."

So. The cursed old man is slipping away from his grasp. If Balthasar is not robust enough to win this match, he will need Elsbet's help in dealing with her father.

"Master, I would like to remind you of what Elsbet said to you about the matter this morning."

"What . . . ? Elsbet . . . ? To me . . . ?" (Ah, so this fellow knows word for word what my daughter has discussed with me . . .) "What did she say, then?"

"She said: Father, it's not that I am in a hurry because I have sins to conceal. For I am a respectable girl and he is a respectable man. But we are all likely to be facing difficult days ahead, and I beg you, don't leave me suspended in uncertainty at this most trying time."

Yes, there it is, word for word. The old man recalls how, as she spoke, she buried her nose in his coarse scarf, how the scent of her hair (washed with pine-resin soap the night before) rose to his nostrils, and how his old heart softened . . .

He glares at Balthasar, realising just how objectionable he finds this would-be gentleman, this quintessential yokel, this educated boor with sly eyes and a mocking mouth, this fellow with his sinewy build and strutting confidence . . . and how close he is now to becoming acceptable because there's no escaping it, for he is the one whom Elsbet has chosen . . . Oh, confound it . . .

"Maijke! Come here, Maijke!"

The housekeeper's broad face and ruffled hair appear between the dogskin hangings on either side of the door.

"Maijke, bring us some *klarett!*"

Maijke quickly brings a flagon of *klarett* and delicate silver goblets to the table. Silver, because she is a woman who understands what transpires in this house and has immediately grasped what her master is discussing with the Pastor, including the significance of the request for *klarett.*

Gandersen fills the goblets. He does not stand up or put his arm around Balthasar, as he by rights ought to. He looks at his future son-in-law with narrowed black eyes and a sour smile, and says – displaying a mixture of dislike, acceptance, respect and judiciousness, which Balthasar cannot but admire, even though in itself . . . ah well. Goblet in hand, Gandersen says:

"It is a great honour for my house that Elsbet is to have a member of the clergy as her husband – that goes without saying. But the fact that it is *you* – well, that is her business. Let's drink to it!"

They clink their goblets; Balthasar is silent. He makes his father-in-law wait before he speaks; he, who is so fluent with words, makes him wait. Lets him understand that this son-in-law does not feel obliged to say a word. They are both aware that the silence is a slight, a retaliation. And they both think: if this test of strength, this knife-throwing contest that has just begun, continues, will I be the one who comes out on top in the end? Ganderen tells himself there can be no doubt about it, though he is only vaguely aware of just why he is so sure. This whole, beautiful, honourable old German town of Tallinn and its social order are all solidly behind him . . . And Balthasar, on the other hand, says the same thing to himself, that there can be no doubt about it as long as Elsbet is behind him. But where else would a wife be?

And then they grapple with the question of the dowry.

Balthasar could of course be more compliant, in fact, wholly compliant. Actually, he sees only two possibilities here. On the one hand he need demand nothing at all, just shrug it all off as dispensable and be completely satisfied, completely happy just to have Elsbet as his own – this gentle, elusive girl in whom he senses a resolute strength, this girl after his own heart. He could declare that to be sufficient. Or he could say to himself: Wait a minute! Why should her father, this reasonably rich man who is at least a hundred times richer than a church mouse like me, benefit from my indifference? Why? Especially since every little bit of the dowry would be not just for me, but also for his daughter. So speak up and seek the maximum . . . Both possibilities appeal to him. But though the arrow on the scales swings back and forth for a long moment before it comes to rest, he chooses the latter.

And so the bargaining begins. Gandersen starts by talking at length, with some enjoyment and even sincere regret, about surrendering this fine old house, in this most desirable location in the neighbourhood of the venerable St Nicholas' Church and the artillery yard. Balthasar, coolly polite, deflects the old fox's sly argument:

"True enough. But we'll talk about the house later. The house is part of Elsbet's inheritance. Is it not so? At the moment, let us discuss the dowry."

The old man does not take it amiss. He has seen enough wet-behind-the-ears blowhards to be pleased by his son-in-law's tenaciousness.

However, by no means does he want to engage in prolonged bargaining with this much younger man.

"You mean, ready money? *Hmm*. Of course, a certain amount. But you know better than I what the times are like. Everyone is having helmets made instead of bearskin hats, and armour instead of fur coats. And consider the moment you have chosen to broach the matter. A time of such complete uncertainty. So – two hundred marks – that's it."

Whereupon the son-in-law (this ill-bred cur of a cleric) says:

"*Hm*. That's exactly half my yearly salary. And my salary is paltry."

Gandersen is somewhat taken aback. He imagines Elsbet feeling dismayed by his offer, so he hastens to add:

"But of course, Elsbet is also getting what remains in her mother's jewellery case. Agnes got her half last year, but Elsbet's share is not less than hers. For my Kati loved beautiful silver . . ."

Gandersen stoops to lift his departed Kati's jewellery case out of a riveted trunk behind the table. It is a stiff, old-fashioned chest, two spans long, with red and green flowers painted on its surface. He lays out, slowly – whether with a husband's tenderness or a salesman's calculation – the necklaces and brooches in the chest.

"This – all of it."

"This is worth about forty thalers," says the son-in-law calmly, "but could you really bear to sell them?"

"Sell them?! Of course not. They were my Kati's, after all . . ."

"That's it. Neither could I. They are my Elsbet's, after all. And besides, your Kati is long since dead, but Elsbet is as alive as can be. So neither for you nor for me is there any monetary value in these things."

"What do you mean . . . ?" For a moment, Gandersen fails to comprehend, or pretends not to. Balthasar suddenly recalls an allegory. It is a little preacherly, and God knows whether it is entirely appropriate in this context (the stories of Pygmalion and Midas combined, plus something else as well) – but in any event, he plunges in:

"What do I mean? This is what I mean: if you set the value of the jewellery as part of Elsbet's dowry very high, you are like the king who wanted to marry off his golden daughter and instructed her suitor to take her as a wife with one hand and as a lump of gold with the other . . ."

Gandersen does not quite get the drift of this. In his view, all suitors mean to get both from the fathers – the girl and the gold. He says:

"Well . . . and what, in your view, should we do? Cancel the agreement?"

"No, not at all. But the sum for the wedding, which is the responsibility of the bride's father, should be – well – proper."

"*Hm*, and just how much would that be?"

"Not less than four hundred marks."

"Four hundred marks?! In these times?!"

The old man is stunned; his dismay arises in part, of course, from his stinginess. But also from an old artisan's sense of measure. Oh, he is quite familiar with the pitiful glitter and fanfare of the Greys' weddings, the revelries, staged by people nearly destitute, that go on for three days running. And is not this former Grey, in his lust for show, for living beyond his means (at the expense of his father-in-law, no less!) – evincing much the same spirit – a disagreeable, childish, offensive lack of restraint? A trend which has lately been spreading even among the half-German and pure German artisans?

"If the dowry is worth two hundred, and the wedding costs four hundred, that adds up to a more or less decent sum. Don't forget, the exchange rate for the mark is lower now than it has ever been."

"No. Four hundred is out of the question."

"Really? Are furriers that much poorer than other artisans?"

"Listen here . . ."

"Or is Elsbet Gandersen not worth as much as, let us say – there are several I could name – for example, Krõõt, daughter of Mats, the bumpkin tailor?"

"Did he spend four hundred on his daughter's wedding?"

"Absolutely. I know it for a fact. They're in my parish."

"*Hm.*"

The old man feels like spitting. But he cannot very well spit on his worktable. And to spit on the floor, he would have to push back his stool . . . But before he does that, he realises that he would be spitting not only at the shameless demands of this cur of a cleric but also at the life and happiness and future of his youngest daughter. Regrettably. The old man's resistance melts away. He even enjoys a slight, sweet satisfaction in capitulating – on account of that fateful softheartedness that has prevented him, at other moments in his life as well, from defending his own advantage with Old Testament-like severity.

"Fine. But not before Martin's Day. *If* we are still alive then, and *if* the siege has ended."

And now St Martin's Day* had arrived. And they were still alive. But the siege was by no means over. On the contrary, in the previous three weeks it had grown ever more fierce. Especially since the sixteenth of October, when the Grand Duke's special forces, known as the *oprichniki*, had come to reinforce the army of five thousand besiegers. They had chopped down the beautiful forest at Telliskoppel and set up their encampment on the peninsula. And Balthasar would never forget what had happened two days later, on the eighteenth of October.

In the first seven weeks of the siege it had seemed that the town could hold out against the enemy. In the eighth week, ships with provisions had arrived from Stockholm and, under the protection of warships, their cargo had been unloaded and carried to the safety of the town with no losses: several hundred barrels of flour and butter, and, most important, gunpowder, iron, lead. And this had so relieved and cheered the spirits of the townspeople that the arrival of the *oprichniki*

* November 11.

107

at the town walls would not have overly alarmed anyone. But the following day, Herr Sandstede had sent men into the abandoned village of Kalamaja, to burn it down – unbeknownst to the townspeople, of course. Every nook and cranny in the courtyards and gardens and cellars and huts of the entire area around St Olaf's Church and behind Holy Ghost and in Luts Street was now crammed with refugees from Kalamaja, who, in their ignorance of matters of war, might have protested Sandstede's decision, and God knows what they would have undertaken had they learned of it beforehand. For until now, the buildings in the villages of Kalamaja and Nunnavalli – nearly two hundred dwellings with their outbuildings and the church – had remained intact. And while Magnus constructed earthworks and bombarded the town from the east and north-east and finally from the direction of Tõnismäe, there was no sustained siege at all from the sea. The result was that until the first snows fell in October, the men of Kalamaja had been able to sprint out of the Great Coast Gate on several occasions in the pale light of dawn, to gather their turnips from the fields and cart them off to town. The cellar beneath the altar at Holy Ghost Church was now stacked man-high with turnips, and men appointed by the elders of the village distributed them daily. But on the evening of the sixteenth of October, Berend Leichtblut of Westphalia, a militiaman who had married the widow of Valgepea-Madis of Kalamaja the previous year, had come at the behest of his wife to Balthasar and in the secrecy of the confessional told him that ten of the town's militiamen, himself included, along with the provost of the company, had been ordered to appear the following morning at dawn at the Great Coast Gate, with buckets of tar and torches and flint and steel, to be prepared to dash to Kalamaja upon command and set fire to as many places as they possibly could – and, in the name of God, to keep their mouths shut about it until they had returned! That same evening, Balthasar had gone to the Town Hall, looking for

Herr Sandstede. He had found the man very busy, holding discussions, shouting reprimands at the company captains, paying out money, cursing and arguing over some kind of cannon. Yet Balthasar had managed to waylay him at the door of the Small Council Hall and ask:

"Herr Sandstede, tell me, is the decision to burn down Kalamaja the right one?"

"Of course it is," Herr Sandstede had replied, "but I'm astonished – how does Herr Balthasar know about it already?"

Balthasar had not answered the question, saying instead:

"I understand that you are afraid the Muscovite might take the houses apart and use the logs to build blockhouses. But in Kopli they chopped down an entire forest. They used a third to build their shelters and huts. Two-thirds are strewn about on the snow. You can see it all from the steeples. That means they have no shortage of material for blockhouses."

At which Herr Sandstede had said, smiling:

"True enough. But Herr Pastor is forgetting one thing. The Muscovite would have to travel three-quarters of a league further to haul the wood from there."

A sudden animosity had flared up in Balthasar's heart at this greenhorn would-be warrior, this long-time sword-clinking grand lord, and he had asked sharply, in the tone he used in church to address scoundrels condemned to sit on the stool of shame:

"Is this distance great enough, Herr Sandstede – this three-quarters of a league – I'm asking you, to justify feeding to the flames two hundred homes and a house of God?"

At that Herr Sandstede had pulled his helmet onto his head to go and watch the exchange of fire from the top of the wall at the Karja Gate; he raised and lowered the visor and said, in a voice altered by the iron screen covering his mouth:

"Yes, Herr Pastor. The distance is sufficiently great. But as I recall, you yourself, Herr Balthasar, by the mysterious will of God, come from there. And therefore you should be able to understand that you, of all people, are not the man to decide the fate of that huddle of hovels."

"And why not . . . ?"

"Because you would, without hesitation, sacrifice the interests of the town – the more worthy interests, for those of that flea-bag village – that much is clear."

Balthasar had decided to go immediately to Toompea and ask Herr Leion, the new vicegerent who had arrived the week before, to reverse the decision. True, Herr Leion did not know him the way Herr Horn once did. But one could hope that he was not insolent, like the local gentry, towards the poor. He said:

"Well, I would be interested to know what Herr Leion thinks of all this!"

At which, raising his visor to his forehead, Herr Sandstede had replied bluntly, without attempting to conceal a smirk:

"You can spare yourself the trouble of climbing the hill. We reached an agreement about the affair this morning. When I told him that, in my opinion, Kalamaja should be levelled, he said that that was exactly what he was going to propose to the town today."

By dawn of the eighteenth of October, the designated arsonists had for some reason not yet carried out their terrible deed. But around noon, people in town noticed smoke rising against the dark-grey sea, from three or four of the nearer huts on the snowy shore in Kalamaja, and immediately thereafter in six or seven other places. Many of the Kalamaja folk who had escaped to town tried to rush out of the Great Coast Gate, but it had been bolted, and no-one was permitted near the walls on the seaward side, from which they would have had a better view.

Balthasar and Märten had climbed up into the bell tower of Holy Ghost Church. They could see Kalamaja burning as if in the palm of a hand. From seven, eight, from twenty houses downwind, the smoke had begun to rise. It was not the serene, grey smoke of everyday life, not the peaceful smoke of hearth fires that once rose from the living village as a daily offering towards God's low clouds, but black and white streaked columns of frightening, swirling smoke above the lifeless settlement – black streaks from the pitch of the torches, white ones from the partly wet thatch of the roofs. Down below, knots of Kalamaja's inhabitants thudded along Saiakang Way, past Holy Ghost Church. Tattered cries, curses and laments echoed between the narrow walls and stone roofs and rose through the veil of a lightly falling snow. The sky above the sea grew darker under the snow clouds; red roosters of flames flew up from the windows and attic openings of the burning houses. Balthasar realised that his body was damp with an odious turmoil of agitation and dread, and to his own surprise, he found himself still arguing against Herr Sandstede's arrogance: So, these people whose homes are burning today, whose childhood dwellings are in flames, are not permitted to raise their voices in defence of their lives and homes? Because they cannot comprehend the "higher interests" of the general welfare of the town? That is to say, that these higher purposes are clear only to the likes of Sandstede, that Saxon slacker of a knight, and those Brandenburg beer barrels Schleyer and König and their ilk . . . (He was vaguely aware, but tried not to acknowledge that he was relegating Herr Leion's role in this course of events to the background. He remained silent with regard to him in his own thoughts. In order to save both Leion and himself – which actually meant the king and the established world order and himself.) Lord, to speak of a higher purpose would be to speak of none other than Your purpose, which is surely at one with the interests of the lowliest and most humble of Your creatures, as Our Saviour has given us to know . . . But here, if I wish to ring the church bells on the occasion of this terrible event . . . I am expected to obtain the permission of these gentlemen . . .

"Märten, go down! Run! Take Traani-Andres' boy Päärn along. Toll the bells. Make them boom!"

"You mean the fire bells?"

"The fire bells. And the funeral bells. Both at once!"

Märten hurried down, and as the bells began to toll, Balthasar watched the village burn. But he could not see the house or sauna of Mündrik-Mats, where Märten had lived until he moved into the parsonage; they were hidden from view by Hundimäe Point. But the homestead of the departed Siimon Rissa, the last one on the point, right on the water, was visible to anyone who knew it, even in the dim light of dusk. He watched the cottage of Traani-Andres next door go up in flames and saw a strong east wind carry burning stalks of straw from his roof to Siimon's, saw the flames advance along Andres' rail fence to reach Siimon's barn. And saw the houses, partly in ruin, several times sold, and perhaps even renounced and abandoned as well, blaze into flame and become one with the huge, furious fire . . . The bells pealed next to Balthasar: bright little Seifert with its *cling-clang-cling-clang* and big Kemming, at every sixth – no, at this moment it was at every tenth – heartbeat: *boom-bam-boom-bam* . . . Balthasar stared so hard that his eyes began to sting, and he squeezed them shut and thought about everything that was in flames and everything that would be forever lost to him . . . But the thing he recalled first, and which absurdly overshadowed everything else, was the little wooden cow from the herd that Paap had carved for him long ago, the herd that he had left on the shore that time, thirty years ago, and which the tide had washed away – God knows where. Later he had found that single cow and hidden it, for fear of losing it, between the roof battens above the stone wall of the barn – and forgotten it until this day . . .

The fire raged for several hours under the whirling snowfall. For some reason, the church alone was spared, nor did it catch fire of itself – situated as it was in the middle of the graveyard, at a distance from the houses.

By midnight, what remained of the site where the village had been was a glowing red wound, five hundred fathoms long, surrounded by darkness.

That wound was still there in Balthasar – he could feel it. It no longer throbbed with the stinging pain of those first days of the blowing north-west winds, when the stench of the burnt village hung in the air and all that remained were ashes. The wound had become for him a strange, empty place, peculiarly disorienting, an absence almost imperceptibly palpable, each moment of recollection accompanied by a stab of pain. Like the loss of a limb, not of a vital limb, to be sure, but of a part of his own body nonetheless. Nor did he find comfort in the news, delivered a few days later by Leichtblut, that the Kalamaja church had been spared, not by chance nor by some early decision, but by an order from Herr Sandstede, which had arrived at the Great Coast Gate half an hour before the men were sent out to burn down the village. It was a deplorably small concession, and it was not clear that Balthasar's intervention had played any role in it. In him the fire left the feeling that he had been somehow maimed, though some at the Town Hall claimed that Tallinn was now much more secure. It undermined his hope and belief that the siege would not last long. Furthermore, if someone like Balthasar – a man living, after all, on this side of the walls – could feel as he did, how much more pain-ful must the burning wound be for the inhabitants of Kalamaja, and how much darker it must have made their view of the future. Balthasar saw it every day. The Council of Clergy enjoined him to hold daily services as long as the town was under siege, even twice a day on Saturdays and Sundays. The church was now full to overflowing at every service. With the enemy just outside the town walls and cannon-balls whizzing overhead, the son of man feels closer to his stern God than at other times. In part, these homeless fugitives were drawn to the church by a sincere desire for the Word of God. But even more by their need to lean against each others' shoulders and be warmed by each others' breath. For with the coming of the chill days of autumn, the refugees, sheltering in the outbuildings of the town's gentry or in their courtyards under the open sky, were in dire straits. But the walls of the church had not yet frozen through, nor had Balthasar in any appreciable measure curtailed his expenses for candles, and the more people inside, the warmer and more comforting it was. Furthermore, it was the only place the refugees could gather where they were welcomed – not shunned, as they were in taverns and alehouses whenever five or six Kalamaja folk gathered there to sit for a spell . . . Counting women and children, the people displaced from unfortunate Kalamaja alone numbered over a thousand. Balthasar had succeeded in finding shelter in the Almshouse, behind Holy Ghost Church, for a few dozen of the weakest of the sick and the aged. And he provided refuge at the parsonage, in several shabby little rooms and even in the great-room, to some of the families he knew – Traani-Andres with his old wife Krõõt, and the children of the departed Mündrik-Mats, along with their husbands and wives and children. It is true, he did it more to forestall grumbling against him or around him or within his own conscience, more from a sense of duty than from satisfaction at being charitable. He established a work schedule for the women: the more vigorous among them were charged with cooking. Using the flour stored above the church and the pastor's firewood and his hearth, they prepared several kettles of thin gruel and distributed it in the church-yard to those in need. And so, nearly every day, in addition to his other duties, Balthasar made the rounds of the refugees, advising and comforting them . . . Good Lord, there was plenty of trouble and more than enough inconvenience with them around. To tell the truth, there were not many among them with the kind of serene and steadfast nature that was pleasing to God. But perhaps it seemed that way because serenity and steadfastness and faith in God become less readily apparent the deeper they are . . . What was quite apparent (and what, day after day, angered him about his new flock) was the deplorable complaining and whining of some of them: "Oh, we miserable worms under God's angry heel, ground into the dust . . ." And the pitiful, empty bravado of others: "Wait'll I get the whole lot of the damn bastards and thrash 'em till the swine foul their pants." And then the total apathy of yet others – worthy of a good thrashing: "We don't need much mores'n a swig o' ale to warm our bellies and it's a whoopdee-do." . . . Loafers and idlers in the eyes of God . . . But it was, after all, his duty to comfort and support those who *truly* suffered. And, in the midst of all this disorder and hardship and uncertainty, to endure. To comfort Elsbet. To endure.

"Elsbet – you do love me, don't you?"

He asked the question with a pleasant sense of confidence and curiosity, and yet, at times he could not entirely suppress his unease. Now, in anticipation of her response, his uneasiness suddenly overcame him – here, in her little room, marvellously quaint, and yet astonishingly real, solid, with its whitewashed walls, a maiden's narrow bed, a wobbly table and stool . . . Above the stone window seat, the rough plastered wall behind Elsbet's hair, within easy reach of his hand; above the table, on the opposite wall, the tiny dull mirror in a patch of light; upon the table, an octavo edition of Aesop, bound in white leather (the Frankfurt edition of Burkhard Waldis, *Anno MDXLVII*, the sight of which startled Balthasar for an instant, even though it was his own gift to Elsbet – given to her with the not especially humble thought that, though other bridegrooms might give their brides slippers and hand-kerchiefs and gauze breast bindings with silk ribbons – he would give her all these things someday as well – but at present, he would give her this book) . . . And yet, he felt uneasy as he awaited her response, here in the tiny, second-storey room of the furrier's house, with his arms around Elsbet's waist, feeling her startle and shrink a little with each boom of cannon-fire.

"Don't you?"

"Of course I do, Balthasar."

It was said with the kind of gentle forbearance that intimates the insignificance of the words, given the truth behind them. And with a love that forgives the words for the anxious vanity underlying them.

Balthasar kissed Elsbet again, feeling that he owed something to the world and to God for all the blessings that, despite everything, were his. He was ashamed of his doubts and anxieties about the future and his feelings of fatigue. For what, actually, did it all add up to: the morning service and the dispensing of advice and comfort in a dozen refugee shelters, the christening in a sheep stall on Luts Street (like our Saviour's birth!), all the rushing about atop the city walls to peer at the enemy forces and new fortifications and the entire panorama of the siege, the discussions with the ensigns and quartermaster-sergeants of Herr Schleyer? What was all this to a man whose beloved had such deep-grey eyes as these and such black lashes, and when nothing more was asked of him but patience, when he was alive and healthy and his standing with the congregation and the town was steadily rising, and when locked within the walls of his study lay a few hundred pages that he had already written about things that had happened and were happening in this land – waiting to be polished and organised and expanded . . .

Knock-knock-knock . . .

They drew apart and Balthasar went to open the door. It was Maijke.

"Herr Pastor – that fellow Märten, your bell-ringer, or whoever he is, came to say that you are summoned . . ."

Märten was waiting downstairs on the snowy front stoop. Old Tibi-Toomas, who lived near the Small Coast Gate, had come to the parsonage to implore the Herr Pastor to come, for God's sake, to serve Communion. Yes, Märten had already grabbed the necessary communion implements.

Before leaving, Balthasar went back upstairs:

"Elsbet, I will be back right away."

He did not exactly know why he said that. The words simply slipped out. Because he meant it: he would come by again afterwards. And yet, there was also another reason, one he probably already had in mind. For just now, in an elusive moment, somewhere deep inside he had reached a decision: he would not endure this waiting any longer! Already imagining his return up those stairs, he went downstairs, thinking: The reason I've been patient until now is not that it would be sin in my view if it happened before that fat Gerstenberger of St Nicholas' blessed us . . . He stepped out onto the snowy street and followed Märten's bobbing circle of lantern light and the sound of his tinkling bell along the pedestrian paths trampled deep into the snowbanks. He imagined hurrying back along this same path . . . And not because, not only because Elsbet would most certainly consider it a sin . . . He watched a hissing Muscovite fireball fly from the right, from the direction of Bremen Tower across town, landing somewhere in the vicinity of Kuldjala Tower . . . Rather, it was because Elsbet, of all the women Balthasar had known, was to be his wife, and thus had to be different from all the others . . . A group of five or six boisterous youngsters wearing masks made of rags and straw, and smeared with some kind of paint, rushed towards them from under Brockhusen's gateway, pale-yellow spectres bobbing in the dim light of their swaying lantern. "Ah, so it's the day for playing your pranks . . . ," murmured Balthasar amiably. For what can one expect of children, when grown men – and in particular the hangman's henchmen, there were two of them right over there – still observed this silly custom of Martin's Eve with the usual frivolity, as though this were peacetime and a

117

time for revelry. They were walking about town this evening in their black capes, knocking on doors and begging for shillings, each one saying as he did so, "I am poor Doctor Martin Luther . . ." He had no idea how such a stupid custom came to be . . . nor why the Council of Clergy had not demanded that the Town Council prohibit this unseemly mockery. But just how long was a man supposed to wait, a man who, moreover, in the sight of God and other men, had the *ex officio** right to join in wedlock both the sinful and the virtuous, and the power to absolve sinners, to boot? How long? And his chosen bride, as well . . . How long was he meant to permit the Muscovite with his German and Danish dogs to taunt him, make a fool of him?! Out of the darkness emerged a sister from the Red Cloister, laughing fitfully as she and a tipsy mercenary soldier, arms around each others' necks, lurched unsteadily back into the shadows. "Oh, you little strumpet . . ." muttered Balthasar. "The fellow's no doubt supposed to be standing watch behind Hattorpe Tower or at Stolting . . ." He shrugged, forgiving them in his mind, then realised with some embarrassment that such forgiveness was nothing more than bribery, bribery . . . So be it . . . but for how long must a man make his bride unhappy by persevering in their absurd situation?! . . . Alright, that last was probably only partly true, for it would perhaps make Elsbet even more unhappy if he attempted to take her, in spite of the circumstances, without the ordained blessing . . . But could one really know what girls were like deep down? Maybe every one of them, including Elsbet, was the same kind of conflicted creature as he himself: with a soul willing to wait, to accept chastity, and a body ready to trample down all fences. Until the *spirit* stepped up (Why the Devil? Why God? Why not a person's own clear, mature, superior spirit, as godlike or devil-like as it might be?) and reached a decision, saying, *Seelah!* . . .† Several citizen patrols

* By virtue of one's office (Latin).
† Stop (Hebrew).

118

recruited for the defence of the town crossed the street in front of them, trudging in the snow banks at the heels of their commanders. They were mostly journeymen, with a few mature and portly master craftsmen among them, halberds carelessly slung on their shoulders, swords askew at their sides . . . And a bride must be led, a virgin, to the altar . . . ? That old Catholic cry of virtue – even in the midst of the popish obscenities of the time . . . Whereas even Moses had said, with utmost simplicity, with respect to a woman not betrothed: "And if a man entice a maid that is not betrothed, and lie with her, he shall surely endow her to make her his wife." And that is what we too shall do.

Tibi-Toomas lived in a common caretaker's hut in merchant Hehn's courtyard, opposite the old Russian church, at the end of a long, vaulted passageway. The wooden hut was flanked by stacks of wood and piles of rubbish, a wagon shed, stables and an outhouse. Toomas, with his wispy goatee, and his old wife, bent and swaying as she walked, guided the pastor and the bell-ringer to the back corner of the chamber, lit only by the glowing coals on the hearth. Toomas blew on the coals to ignite a pinewood splint. The patient for whom Balthasar had been summoned lay on a pile of straw on the floor. She was a fifteen-year-old girl by the name of Liso, who had run away from somewhere beyond Pleekmäe, as Toomas told them. She had been with him and his old woman since the start of the siege, earning her daily bread by helping the housekeeper of Herr Hehn's household. Now she lay unconscious, breathing in rasping, fitful gasps. Balthasar touched her forehead. It was on fire. Toomas said:

"Yestermorn', she was washin' the floor over at Herr Hehn's. In the storehouse or some such place. And fell down the cellar hatch, hard on her right side. Bruised clear up to her armpit. And since yestereve', her mind's been gone . . ."

Balthasar had Märten clear the low worktable and spread a white cloth over it, as was right and proper, and set upon it the wine and

119

bread. Everything as it should be, even though it was clear that he could not give Liso the sacrament. He knelt by the girl, and the others did the same. He started the "Our Father" out loud and the others murmured along with him. He banished Elsbet's face from his mind. He looked at the dying girl's burning visage turning grey now, and he prayed with concentration, something he was still capable of doing, even if at times it might have been more a matter of concentrating his eyebrows and facial muscles and will than his mind and heart.

There was no-one here to be consoled – not even in a few simple words and without much ado – as church rule prescribed. For the sick girl would not have heard them, and Toomas and his wife did not need them. Balthasar folded his hands over Liso's shockingly clammy fingers, and prayed:

"Lord God, Heavenly Father, who has promised to us in the words of Your son Jesus Christ, whenever two are gathered together to pray, my Father in Heaven will heed their prayer. This, Your promise, we ask too for Your servant, Liso, baptised in Christ . . ." (He could assume this to be true, but he could not very well continue with "who has openly before us acknowledged You, Eternal Lord, and Your Son and the Holy Spirit".) He continued simply, "That You have mercy upon her, and if You truly call her to Yourself, grant her eternal bliss through Your Son, Jesus Christ, Our Lord. Amen."

He had prayed so fervently – believing it would somehow protect this sick girl and Elsbet and himself (Bribery! Bribery!) – that not until the end of the prayer did he notice that the three siege-culverins in the rondel* at the Karja Gate had begun, in the dark of evening, to bark at the enemy in full voice.

He made the sign of the cross above the patient, his arm stiff, his jaws clenched – displaying none of the effortless ease of a bishop's practised gesture, which he had never forgotten after once having seen

* Round tower.

the way Herr Geldern made the sign . . . He stood up, refused the farthing Tibi-Toomas tentatively held out to him. (Bribery! No, he is not trying to buy me off with this money, rather it is I who am trying to bribe – whom? – by refusing to accept it.)

When they had reached the Kanuts' Guild, he said to Märten:

"Go to Barber Dietrich. Ask him to go – at my request – to take a look at Liso. Perhaps bloodletting would do some good."

Elsbet whispered, with despair and, thank God, not only despair:

"Good Lord, Balthasar . . . is it really permitted . . . ?!"

"It is!" Balthasar replied.

"Having just come from a deathbed . . . ?!" she whispered.

Balthasar was silent. He struck a spark with flint and steel to light tinder for the candle. Had an observer chanced to look at him closely, he would have seen, by the light of the flint spark, a mischievous little-boy's glint in Balthasar's eyes as he said:

"But I will perform two christenings. Tomorrow morning . . ."

He managed to light the candle, lifted the candlestick from the table, and looked into Elsbet's face – with its quite peculiar expression, oddly absent and at the same time present. He saw traces of tears on her cheek. He wanted to say, My beloved, my beloved . . . but remained silent. For he suddenly felt that he was perhaps not as entirely sincere as he would have wished – for otherwise, would he not have waited, in spite of everything . . . ? He was silent. He had to say something, but did not know what. At that moment, someone knocked at the door. Moving to open it, he felt relieved, grateful for the knock. At least for a few moments, he was grateful . . . It was Majike again. And again Märten was downstairs, asking to see the Pastor. Balthasar went down.

When he returned, he paused at the threshold. Elsbet was sitting on the three-legged stool at the table where the volumes of Burkhardt lay, looking into the dusky little mirror that hung above it as she secured some loose strands of hair. She saw Balthasar's face in the mirror. She could not have seen it very clearly. The mirror was too small and the room too dark. But for some reason she turned around and was about to rush towards him.

"Balthasar – what is it?"

"Don't come any closer!"

"Jesus – tell me – what is it?"

"The girl is dead. She had the plague."

The dreaded word had been uttered. (Oh, Elsbet had sensed it, intuited it, when she surrendered to him – although she had not understood the significance of her intuition . . .) The scourge of God had struck close – it was significant, how close. And of course, the dreadful affliction in itself was neither unprecedented nor unheard of . . . Still, it had never before come this close to Balthasar. Not even in '49, when it carried off Superintendent Bock, along with several hundred other people. Balthasar clearly remembered the general despair throughout the town and the rows of grey coffins lined up at the edge of the cemetery and the plague barbers in their beaked masks. In '58, when he had arrived in Stettin, a plague epidemic had nearly subsided. And in '61, when it took Meus, Balthasar was in Germany. But in '66, it had taken only twenty or thirty people here in Tallinn, even though it had been fierce further inland. And the seven or eight members of the Holy Ghost congregation had belonged to the departed Bushauer's flock.

"Wash your face and mouth and hands with vinegar right away. And fill your chamber with smoke. Laurel and juniper. The peasants believe in juniper above all. I am leaving now. I won't come back until my condition is clear. That will probably be in three days . . ."

"Balthasar, this is God's punishment for our sin . . ."

Balthasar stopped on the threshold. "Well, if the plague spreads throughout the town – as I fear it will – do you really think God would punish the entire town on account of our sin? Do you?"

122

O Lord, the way this man – with the whiff of stables and grain about him and other strange and unfamiliar scents, this untamed, sinful, beloved man – the way he looked at God's actions through the lens of human reason was truly not the way of a pious soul. But however unsettling it might be, it was also reassuring and encouraging. If the plague should spread throughout the town . . . ? Lord, tell me, which I should wish for, in that case. O God, what thoughts . . . I do not wish for anything, not for anything. I put this and everything and myself in God's hands. I pray only that he remain untouched by plague and that he commend himself to God . . . and that he not, like a fabric merchant, apply a measuring stick to God's judgments nor attempt to draw inferences from them . . .

But the Lord had decided, and the plague did spread through the entire town. As if Balthasar and Elsbet truly needed this for their absolution.

By the third day, the number of the dead in all the congregations had risen to twenty or so, including old Tibi-Toomas and his wife. And death came with unusual rapidity this time. One woke up in the morning with a fever and a tight iron band clamped around one's head. By afternoon the sufferer felt that the relentless pounding had caused the band to become thinner and increasingly fiery. By evening the swelling began, either in the groin or armpits. During the night the patient lost consciousness. By next morning the buboes, having turned brown, burst, releasing an unbelievable quantity of pus; this sometimes brought relief and recovery to one victim in twenty, the other nineteen were dead by the third morning, as if their insides had simply putrefied and burned, leaving but the shells of their bodies behind . . . In a week there were nearly a hundred dead; in two, three hundred; just before Christmas, the number of dead had grown to six hundred. In the first week the burials were conducted to the accompaniment of church bells. Then Herr Leion forbade the ringing of bells at any time except during the sermon. The burials were to be carried out in silence – to prevent the enemy beyond the town walls from calculating how many were dying within, lest this embolden them. The Town Council compelled three barbers to minister to the afflicted by threatening to revoke their licence to practise if they refused. In order to prevent them from carrying the disease to their families or spreading it around the town, provisions were conveyed to a ramshackle wooden house at the walled-up Harju Gate where they were to live, keeping their distance from all healthy people until the scourge had been lifted from the town. In one respect, there was an advantage to the enemy siege: the barbers could not flee the town, which at other times had often happened. But in another respect, it was a disadvantage: there was nowhere to bury the dead except inside the walls, and the living, who at other times would have been allowed to flee, could go nowhere. Everyone had to sit in the plague-ridden, locked-up town, like people in a burning house with barred windows and padlocked doors, waiting to see whether God would send clouds and rain to quench the flames or whether they would all be burned alive . . . the situation of the townspeople was even more dire than that of people in a burning house, for a fire can at least be combated: a prudent homeowner would have barrels of water stored in the attic, and axes for hacking burning timber into pieces which could be flung out through the window bars. Cries for help could summon nearby neighbours to break down doors. But what could people in a besieged town do? Those hearing cries for help were likely to fire more arrows from their crossbows, more whistling shots from their arquebuses, more terrible volleys of cannon-balls – unless, perhaps, the cries for help were accompanied by clear cries of surrender – may the Lord God save us from that . . . And even if some kind of dubious remedy to ward off the plague happened to exist, it would only be available to those with a prominent enough name and a heavy enough purse to reach Apothecary Dyck's stores and the fruits of his learning. He had walnuts and almond milk and dried chanterelles . . . alongside something reputed to be even more effective – a powdered concoction of seventy components, a cure-all called *electuarium theriacum,** to be swallowed with rosewater or Spanish wine. But for the poor, among whom the disease seemed to be raging with the greatest force, all these remedies were so far beyond reach that it made no sense even to mention them. And this was so not just for medicines, but even for the recommended daily regime. For where, packed into their miserable little hovels and shacks and cellar shelters, were these people supposed to take the recommended measured walks and horseback rides? How were they to avoid the thick air, the manure, the run-off from the barns, and keep their windows open to admit cold, dry air, and inhale the smoke of burning bay laurel and juniper, and wash their hands and faces often with vinegar, and above all, avoid crowds – even saunas – not to mention everyone suspected of the affliction? . . . Consequently, the main hope of the poorer population lay in the common practice of smoking their rooms and, above all, in prayer.

Balthasar could not, of course, say that he was entirely lacking in remedies. True, he did not have the money for *theriac*, there was no doubt of that. But the women of his congregation brought him several small bags of dried chanterelles. And he had the means to procure vinegar, even though it was not entirely clear if what Herr Dyck had sold him was pure four-thieves' vinegar – plague vinegar, in other words, which was purported to contain all kinds of costly oils of lavender and rosemary and lemon, and other such. The storerooms of Herr Dyck hardly contained supplies of these oils adequate to meet the demand during an outbreak of the disease. The juniper branches for smoking the parsonage were not much to speak of. But fortunately

* Ancient panacea made from seventy ingredients – reputedly invented by Emperor Nero's physician.

there were at least some to be found (Balthasar had been using juniper branches for three or four years in his sauna, and there were now so many stubby old bundles thrown onto the topmost planks, that he sent half of them to the Gandersen household). So, Balthasar was not without several remedies – and the power of prayer would, it was assumed, better protect a man like him than some other common sinner further removed from the Lord. And yet, it seemed to him, especially in the first days of the outbreak, that he was entirely defenceless and vulnerable. Especially as his official duties grew more grievous and more difficult day by day.

In the second week, the duties of plague pastor were assigned to Pastor Bussow of St John's Almshouse. He had fled to town at the beginning of the siege, and his church, along with the entire Almshouse, had been held by the besiegers for three months. But he could barely manage the task of administering last rites and conducting funerals for the sick refugees. Among the parishioners of Holy Ghost, the duties of *pastor pestilentiarius** were entirely on Balthasar's shoulders. In the first days, two, three, four dead, and by Christmas-time, seventeen . . .

In the bitter cold of the dark early morning, by the guttering flames of tallow candles – cropped to half their length now – ancient words of hope spill from the pulpit into the bone-chilling gloom of the church unto the congregation, that great grey creature, stirring, desperate, hungry for salvation . . . Would that it not hold these words to be chaff, but find in them sustenance for heart and soul at this dreadful, most dreadful of dreadful times: "And the angel said unto them: Fear not. For behold, I bring you good tidings of great joy, which shall be to all people: For unto you is born this day in the city of David a Saviour . . . Truly I say: unto us, unto us too, the people of Tallinn!" (Oh, would that this give them strength, those to whom I speak, as it gives me strength – for whence comes my strength if not from my faith, whatever

* Plague-pastor (Latin).

little I possess?!) Yes – unto us too, whosoever we are, lying face down in the snow and the mud under flying cannonballs and in the putrid mire of this disease, yet daring to lift the face of our spirit, in faith and hope, towards the Light that is Christmas. (There, on the left near that column, there's a disturbance of some sort among the people. I cannot tell in the half-dark what it is. Did someone collapse on the floor? Are they dragging someone out of the church? That's what it seems to be. Someone overcome by the plague in God's House? Can they do that? Drag out a dying one in the name of life, away from the altar, out of God's House? . . . I don't know, I don't know . . . when I know that I myself see their breath rising towards me and ask myself: which one of them, unbeknownst to all, already carries the *contagio* of the disease in himself?)

The organ begins to sound, wheezing and wavering. For there are inexperienced youths from the town school treading the pedals today; the others are fled. The organist himself is new – a fumbling former organist from Kalamaja, with just two days' practice on the Holy Ghost registers. After the *köster*, Caur, was laid into the ground the day before yesterday . . . "Lo, how a rose ere blooming" . . . The hymn, trailing behind the organ, rises barely audibly from a thousand throats hoarse with despondency: "This rosebud small and tender" . . . The one upon whom we lay our hopes – the only one we can lay them upon . . . even in this dread time . . . Get thee behind me Satan, you who whisper in my ear: But what if the little rose has plague-poisoned thorns? . . . "Amid the cold of winter . . . behold Our Father's glory" . . . A fearsome glory such as to make one quake, if judged in human terms . . . But man must not judge God, he must do his duty . . . Despondent grey faces, grey shapes grouped around the door behind the altar. Behind them, in the middle of the small graveyard, in the shadow of chill grey houses, under the grey sky streaked with blood-red – how many this morning? – Five, six, seven, eight, nine grey coffins alongside the long, low grave between frozen mounds of earth . . . Funerary words. Again and again. Spoken to the hissing wind. To the yellowish, tear-streaked faces. Today, at least, not to the thundering of cannonballs. Odd that the Muscovites are not firing today – can it be that they too observe Christmas? . . . Frozen clods of earth thudding upon the coffins. Week after week. Frozen clods of earth echoing through my chilled body. And then the wrenching moments at the sickbeds. The dying, breathing their last on rotting pallets in their pitiable shanties. Words of condolence – words, mere words. God, are they of any use . . . ? But they have to be. They are! A hundred times, he had seen with his own eyes how the awful suffering of the dying abated when he took their hands into his own and said: "Your sins are forgiven," and how eyes that had nearly turned to stone quickened, and then were extinguished before the miracle occurred when, with trembling soul, he said to them, "Resurrection and eternal life" . . . And at the same time, there was his own fear of death . . . Fear – grey, dark-grey, black, blazing out at times into fiery purple . . . Good Lord, the plague barbers had tried to flee town in their deadly fear. The Town Council did not accuse them of planning to go over to the enemy, which they would certainly have done in other circumstances, but the disease was rumoured to have broken out in the enemy camp as well. They were permitted to continue working and were spared the gallows because they were needed at this time. Relief was provided for them and assistants sent to aid them: three murderers in the town stables awaiting hanging. The bailiff had promised to spare their lives if they faithfully fulfilled their duties and if they did not succumb to the disease, which the bailiff would take as a sign from God . . . But were Balthasar's duties any lighter than those of the plague barbers and their aides? They at least had long leather gloves to wear when they treated the pus-filled buboes and carbuncles of the ill, or lanced those that failed to break open of themselves. And when they bent over the afflicted, they wore long-beaked masks, enabling them to turn the beaks to one side to avoid breathing the exhalations and vapours of the diseased body. And inside the beak they even had a rag soaked in vinegar to filter the air they breathed . . . But when Balthasar laid his palm on the foreheads of the plague-stricken or took their hot hands, damp or icy, into his own in prayer – that the solace of God might pass from him to them – he could not very well interpose a goatskin glove between himself and the patients! And when he bent over a sick man that he might convey to him the promise of Jesus Christ, "This day shall you abide with me in Paradise", it was quite unthinkable for him to murmur from behind the barrier of a leather beak and a vinegar-soaked rag those words spoken by the Saviour from the cross . . . O Lord God, at each such occasion the stony hand of fear gripped his heart. And each time, he was miserable, wretched, that such fear should come upon him and that the words of God, which he uttered to comfort the sick, were powerless to dispel his own fear. Often, too, the devilishly ominous *interpretatio*s of the Scriptures, which flashed through his thoughts like unclean, elusive birds, vexed him and made him flinch. "This day shall you bide with me in Paradise" – you, who in an hour or two will be stiff and cold . . . Do those words not mean – with me, who is kneeling here on the muddy floor, in the stench of pus, choking with fear, and groping for the iron links of the chain behind the words of the prayer: *to do my duty, to do my duty, to do my duty* . . . even as I resist, in such a wretched manner, the idea of entering today the joys of Paradise?

In effect, Balthasar had less material protection against the deadly disease than even the plague barbers. He was on the same footing in this respect with those murderers whose fate the Council had consigned to the wisdom of God. For, like Jakob of Montpellier, during that town's dreadful epidemic a hundred years ago, who knew no other remedy than to rub his hands and face with a rag steeped in vinegar, neither was there any other remedy in the town of Tallinn for Balthasar, nor for the murderers tending the stricken. Yet it must be said that the fear of the disease began to wane in Balthasar as the weeks of the epidemic wore on.

Perhaps this came about, to some extent, from a deepening trust in God, who had protected him until then. But that was not likely – not after the hellish scenes of misery he had witnessed. More likely, his terror gradually abated simply because of fatigue and the numbing effect of daily exposure to a silent and invisible danger lurking everywhere. To dwell on that danger would have meant burning his own spirit to ashes, the way the disease consumed bodies. In any event, Balthasar noted that his frame of mind was very different when he entered the house of a plague victim now, from what it had been in the early days of the disease. In those first weeks he had recoiled each time he caught sight of the ochre cross painted by the plague barbers on the doorposts of houses to which they had been sent or summoned. When he entered such a house he was greeted sometimes by weeping family members paralysed by fear; at other times his footsteps echoed through a bleak dwelling deserted by its inhabitants, as he strained to hear the groans of the dying person and groped his way in the dark, only to find a cold corpse. When he entered such a house, he felt, whether it was a shabby hut or the spacious home of an artisan, as though he were stepping into a trap. A kind of ferret cage that would snap shut with a click, a trap with no exit, with a huge, crushing stone suspended overhead that for some reason would not fall immediately, but would slowly and *visibly* begin to descend . . . In the third week of the epidemic, he began to feel that there was no back wall to the plague houses he entered. That the slimy floor, covered by a mix of snowmelt or frozen mud from the plague barbers' boots and the pus of the disease and the spit of the barbers' aides, was dangerously sloping towards a bottomless pit. And that any careless step could send him plunging over its edge . . . And yet, the fear of a fall did not now torment him with its former force. The feeling of horror, however, persisted, and with it the indefinable attraction of things unknown and unknowable . . .

Perhaps a sense of shame also lent him courage. Shame, that he was still alive. Shame, that he was still able, be it late in the evening or at midnight, to wash his hands and face with vinegar and to walk past the sleeping members of his household (the disease had not yet touched them) and go up the stairs and close the door of his study behind him . . . Shame, that he could still open the iron door of his wall cupboard and spread out the grey sheets of paper upon his lectern and read them by candlelight – as though there might be something significant in them *sub specie aeternitatis* . . .* That he could even take up his pen and continue writing:

In the year 1571, on the 12th day of new-year-month,† yet another company of Muscovite forces arrived at the city walls with heavy cannon and fire-mortars. Towards nightfall of the 13th of January, they entrenched themselves in the bitter cold, between St John's and the Copper Mill, and began that very night to bombard the town with six- and sixteen- and twenty-five-pound cannonballs, though these did no great harm to the populace. Only one musketeer on the wall was killed and two poor women, sisters, lying asleep atop their stove.

On the 16th day of new-year-month, the Muscovite constructed another emplacement at Pleekmäe in front of Viru Gate. From there they fired stone cannonballs and fireballs into the town, but damaged no buildings or people.

On the 17th the Muscovite captured the splendid hospital, the Pox House, and conveyed several cannons into it and took cover

* Under the aspect of eternity (Latin).
† January.

there. The men of Tallinn did not grant them much respite, however, but sallied forth that very day through the Great Coast Gate, and in full force engaged them in battle. But the Muscovites had the advantage both in their location and the buildings they occupied, being protected by a heavy wall on one side and a strong board fence on the other, and so put up vigorous resistance from the cover of their position and wounded many townsmen, until the latter were forced to retreat, taking one prisoner back with them. They interrogated him thoroughly, gleaning much useful information about the enemy, and at twilight sallied forth once more. They now stormed the Pox House and dislodged the enemy, slew many Muscovites, and set the hospital aflame

On the 30th of that selfsame month, the Tallinners dispatched their arsonists to burn down the church in Kalamaja, which one man had succeeded in saving in October, and they levelled even its ruins. I say it was a witless and utterly senseless act.

On the 3rd of candle-month the Muscovites dispatched to Russia from their camp more than two thousand sledges laden with booty.

On the 22nd they constructed yet another emplacement on Köismäe opposite the Great Coast Gate, and bombarded the town even more fiercely than heretofore with fireballs and cannonballs, but inflicted no great damage. Only one musketeer in St Olaf's steeple and a Swedish mercenary and a manorman on the Systervall Wall were killed.

On the 25th Heinrich Harder from Sweden, the assistant pastor of St Nicholas and a preacher of solemn sermons, died of the plague, which he had contracted serving Holy Communion to the afflicted . . . Even though he had had much less contact with the sick than some others . . . (By the end of candle-month, the number of those having succumbed to the plague in all the congregations had risen to nearly a thousand . . . of which fact the Council had forbidden open discussion.)

So perhaps, indeed, it was sometimes nothing but shame, at least in part, that gradually shored up Balthasar's courage. For at times, at exceedingly grave moments as he prayed with a dying patient, he had to utter a prayer for himself as well: "Lord God, help me – take from my heart this damnable, wretched, gloating sense of relief . . ." He was compelled to utter such words, for example, on the last day of candle-month, when he was summoned to the deathbed of Herr Martin Loop.

Martin Loop, as former assistant-scribe of the Town Council, was a member of the Holy Ghost parish. Balthasar had not seen him for many years (like Herr Topff, Herr Loop was now in retirement), but recognised the man immediately, in spite of the swollen neck that considerably altered his appearance. It was the same old man – with the face of an aged child and the same forlorn mien, who, on that distant, dreamlike early morning had been waving the letter from Order Master Kettler under the noses of the surly, shaggy, furious peasants, and had thrust it into their hands, so that they could touch the wax seal, and had lied to their faces, as he recited its non-existent promises: ". . . and I shall see to it that all the complaints of the peasants brought against arrogant manor lords be thoroughly examined, and that justice according to God's Will shall reign between them and the lords and that it shall remain unto them and their children and their children's children . . ." A lie uttered ten years ago, not even of Loop's invention – deceitful words in a delusive dream that no longer had the least importance, a dream that the millstone of time had crushed to dust, obliterated more thoroughly than dust. And yet . . .

Herr Loop was lying on a rumpled canopy bed, his wasted body oddly straight, his bony chest taut under a purple shirt, his grey chin jutting up, the black toothless cavity of his mouth drooping downward (resembling the dog-like face of the lion battling with Samson in a scene carved into the armrest of one of the Council chairs) . . . Balthasar tilted a goblet of communion wine to Herr Loop's lips and murmured: "Your sins are forgiven" . . . even as he was thinking: Lord God, You, up there above the clouds, You will forgive him – forgive me also, for I, down here in this wretched dust where we all trudge, cannot manage to forgive him wholly . . . Just then Loop wheezed his final high-pitched breath, stiffened and stared – wild-eyed and distraught – at Balthasar, as though he had sensed the reluctance in the Pastor's words of absolution – and was gone before Balthasar could overcome his reluctance . . .

Perhaps it was out of a sense of debt to Herr Loop that Balthasar, on that same afternoon, took special care at the deathbed of the baker Slahter in Rüütli Street.

He had known the old man, whose sparse white hair and flaccid white face gave him the look of someone steeped for many years in milk. He had noticed the old man's son, Mihkel, performing in a play by Plautus with the town schoolboys seven years ago. And just before the plague outbreak, and even now, in the course of these last weeks, Balthasar had had Märten deliver some of baker Slahter's cardamom buns to his father-in-law. (Even an uncouth, prospective bridegroom knows some of the tricks of the courteous bridegroom!) And as he now stood at Slahter's bedside, he counted, with relief, the days since he had last ordered the cardamom buns for the Master Furrier – eight days ago. Thank God. At that time Slahter had been in full health.

Balthasar served Communion to the old man, who seemed to have been momentarily freed from his fiery fever by the miracle of God's body and blood. And Balthasar prayed with him, in German, as was fitting in the case of Herr Slahter. But when the prayer ended, the old man would not let go of Balthasar's hand, gripping it hard in his own, smooth from kneading dough but burning with plague fever, and he suddenly whispered, in country-tongue:

"Pastor – I beg you – there is something I must ask of you – before I . . . I knew your father – old Siimon . . . He was – a man of his word. Only God can hear us . . . I have become a German . . . in the town of Tallinn . . . But I come from the same place . . . near the Harju-Jaani Church . . . that old Siimon came from . . . though not from Kurgla . . . but from Haljala . . . But you are . . . also a German gentleman – there's not a whiff of the country left about you . . . And my son Michel . . . you must remember him – from the town school . . . ? He too has the good fortune . . . to be on his way to becoming German . . . at the university, in Rostock . . . And I beg you . . . when he returns . . . he has neither kin nor friend in town . . . watch over him . . .Give me your word—"

"I give you my word," said Balthasar ardently, and not just because he wanted to free his hand from the old man's grip, nor just to redeem himself before God for his arrogance at Herr Loop's bedside, but also because he remembered Mihkel Slahter as a fine young man.

When news was brought to Balthasar the next morning that old Slahter had been called to his Lord during the night, Balthasar reaffirmed to himself his vow regarding Mihkel, and experienced thereby (as is often the case in such circumstances) a slight renewal of spirit. As for his spirit, God alone knows what fed its sustaining rivulet, for it did not entirely dry up even when the plague deaths were at their most terrifying. It was likely not only shame but also hope that sustained him. Blind human hope. Hope that is said to grasp at a straw but does not in fact need a straw, for it is itself much more than a straw: it is itself at least the magical willow pole, the balancing beam with little lead balls, little worry-balls affixed to each end, as one flies along the dizzying rope stretched between towers . . . Or is it, after all, that dizzying rope itself that one walks between life and death? Or perhaps it is the ropewalker himself: hope, which is ultimately the human self . . . ?

And so, on many an evening Balthasar would douse himself with several wooden buckets-full of hot water sudsy with resin soap, and swat his steaming body, reddened and splotchy, with soft-soaked juniper branches, to rid himself of the seven plague-and-deathbed visits and nine funerals of the day, and to banish the fatigue of sleepless nights from the back of his neck and the stiffness from his calves, sore after climbing towers and mounting defence galleries on the town walls. He would put on clean clothes that had been exposed for long hours to the smoke of burning bay-laurel branches, and then go to Rataskaevu Street, to the Gandersens' house. There, he sat on the stone window seat in Elsbet's upstairs room, with her sitting across from him, next to the mirror, for he had vowed not to touch her again until they had been blessed at the altar. He had made the vow voluntarily, to punish himself, and to increase the likelihood – in a bargain with God – that he would be spared death and survive the war and ultimately arrive at the altar.

Sometimes he would still be there late at night. Or downstairs, in the great-room with Master Gandersen and his journeymen. Elsbet, at her father's behest, would bring them a pitcher of clear ale mixed with ginger – which was said to fortify the heart against illness. Balthasar drank this heart medicine and gazed at the candlelight flickering in Elsbet's dark eyes and glowing on her darkening, yet increasingly transparent face, becoming more distant and more desirable than ever. And he tried to toss something into the conversation that would bring even a hint of a smile to her ever-so-serious lips. He enquired, naturally, about the state of the household. No, the Gandersen house had not yet – thanks be to God – been afflicted by the disease. Even though, right here in Rüütli and Rataskaevu streets several dozen people were known to have died. After his tanning sheds at the back of Pleekmäe became inaccessible at the start of the siege, old Gandersen had buried some of his indispensable barrels of tannic acid in the big stone barn right here in his courtyard. In his view it was the strong stench of tannin (and of course, the Grace of God) that had kept the plague from his house till now. Balthasar mentioned briefly the latest cases of the plague, as many as he had heard of (with the help of God, their number seemed to be decreasing in the third week of candle-month). He spoke with enthusiasm, taking comfort in relating the cases of one here and another there, whose recovery he had heard of or witnessed for himself. One such story was the miraculous tale of his own bell-ringer and assistant, his old friend Märten Bergkam.

They had been on their way home, he and Märten, in the middle of candle-month, on one of the most terrible days of the raging plague, walking back from several deathbeds in the shacks somewhere in the vicinity of the Harju Gate, as was usual these days. Without warning Märten stopped on the corner of Rüütli and Harju streets and leaned against a wall. It was dark, and the lantern light on Märten's face was too unsteady to reveal what he actually looked like as he pressed his bell and lantern into Balthasar's hand and said:

"Bal, go home. I'm not coming."

"Why not?"

"I don't feel well. I'm going – over there – around the corner. To the Almshouse. They'll let me in, sure."

"You're mad! What's the matter?"

"Don't bother asking . . . It's the same . . ."

"Come home," said Balthasar, his throat hoarse with fear, and gripped his friend under the arm. To his dismay, Märten, who was leaning against the wall, crumpled onto the street. He had been about to put down the communion chest, still dutifully slung across his shoulder, when it clanked onto the cobblestones with a sound like rocks hitting the sides of a wooden coffin.

"No I won't. What for? Your house is still clean. But there are over a dozen sick at the Almshouse."

"Come home with me," said Balthasar. He propped Märten up against the wall.

137

"I said I won't, confound it! You have a house full of people. Help me to the door of the Almshouse."

Balthasar guided Märten to the Almshouse. He pounded on the door until he woke the night watchman and finally also the warden. He saw to it that Märten was given a decent pallet. He said to them: "Hold your tongues. Five thousand people were fed on two fish, and you are to find clean straw for him and a private corner!" By the time they had managed to accomplish this, Märten was already barely conscious. When they laid him down on the straw, Balthasar examined him by candlelight. His groin was swollen and blue. Märten clenched his teeth in pain and muttered:

"Go on home . . . Let Päärn toll the bells . . . That way . . . I'll be . . . everywhere . . ."

Balthasar sent for a barber, who lanced Märten's buboes. The next morning when Balthasar came to see him, he was unconscious, his face white and peaked. His lips were puckered and his eyes shut tight in an angry squint, as if he were staring into an invisible sun. And although he had witnessed so many such scenes that he had become numb to them, Balthasar felt, as he stood at Märten's bedside, that he only now fully suffered what he had first experienced as Kalamaja burned: the feeling that he had lost one of his own limbs. But all he could do was clench his jaw with the pain, just as hard as his dying friend had done, and repeat to himself: "Whatsoever God does is ever good – this I believe, I believe, I believe – *credo, credo, credo – quia absurdum** – spitting out the final words . . . He wanted to prepare the unconscious Märten for death, but of course he could not yet give him the Sacrament. He folded Märten's cooling hands on his chest, bent over his white cheekbones and spoke: "Repeat after me: Into Your hands, O Lord . . ." but then realised that the other could not hear him, and stopped in mid-sentence – not only because of the realisation,

* I believe – because it is absurd (Latin).

but also because of an impious flicker of hope, as if it might make a difference whether he finished the sentence or left it incomplete . . .

When he returned the next morning, he learned that Märten had died during the night and been buried at dawn. Pastor Bussow had overseen the burials of three plague victims at the Almshouse who had succumbed that night. The housemaster of the Almshouse could show him only a plot of freshly dug earth near the Assauwe Tower, quite close to the wall, a spot trampled by the town's guardsmen. Staring at the gravelly patch of dirt, Balthasar vowed to himself that on it he would have a stone tablet erected, God willing, with the words: *Hic requiescit in pace Dei Märten Bergkam, Aeditus Sancti Spiriti . . .* * But then he recalled, with a stab of contrition, that on his father's grave, protected now from the trampling feet of the enemy only by the ashes of Kalamaja, though there was indeed a stone, the promised script had still not been chiselled upon it . . . so he refrained from making another vow.

And a good thing it was. On the eleventh day after Märten's death, at ten o'clock in the morning, Balthasar was standing in the sacristy, turning the key in the iron door of his wall cupboard. He had just finished rereading the last testament of Master Baker Slahter, which had been given to his keeping, and he now locked it away once more. The congregation had been bequeathed five hundred marks. Just then there was a knock at the door. Balthasar turned around – and for the first time in his life he actually saw a ghost. It was Märten's ghost. Stinking of the grave, and terribly bony. Transparently grey. But since it was Märten's ghost, Balthasar was not greatly alarmed. For Märten would not harm him even from beyond the grave . . . though Balthasar knew that the sudden appearance of a ghost (especially at such an hour as this, in broad daylight) could mean but one thing – that his own time had come. He made the sign of the cross. It seemed to him that in one instant, his mind, like a huge fishing net, embraced his entire life –

* Here in the peace of God rests Märten Bergkam, Bell-ringer of Holy Ghost (Latin).

from Hundimäe Point and the clearing at Kurgla to universities and dukes' castles and Kolovere and the pulpit of Holy Ghost Church; and it seemed that the net was too loosely woven to catch the baby fish flashing by in the insubstantial, shimmering grey water, and that everything was flowing through the net and back out to sea, even as the net itself shrank in his chest to a pulsing clump the size of a fist.

"Why have you come?"

"Where am I supposed to go then?"

"Did Bussow not bury you in accord with Christian rites . . . ?"

Perhaps Märten had not come to deliver a death notice after all . . . Perhaps he had come on his own account – because of some error in the official rites that Balthasar could correct . . .

"He never buried me."

"But how can that be? They told me that . . ."

"It's of no account what they told you. I realise you think I'm a ghost. But I'm alive. See here, touch me!" The ghost stepped closer to Balthasar and extended its right hand towards his face, and when Balthasar hesitated to touch it, it grabbed hold of his hand and shook it. "See now – it's true, I'm like a skeleton, but I still have a bit of life left in me . . ." Balthasar was still silent and the apparition continued:

"Fool, if you don't believe me, what kind of ghost slurps broth?" Only now did Balthasar notice that the apparition was holding a bowl of soup in his left hand – he had grabbed it in the courtyard from someone distributing soup. Now he pulled a tin spoon out from under his coat and began to slurp the flour broth, standing where he was.

"It's the second day already that my body's as hollow as a dead man's flea!"

"Tell me right now, how could something like this . . . ?"

But there was not much to tell. Balthasar had paid the housemaster of the Almshouse half a mark for a private corner and bed for Märten; at the time there were three hundred sick and needy people in the

Almshouse, and only a hundred pallets. But as soon as Balthasar left, the housemaster had ordered the half-drunk descendants of the Good Samaritan to carry Märten into the large common room, from which a corpse had just been carried off to the chamber of the dead. In the morning, when Märten was quite unconscious and the Samaritans completely drunk – for they could not have persevered at their work otherwise – they thought that the body in the chamber of the dead was the one delivered by Herr Balthasar. But such cases, where one of many dozens of plague-stricken patients at the Almshouse continued to breathe for several days and finally sat up and asked for food, well, such cases had surely been heard of from time to time . . . Balthsasar thought to himself: the Franciscans and disciples of St Rochus, the Beguines and the Singing Brothers of Cologne – pure Catholic nonsense, surely – and yet, did they not provide greater comfort to the ailing than nowadays, when such nonsense does not exist? He asked:

"But why did you not send me word the moment you regained consciousness?"

"What for? Especially since God had decided that I was not to die."

Märten had risen from the dead. He had survived the plague. Märten was alive. Balthasar took special pleasure in recounting the tale in the Gandersen household, in Elsbet's hearing. Not only because it provided comfort and encouragement both to his listeners and to himself, but also because the story brought the tremor of a smile to Elsbet's lips.

And, even more, because Balthasar could also declare there were signs that Magnus was wearying of the siege. Yes. The plague was apparently raging in his camp as fiercely as in town, or even more fiercely. It was said that his chancellor, Conradus Burmeister, had fallen ill and was now under the sod. And all the quartermasters and ensigns and fire chiefs assured Balthasar that the enemy's assaults were more haphazard than at the beginning of the month. Never mind that just last week they set up new blockhouses (and two days earlier they were driven out of them again!), and never mind that at this very moment one could hear some of their cannons barking at the town. Balthasar could say: Let us be filled with hope.

When he had trudged home through the snowdrifts behind the church, the snow smelling curiously of spring, and hurried between the sleeping refugees in his parsonage, and up to his study, he could still (or once again) take out his greyish sheets of paper late at night and with renewed hope write on his creaking lectern, by candlelight:

> In the course of this great siege there were so many skirmishes and battles around the town walls that it is not possible to describe them all, and soldiers and young journeymen, house servants and boys raced to join the battle, whether to the town gates or as far Tönismäe, as if they were heading to a wedding feast . . .

He wrote, and had the sense that in his words (but that means, within himself, in his mind and body and blood) there was a kind of frivolity worthy of reproof, a superficiality that deserved the lash. But he continued to write and could not bring himself to cross out a single line.

CHAPTER FOUR,

in which, abruptly and to our own surprise, we leave for a time the man whom we have faithfully been pursuing and follow a new set of tracks – those left by a pair of high, moose-hide boots that creak as they stride across age-old, admirably restored slate floors and past walls hung with coats-of-arms carved long ago – tracks left by boots, hearts, memories, aspirations and intrigues, of which that stubborn man, whose affairs have occupied us to now, has at best a foggy and only partial awareness, despite his childlike curiosity.

"Herman! Jürgen! Your father is waiting!"

It is the voice of Hofmeister Fabian, calling from a door he has just opened to the courtyard. And from an open window in an upper storey, the father watches the boys appear from around the corner of the house, in response to the summons. Of course, they have been in the narrow yard facing the sea, practising duelling with their blunted swords – their clanking has been audible since the midday meal, and audible, too, the boys' delighted cries during the pause in their battle when they chanced to look over the stone wall and caught sight of three Swedish carracks just about to enter the bay, near the island of Naissaare. Since spring, thank God, the shipping lanes to Sweden have once again been open. Yes indeed, the boys are excited, worked up, but they are responding to his summons, as is proper. Without dawdling – *one-two-three!* – for Fabian called them and it is time: the shadow of the Dome Church steeple stretches cross the rosehip bush in the middle of the courtyard. The boys will be interested in what awaits them. The father has not required that Fabian address them as *Junker** Herman and *Junker* Jürgen, despite the fact that at one point he had thought it appropriate, especially when he recalled that in Spain every young man like them would have without question been addressed as "Don" . . . but he has long since realised that this is by no means Granada or even Sicily, but our uncouth, unrefined Livonia and, in its own way, proud in its simplicity. Fine. The boys are crossing the courtyard. Herman and Jürgen. Fifteen and thirteen, both fine straight-backed youths, the older one already on the cusp of young manhood. Heaven knows, neither is exceedingly bright. A little rougher and rowdier than necessary (a generation ago such colts were more polished than nowadays), but they will soon be prepared to serve whichever king they prefer. They are certainly sufficiently polished for this Livonian land of ours. Their mother comes, after all, from one of the most prominent families of prosperous old Bohemia, the von Schnideck family . . . And their father . . . third generation no less . . . what the devil! – just how many sons of Livonian nobles can boast of a father with that kind of lineage, eh?

The boys knock on their father's door – it would not do to enter without knocking – and Herr Tõnis Maidel turns towards his sons.

"Good day, Father."

"Hello boys. Take a seat."

The boys sit down on a heavy, dark-brown wooden bench set against a whitewashed wall. From the rim of the wainscoting they each take a wax tablet and stylus to write down questions that might occur to them, for they always do occur. The boys smell of dust, sweat, and of interest – yes, of interest. Thank God. It would be foolish, *exempli causa*,[†] to be telling them his life's story if it made them yawn.

"Herman, how far did we get last time?"

"To the Kaiser. To that island called – what was it . . . ?"

* Squire (German).
† For instance (Latin).

"Mallorca," says Jürgen.

Herr Maidel looks out of the window. In the bright June sky, the blue-grey steeple of the Dome Church rises above the red roofs of the bishop's courtyard. Doves bob along the ledge below its lead spire. In the distance, under the pale sky, the land lies green and misty, and an indistinct road winds across the fields behind the town – the road to Harku, Keila and Padise . . . Herr Maidel furrows his brow and shuts his eyes tight:

"Right. And your father was then twenty years old, his first year of sailing under Spanish banners. The day before yesterday, I was telling you how I came to be there. By dint of my own will, your grandfather's permission, and the recommendation of the castellan of Tallinn. First, I went to Germany to join the forces of the Duke of Braunschweig. He was recruiting foot soldiers for the army of Kaiser Karl* at that time and needed young noblemen as officers. Then, from Germany to Holland. And there, Admiral Perez placed me with the naval fleet. He held that all Livonians were great seamen. In such matters chance usually plays the greatest role. And in the spring of '41, when the Kaiser was beginning to prepare for his great foray into the Barbarian lands, I was already in the Mediterranean, on the *Despejado*. A small, very fast galley. Eighteen fathoms long and three wide, only one fathom in depth. With forty oars, and four men on each oar. In the bow, three cannons – a twelve-pounder and two at six pounds each. And your father, in charge of them. But the ship itself was more for show than for war. Like most of those galleys in general. And *our ship* was to serve, above all, as liaison between the ships carrying the army. Two masts. Triangular Latin sails, striped red and yellow. Banners, red and gold, four fathoms long on the yards – like all the Kaiser's ships.

"That's how it was. My captain, as I've already told you, was Enrique Cortés. Apparently the grandson of the famous Hernán's older brother.

* Charles V, Holy Roman Emperor.

Barely older than I, but definitely more of a greenhorn. '*Capitano*', of course, thanks to his family connections. *Ahem*.

"So. The *Despejado* rocked there at anchor for a week, off the coast of Palma de Mallorca. The officers rowed to town in a *caïque** – nothing noteworthy about the town. Whitewashed walls. Narrow streets, an imposing cathedral, an old *castillo*,[†] cheap taverns. Beautiful girls too, of course, black eyes – a blink and a flash from behind their *rebozillos*[‡]. In the distance, at sunset, hills the colour of oranges. Oh, of course – you've never seen an orange . . . And on the shore, salt marshes, whose vapours cause malaria. Well, the Kaiser finally arrived from Sardinia with the main fleet. All at once the bay was humming with activity – ships, boats, rowing, swearing, music, noise. And even though going ashore was strictly curtailed, and a double watch was set up at eight town gates, there were, in all the drinking houses of Palma and also in the other houses . . ." (He pauses, clears his throat.) "Well, anyway. On the fifteenth of September, we set out to sea from Palma. The bishop himself came to the harbour with a procession, to sprinkle the Kaiser's flagship, and we sailed out to the accompaniment of bells pealing from seven churches.

"You can picture the scene for yourselves!! Two hundred large warships and a hundred smaller ones and seventy galleys. It was the most massive fleet ever to set sail from Christian Europe against the Muslims. Twenty thousand German and Spanish and Italian foot soldiers and two thousand mounted knights. The magnificence and marrow of the nobility of Germany, Spain, Italy, Malta and Rhodes. And the commanders! Kaiser Karl himself. And under him, who? Alba! Cortés! Seisenegg! Gonzaga! And old Andrea Doria as Grand Admiral. Boys, I'm telling you, you'll hear all kinds of unflattering stories about

* Yawl (Spanish).
† Castle (Spanish).
‡ Shawl of white muslin or lace (Spanish).

these men: people will say that Kaiser Karl suffered from a liver ailment all his life and was incapable of making an independent decision; or that he was a fool who held on, tooth and nail, to every misbegotten decision he'd ever made – assuming, that is, he had ever actually managed to make a decision. Or that Duke Alba, right now, is ordering thousands of people in Holland to be impaled on stakes and sent to the block. Or that the armoured warriors of Cortés have chopped up naked Mexicans, the way a meat-grinder chops meat. Or that Andrea Doria was a soldier of fortune who transferred his services to five different rulers in turn, whose causes he had agreed to defend. . . What I'm telling you is this: listen to what your father has to say about these men. For I have seen them all with my own eyes and have fought in their company. And I can tell you that these men are pearls in the crown of knighthood in our century. Take Alba, for example. His devotion to his monarch is the most ardent ever seen. And Cortés. He was inexhaustible, as though his armour were inhabited not by a man but by a magic machine. And Doria – what extraordinary capabilities! . . . But as for the accusations so volubly voiced against them, I pose this question: What should Alba undertake against the cheesemongers who are rioting against their king? And how else could Cortés, in his time, with but seven hundred men (for he had no more in Mexico) – how else could he have laid an entire sector of the world at his Kaiser's feet? He apparently said to Karl (as he himself told me): 'An entire sector of the world, like a green carpet, and there is still less blood on it than gold embroidery . . .'

"So. We set sail on the fifteenth. And we could have arrived by the twentieth. Even the slowest of cargo ships could have done so. Had the weather been the least propitious. For from Mallorca to Algiers is just a little over fifty leagues, measured in our Livonian leagues. But it took us three days and nights to get past Cabrera . . . Yes. Doria had warned the Kaiser in all urgency that at such a late time of year one ought not subject oneself to the moods of the Mediterranean. But the

Kaiser paid no heed. He had said: 'Andrea, the timidity of old men is a disservice to our warriors.' (Doria himself was past seventy, and at that age men of lesser mettle sit at home like decomposing stumps.) But from the first day on, it seemed as though his warning had cast a curse upon our venture.

"Above us the sky was the colour of a grave-marker hewn from Tallinn's damp grey limestone. And the further south we sailed, the blacker the sea became. But there was only the lightest breath of wind, and only as far as Cabrera. As soon as we had idled past it, the last breeze expired and we were becalmed. Those vessels under oars continued on at first and the fleet dispersed, becoming scattered over many leagues . . . The galleys moved onward in the sultry, stifling heat, propelled solely by oars. And boys, you cannot imagine the stench . . ."

"Father, what was the stench from? Was it the sea?"

"Foolish boy . . . It was the stench of the oarsmen. When there is wind you don't notice it so much. Especially when it blows across the ship or from the stern. But when there's no wind, and the oarsmen are propelling the galley at full speed in the dense, humid air . . . you smell it. The ship is flying, but the stench of the ordure and urine and sweat of that rabble is awful. The officers' quarters in the stern are afloat the whole time in that river of foul odours. Our Capitano Enrique had grown up amidst the fragrance of Andalusian roses, and he heaved three times a day. I myself don't have as refined a nose. But even so, I insisted that I be near the cannons, and moved in with the surgeon and boatswain, in a forecabin. There, it wasn't so bad. But the true hidalgos claimed that such a move was beneath them. Oh well. And on the fourth day came the storm. The first storm. Three or four days. Almost drove us back to Sicily. And then another week of incubation: you could actually watch the mould growing on bread. And then once more, a week of storm. So that we traversed this distance not in five days, but in a month and five days. And no-one doubted that a curse had been laid upon our endeavour. Although we did not think that it was the doing of our Admiral. Even though he had fought with the French against our Kaiser, and with the Pope against the French, and with our Kaiser against the French and the Pope. But definitely not with the Muslims against the Christians. So, it was evidently the Muslims who were responsible for the curse. The sorcerers of Numidia and Kabylia and the Atlas Mountains – they're everywhere in the markets and caves and gorges of those lands – *they* were the ones who had unleashed their demons upon us! And they'd long known about our arrival, of course. We'd seen their sails almost daily on the horizon.

"Well, on the twentieth of October, we arrived at last. In the morning, the hilly shoreline came into view. Strange-looking grey slopes under a clouded grey sky. All we could see of the town was a hazy, white mound that looked like ants' eggs. A fairly large mound. Its peak reached halfway up the grey slope. We did not of course sail directly under the cannons of the town. We turned to the left in good time and proceeded half a league to the south, into the bay.

"Our forces started to row to shore under cover of cannon fire. The *Despejado*, with its draught measuring a fathom, was in the row closest to shore. I was standing next to our three cannons and directing the fire. All the ships were simultaneously spitting iron balls onto the beach. There were, no doubt, a thousand cannons firing. It was many times what was necessary for the landing. And a couple of ragged companies of Turkish horsemen immediately fled the beach.

"Capitano Cortés summoned me to him; he was, I must say, quite pale. But a beaker of Malaga was on the table in his splendid cabin, and it seemed to me that he grinned as he spoke: 'Dionysio, I have an assignment for you. I had a dream this morning. My Uncle Hernando is in grave danger on this shore.'

"He paused, for the cannon thunder was deafening. When the rumble subsided somewhat, he spoke into my ear: 'He is protected by only one thing. It was revealed to me in my dream. See, it is this holy relic. This arrowhead torn from the body of St Sebastian. When he carries this in his breast pocket, neither sword nor bullet can touch him.' He pressed a beautiful wooden box containing the arrowhead into my palm. 'You understand, one must take care of one's uncles. Especially when they themselves forget to. And even more so if they are the kind who would never, in all this world, forget those who show concern for them. But of course, I myself cannot set foot on land. So I am asking you to deliver it into his hands. And tell him about my dream, about my concern for him. *Et cetera*.'

"Well, I responded: 'It will be done, *Capitano*. But, if I may ask, why me?' (For I had not been a special friend to this young gentleman.) But he said: 'You, though you are Catholic, as a nobleman should be, hail from a land corrupted by Luther – and you are so sceptical of relics that you would not steal them.'

"Ha-ha-ha. Well, an order is an order. It would of course have been less dangerous for me on the ship. But a lieutenant who wants to become a captain as quickly as possible does not make a point of looking to safety for himself. And the name of Hernando Cortés has greater resonance than any other among the Spaniards. It can only be of benefit to a young man to have contact with great men. If he is sharp enough . . . and if these gentlemen are truly gentlemen – keep that in mind.

"I hopped into the *caïque* and four men proceeded to row me ashore. It was only a distance of three or four hundred cubits. And I can tell you this: at once, the spell that had been cast to bedevil us on this entire campaign unleashed new forces. No sooner had I stepped into the boat than a driving rain fell upon us. With the tenth pull of the oars, the downpour was so dense that it obliterated both the fleet and the shore. My goatskin doublet was quickly sodden, and water flowed over the brim of my hat.

"We landed somewhere at the mouth of a small river, and I sent the boat back, for it was clear that I could not carry out my mission until the next day. The first men that I found in the downpour, of those who'd come ashore, were the Germans from Seisenegg, who told me that the Spaniards were somewhere to the north of us. I still could not see a thing for the rain. The Germans were trying to set up camp and, as I walked past, I heard them shouting and cursing, for they could not find their tents and were getting wetter by the minute. And north of their camp, I sank into the most awful quagmire of mud and salt. (Afterwards I learned that this was a marsh by the name of Hamma, quite close to the sea.) Then I sloshed back, sodden to my groin, and along with a few officers, slept in a house abandoned by Arabs. The next morning I found the Spanish camp on the other side of the Hamma marsh. But by then Don Hernando and his troops were already headed for town.

"Well, I pursued him for almost that entire God-given day. With a motley confusion of Germans, Italians and Alba's Spaniards. Over a jumble of rocks and boulders and sunken roads. All the while, throughout the day, you could hear skirmishes, big and small, breaking out in the hills that surrounded the town. And the rain fell in fits and starts, and a bone-chilling rain it was. The clouds dragged themselves along the tops of the hills and the wind howled in the valleys. And I was so hungry that I could have eaten my own boots.

"Not until after midday did I reach Don Hernando at the Sidi Medjabar Hill to the west of the town. He seemed indeed to be amused by St Sebastian's arrowhead. He stuck it into his breast pocket and inquired about his brother's grandson and whether I had had dinner. I tell you, a true commander! With shells exploding around him, he could find time for *that*. And at the same time, he was signalling with his other hand to his *capitanos*, indicating the direction they should take to get behind the Arabs!

"You want to know what kind of man he was? A nobleman of

Estremadura. Approaching sixty at the time. Nothing much to look at. A sparse, greying beard. Brown eyes. Yellow teeth. But I noticed one thing: whenever he looked someone in the eye for any length of time, that man eventually averted his eyes. And when he laughed his hoarse laugh, everyone laughed along with him. Not from amusement, but out of respect. I told him I would return immediately to my ship. To which he said: 'There's nothing for you to do there. But here we have a town to conquer. Stay here with me.'

"Well, as you can imagine, I had no objections to that. Don Hernando said: 'We have some hard work to do before we can lay siege to the town. For we cannot move our cannons along these cursed marshy roads. And I don't understand why the devil we haven't been sent horses. There are Arab horsemen behind every knoll and rise!'

"Anyway. He had a helmet and light armour brought out for me. It fitted me perfectly. Only the wrists of the Spanish armour were a bit tight around my Livonian bones. And I was with the Spaniards who pushed through to the Medjabar Hill before evening. Those confounded Arabs dispersed like the fog before we could cross swords with them. But from there we had a clear view of the west side of town. Their moat was wretched and filled with rubbish. But the town wall on that side was thirty feet high. Well, that evening I spent an hour cleaning mud off myself and then went, as summoned, to the tent.

"What did I find there, you ask? Nothing much. The evening meal was meagre. As it commonly is among the Spaniards. And Don Hernando was a true ascetic. By the way, a refined gentlemen, though he doesn't need to be an ascetic, shuns the kind of gorging that goes on in Livonia. But Don Hernando was interested only in *power*. In power more than in gold. And in gold only because it is power in metallic form. But I was so confoundedly tired that I remember only some of what was said there. There were a few officers who had fought with Don Hernando in Mexico and he and they were asked to tell their stories. My eyes kept closing and I pinched my thigh so as not to fall asleep. I remember talk about the awful human sacrifices of the Aztecs and about their pyramids rising from lakes of blood, and of how unspeakably treacherous a people they were. So treacherous, that the only way to govern them was ruthlessly – without mercy. It's the same with the non-Germans here in Livonia. And there was talk about the quantities of gold they have. But how much gold he had brought back for himself or for his Kaiser, he did not say.

"And the next evening, when the town was to be properly surrounded and in our hands, Don Hernando promised to tell us about the Night of Sorrows. That is the night, in 1520, when he and his small force fought their way out of the capital city of the rioting Aztecs, spilling blood every step of the way. So that the night of the greatest disaster became their greatest triumph.

'Here in Algiers,' remarked one of the *capitanos*, 'we can expect neither such triumph nor such disaster. Unfortunately, and fortunately as well.'

"And then they spoke of the situation in Algiers. After all, we were in Africa to put a stop to the shameless piracy of the Algerians. That was evident to everyone. It was clearly impossible for the Christian world to tolerate those outrages any longer. But in the company around Don Hernando it was said (I remember that we all roared with laughter at this) that the Muslims claimed they were waging a righteous war against us, for the Christian dogs were trying to take over the Muslims' ancestral lands and stifle their rightful freedom to sail the seas.

"And I remember that when I turned in to sleep in the adjoining tent, I did indeed have a sense of being a participant in some fantastical tale . . . I heard the wind whistling down the mountain gorges, the tent canvas flapping, the guards calling out their watchwords* . . . And I thought of Mexico and Kabylia and Livonia. And about this old

* Military passwords (archaic term).

153

stone house at the edge of Toompea, in Tallinn, where our ancestors have lived for five generations—"

"This same house where we are now?"

"Indeed . . . And about the wider world where those gentlemen performed their heroic deeds and amassed their riches and where I was, too . . . like an arrow on a taut bow . . . And about St Sebastian's arrowhead, which was no longer in my bosom pocket. For who knows . . . perhaps it did indeed provide some slight protection . . . But the next day, it became clear to me that all the holy relics in the world were of no use whatsoever against the witches and demons of that land. Not there, in the very homeland of the demons. Even though our Spanish and Italian soldiers had all kinds of holy artifacts with them, several wagonloads in fact . . .

"The next morning the Kaiser sent a messenger to town warning them not to be foolish, and to surrender. But their chief commander, Hasan Agha, had spat – no, not in the messenger's face, but onto the ground in front of his feet, and had retorted: 'Pick up my answer and take it to your Kaiser.' And, in retrospect, it is of course clear upon whom and what he set his hopes. For his eight hundred Turks and five thousand ragged Mauritanians could not have been the mainstay of his arrogance.

"Before evening the Kaiser summoned his war council. Don Hernando asked me to come along with his entourage. The Kaiser was quartered in the centre of our ranks, over half a league south of the Spaniards. His tent was on a hill called – this I found out later – Kudiat es Savun, which means 'soap hill' – as though in mockery of how utterly unlike a smooth advance our enterprise was turning out to be . . .

"Lieutenants were of course not invited into the Kaiser's presence. I remained outside with the younger officers. We dismounted and looked around. And I was nearby when the Kaiser came out of his tent to receive the commanders – lanky Alba and rotund Seisenegg and Gonzaga and

154

the rest. But Karl himself was a tall and most dignified gentleman. Pale from lack of sleep, and with a growth of black stubble – as though he had given no thought to shaving, burdened as he was by the cares of war.

When they had gone inside and there was nothing more for me to see, I raised my eyes to the hills and, by God, I quailed. To the south, above the mountains, a black wall of clouds had risen to the skies, the likes of which I had never seen before and have never seen since. I was about to hail the others to look and listen, but managed to grab the words by the tail just in time: it is not seemly for a man to appear overly excitable and fearful among his peers. But by then other officers had also noticed the sky and were crossing themselves. One of them said: 'But from up there we're going to get . . .' and with that, the first blast was upon us. The Kaiser's tent remained standing for the moment, but the wind ripped off its flapping imperial banner with its golden eagle and golden cross, flinging it downhill amidst swirling dust clouds, like a torn kite . . . It was retrieved several hundred paces distant, in the Muslims' graveyard, where Seisenegg's men were encamped, and returned at a run to the hilltop. So that when the Kaiser emerged with his council a half hour later, the banner was back in place. And even if he had witnessed the event, he would not necessarily have deemed it an omen. For he had made the decision well before the council arrived at it: they would storm the town at dawn.

"The Kaiser held on to his beret, for the wind was fierce, and his gaze was somber as he looked at the sky. But then he smiled and said: 'Look, gentlemen, what a storm our Lord has sent to aid us – to strike fear into the hearts of the Muslims!'

"They all smiled bravely. But I do not know how many still believed that this storm and these clouds were the work of God . . . Three-quarters of the sky was entirely black, and only by shouting could one be heard above the roar of the wind. But Karl now requested that the younger officers be introduced to him. There were several dozen of us gathered between the tents. The Kaiser came to us and spoke with each one of us—"

"With you, too?!" ask Herman and Jürgen in one voice.

Herr Maidel stands up, recalling the event with great pleasure (even though this recollection has its own Achilles' heel). He looks out of the window into the distance, beyond the Bishop's Grove and Lake Harku gleaming in the light of the afternoon sun, and turns to his excited sons:

"Of course. He walked right up to me. And stood as close to me as you are now sitting. The wind blew the scents of musk and garlic from him straight into my face. Don Hernando said: 'This is Don Dionysio Maidel of Your Majesty's fleet. He is under my command at the moment.'"

"And what did the Kaiser say to you?" the boys ask eagerly.

"He asked where I was from. I was standing in front of him, very straight, and I replied: 'From Livonia, my Kaiser.' And then he began to speak to me in German."

"From so far away?", he asked. "That is indeed admirable. When I was young, there was a painter in my service. From Livonia. Michiel Zittoz.* Have you heard of him? No? Ha-haa. No prophet is ever famous in his own land. A very gifted man. In some ways, I liked him more than any of my painters. Even more than Titian. But *Maidel*? That's not a German name either, is it?"

"But it is, my Kaiser."

"And what does it mean?"

"It is a fish."

"In *German*?"

"*Jawohl.†*"

"*Hm*. Even the Kaiser learns as long as he lives."

"Then he walked on through the storm to the next officers. And

---

* Michel Sittow, Estonian Renaissance painter.
† Yes, indeed. (German).

the others looked at me with envy. For he had talked to no-one else at such length.'

"But father, *is* our name a German name?" asks Herman.

And Jürgen says: "I've heard people say . . ."

"Boys," says Herr Maidel, with a gravity that brooks no further discussion of the matter, "if your father said as much to the Holy Roman Emperor, then it is indeed a German name. And now I will continue.

"I rode back with Don Hernando and his officers to Medjabar Hill. The wind whipped at our backs, in effect pushing us onward. We were but halfway there when everything grew dark. And then the rain started. The most wretched rain I have experienced in my lifetime. The storm lashed and beat us, soaking us to the bone. Inside the tents, the force of the wind was such that we could not light a candle. On the floor there was half a foot of water. And as we were looking for torches, someone shouted, 'Look! Look!' We rushed outside – and by God, in the raging tempest, in the near-dark, enormous black birds of some kind were flying over our heads. There were five or six of them, and they flew so low that we dropped to our hands and knees. These could be nothing other than the abominable Arabian rocs, capable of picking up a lion in their claws as though it were a mouse! We crossed ourselves and crawled back into our tent to look for torches, and then the storm ripped a corner of our tent loose from its stake. Immediately all the other stakes were jerked out of the ground and our tent ballooned with wind and flew off, flapping and snapping. As for the birds – they turned out to be the tents of our troops below us at the foot of the hill . . . But the gusts were so strong that they threatened to flatten us to the ground, and so heavy with water that we felt as though we were suffocating and drowning. You could not lie down. We tried. We were in a foot-deep stream of raging waters. But I have to say, even in this most awful situation, Don Hernando did not lose his head. It was impossible to talk. I heard Don Hernando shouting into my ear: 'Your lances! Blades into the ground! Hold fast!'

"We were eight or nine men. We threw ourselves down into the muddy rapids and groped around the place where the tent had been. We found five or six lances and halberds. We drove their blades into the rocky soil and stood up, holding on to the lance handles and to each other. There was no way to find out what was happening with our men below. I pulled myself to Don Hernando's side, moving from one lance handle to the next:

"'Don Hernando,' I asked, 'what will become of our ships?'

'If the *Doria* . . . sets sail. . . early enough . . . they might survive . . .'

"After an hour we were utterly exhausted. And then came the thunder . . ."

"What thunder?"

"A deafening roar of thunder."

"And lightning too?"

"No lightning at all. Lightning is God's weapon. But this was the work of devils. A terrible, roaring thunder in total darkness. And then the earth began to shake. Making our lances wobble, the ones we were holding on to. We were like flies on a huge horse, with the horse rippling its hide. Boulders rolled past us in the dark. Boulders, like black cats, completely silent. In the midst of a mighty roaring. Three times, the earth shook."

"How long each time?" ask the boys. For they live in a land where many have quaked, but where earthquakes are not known.

"How long? Well, it seemed to us that it lasted a quarter of an hour each time. You know, when boulders are moving underfoot – it's a devil of a long time from one heartbeat to the next. Something like that I would wish only upon my enemy."

"And then?"

"Then it began to subside. Even so, the storm continued for half the next day. At dawn we began to see what had become of our ships. For from the top of Medjabar, the bay would be visible, and a few of us climbed the hill before daybreak to take a look. Not a single ship on the sea. But the remains were strewn on the shore, where groups of Turks were busy impaling on their pikes any man who had reached land, for those who had managed to escape from the ships were half-drowned and nearly dead anyway. There was no point in even talking about an assault on the town. Instead, Hasan Agha and his men came from the town to attack us. And after the nightmare of our own 'night of sorrows', we were so thoroughly enfeebled that at first Hasan Agha, with about a thousand of his men, drove us into retreat. What made it even easier for him was that the news had already spread through our forces: our ships were gone . . . We had to expend extraordinary effort – severely debilitated as we were by the malefic terrors of the night – to check the advance of the Turks. The Kaiser himself joined the soldiers, his face green and eyes feverish. Don Hernando shouted until he was completely hoarse, and Seisenegg sweated off five pounds of beer belly. Finally Hasan Agha pulled his forces back and withdrew into the town. But our condition was worse than miserable. It's known that extreme hunger can drive men to slit the throats of their commanders and go over to the enemy. For what a mercenary believes in and holds true is determined by his stomach. And it was old Doria who saved us in the end. Which I encourage you to remember when you pass judgment on old men.

"Before evening a boat came ashore near the Italians, with the news that the fleet was not totally lost. A hundred and forty cargo ships and fifteen galleys had sunk, among them the *Despejado*, and about eight thousand men altogether. Old Andrea had managed to assemble the rest and was waiting for us at Cape Matifu. Well and good. But it was a three-day journey from the town to the headland.

"Well, we struggled through those three days somehow and crossed that abominable land. The cursed Turks firing at us without cease and threatening to fall upon us. The mud on the roads was knee-deep. Bridges across the mountain streams had been washed away. Grass and roots were our only food.

"Ahem. Don Hernando chanced to notice me as I fought off the Turks attacking us. When I returned from one such battle, he said, in everyone's hearing:

"'Don Dionysio, I will deliver a report of your bravery to the Kaiser.'"

"And did he do it?"

"I – I don't know. Anyway, it was of no benefit to me, for this very promise – oh well. On the fourth day we finally reached Cape Matifu and began boarding the boats. We had in effect escaped, though more dead than alive. But as the presence of our army upon the grey sand shrank, the Turks grew more zealous in attacking us. The Kaiser, like the captain of a ship, wanted to be among the last to leave. It would not have been appropriate for Don Hernando to get into a boat before him. That was a given. Nor could I board before Don Hernando. That was also a given. Our ships fired at the enemy, providing us cover for boarding the boats. But our cannonballs were already landing behind the ranks of the Janissaries. Otherwise, they would have endangered our lives. In effect, removing the last remnants of our forces from this infernal Barbary Coast was a difficult task. Finally there were only about a hundred and fifty men left to provide cover for the Kaiser's departure. Arquebusiers in the boats and on the shore fired at the enemy with all they had – the top layer of powder in their powder horns was more or less dry. And then a more virulent contingent of Turks descended, bearing down on us from the right, along the sandy beach. Just two days earlier, Don Hernando had promised to inform the Kaiser of my courage. But now the Kaiser was right there, near us! He had just ridden his horse into the water and stepped from the stirrups into a boat. He was standing there, gesturing towards the shore . . . and your father decided that the Kaiser should see with his own eyes just what kind of man this Lieutenant Maidel was, of whose courage Don Hernando had told him (or would soon tell him)! I shouted for a dozen soldiers to follow me and stormed towards the approaching Turks.

"Well, as I told you, I was twenty years old at the time. Now I am almost fifty, and now I would no longer behave that way. But if I were twenty again, I'd do as I did then. For a young nobleman must be prepared to undertake acts of bravery. All the more if fate grants him the opportunity to accomplish them in full view of his Kaiser.

"I remember the first Janissary and his horse's bulging eyes and the clash of our swords – and I must say, such stunts often do turn out better than that one did.

"When I next awoke to the world, my face was bloody from an awful sword-wound to my temple . . . That was, of course, to be expected. The Turks had been on horseback and I on foot. There were several dozen of them and I had only a dozen lazy, waterlogged mercenaries straggling along behind me. And now, my head bound, I was dangling across the rump of a Turkish horse. Bushes sped past my eyes. The sea glinted through the bushes. And ships. Ships already at a distance. I was a prisoner of the Algerians. Yes indeed. Altogether there were several hundred of the Kaiser's soldiers. My sentence – five years. Until the Trinitarians managed to deliver the ransom for me. So. That's enough for today."

Herman asks: "And after that you served the Polish King Sigismund. Right?"

"Yes. Both Sigismunds. Father and son." Herr Maidel has already risen to his feet in all his sinewy length. His sons too have stood up. Jürgen asks:

"And under them you rose to the rank of colonel, right?"

"Right. Colonel of the Rzeczpospolita. But of that I will tell you another time. For now, I must go and see the vicegerent. I'm expecting a few gentlemen here this evening."

Herman asks, or attempts to ask, another question: "But Father, in Algiers, weren't you – when Berend was our tutor, he once told us that…"

Herr Maidel has been accompanying his sons to the door, enjoying his status of father, but now he starts and comes to a standstill:

"And just what did Berend, that maggoty gudgeon, tell you? Eh?" Herr Maidel's voice suddenly rises to a falsetto. "Was it, perchance, that your father served as a gooseherd in Algiers? Was that it? Was it? I knew it! And let me tell you – that is shameless slander! And God has already punished him, that foul mouth! For the plague got him! And just you remember – this story of the gooseherd – I know there are those that bruit it about – it's a miserable lie! A Livonian nobleman would never let himself be so debased! The steward of Hasan Agha's manor – yes, that I was, for he asked me to be! But whoever's been gabbling to you about these geese, send him to me! So that I can wring his neck! And when you become men, you do the same with any such man! Well then. Now I am going. The summons from the vicegerent came at noon."

To be precise, it was not the vicegerent himself who had summoned him. But Herr Maidel felt no compunction about his little inaccuracies, particularly when they served to elevate his standing. Besides, it was not at all clear just who in Tallinn *was* the representative of the king at this moment. Until '68 it had been old Herr Horn, a chap the nobility found somewhat annoying, with his Finnish–Swedish peasant manners, but admittedly a clever and skilful fox in matters of state. When Johan III ascended the throne, however, this formerly most trusted of Johan's confidants, who had in the meantime retired from service, inexplicably incurred the king's wrath. So that Dobbeler and later Oxenstierna were hastily dispatched to Tallinn. And then, during the recent siege, even as the town was going up in flames, Oxenstierna was recalled and replaced by Herr Hans Björnson Leion. And all these substitutions were only evidence of the king's insecurity and suspiciousness, thought Herr Maidel, as he pulled on his boots. They showed that it was high time for the nobles in the territory of Estonia to dig in their heels, firmly. Especially since Herr Björnson Leion – in spite of the "bear" and "lion" in his name – was a man without horns, and even less courageous than his predecessor, the "ox-head". And by now, this same Herr Leion had spent several months in Stockholm. But the previous week, Karl Henrikson, the son of old Herr Horn, had arrived in Tallinn and established himself at Toompea castle. Some said it was to secure the seat of vicegerent for his father once more. Others maintained that he intended to head straight for Finland to set up an official position for his father there. Apparently old Horn had straightened out his affairs in Stockholm, winning the confidence of the king once again. And it was Karl Henrikson himself who had summoned Tõnis Maidel to the castle today for an undisclosed purpose. As for Karl Henrikson, he was merely a twenty-year-old greenhorn. But it should not be forgotten, he was his father's son. It was said he had a brilliant mind. But then, such things – or the opposite – were often said of the sons of powerful figures. People generally describe the sons of prominent men as either heroes or ne'er-do-wells. Herr Maidel had pulled on his boots, musing: My Hofmeister,* Fabian, tells me that Jürgen and Herman are exceedingly gifted. But Berend, that impertinent lout who came before Fabian and then caught the plague and croaked, used to say, at least behind my back, that they're thick-headed dolts and that Herman tended to get himself drunk at feasts . . . *Hm* . . . But what matters now is that old Horn once more has the confidence of the king, as he did fifteen years ago . . . when the king was the Duke of Finland and Herr Horn accompanied the duke to Poland to help him woo the Polish king's beautiful sister, our present queen . . .

It was then that Colonel Maidel had impressed upon his memory the attentive peasant face of Herr Horn in the great wedding procession in Vilnius.

* Private tutor (German).

And that is why Herr Maidel had the gleaming chestnut bay saddled and brought round to the entrance. Even though it was barely two hundred paces to the castle. But too little attention in general was paid in this land to the proper formalities between gentlemen. Much too little! And yet, what could one expect? The local gentlemen, after all, had been schooled neither in Valladolid nor in Krakow. And the royal court that the sons of that grease merchant Gustav (as the Grand Duke of Moscow had purportedly remarked), were attempting to establish in Stockholm was still merely a clumsy beginning. At least in the view of the hereditary nobility of Livonia.

Herr Maidel was directed to the rear of the old chapter house, to a small room with vaulted ceilings, next to the vicegerent's study. Consequently he could not tell, from the rooms in which Karl Henrikson received him, whether the Horns were departing or arriving . . . But with respect to manners, this young man left nothing to be desired. For when one of the most influential members of Estonia's knighthood appeared in response to his summons, Henrikson did not keep him waiting long:

"Ah, Herr Maidel. Very good. Let us sit down. And with your permission, I will get straight to the point."

These were so obviously words learned from his father that it was difficult to suppress a smile. The person of this young man made it more difficult still – a mere boy, notably shorter and stockier than his father, with a jaunty, golden brush of a moustache sprouting under his pink nose. But Herr Maidel did not smile at all. For this was Herr Horn, Junior, after all. Were his ancestors two hundred years ago really simple peasants? They were hardly the only ones . . . And at the moment, in the presence of this boy, he was, in a certain respect, in the presence of the king. Had Herr Maidel observed himself, he would likely have noticed that he actually felt a bit . . . how to say . . . fluttery inside. And there was in him an interesting combination of an arrogant, older gentleman swallowing a smirk, and a man eager to demonstrate long-practised, ready obedience to his superiors. Herr Horn said:

"A letter arrived today from Henrik Klausson. I want to inform you of its contents."

Aha. He's talking about his father as if he were someone else. Such striplings always imagine themselves to be independent. I'll put him back in his place as the son (*he-he-he*) and maybe I'll find out something at the same time.

"Is your father – writing – in his capacity as our next vicegerent?"

"He is writing as the king's counsellor. Also about the affairs of this land. Herr Leion is apparently sick, in Stockholm. And the king has asked Henrik Klausson to recommend someone from among the suitable candidates in this land to become admiral of the royal fleet's squadron in Tallinn. Henrik Klausson has thought it over and recommended you. The king is in agreement. But he does not wish that it be a behind-the-scenes appointment. He would like to offer you the opportunity to accept or reject the offer. So. I ask for your response, that I may convey it to the king. If you accept, you are to set sail immediately for Stockholm, to swear an oath to the king."

... Wha ... wha ... what? Can it be? ... Me? ... Well, and why not? Why not? They couldn't, in fact, find a better man in this land ... But still ... This preposterous boy comes out with a proposal like this without any advance notice ... Me? To tell the truth, given my attitude to this whole Swedish business ... ? *Ha-ha-haa*, old Horn must be blind ... But why blind? For I have not revealed to him ... that I didn't leave Sigismund for love of King Johan, but solely for love of my estates at Maidla and Päranurme, which would have gone to the state if I had delayed ... And now, if I were gratefully to decline ... ? This stripling would no doubt say: Aha. Pity. I shall relay your answer, and that would be that. But in time I would begin to notice that various of the Tisenhusens and the Tuves were being summoned for consultations to which I was not invited . . . And then it might suddenly happen that . . . well, for example, that a Tisenhusen or a Tuve stirs suspicion concerning one of those promissory notes that name me as title-holder to numerous villages and mills in Keila . . . and legal proceedings with an unforeseeable outcome could be set in motion against me, and complaints against me and the legality of my claims could reach the vicegerent and the king . . . At first in one case, and then in a second, and a third . . .

The boy says: "Henrik Klausson has informed the king that no other member of the nobility in the territory of Estonia possesses such broad military experience, especially naval experience, as you have had aboard the ships of Kaiser Karl against the French and the Turks and the Algerians, and on Sigismund's ships against the Hansa and Denmark. And you have also fought in the Polish army against the Muscovite."

"True enough," says Herr Maidel, "but I still need to think it over . . ." And it takes real effort to control the corners of his mouth in his roughened, ruddy, scarred face. For he can vividly picture just how his standing among the knights of this land will soar when the king names him admiral of Tallinn's naval squadron.

And while Herr Maidel is thinking it over, Karl Henrikson is thinking too: Well, this fellow has pretty well taken the bait if I am any judge of faces. Father writes: "Praise his military experience, for he is not wholly lacking in it, and he is exceedingly vain. The king has need of him, not primarily because of his military exploits but because of his wide-ranging travels and his agile tongue, and especially because there is a dearth of better heads among the Estonian gentry – he is one of the more capable men. And at this time of tumult, when they are inclining not only towards Krakow but also towards Moscow, elevating this gentleman could have a beneficial effect upon the general mood of the knighthood in the province of Estonia . . ."

Herr Maidel then stands up and says, without ceremony and fairly quietly, yet in a voice gruff with resolve:

"Let your father inform the king that I am agreed. When does the ship sail?"

"The day after tomorrow, in the morning."

"Fine. I shall sail for Stockholm. You may give me the letters to be delivered to your father."

When he arrived at his gate, Herr Maidel sprang from the saddle, threw the reins to the stableboy, strode, boots clacking, across the paving stones of the high-walled courtyard, stepped into the house and locked himself in his study – a room with windows facing the sea.

He sat down on the stone window seat, still warm from the afternoon sun, pushing to one side a little table with the rolled manuscripts of his unfinished *Bauernordnung.** For three months already he had been struggling to formulate disciplinary guidelines, that there might finally be strict and clear procedures set down on paper concerning the peasantry – those pigheaded yokels – guidelines that he hoped would be adopted by all the knights. Now this work would, for the time being, once more have to be put aside. Because there were more important matters to be addressed. *Khm.*

Herr Maidel stretched out his legs, resting his new boots of tan moosehide on the bearskin rug. The right boot was quite tight, and he imagined the pleasant tickle of the bearskin against his bare feet. But it would have been unseemly for a gentleman to bare them in broad daylight. Besides, he had too many serious matters to mull over.

Hm. Perhaps he should not have accepted the Swedes' offer after all? Perhaps he should have held back from committing himself? And just waited? But waited – for what – confound it?! After all, half the Maidel clan were subjects of the Polish Sigismund, either in Poland proper or with domains in Kurland, thanks to Duke Kettler, and quite a few held

* Peasant Regulations (German).

influential positions in Poland. His, Tõnis', own children would soon inherit sizeable tracts of land in Pilten, from an uncle. And his own dear nephew, Johann of Volluste, a real airhead, a clod with bulging eyes and a ruddy peasant face, was head of a company of manormen and was with Magnus now (that milksop king, who was driven out of the Tallinn area and was now happily ensconced in Põltsamaa) as one of his top men – but that meant, one of the Grand Duke's own men – and on occasion, one of the Danish king's men . . . But with the Swedes, the Maidel family had precious little clout. Even though in Harju and Järvamaa counties – Herr Tõnis counted them on his fingers – there were seven families in eleven estates. In the past nearly two hundred years, they had quite energetically attempted to carry out God's word: "I will make your seed as the sand of the sea . . ." The children of the butcher Villeke had spread out across all of northern Livonia. However, there was not a single Maidel close to the vicegerent. Not to mention in the retinue of the king in Stockholm. Consequently, what Tõnis was taking upon himself this day was, actually, wholly in the interests of the family . . . And, upon closer examination, it would be seen less as a step designed to further his own ambitions than as an act of self-sacrifice for his family (yes, precisely so!). Of that there could not be an iota of doubt in anyone able to imagine the kind of envious murmuring that would now break out among the knights . . . A murmur quite pleasing, in fact, to a man of experience who knows that the matter would not spur anyone to reach for his dagger, something that might easily have occurred in Spain, for example, but would not happen here, in our more dispassionate Livonia. And yet it could be irksome, even dangerous – if one also recognises how easily the weeds of intrigue burst forth and grow rampant under a murmuring drizzle of envy: with the Zoyes rushing to the Wrangles, the Wrangles to the Yxkylls, and the Yxkylls to the Tisenhusens, crying: "Knights, Brothers, have you heard?! Why he, of all people? That descendant of

God-knows-who . . . ?!" *Hm* . . . But tonight he would at least have the pleasure of announcing the news to them himself.

Herr Tõnis clapped his hands once, and when the servant shuffled to him, bade him summon his wife. She came promptly, knowing from experience that her husband was a man of limited patience. He looked at his still very young and pretty wife, Margarethe, with a mixture of pleasure and irritation, as always. Looked at this woman, a mere thirty-odd years old, with her prematurely self-important, haughty mien, whose dowry of chests of silver had once inspired Tõnis to be a most zealous and attentive suitor in Poland . . . And whose manners, polished in the southern palaces of Braunschweig, still charmed and annoyed Tõnis, and intimidated him . . . So perhaps his acceptance today of Horn's proposal . . . But no! No! By no means was his assent an effort to raise his own social standing closer to that of his prominent and refined wife – no! A foolish idea like that could only enter the heads and leap to the tongues of those Tuves and Tisenhusens and others bristling with envy . . . What of it that he had at his side a wife who had been born a von Schnideck . . . What kind of sense of inferiority could be imputed to him to explain his decision? To him – the owner of three estates, the kaiser's lieutenant and the king's colonel! Sheer foolishness. Nothing lay behind his decision but the interests of the family. More broadly, the interests of the clan. And, of course, the interests of Livonia. For, actually, King Johan was now the only force of justice and order here. (*Now* of course meant *right now*. Nothing more than that. And nothing less.)

"Margarethe, I have just come from the castle. Young Horn has conveyed to me the king's request that I become admiral of the royal squadron in Tallinn."

"Oh . . . and what was your response?"

There was a faint ring in Frau Margarethe's voice, revealing her reaction to his news. If Tõnis accepted the Swedish proposal with the intent of impressing his wife, he had achieved his purpose, at least to some extent, whatever other intentions he may have had. And whatever further direct acknowledgement might or might not be forthcoming. For Frau Maidel's rosy face, reminiscent of the pink-veined rock of Vasalemma, did not manifest enthusiasm for longer than an instant.

Herr Maidel said: "I was thinking of . . . um . . . of the fate of our land. And the position of generations of our family here at the border of the Vasa kingdoms—"

"And . . . ?"

"And . . . so I decided that it was my duty."

"Well, well . . . But aren't you afraid that an admiral in a land with such meagre resources will have to pay more for the honour of his position than he receives for it?"

Tõnis snickered (for he had caught the glint of surprise and gratification in his wife's eyes). "If I put *you* in charge of adding up the costs and the benefits of this honour, there'll be no such danger." He grew serious again. "But at the outset we will have to spend a little. Starting today. See to it that the gentlemen who are coming this evening sit down to a festive table. In accord with their gluttonous tastes. Ham, roast moose, almond cakes, Rhine wine. Something like that – you know how to do it. They need to have something to chew and something to wash it down with, so they don't choke on my news when they hear it."

. . . And *if* that little man who climbed up from the lower town in the summer twilight this same evening and knocked on the door of the Maidel house was let in, directed to the yard on the sea side and asked to take a seat on the stone bench under the rose bush until the master was summoned – *if* that same little man had arrived a few hours earlier, and if he had heard the conversations of the illustrious company before the meal and during the drinking party, this confoundedly attentive, sharp-eyed man would have noticed much, and in his genial, elusive manner would have had much to relate afterwards to a certain someone.

He could have recounted how the eighteen or so knights exchanged murmured greetings and conversation as they gathered in the great-room and took their seats. And how they sat there, those of higher rank on the seats with high backs, with their scraggy limbs casually outstretched or their knobby knees comfortably widespread . . . the younger men perched slightly less steadily on stools covered with elk- or bear-skins . . . all around an open hearth, where the master of the house himself ignited the fire already laid for him . . . And how it suddenly became obvious, in the firelight, that the seating arrangement had not occurred at all by chance . . . But that Herr Zoye and Hastfer and one or two others were seated to the left of the fire, and Herr Yxkyll and his confidants to the right, and Herr Tuve with his men more or less in the centre, and Tisenhusen, of Metsamõisa, whose sister was married to the famous or infamous Elert Kruse, was behind Tuve's men, a little off to the left. By chance or not, they were in fact grouped according to their sympathies towards Poland and Denmark and Sweden and Magnus and Muscovy.

Indeed, if that little man had only arrived in time, he could later have recounted it all to someone eager to know everything (for a few jingling coins, to be sure):

. . . How, since Tõnis Maidel had long been known as an upstanding knight of Livonia, and not one who could be bought off by any lord, and in whose house matters pertaining to the fate of the land had always been openly discussed without anyone having to mince words – how, on this occasion too, these themes were immediately taken up for discussion . . .

How Herr Maidel had the wine pitchers and goblets brought to the hearthside: "So far as I know, Margarethe's plan is to treat us to smoked wild boar, and the dry Rhine wine prepares the stomach better than anything else . . ."

How Herr Zoye, sipping his wine, remarked: "Herr Johan, with God's help, holds our town securely in his hand. That is true . . ." And how another interjected in response: "But abroad in the countryside, no soul feels secure with respect to his treasure or his life." And how Lord Tuve then took a sip of wine and replied: "Only the inhabitants of Saaremaa under their Duke Magnus are safe and secure . . ." And how someone immediately countered: "But that is not because Magnus is protecting the island's inhabitants, but because the *sea* is their moat. And furthermore, the islanders are in fact more subjects of the Danish king than of the duke . . ." – "But around Põltsamaa, the way Magnus' manormen are pillaging the land is terrible to behold . . ." – "And those of the Grand Duke are said to be preparing again for an assault on Tartu!" – "In my opinion, we can hope for nothing better than that the Poles push on northward of Pärnu and settle the matter . . ." And how someone called out: "Oh God – a thousand marks in pure silver to whoever can predict which sovereign will come out on top in the end!" And how another retorted: "Come, come, come – in that case you would need a purse bursting at the seams with silver . . ." And how one of the guests then turned to their host: "Tõnis, you've got a head on your shoulders sharper than most . . . And you've probably – um – seen more of the world than many of us. What's your view?" – "Right. What do you suggest?"

And how Tõnis then replied: "Esteemed friends, I suggest that, first of all, we drink to the pleasure we all share in this company of the honourable Knights of Livonia."

"That's the God's honest truth."

And how the goblets were raised in unison – held aloft in the sinewy hands of swordsmen, in the stubby fingers of gamblers, in the soft palms of gourmands. Moist lips moving. Pale droplets of wine glistening on grey and brown and black moustaches. And there appeared upon the faces hardened over time by the arrogance of unchallenged power – faces in fact quite various – an almost identical expression of childlike eagerness to embrace the idea:

"That's the God's honest truth! Honourable Livonian Knights . . . every last one of us . . ."

And how, just then, as the nobles were noisily drinking to their brotherhood, Frau Margarethe entered. How the more well-mannered and better-known gentlemen stood up, their chairs scraping the stone floor, to greet the mistress of the house, some even planting a kiss on her white brow. And how Tõnis caught the eye of his genteel wife from beyond the gentlemen's eyebrows and moustaches – and winked, so that the lines at the corner of his left eye merged with the long sword-scar on that side of his face, and there was only one way for her to interpret the wink: You are about to witness, right now, how your husband will make every one of these gentlemen fall on his arse.

And how Tõnis continued: "But if you are asking me what I would suggest at the moment, then I can only respond by telling you what I have done. For each of us does what he thinks is right. The king conveyed to me a proposal today . . ." he paused briefly, and, with each succeeding word, struck the stone fireplace with the empty silver goblet, ". . . that I assume the post of admiral of the royal squadron in Tallinn."

"You?!" – "An admiral?" – You jest . . . !" – "Over all Tallinn's warships?!" – "I'll be damned!" – "You really mean it . . . ?" – "And you replied . . . ?"

"I considered the matter from every angle."

"As anyone would. But what was your response?"

"That I would accept."

Yes indeed. And the little man could also have related how Frau Margarethe asked the guests to the table at this point, so that their exclamations and mutterings were muffled by the clatter of chairs on the stone floors and only partially audible: "Oh Tõnis, you ought not to have . . ." – "Well-well-well-well . . ." – "Good work! Bang! And in the bag!" The man could have recounted, too, how towards the end of the eating and drinking, expressions of praise for the decision their host had taken increased steadily in frequency and volume – accompanied by the clinking of goblets – and expressions of disgruntlement simply melted away or were swallowed. For the words of approval grew ever louder, and the reasons behind them were freely given voice:

"You know, Tõnis, we Wrangels have always said, there's no man among us like you! At last we'll have a Livonian in the Royal War Council! As admiral, you'll be a member, right? So that you'll at least be able to talk some sense to the keepers of the purse in Stockholm – set them straight on the matter of our taxes to the crown . . . isn't that so?" And so it went.

But, as we mentioned, that little man, the man with the grey-cat face, had unfortunately arrived at the Maidels' door and at the stone bench facing the sea only after the guests had long gone their separate ways, after even the dining table had been carried off and the flagstones swept clean of the bones and pork rinds that had fallen to the floor.

Herr Maidel kept the little man waiting, of course. As was only natural, given the difference in their social standing. And longer, much longer than usual today, even though he had come, as always, in the evening, as Herr Maidel had specified. Yet it cannot be said that the wait was of *humiliating* duration. Not at all. He stood up when he heard the master's steps on the sandy path.

"Esteemed Sir, here I am, at this late hour."

"Right, right." Herr Maidel spoke more curtly than usual, and his expressionless face seemed to reflect, with unusual intensity, the violet-red glow of the sunset. *The old devil's been swilling wine*, noted the little man, relishing the impertinence of the thought.

"So, and what have you brought me today?"

"Something quite new. The statement of the Kaiser's envoy to the Town Council. The report from Tuesday last."

"Maximilian's dispatch? The one delivered by Offenbürger?"

174

"The very one."

"Ooh, I have already heard that it boomed like a bell and was just as hollow." Herr Maidel yawned as he took the sheet of paper. "But since you are here – there's nothing more exciting?"

"I wouldn't know . . ."

"Everything as usual at the Town Council?"

"Same as always, at the moment . . ."

"What about that fellow – Russow – is he still coming to you, snooping around?"

"Persistently."

"What is he interested in?"

"Everything. As always. Procurement of military supplies. Matters of trade. Official appointments."

"Surely you do not show him information on such matters?" Herr Maidel waved the copy of Offenbürger's report in front of the little man's grey-cat face.

"God forbid – no!" replied the man in alarm, and blew out his breath as though to blow something off the paper being waved under his nose – who knows whether something imagined or real, perhaps a crumb of communion bread from someone's fingers . . . And he bit his lip at the same time, to suppress the smug smile twitching at one corner of his mouth, for all of a sudden this obviously worthless sheet of paper seemed to acquire in Herr Maidel's mind such significance that . . .

"Fine. Wait here. I completely forgot . . ."

Herr Maidel left the little cat-like man standing among the bushes and went back into the house. It seems he had drunk such a quantity of wine that he had forgotten to bring money along for him. So Herr Topff stood among the rose bushes and waited.

He could hear horses snorting in the stables. A night bird fluttered in the branches. He heard waddlers or waterfowl quacking in the moat at the foot of the hill. And Herr Topff stood among the bushes thinking: I don't even know the names of the waterbirds. How is a townsman to know such things? Living these twenty years in the Markvard house behind the abbey. The birds quacking in the moat – they're all ducks to me . . . But these bushes now, giving off this fragrance in the twilight, these are brier roses, the buds already bulging . . .

Reaching out his hand, he pulled the fragrant branches down closer to his face. They pricked his fingers.

Deiwel!* Even a townsman should know that roses have thorns. Our Saviour's crown was of these very branches . . . No, no, Herr Maidel did not keep me waiting for an insulting length of time, not at all . . . But on the other hand, just how long a wait is insulting and how long a one is not . . . ? That of course depends on who is keeping whom waiting . . . Wait, what's that droning? Dung beetles, that's it! Yes indeed . . . They must have good eyes to be buzzing about in this half-light . . . No, no . . . Maidel treats me just fine. No shouting or such. The knighthood wants to keep abreast of the town's affairs. What could be more natural? They're the lords of the land, after all . . . They could, of course, at some point, just say to me: If not you, then someone else. Hah! Just where would they find another man who handles as many papers as I do and who can be as discreet . . . ? Anyone else would fall to boasting about the thalers he's earned! But not me. All I want is to save the money bit by bit, and buy the Markvard house when I retire, and then live in my own house and grow rosebushes on my own soil . . . *Bzzzz-zzz-zzz* . . . it's coming back. A pox on you! Away from my beard, you dung-devil! It's not easy to say whether I prefer coming here or going to Holy Ghost . . . Herr Maidel considers me useful. But the one over there, behind Holy Ghost Church . . . he considers me a soul gone astray, whose missteps are useful to him – so he buys them from me (even today I don't know whose money it is) and thus pardons me at the same time . . . And he's made it so simple that it's not even necessary

* Devil (Middle Low German).

for me to confess, for the pardoner already knows everything . . . He has an even more open hand when it comes to paying me than this lord here . . . and I cannot truly say what I dislike more – the way Maidel always sets the money down on one end of the bench, instead of handing it to me, or the way Herr Balthasar, after he has pressed the money into my fist, sometimes grabs hold of the front of my *Schaube**and for no good reason simply starts shaking me, and so hard, the big yokel, that my farthings fall clinking and plinking to the floor and I have to stoop to pick them up . . . I do not know what goes more against the grain with me . . . But I have arranged things quite cleverly. If I should be found out, I have Maidel as protection against the earthly authorities and Russow against the heavenly ones – and they cannot deny me protection without compromising themselves . . .

Herr Maidel returned. He had quenched his thirst in the meantime with another good draught of wine, and his words smelled even more sour than before: "Here's for your trouble." He set a low stack of farthings onto the stone bench between himself and Topff. "And with respect to that . . . that fellow Russow . . . continue to keep an eye on him. Understand? And you're to report to me immediately should anything come up. He still tells you he's gathering information merely out of curiosity? Just for himself?"

" Yes."

"That's sheer nonsense, of course. Find out who he's working for – Sigismund, Gotthard, Frederik, Magnus, Ivan, or for our vicegerent and our King Johan – whoever it is! It is of utmost importance at this critical time that we find out. But better not to probe too aggressively either. Understood?"

"Understood. Long since, Your Honour."

Herr Maidel inclined his head – he did not, of course, deign to proffer his hand to Herr Topff – and went back into the house. Herr

* Cloak (German).

Topff slid the silver coins from the bench into his pocket. It was just the amount he needed for the second-storey window frames on the north-east side of the Markvard house. Indeed, he had long ago parcelled his dream house into sections and played a kind of game in which he designated for specific structural elements the money he earned by his, how to say – *little services*. And so, he put the window frame into his pocket, so to speak . . . He let the servant see him to the arched gate and close it behind him. He did not even notice how the quacking of the fowl in the moat was muffled by the walls and the gate, and only the tapping of his own careful steps in the twilight echoed from the walls of the houses and the Dome Church. For he was thinking: Now I have the jambs for both north-east windows. For the upper one – jingling here in my pocket. And for the lower one, I even have enough – with the thalers that Herr Balthasar gave me yesterday – for a limestone sill and iron grating. All I need now are the glass panes, may God forgive me . . .

And when the little man with the grey-cat face had paid his shilling at the Lühike Jalg Gate and started down the steep limestone steps, he realised that he was carrying two stone pillars on his shoulder, each three cubits long, and that in spite of their weight, they were laughably light and easy to carry. Two hewn stone pillars on one shoulder, for some reason, causing him to stoop more than usual . . . Two pillars, not properly parallel or side by side, for some reason, but lying at an angle, at a diagonal, across each other – forming a cross . . . And he was overcome by a sudden fear of the end of the world, on account of his arrogance in comparing himself, on this shameful errand, to Jesus Christ carrying his cross, though it was Satan himself who had injected the thought into his mind, even if for a mere instant . . . So there, near the parsonage and churchyard of St Nicholas', where the rain-streaked sandy soil muffled the sound of his footsteps, he came to a standstill and, with a shiver of fear, crossed himself . . .

CHAPTER FIVE,

in which we return once more to the man whose trail we have been following between the covers of this book, in which our main goal has been to give an account of his life to the extent that he himself is aware of its motives and limits and goals (an awareness inevitably inadequate in mortals). Neither do we entirely overlook life in his town – the struggles of crab and pike and swan within the small space and brief time allotted to them: the crab and pike are unaware that they themselves can choose only in part (and therefore not at all!) which way to swim with their meagre catch, for there is no escaping the river's current; nor does the swan understand that it cannot decide where to fly with its portion, but that its course will ultimately be determined by gale winds from the storm clouds overhead . . .

What is it that a man might mean when he pauses to look around him and says, in the words of Samuel: "Hitherto the Lord has helped us"?

If he is a complainer and given to grumbling – that is, if he views the world and other people with the doubt and scepticism born of his own bitter life experience, he might understand Samuel's words to mean: Well yes, the Lord has helped us somewhat until now, but what we still have to face will not be half so easy. However, if he is one whose mind and spirit turn towards hope the way the heliotrope turns towards the sun (and this, with the help of God, is more often the case), then these words will mean to him what they did to Samuel himself as he placed upon the battlefield the stone Ebenezer, "the stone of help", after his great victory over the Philistines: Hitherto – and hopefully from this time forward as well . . .

Balthasar could claim no great victory over the Philistines – none whatsoever. If anyone could speak of victory, it was the town of Tallinn as a whole, and the retreat of Magnus provided plenty of fodder for such talk for many months and more. Balthasar's role had been very small indeed, though probably not negligible. The question of *who* had played the greatest role was fiercely debated: was it Herr Sloyer's municipal guard, or the Brotherhood of Blackheads, or the army of citizens, or the unwaveringly resolute Town Council, or the gentlemen Oxenstiern and Leion and the castle garrison? The arguments became ever more vehement and contentious. The disputants "up above" consumed wine by the mug and grew hoarse with quarrelling, while those "down below" emptied numerous tankards of ale, which they then brought down upon their opponents' skulls, ostensibly to knock the plain and simple truth into the ignorant blockheads . . . (Luckily, no-one was actually done in.)

True, Balthasar had at last gained the upper hand over a Philistine. But this could hardly be considered a great triumph. For, as we know, his opponent had in effect been overcome before the final victory, since he was none other than the furrier Hans Gandersen of Rataskaevu Street, Balthasar's increasingly sullen father-in-law.

It had happened in the spring, during the heady celebrations after the great victory of the lifting of the siege, when windows, doors, gates, docks and roads – at least those leading to the nearer villages just outside the town – were once again opened. When townspeople, and not just young colts and fillies and new apprentices, but respectable masters with their wives, and even the elders of the guilds and the burgomasters with theirs, hurried out, day after day, through slush and mud, with the church bells booming in great peals of thanksgiving, to the top of Lasnamäe Hill, to gaze fondly upon their resolute town, as they poked a stick or the toe of a boot into the mounds of ash that were the remains of Magnus' camp.

Then it was, during the thanksgiving services and drinking bouts in celebration of victory – at the most opportune time, in other words – that Balthasar appeared at the furrier's house and said:

"Now."

The master sniffed and looked past him – past this obstinate cleric who had become ever more sinewy during the many months of war and plague, yet who still exuded health and vigour, this annoyingly single-minded pastor who was so relentlessly pursuing his goal – and then looked straight at him again, responding with a slight quaver, which perhaps revealed that the old man considered his assent not only a matter of honour for a man of his word, but also an offering of gratitude to God that he and his household had neither been touched by the plague nor harmed by the besieging army.

"So be it. Since I promised."

But when it came to setting a date, Gandersen managed to haggle and complain and prevaricate so long that not until mid-July was it settled. It seemed to Balthasar that Gandersen was behaving as if his daughter were a sack of silver, for which he wanted to collect interest another month or two before yielding it up . . .

At last, with God's help, everything was settled. Details of the marriage contract were on record. The large guildhall was reserved for the wedding feast, and the tables laid for fifty guests. Annika, now married to Winkler, a teacher at the Dome School, had taken charge of the table settings, contributing platters and goblets from her own household to supplement those of the guild. The bridesmaids and groomsmen had rehearsed their parts; four council musicians were to play that evening, and six boys of Holy Ghost Church, for whom Balthasar had had new coats and trousers made for the occasion, would add their voices in song to the instrumentalists. The wedding feast did not include bewildering varieties of almond cakes and marzipan confections, but there was plenty of fried ox and pike and goose, and no shortage of ale. For the ladies, there was sufficient Malmsey wine stored in the guild's pantry . . . Balthasar could not quite understand just how the devil this whole affair had grown so grand. Half in jest, he had managed to squeeze out of Gandersen a four-hundred-mark wedding for himself – for himself and Elsbet, *nota bene*! But in the hands of Frau Horstmann, Elsbet's older sister, and Maijke, Gandersen's housekeeper, the wedding avalanche had been loosed, and though its immodest proportions went against Bal's grain, he was also oddly pleased . . . The extravagance was contrary to the fundamental modesty of his habits, which he himself had disregarded when deciding to hold the wedding feast not at the Kanuts' hall but at the Great Guild. As a man of the cloth, he had a traditional right to that. True enough. Nonetheless, others of his standing, meaning local country pastors like Huhn and Mündrik and a few others, had not availed themselves of it. For, lawful though it was, there was a faint whiff of effrontery about it. Besides, he had then yielded to persuasion – agreeing to Malmsey wine and musicians and various other unusual indulgences. Well, he had not exactly been persuaded, but he had pretended not to notice when his sister-in-law, Agnes, and Maijke and Elsbet herself decided in favour of more of this or that luxury than the bridegroom ought in fact to have approved . . . He was pleased, however, to have at least forbidden an excess of sweets, and to have used that money and much more – over a quarter of Gandersen's four hundred marks – on coats and trousers for six schoolboys, a purchase his father-in-law was reported to have derided as money "senselessly squandered".

And so, on Sunday, 14 July, 1571, at ten o'clock in the morning, at an hour when the dense morning fog still hung so low that it muffled even the words uttered between the town walls – like cottony fingers closing over their echo – Bishop von Geldern of St Olaf's Church joined in holy matrimony Balthasar – his "no longer so very young colleague in the Lord's service, God knows" – and Elsbet, "daughter of Master

Furrier Gandersen, henceforth to be his lawful wife before God and man". Since the ceremony involved a colleague, the bishop did not stop once he had heard their vows and pronounced them man and wife, but delivered a little sermon as well. In addition to the members of St Olaf's congregation who were present out of sheer curiosity, many more had come than Balthasar had anticipated. Half of his own Holy Ghost congregation, half the women at least, had also come to see him wed, not to mention Meckius, the new *köster* of Holy Ghost and the servants of the church, including the bell-ringers, with Päärn, son of Traani-Andres, at their head and Märten somewhere behind the others, leaning against a column, eyes half-shut, with a St John's carob pod between his teeth. At the back of the church stood a large crowd of Kalamaja folk, their number perhaps swollen because most of them were still sheltering in town – only a very few of those more energetic had managed to cobble together new huts on the ashes of their former village. Naturally, they could not understand what Herr Geldern was saying to the couple in German, especially to the groom. For some, it was simply too hard to hear the bishop. The damp morning fog had penetrated the church, making his words sound oddly muted. Perhaps Balthasar alone understood what Herr Geldern was thinking – as of course did his sister Annika (sitting in front, to the left of the altar, next to her grey-haired, earnest husband). She was his sole relative at the occasion. Indeed, Annika could no doubt surmise what Herr Geldern was driving at when, speaking in a near-whisper in his practised pulpit voice, and wrapping a barely perceptible sneer in an aura of ceremonial solemnity, he said:

"And it gives me joy to remind my dear young colleague, who has stepped to the altar with this lovely maiden . . . it gives me joy to remind him of the words of the Apostle Peter as written in his First Epistle, chapter 4, verse 3: 'For the time past of our life may suffice us to have wrought the will of the Gentiles, when we walked—' But indeed, our young brother himself knows better than anyone of what Peter speaks ..."

Balthasar stood next to Elsbet at the altar, staring at the hem of her flowing dress, shimmering, alive, stirring on the grey limestone floor, and he squeezed her hand. Squeezed so hard that he hurt her – distressed as he was at the helplessness he felt before Herr Geldern's damnable, mocking words that were, of course, intended to invoke his sins with Frau Friesner and God-knows what other missteps of behaviour or frailties of character. For the sins that St Peter had listed, but Herr Geldern did not name, included "lasciviousness, lusts, drinking excess of wine and abominable idolatries". Lasciviousness and lusts ... alright. But excess of wine? How often had he sinned with drink anyway ... ? And worshipping idols – that was utter nonsense in his case . . . Or was it an allusion to something he had in fact wondered about on a number of occasions, namely, the earth-gods of this land? (Where *had* they hidden themselves, if they did at one time exist? Were they perhaps still around, somewhere? He himself had seen one of them – long ago, to be sure – with his own eyes, and the peasants everywhere in this land, under their veneer of Christianity, did still worship them.) But it was not only from distress that he squeezed his wife's hand. It was from the realisation – it almost made him laugh to think of it – of just how distant were the things to which Herr Geldern was alluding. And he squeezed Elsbet's hand again, out of sheer joy, a simple-minded joy (which he recognised as such, standing there at the altar, and delighted in, though it also struck him as unmanly); joy, that her warm and astonished hand was there for him to squeeze, his at last – all of her, his.

This state of true happiness helped Balthasar surmount the absurdities and tedious obligations of the festivities. By evening the large hall was buzzing with wedding guests and the instruments were singing. When he had finally satisfied his hunger with a goose leg, gnawing it to the bone, and had downed a tankard of ale, and even emptied a goblet of wine with his father-in-law, he gradually began to feel like himself. Especially when he and Elsbet led the rows of dancers in a rhythmic chaconne. This way of dancing was actually a kind of tame, side-by-side walk, with the partners bowing to each other from time to time. (Now, a real dance, with his hands on Elsbet's hips, and the bagpipes blaring above those *à la gamba* viols – or whatever they were called, *ha-ha-ha-ha*, that kind of dance was unthinkable at the wedding of a town pastor . . .) Still, he could hold Elsbet's hand during this high-class dance and draw her to him, and with a bridegroom's ardour and anticipation gaze into her soft, dark eyes gleaming in the candlelight. He chatted with several men too, of course – his brother-in-law Godert, for one, and the baker Horstmann, a noisy red-haired fellow who was soon drunk and trying to paw the rotund wife of *köster* Meckius, until Balthasar growled at him. He also talked with Pastor Walther of St Nicholas' Church, an irritatingly pedantic, large but weak man, who was attempting to ingratiate himself with Balthasar. (The reason was not difficult to fathom: the bishop himself had deigned to be a guest at the wedding, and the fact that he was accompanied by his wife and all three daughters indicated he was there not only to marry the couple, nor just as the groom's superior, but also as his colleague and associate. Indeed, judging by the bishop's jovial talk, his robust appetite for goose, and his delight in drink, he was present, if you please, as the groom's honoured friend . . .) Balthasar, of course, exchanged more than a few appropriate words with him, and perhaps some that were not especially appropriate. For, in spite of his professional success and maturity and his new status now as a married man, Balthasar had not yet managed to overcome that childish Old Testament principle of "an eye for an eye", which principle a man of his standing, whose calling it was to impart the spirit of the Gospels to others, should have overcome. Instead of exercising true Christian forbearance, he felt himself bristle. He did not see why he must turn the other cheek. Must a peasant-pastor swallow everything meekly while a bishop does nothing of the kind? No doubt Balthasar realised full well the fallacy of trying to take refuge in his role as a peasant-pastor to justify pettiness, but it was not a realisation that moved him to change his attitude one whit. Rather, it provoked him to recount to himself the reasons for his unreasonableness and thereby stoked his ire: this lout, playing a genteel lord, has the gall, at the sacred moment of my marriage ceremony, to chide me for my youthful indiscretions instead of holding his tongue and recalling his own sins, which he, as a bishop, committed at the same well . . .

In this foolish, benighted frame of mind, Balthasar pursed his lips a bit, narrowed his round eyes a little, and allowed an impudent smirk to spread to the corners of his eyes as he said:

"The fact that Your Most Serene Eminence chose precisely those words of Peter's that say not 'you' have done this, but rather 'we' have done this, and that suffices – that was so fine. So encouraging. To our sinful souls."

Herr von Geldern paused at that to swallow an especially long draught of ale. Balthasar did not wait for his response, but turned to the bishop's wife:

"And if the gracious lady has no objection, and this young maiden agrees, I should like to dance with her."

The gracious lady had no objection, at least none that she would voice outright. The young maiden's blush spread up her neck and all the way to her ears, and Balthasar led the bishop's daughter out onto the floor, to dance with her between the columns of the Guildhall. When, after separating to form their figure eights to the strains of the viols, they met again at the centre column, Balthasar began:

"Does the young lady Magdalena remember—?" Upon which the young lady interrupted:

"But I am not Magdalena. I am Agneta. Magdalena is my younger sister."

"Really?!" Balthasar was taken aback, his face reddening. "I have thought of you as Magdalena for thirteen years. Since May of '58, as I was about to mention, when your father delivered the sermon at our graduation ceremony at St Nicholas' Church, and you and your mother were sitting there . . . I recall someone saying: 'That's little Magdalena with her mother, the pastor's wife.'"

"We didn't have little Magdalena then – not even in a basket at home. It had to be me at the church."

"You're right, no doubt," said Balthasar. "And where is little Magdalena today?"

"Oh she's still a baby, only eight years old. She's at home, wailing: 'I wah-ah-ant to go to Herr Baltass-saar's w-eh-eh-ed-ding!' But Mother said that girls so young were not allowed to attend. And I promised Magdalena that, in autumn, at my wedding to Herr Joachim, she could be my bridesmaid."

"Ah, so you're going to marry my colleague Herr Joachim in autumn?"

"Yes, at Martinmas."

"Well, well. So that explains why Joachim is so energetically whirling your mama around the dance floor." This is what Balthasar said to Agneta, but to himself he said that he ought really to take more care and be better informed about the doings of his superior's daughters. Especially as a married man. First, out of basic courtesy, and second, to avoid putting his foot in his mouth, for he had been about to refer to Joachim, in the presence of his future bride, as a tiresome scarecrow . . .

The viols grew silent and six boys in black coats replaced the players in the gallery. The dancers returned to their tables. By the time Balthasar and Agneta reached theirs, the basket-weaver, Peeter, was singing, his voice so high and bright that the murmuring of the guests subsided:

> *In meyner bolen garten*
> *Dar sten drey bomelyn.*
> *De eyne de dreget muschatenblomen,*
> *De ander negelkyn . . .**

From the pewter tray on the table, Balthasar picked out two of the largest sugar confections – heart-shaped, weighing almost half a pound each.

"Fräulein Agneta, eat this one for my health and your happiness. Take the other one home to little Magdalena. As consolation for not being able to come to my wedding."

Then he drank a mug of ale with Winkler, his sister's husband – young-looking though grey-haired – whose Adam's apple moved up and down when he swallowed, in a way that awakened a slight sense of sympathy in Balthasar but also seemed comical and comfortably familiar. In fact, the world around him gradually seemed to be flowing ever more smoothly. Not that the banquet tables began to sway or levitate. Not that the wedding guests, the solemn lords and prominent men in coats with slashed sleeves, and the women with their gold and silver (mostly silver) jewellery, merged in Balthasar's eyes or rose up to float in the air. Not at all. They remained clearly grouped and individually defined. And arrayed in front of the blue–green–brown foreground of lay folk – the merchants and artisans – were the black coats of his colleagues, and, far to the back, the short dark cloaks of the servants of the church, all nicely interspersed, all in their proper places . . . No, there was nothing seriously amiss with the world . . . At the moment, Balthasar was not even especially irked at his father-in-law

* In my beloved's garden / Three small trees are growing, / Muscat blossoms bloom on one, / Carnations on another (Middle Low German).

188

for having failed to deliver the promised silver chest, Elsbet's dowry from her mother, as specified in the marriage contract, and for having grunted instead and asked Balthasar to wait a while longer . . . Fine, so be it . . . Staring at the wedding guests in the midst of the dizzying buzz and din of the hall, Balthasar mused on the world and its people in general, as was his habit on occasion, telling himself that the Lord's zoo was truly more varied than that of the Pomeranian duke in Stettin . . . *Just look at my dear brother-in-law there* . . . for Winkler looked to him like a large, bony grey rabbit. Of course, he did not know if the man's heart was as courageous as a rabbit's was said to be . . . Apothecary Dyck, after all, sold desiccated rabbit heart to many of his patients as a cure for sundry fears.

Balthasar led his wife onto the dance floor, again ruminating: There's my neighbour Dyck, cheerfully dancing with his notorious wife – just like a sparsely whiskered old seal with a big cat – his whiskers twitching and her blue silk veils flying. Would I be capable of taking back a wife who'd run off, let us say, to my *köster* Meckius, and then come back to me after she'd been condemned to sit on the stool of repentance at the church? . . . Would I be able to do that, as Dyck here has done? Would I? No. No – never! But then, it's not something I'll ever have to do . . .

"Balthasar, why are you squeezing me so hard all of a sudden . . . ?"

"I'm happy you're so close to me."

In the meantime, Balthasar was also busy maintaining a level of seemly behaviour among those at his wedding. He sent Märten to tell the organist of the Almshouse church to play more softly, for the fool, flushed with ale, was drowning out the viols with his raucous outbursts of song. And then there was Master Cooper Falck, whom Balthasar had invited because it was at Falck's wedding that he had become better acquainted with Elsbet. When this red-faced, bushy-moustachioed Kristjan Falck, voicing his praise of the king (it was hard to tell whether it was some foreign king or our own Johan), pounded the table and demanded to be heard, and when the fool then landed a crashing blow to the oak table, setting the plates clattering, and when he had knocked over a second mug of ale, Balthasar went to him and said icily – no matter that Kristjan was one of the church wardens and a pillar of Holy Ghost Church and in the leadership of the Kanuts:

"Kristjan, this is an occasion for rejoicing, not ranting. Get along now, go home!"

And Master Falck went home, snuffling and muttering loudly. But he did not dare to growl at the pastor-bridegroom.

After all, there had to be *ordnung** in the house. For otherwise, how could Balthasar have stood at his creaking lectern just a week earlier, writing upon one of his grey sheets of paper, feeling that *that* piece of paper and others he had recently completed were more alive and contained details more vivid than anything that he had written to date:

> At these Livonian weddings of old there was endless drinking and boozing, where a man would drink to another's health by guzzling half or even a whole measure of ale, beaker after beaker, without pause, holding one to his lips as another was emptied into it until he had quaffed it all in one uninterrupted gulp, so that the guildhall floor was awash in spilt ale and had to be repeatedly strewn with fresh straw, that people might walk and dance upon it . . .

At Balthasar's wedding, thank God, the floor was fairly clean, and he danced on it with his sister-in-law Agnes. This baker's wife was much more withdrawn and stiff than Elsbet, and he could see, looking closely at her, that living with Godert these couple of years had etched care lines at the corners of her mouth, though she was still a fresh young wife. So, if Elsbet looked like her when she reached that age – which would be in seven years – it would be just fine. He certainly had no

* Order (German).

intention of causing her such worry lines . . . Then he danced with his sister Annika, who was becoming more of a stranger, but she was still the one truly familiar part of his own flesh and blood and child-hood, here among all these strangers and all the noise and commotion, which was making his head spin . . . And then Annika suddenly asked him, so suddenly that he could not be quite certain whether, or to what degree, her question had the familiar, slightly mocking tone of an older sister:

"Well then, Bal, have you now reached the pinnacle of happiness?"

It took a moment for Balthasar to respond:

"And why not?" – even as he felt that his response might also seem – how to put it – somewhat naïve . . .

But truly – why not, indeed?

He had recently been punished a little, but as he had to admit, not excessively. For he had grown impatient and yielded to the ignoble whisperings of the flesh, and had sinned with Elsbet before their wedding. What happened in the two weeks that followed could by no means be deemed severe punishment. It was this: it took nearly two weeks, in spite of all his efforts, to reach the moment when a man can say that he has succeeded in handing his wife the topmost apple from the Tree of Paradise.

And now, in the early morning of St Olaf's Day, Balthasar's fifteenth day as a husband, he was standing barefoot, wearing a loose, brown, calf-length housecoat, his strong legs firmly planted on the wide, uneven floorboards of the bedroom, gazing at Elsbet's face as she slept, at her peaceful, contented, faintly smiling mouth, lips parted – moist, alive, real and tangible – and at her eyes, darkling, he knew, behind her eyelids.

Balthasar tried to find a place on the bed to rest his hands as he leaned over Elsbet, but since he was unable to find a spot where his weight would not wake her, he put his hands on his hips and bent his face over hers. Breathing in the scent of her loose hair and the warmth rising from the neck of her nightdress, he lowered his mouth so close to her eyes that her lashes might have tickled his lips. But he did not wake them with a kiss. He straightened up with a contented smile, raised his square fists to his shoulders and, extending his elbows to either side, inhaled the dust motes in the sunlight and the smell of the feather pillow and the stone walls, so that the front of his cloak fell open to reveal a muscular chest, with a few stray grey hairs among the red-brown.

He stretched himself at length and then walked out of the chamber and down the stairs to the great-room. Stepping into the dooryard, he turned towards the back of the house, towards the sound of an axe near the sauna and shed. Märten, in his homespun shirt, was chopping wood for the kitchen hearth. Balthasar said: "More power to you!" and was about to pass by, but stopped instead.

Perhaps it was a flash of guilt – groundless, to be sure – that made him pause. It would truly have been silly to feel guilty somehow, because he was who he was and where he was, and his friend was chopping wood for him in front of his sauna . . .

Balthasar stood there, listening to the faint voices on the other side of the Almshouse wall, singing a chorale after the breakfast prayer, and watched Märten chopping – calmly, skilfully, and with a kind of shameless complacency . . . Only God knows whether there *was* a faint trace of envy in Balthasar's question, or none whatsoever:

"Märten, haven't you thought of building a nest for yourself as well?"

"No, not yet—" glancing briefly at Balthasar while swinging into another log.

"Ah. You once said to me, when you were talking about the sauna girls at Kruwel's, that what's acceptable for a bell-ringer would be wrong for a pastor. Remember?"

"I remember," he said, burying the axe in the stump.

"Maybe it'll eventually be wrong for a bell-ringer as well?"

"Are you trying to get rid of me?"

"What kind of talk is that?"

"Perhaps I'm too much of a sinner for your pious household?"

"Don't talk nonsense. Is there somewhere you're wanting to go?"

It appeared that Märten was extending the thread of a storyline he had been handed and was enjoying teasing his friend. Even so, his narrow face remained wooden, utterly serious.

"Well, the world's full of places . . . Out at Hundimäe there are plenty of partly burnt old logs strewn about. It would be child's play to cobble together a hut."

"And you wouldn't mind leaving?'

"I'm not about to leave."

"Well, stop jabbering about leaving then . . ." Balthasar changed the subject. "Tell me something – I haven't had the chance these past several days to ask you – is it true that someone from the wood-carvers' guild has been nosing about lately?"

"True 'nuff."

"Who then? And what about?"

"Oh, it's that tiresome loudmouth Meldrop. Complaining about my selling a rough piece of mine to the church on Prangli Island."

"What piece was that?"

"A small lindenwood carving of Moses."

"And why do the men at Prangli want it?"

"Seems they've got a pulpit that's held up by Moses, Joshua, Elijah and Jeremiah. But the Moses has fallen apart, and they're afraid the pastor'll come tumbling down along with the pulpit."

"And how did they happen to find you?"

"I ran into their bell-ringer at Kalarand. Reasonable fellow. Klaasman by name. Well, we had an ale at your sauna here. He saw one o' my unfinished old-man carvings. The next week the church wardens of Prangli came for a look, and offered to buy it."

"And why did they not go to the wood-carvers?"

"Listen, Meldrop or his like would've asked twenty marks for such a piece. They offered me two."

"And you sold the Moses to them?"

"Didn't sell 'em a thing. I knew the guild would raise a row."

"What's the problem then, if you didn't sell it?! Show it to me."

"There's nothing to show. They've got it now . . . A carpenter in Prangli made a stand for it a span high – otherwise the head wouldn't have reached the pulpit."

"How the devil did they get it then – if you didn't sell it?"

"I just gave it to 'em for nothing! But try to explain that now . . ."

"Come, come . . . that's something that can be explained."

"The devil knows what they'll do. Maybe I won't be put in the stocks for it. But this confounded explaining is even worse than the stocks!"

"Don't worry. I'll talk to the guildsmen. And even to the leadership of the Kanuts. And I can write to the pastor at Prangli too. I'll ask them to send you ten marks. Agreed?"

"No! Don't you do any such thing! I won't take the money!"

"Fine. That's one thing I won't do then."

Balthasar walked from the sauna back towards the house and past it, continuing barefoot between the graves, along the limestone slabs still cool at that early-morning hour. The knowledge that he could do something concrete to help Märten was gratifying, liberating, as though he had been forgiven . . . He walked cheerfully out of the churchyard, out on to Saiakang Way, where bakers were just opening the half-doors of the cellar shops that sold breakfast buns or rolls or scones or raisin braids. They greeted him, staring in astonishment to see him walking about barefoot . . . Let them stare at my bare feet, he thought, let them stare as much as they like! We are what we are, and why should we go about otherwise if it pleases us to go about like this? He entered Herr Dyck's Apothecary, the doorbell tinkling as he stepped into the empty shop.

He sat down at a table under the window usually occupied by wine-drinkers. The yellowish belly of a stuffed crocodile suspended from the ceiling hovered above his head. Through the clear middle pane of a brightly painted window, he could see the early-morning market-place – the matrons of the town and servant girls bustling about the market stalls and farm wagons. It was a wonder that even though all of Harjumaa had been pillaged and laid waste by the enemy in winter, in the granaries there still remained grain to be hauled to market. And the will to live survived even now in the countryside around Tallinn, in the villages beyond the marshes and on the limestone flats – in those, that is, that the besiegers had not burned down. This time, fortunately, the village of Kurgla had escaped. Nevertheless, the war had brought heavy losses to Uncle Jakob. For some reason, that fellow Magnus – bishop or duke or king, whatever he was – considered the Raasiku estate and all the surrounding villages to be his bond, in effect his property. In the middle of new-year's-month, his military commanders had received orders that half the livestock and foodstuffs and other goods from the countryside around the Raasiku estate, including Kurgla, were to be hauled to an encampment on Lasnamäe Hill. It was some consolation that the demand was only for half, considering how many other villages had been emptied of everything. But since the taxation was in fact carried out thrice, by the end of it, Uncle Jakob had just one of his eight cows and heifers left. The same thing happened with everything else edible and usable that he possessed. And so, the hundred marks that Balthasar had generously pressed into his uncle's hand on St Ambrose Day,* when he had been in town – half his yearly salary, half Elsbet's dowry – was urgently needed by the Kurgla folk.

* April 4.

Granted, the giving of it was also an urgent necessity for Balthasar – as a way of fulfilling an obligation to his kinsfolk. It is what he had told himself, and as he watched the market-goers from the Apothecary window, he felt their very blood, his own blood, flow in his body more pleasantly and easily at that morning hour. When Herr Dyck emerged from his laboratory at the tinkling of the doorbell, Balthasar tolerated his overly friendly tone without irritation and even with a degree of pleasure.

"Well, a good morning to you, a very good morning! Up and about so early, Herr Balthasar?! Isn't it a pity though, to have to rise from beside a young wife, *he-he-he* . . . Mouth's a bit dry? Right away! We've a bottle *specialiter* put aside for you!"

Herr Dyck brought out a square green bottle and a pewter mug. He used a curved blade to cut off the wax top of the bottle and filled the mug with a sparkling, pale-green liquid.

Balthasar sniffed the drink. It was difficult to identify its smell in the cloud of God-knows-what odours filling the Apothecary. The cinnamon and pepper and vanilla and other fragrances made it seem not at all like an apothecary in Livonia at the edge of a grain-and-fish market, but more, let us say, like the storeroom of the Spaniard who had returned a year ago from the islands they named after their king, that Catholic monkey Philip – in any event, like the storeroom of that skipper – what was his name again – ah, Legazpi – *ha-ha-ha-ha*! And revelling in recalling the name (Heaven knows where he had heard it), Balthasar also identified what he detected in Dyck's drink: worm-wood and mint, mainly mint, and perhaps a touch of something else as well . . .

"As I was saying – aren't you sorry to have to leave the side of a young wife . . . and what a wife! I say, like the young Queen of Sheba herself . . . and what an amiable manner as well! And they say her papa's even richer than one might suppose . . . Yes, yes . . . So that you, Herr

Balthasar, are now – how should I put it – well set up, what with money in your purse, a bride in your arms, and May Day revelries without end!"

On the subject of Elsbet's papa's wealth, an inebriated Märten had come to Balthasar on the evening of the wedding with a story to tell: on his way to the Green Frog to refill a wine keg for the wedding guests, he had just emerged from the Great Guild as two men, apparently merchants, were walking past. One had observed, "See, here's where that country bumpkin is holding his wedding feast, squandering his father-in-law's money." The other had added, with relish: "I've heard that he stripped poor old Gandersen bare in the dowry settlement."

"And what did you say to that?" Balthasar had asked Märten.

"I burst out laughing behind them – startled them, I did."

"But what did you *say* to them?"

"What was I supposed to say to the fools . . . I said, have it your way, but this bumpkin will be famous one day and *everyone* will know him. Whereas not even the Creator Himself will be able to identify you, neither you, my dear sirs, nor me, even in the Creator's own pastures. *Heh-heh-heh!*"

"*Hm.* You really think people will know me?"

"Well, once you finish that chronicle of yours, I should think so . . ."

So, Balthasar did not take offence at Herr Dyck's talk of his father-in-law's wealth, nor at the simpering smile that accompanied his mention of the Queen of Sheba. He thought: So now Herr Dyck, who for twenty years has been thrashing about in the same woman's skirts, is an authority on young wives! Balthasar took a sip of Herr Dyck's pale-green drink and felt suddenly infused by a sensation of something at once warm and cool, something magical, from long ago. What is that taste, he thought. What in the world is it?! And then it came to him: the flavours of mint and of wormwood, hot and cold – the very taste he had once expected, high up in the steeple of St Olaf's Church – which would have enabled him to fly without wings . . . The very same!

He swallowed a draught of Herr Dyck's liquor slowly, tensed his shoulder muscles, stuck out his lower lip and breathed in deeply, filling his nostrils with the mint–wormwood scent. He said slowly:

"Mmm. Hitherto the Lord has helped us."

Just then footsteps sounded on the stairs and the doorbell half-trilled – for the woman in black who entered did not shut the door behind her . . . And here we must note: whenever there is talk of situations where the Devil grabs the stage director's baton during a scene on the world's stage and strikes with what seems like a whip – *crack!* – right through what a moment earlier we had understood to be the very spirit of a scene, both in language and staging . . . in short, whenever there is talk of such situations, it is not possible, at least not for one disentangling the thread of Balthasar's life, to ignore this moment on the morning of St Olaf's Day* in Tallinn's Town Hall Apothecary.

The dishevelled, grey-haired woman in black staggered into the Apothecary and crumpled to the floor, before Herr Dyck or Balthasar could reach her.

"Help me," she gasped from the floor.

"What ails you?" asked the Apothecary, leaning over the woman.

"The pain and . . . Oh God . . ."

Herr Dyck pushed her hair from her face: "Frau Friebe! From my own house – and I did not recognise you! . . . What *is* it?!"

The woman attempted to answer, but could do no more than groan. Balthasar was about to pick her up, intending to carry her to the wooden bench at the wall, but Herr Dyck grabbed his sleeve and pulled him back.

"Wait! Don't—"

He limped out, rather briskly for a man of his age, to his laboratory, and returned right away. But the very fact of his departure was for Balthasar the first of three steps up a fateful staircase, each confirming

* July 29.

the reality of a terrible premonition: The first was Dyck's frightened expression and drooping moustaches as he glanced at Balthasar on his way out, at which look there arose in Balthasar a question and simultaneously an answer that suffocated him: Does this mean that . . . ? Yes, I fear, that it does . . . Next, Dyck's return to the shop – not with his own pallid, human face, but in a black, beaked leather mask. So it does mean . . . ? And finally, his kneeling by the patient – he had pulled on long black leather gloves and was now palpating her neck and underarms. When he straightened himself up – his brown eyes visible in the eye-holes of the mask, bulging, terrified – nodding his head . . . Lord . . . it is not only what is written that must come to pass, but also presentiments! And thunder clouds beyond the horizon of overly presumptuous sunny days must rise and fill the sky and pour out all that they contain, upon those about to be struck by lightning . . .

Herr Dyck's voice was hollow, muffled by the mask, as he said:

"Yes. This scourge is upon us once more . . ."

Again and again and again, morning, noon and night the tolling of funeral bells above the town. (At least the funerals did not have to take place in silence now.) Again, people passing each other in the streets with that fearful-furtive look of wild animals . . . Aa-gain! Aa-gain! Aa-gain! . . . And again, the anguished, secret fear of *contagio*, even harder to bear in the stifling, windless, stinking heat of summer than in the winter months of plague. For it was true that this disease often afflicted those designated by the Lord's punishing finger. But often (and this did not mean that it happened against God's will!) it also struck those who merely chanced to breathe the disease-dispersing miasmas, or those who chanced to come into contact with people already infected but not yet ill – eating or drinking from the same vessels or meeting in the same public sauna or encountering elsewhere those who appeared deceptively healthy. Not to mention the obviously diseased nor the dead. Again this . . . this familiarity with death, this fear that he was bringing mortal danger into his own home every single day after touching those well and those ill, the quick and the dead, and then coming home and touching Elsbet . . . The feeling, for some reason, of having become a much larger, a much more easy target, than during the winter plague . . .

Clearly it was his dream fulfilled – yes, the good fortune that had fallen into his lap utterly unexpectedly and utterly undeservedly, as he secretly acknowledged – it had to be just like an inaudible cry, just like an audible cry . . . On the sultry nights of August, after he had thoroughly swatted his body with juniper branches in the infernal heat of the sauna and opened the north window of the bedroom, he lay next to Elsbet, listening through the sound of her breathing to the sleeping town . . . Yes, the smell of the walls of this old house, this peace, the twilit summer nights deepening into autumn darkness, and the smell of mushroom ink rising from the fresh copy of Bomhower's *Schöne Historie* on the little table between the window and the bed (he had just bought it in Riga before the plague, for ten marks), this dear face in the grey half-light, this hot, slender body which was his, which he took and which yielded to him devotedly, passionately – all this seemed like a silent cry, like an audible incantation directed to the man in the black hat, that he spare them, pass them by. He was said to have rowed ashore a month ago, from a ship that had sailed from Lübeck or Raseborg or Danzig, and was now walking the streets at night, his sooty finger drawing crosses on doors, which three days later the plague barbers would outline in ochre . . . All of this – an urgent cry: Do not come! Please do not come! In response to which, the man would probably be compelled to come . . .

Lord, how easy it was for Elsbet to contemplate death! At first Balthasar had marvelled at it. Then he grew irritated, then he marvelled again, more thoughtfully than he had at first.

Since the town was not under siege this time, those who were most gripped by fear could leave and go where they wished. If, that is, they knew of a place that would not shut its gates against those fleeing a plague-stricken town. Or if they thought it easier to survive in the open countryside, even amongst roaming mercenaries – Russians, Tatars, Swedes, Poles, peasant vagabonds and experienced bandits – than to slip through the bony fingers of the deadly plague inside the protective city walls. The shepherds of souls and plague barbers, of course, had to stay put, but Balthasar had said to Elsbet at the first outbreak of the plague: "I'll take you away from the city. Where? To a place beyond the marshes and forests where the plague, God willing, has not reached. It's four leagues to the east of town, to the village that my kin hail from. I have an uncle there with his wife and son, you know. Yes, they are peasants. And live in a dwelling with a dirt floor and no chimney, true, but comfortably enough. They can even offer you a silver spoon for your broth. Pack up the things you'll need. Märten will saddle the horse, I'll take you there myself."

At that Elsbet had stepped close to Balthasar, raised herself up on tiptoe, wrapped her warm arms around his neck, and said:

"I will not go anywhere without you."

"But you'll be much safer in the countryside. And it's not as though you were living here under just any man's roof. You see how it is – I have to tend to the sick every day, and every day, bury the dead . . ."

"My dear, do you believe anyone can escape God's will? His will shall be done in any event. And I'm staying here."

And Balthasar, doubtful, gazed at her in surprise, for he knew council members' wives who had staged tearful scenes just yesterday and today because their husbands had not managed to arrange for their departure from town with sufficient haste. Elsbet quickly added:

"Dearest, do not think I refuse to leave because I would be living with peasants. Even if you were bishop of Tallinn and planning to take me to the Kiviloo bishop's castle, I would still stay here with you. Because when I pray to God beside you, my prayer carries more weight than anywhere else."

This was the first time Balthasar realised that he and Elsbet could have differences of opinion, and it resounded in him like the dark clunk of an axe hitting rock. But he did not worry about her resistance, for it was a sign of her courage. Besides, whatever else it may have been, it was a decision on her part to stay with him.

And, of course, Elsbet was right. So indisputably right that, when he had the chance, in the midst of uttering words of consolation and biting his lips and listening to clods of earth thudding onto coffins and to bells tolling, he wrote at the creaky lectern in his study, on the next grey sheet of paper:

> In the town of Tallinn, the plague made itself known first at the Apothecary's shop and spread from there throughout the entire town. And countless people, young as well as old, died of it. That this affliction broke out this time at the Apothecary, a place where people seek comfort for what ails them and consolation and medicaments, is evidence that it did not take place without our Lord God's direction. For did not the Almighty seek to show us, thereby, that all man's remedies are powerless against the three main scourges: war and plague and times of want, with which He punishes disobedient lands and cities, and that in times of such affliction there can be found, according to His Word, no other succour than repentance, penance and prayer . . .

Yes, all this was true. Nevertheless, Balthasar adhered rigorously to the regime of washing with vinegar and inhaling juniper smoke and eating chanterelles morning, noon and night. For would not God come first to the aid of a supplicant who, though turning to Him for assistance, nonetheless undertook, with human means, to meet Him, if not halfway, then at least a quarter of the way . . . ?

Elsbet did not refuse to use Balthasar's plague remedies. She dipped her fingers in vinegar. She took care to see that both the rooms and the sacristy were filled with clouds of blue juniper smoke morning and evening. Three times a day she smilingly chewed on chanterelles. But it was clear to Balthasar that she did all this merely to please her husband. She placed her hopes wholly in the Lord. As we mentioned, Elsbet's courage, which came from her faith in God, caused Balthasar to marvel at first. But he could not refrain from reproaching her when her courage seemed to become an unreasonable testing of God. For example, instead of sending Märten or Päärn or a churchman to summon Balthasar from whatever plague house he was visiting (since there were many who came to the parsonage seeking his services for the growing number of the ailing and dying), Elsbet took it upon herself to fetch Balthasar and to smooth the pallets of those in the throes of death and to dry their foreheads and raise a mug of water to their lips, all of which were proper services for a pastor's wife to perform, but not with plague patients. And so he could no longer refrain from admonishing her:

"My dear, you must not put Our Lord to the test in this manner. Do you not understand that?"

Elsbet replied: "In that case, you yourself ought to do but the half of what you do in tending the sick and dying."

Balthasar looked out of the window at the chimneys of the Almshouse across Nunnade Street: "It is my duty to fulfil the obligations of my calling. If I take a little more time with some things, it is because I am ashamed to do my job in haste in order to escape danger . . . But you, who are under no obligation, are attempting to perform the holy deeds of St Catherine of Siena, and you forget that the time of the saints is past."

But no longstanding disagreements about this arose between them. Perhaps because Elsbet became more careful, but perhaps simply because, after the first night-time frosts of October, the epidemic began to abate. Furthermore, when clouds did gather between the two young people as they were learning to know one another during that autumn of the plague, it was for a very different reason.

The epidemic was not yet over. Later, Balthasar recalled that the bells of St Nicholas were tolling for the funerals of merchant Deeters and a few others when Elsbet unexpectedly entered Balthasar's study and addressed his back:

"Excuse me . . ."

Balthasar sensed from her voice and her very presence in his study that something had happened, for the times were such that one had to be prepared for anything.

"What's happened?"

No, Elsbet did not appear to be ill. But she did look pained. She looked him straight in the eye, a dark look:

"Balthasar, why have you not told me . . . why did I have to hear it in town that you've taken my father to court?"

Hm . . . This, of course, was unfortunate – that Elsbet had to hear about it in town. Unfortunate, that Balthasar had at first put off talking about the unpleasant matter, and then, as the plague grew ever more deadly, had forgotten about it, and later, considered the time not right . . . . And, even worse, that it had become necessary to summon old Gandersen to appear before the Town Council. But in the end, what was Balthasar to do, when Gandersen, even after three reminders, had continued to withhold from his son-in-law the promised coffer of silver jewellery? Gandersen had not balked at handing over Agnes' half of their mother's silver to Horstmann. But with Balthasar, he had delayed and resisted. And it was not because of a sudden financial loss or some such serious matter. Not at all. It seemed that he just liked to take out his departed Kati's jewellery box from time to time, from the big chest in the corner of his workshop, and feel the weight of her necklaces and bracelets in his hands. And Balthasar was expected to be affable and obliging in response to his father-in-law's miserly moods! But of course, the old man was *so very attached* . . . Perhaps it would have been worthwhile to take his sentimentality seriously and show him some sympathy, particularly now, at this time of the recurring scourge of epidemics, when one's capacity for empathy was being tested . . . But then, it was not Balthasar who had complained to the Council Court about his father-in-law. It was Herr Boissmann, who had inquired in passing, merely out of politeness:

"Well then, Herr Balthasar, how are things with you? At this wretched time – in your young marriage?" It was a casual question, asked on the corner of Kuninga Street.

Balthasar had answered:

"Not bad. At a time like this, when you thank God every morning upon waking that there are as yet no blains or boils on those in your household."

"But otherwise, as they say – making merry at plague-time, eh?" asked Herr Boissmann, a smirk on his yellowish face.

Balthasar had wearied of this kind of remark. Furthermore, he was still irked at Boissmann for turning him down the year before, even though he had found a much more forthcoming (though more costly) source of information in Herr Topff. But that was no thanks to Herr Boissmann; and there, on the corner of Kuninga Street, Balthasar wanted to contradict his yellow, horsey grin . . . but without demeaning himself by seeming pitiable . . . What he wanted to say was: Aren't you all a contentious, obstinate group here – all you councilmen and master craftsmen, you wool merchants and furriers . . . Whereas he muttered:

"Just what kind of merry-making can one have when one's father-in-law will not yield up the silver he promised as his daughter's dowry?"

That is all Balthasar had said, but Our Lord, who sees the tiniest speck in a man's soul, no doubt saw, as he spoke these words, the calculation that flashed through the vaults of Balthasar's brain: If Herr Boissmann finds out about this, he might talk to the bailiff about it, and the bailiff might summon my father-in-law to appear before the council – and it is likely that Herr Boissmann will do this, because, ever since last year, he has felt he owes me something . . .

Which is exactly what happened.

The bailiff summoned Gandersen to appear before the Town Council, and when he learned the reason for the summons, he immediately brought Elsbet's jewellery box to the Town Hall, spat on the floor, and put it on the table in front of the bailiff. To the faintly reproachful question as to how he, a respected master craftsman and honest man, could have refused, in such a childish manner, to honour a contract, the old man merely sniffed in response, slamming the door behind him with a shameless bang as he left the hall. The councilmen took note of it, of course, but did not make an issue of this show of disrespect: after all, these were trying times, and the man was overwrought and in ill humour.

But then something happened – that no-one saw, by the way, for it occurred after Gandersen had slammed the door of the Small Council Hall. (And we are relating these events only because they give us an inkling of just how difficult it is to understand people and judge them fairly.)

Herr Topff, who had followed Gandersen out of the hall with Elsbet's jewellery box, now glided in front of him, and in his soft, insinuating cat-voice said:

"If the Master Furrier could perhaps step inside for a moment . . ."

They descended the side stairs to the familiar, low-vaulted room that housed the town archives and sat down. Gandersen had acceded only because Topff was still holding that cursed box under his arm and presumably wanted to discuss something official in relation to the whole matter.

Herr Topff opened the flowered lid of the box and played briefly with Kati's or Elsbet's or that damned Russow's – the Devil take him! – jewellery. Gandersen sniffed and waited to see what Topff wanted of him.

"A nasty stunt, this, on your son-in-law's part . . ."

"A contemptible stunt," said Gandersen through clenched teeth.

Herr Topff moved his mouth a bit and then began, almost in a whisper, though he plunged right in, *in medias res,*[*] as though he suddenly recalled the words and the manners of the former vicegerent, for some reason:

"As you know, I am not a soldier – but I will get straight to the point. Tell me, um . . . just what sort of man is this son-in-law of yours?"

Gandersen extended his lower lip and replied, scoffing:

"What sort of man . . . ? He's a servant of God!"

Herr Topff's hand, playing with a silver ring – Kati's or Elsbet's or Balthasar's – hung suspended in mid-air. He closed one eye, holding up the ring to the other eye, and peered at Gandsersen through it, as he asked quietly:

"A servant of God . . . fine, but whom else does he serve?"

Gandersen's slanted black eyes goggled and he stared at Herr Topff in bewilderment. He felt Herr Topff's grey moustache approach his ear. He heard Herr Topff telling him something in a very low voice, and because of his low voice, what he said seemed especially urgent. It was about Balthasar's boundless curiosity concerning all manner of things in the world, things which should not concern a serious man of the cloth. Master Gandersen had no doubt noticed that himself, or had he not?

Gandersen cleared his throat. What the devil was he supposed to

* Into the middle of things (Latin).

have noticed, he wondered, apart from the fact that Balthasar had a good head on his shoulders and was as hard as nails in pursuing his goal . . .

But Herr Topff was already talking about this peasant-pastor's exceedingly questionable interest in the council's correspondence (imagine!) and in the town's supplies of arms and food . . . And all of this, he implied, was obviously not of primary interest to Herr Balthasar, for there was no use for such information in christenings and funerals; it could only be of interest to someone else (as was no doubt obvious to Master Gandersen himself). "Such a fateful time as we're living in . . . with the fate of our whole town and all of Livonia . . . and into whose hands, in the end . . . you, as a German . . . but just who is he . . . ? You saw for yourself just how boorish a disposition he has, that yokel . . ."

Herr Gandersen coughed again.

"But you will of course not cast off your daughter completely because of this?"

"Cast off Elsbet . . . ?! What are you talking about . . . ?"

"Oh, nothing, nothing at all! Of course you won't. So . . . when your displeasure with your son-in-law has abated, you will again visit your daughter's house, from time to time? And she will surely visit yours?"

"Of course, God willing . . ."

"Yes indeed. God willing, the plague pass us by . . ."

Gandersen felt Herr Topff's moustache approach his ear again.

"But if God in His mercy protects us – take a look around at what goes on in their house. Who visits there. What they do, what they talk about. And let your daughter keep her eyes open as well. To see just whose interests your son-in-law is . . ."

Gandersen stood up. He placed his old man's tannin-stained hand on Herr Topff's ink-stained table and said, his voice harsh:

"So I'm supposed to start spying on him? And my daughter, too?"

He tried to summon a proper retort, could not find the words, turned his back on Herr Topff, paused to try again, still could not find words, spat a gob of spittle onto the threshold – considerably larger than the one he had deposited in front of the council table – and left, slamming the door behind him with a force at least comparable to that earlier exit.

But Balthasar knew nothing of this part of the story. He knew only what had happened in the Council Hall, and only from the summoner, Johann, a member of his parish, who had delivered the agenda of the proceedings to him at the behest of the court. Elsbet did not know even this much. And now she was standing in front of her husband:

"Balthasar, why did you not tell me . . . ?"

Balthasar realised that he had perhaps not acted in the best possible way. On the other hand, he himself had not brought a complaint against his father-in-law! And while his father-in-law had not exactly tried to cheat him (eventually he would probably have given him the silver), he had been mocking him with repeated delays . . . So that now he, Balthasar, was in a position of having to defend himself to his wife . . . He would have to say: My dear, this talk of my taking the matter to court is only superficially true – but in fact, it's false even superficially! For it was actually by sheer chance that . . . (Though in truth it was not quite sheer chance!) . . . And in any event I have not appeared before the court with your father for – *damn!* He felt how, in his impatience, the threads of his self-defence became tangled, and they tightened into a nasty knot, which he could neither swallow nor spit out . . . He sensed a sudden little volte-face inside, a change of tactics, which, in the name of righteousness, chooses to launch an offence in lieu of mounting a defence:

"Did you expect me to complain to you about your father?"

"But you did raise a complaint before the Council Court . . . ?"

Balthasar emphatically sidestepped all possible denials:

"Because he did not honour our agreement!"

". . . Alright . . . I don't know . . . But you are a pastor . . ."

Aha . . . So he was the one who, because of his profession, had to understand, accept, agree, smile, forgive, turn the other cheek after being struck . . . Balthasar asked, more aggressively than he intended:

"And is that why a signed agreement given to me does not count?"

"I do not know . . . but . . ." Elsbet spoke so softly that it pained Balthasar to continue, but in order to disguise the pain, he spoke the more loudly:

"But he, by profession fleeces goats – and I am supposed to be the yokel goat that he fleeces?!" A sense of injustice, like water overflowing a dam, threatened to engulf him: Were not Mündrik and Bussow and he – in a word, the pastors of Tallinn's Greys – the most poorly paid in all of Northern Europe, the most poorly paid by far, and with the greatest burden of responsibilities!? (Even that very evening he had to go and serve Communion in two shacks teeming with plague!) And, in addition to everything else, it cost him a huge amount of money to procure what was necessary for the chronicle he had undertaken (whether it was foolhardy or no) – the books and manuscripts and documents and reports . . .

He pulled open the drawer in his lectern and then the iron door of his cupboard, both the drawer and the cupboard full of books bound in wood and leather, and rolled up manuscripts, and said:

"My dear, you know the cost of flour and barley and peas and meat these days. But can you imagine what these cost?"

"I think I can imagine, but . . . Oh, how many you have! I had no idea! . . . And what do you do with them?"

That same evening, lying in the old bed bought from the widow of Tohvel-the-Hatter, Balthasar began to tell Elsbet of his – how to describe it – his "fool's errand", which, if not in terms of time, was nonetheless the work closest to his heart, his "real" work, as he had begun to think of it. Furthermore, perhaps talking about it would re-establish their closeness and help banish the frosty distance between them since that morning.

For a moment, he did not know how to continue, and his thoughts wandered: This very bed had, in the time of its existence (at least forty years), heard Tohvel and his wife talk about their work countless times: about felt, leather, hat-blocks, ribbons, thread, lining material, and ungrateful and grateful customers . . . (What a good thing it was to have your other half by your side as your helpmeet, at times even as your right hand . . .) Yet the planks of this bed could not have an inkling of the fool's work that he wanted to talk about here . . .

"Perhaps you've noticed . . . it's not just sermons or the parish registers that I often sweat over. And the books I buy at high cost and read in the evenings are not only books of Scripture . . ."

Even as he spoke, Balthasar was aware of how he was reining himself in, holding himself in check, though wanting to shout: Wait, why talk about it? . . . And how he argued with himself: I've told Märten about it, after all – why then can I not tell my wife . . . Because he could be certain that, even on the rack, Märten's lips would be sealed . . . But Elsbet was a woman. She might be boasting about something (or more likely lamenting) and happen to say something about it to her friend Birgit, that chatterbox, the tanner's daughter from Pikk Street, whom he did not rightly know. And then the town could, well, as a result of this most innocent exchange, be buzzing a few days later with the news: Russow of Holy Ghost is writing a big chronicle on Livonia . . . !

"What did you want to tell me about, Balthasar?"

Behind the tiny window, the early-winter evening was nudging a towering mass of leaden clouds towards the crescent moon, a sliver curved like the blade of a Tatar's sword . . . I should end this discussion! End it, much as I regret it. Maybe talk some other time . . .

"Umm . . . what I wanted to say was that I have taken up a some-what unusual task: studying the histories of neighbouring lands and kingdoms. It is a confoundedly costly and time-consuming job. With all my official duties I scarcely have the energy for it. Especially during such months as these, which, thanks be to God, are now behind us . . . But it is exceedingly interesting to learn about so many things: about the battles that have been fought here and whose interests have been at stake . . . *Hm*. Oh, I just remembered something: when I was in the sauna, I noticed that the hot-water bucket we use for soaking juniper branches has sprung a leak. Tomorrow morning we should tell Märten and have him caulk it . . . which reminds me, did Märten come by looking for me? He did? What did he say? Nothing? *Hmm* . . . Have you already heard about what's been happening in Tartu? No? Kruse, long-time friend of Tallinn, attempted, in league with Taube, to wrest Tartu from the Russians, with a company of their manormen! Imagine! Kruse, of all people, who for years was crooning honeyed songs about how very beneficial it would be for Livonians to become subjects of the Grand Duke . . . Apparently they were trounced in Tartu and have thrown themselves into Poland's protective arms. So, you see how much words mean. But I don't yet know anything more specific."

Elsbet listened to Balthasar talk. In the dark, her hand under the covers rested on her husband's bare chest. Her fingers plucked at the hair (tenderly, absent-mindedly, just a bit provocatively – Lord knows, in what proportion), as though her hand were a bird pecking at his chest, wondering whether to make its nest there . . . The tower of clouds had taken the moon prisoner. He could not see Elsbet's eyes. Only the pale patch of her face was faintly discernible in the darkness.

"I am astonished, Balthasar, at how much there is of worldliness in you."

The sermon has been delivered. A bit bland this time. Even though it is the first Sunday of Lent. The Gospel of Matthew, chapter 4, verses 1–11: the temptation of Christ in the wilderness and on the pinnacle of the temple. And then Meckius leans on the keys and the organ swells. The schoolboys up in the choirstalls sing with heart and soul, as Balthasar has instructed them, and the sonorous music cascades through the white light of the snowy windows and settles upon the grey congregation.

Balthasar returns to the pulpit; everyone is now wide awake. The announcements today will include something more important than the reading of the banns and the usual admonitions.

"My dear parishioners. The curse of the plague has again, with the help of Our Lord, been lifted from Tallinn and Harjumaa. But it can scarcely be hoped that you have become better Christians than you were before you endured its horrors. And I ask, how is it even possible for me to expect it of you?"

He feels it is utterly wrong to make such an admission if one intends to give the congregation moral guidance. In fact, his purpose is not to scold his flock but to prod their masters . . . For there are two gentlemen who have been sitting up in the right choir, from the outset of the service – who knows what they are doing here, in the peasant church, on an ordinary Sunday no less – Herr Tõnis Maidel and one of the Tisenhusens, presumably.

"And so I ask, yes, how can anyone demand that you more quickly become better Christians when those who have been installed in the countryside as your masters desire everything *but* your betterment. For they hold that the more ignorant a life the peasant leads, the less he honours the sacraments. The more children he has out of wedlock, the easier it is to deny those children their inheritance and the easier to take their small inheritance, no matter how meagre, and put it into their own pockets . . . Indeed it is true that all this pertains mainly to the peasants in the countryside. But I am telling you this, because here, in the town of Tallinn, our situation is only very slightly better."

Balthasar pauses for a moment, considering how to continue.

Whether to spit out something else from his heart and his tongue or to swallow it and get to the point. He sees Herr Maidel nudge Herr Tisenhusen in the ribs, as if to say – just listen to that oaf of a pulpit-peasant, what he has the gall to say, not only about the nobility but also about the town fathers . . . He sees the two prominent men, their lips under their moustaches parted in anticipation, their eyes bright with malice, waiting to hear him continue . . . Well, well, well – after nearly ten years of honest toil, ten years of proclaiming the Word of God, he no longer has to watch his every word in this pulpit! But going too far never helps a cause . . . best somehow to turn back to the matter at hand:

"At one time, on this admirable wood-carving, which, because of its beauty and artistry has been kept here, on this humble ground, since the days of papal doctrine—"

Balthasar turns towards the altar and gestures towards Notke's gilded figures – Mary and the Apostles and Burgomaster Hagenbeck, who, ninety years ago, managed to bargain a place for himself among them . . .

"At an earlier time, the Holy Spirit, in the form of a dove, was also present . . . the scene, after all, depicts the outpouring of the Holy Spirit. But after the Great Cleansing of the Faith, the dove was hung up here, under the pulpit canopy. In either case, it is no more than a mere piece of wood that—" Balthsaar looks around. He picks up a staff leaning against a nearby column (at its tip is an iron clamp for a torch, to be used for lighting the candelabras in the church). He taps the dove's breast with its sooty tip and continues:

". . . a mere piece of wood that emits a *hollow sound* as you tap it. For the spirit must be *in* every human being. I ask you, from where is the spirit to come and descend upon you, how is the spirit to enter you – to guide you towards wisdom, prudence, moderation, and to the knowledge of good and evil – when *schools*, which should be preparing the way for it, are nowhere to be found in this land? And the situation

214

here in our town of Tallinn is worse than deplorable. We all know that we have but one small school here at Holy Ghost Church, which provides elementary instruction to town children who come from the peasantry. It is a most inadequate school—"

Balthasar does not begin to describe it. Most of them know anyway: three dozen boys, half as many girls, in two schoolrooms where the plaster has long since crumbled, where in winter they have to blow on their stiff, frozen fingers so as not to drop their slate-pencils . . . Where *köster* Meckius scurries back and forth between the boys' and girls' classrooms, lamenting, scolding, maintaining order with his rod, and – when he gets a chance – attempts to teach them something.

"And yet, even this poor school has been of benefit to those who have attended it, and through them, in a small way, to us all. With the help of God, some of our brightest boys have from time to time gone on to the Munkade Street school, and from there, even to the institutes of higher learning in Germany. But in order that this small, impoverished school be able to continue doing even the little that it does, we must have the stoves repaired, that the children not suffer from the cold, and the stairway repaired, that they not risk breaking their bones. And, in order that the *köster* might tend to school matters with greater enthusiasm, we need at least to procure the fabric for a new pair of trousers for him! And so on. And so . . . I want to ask all of you who are concerned about your children – those now living and those to come – for your contributions. The mouth of the collection box is open!"

Balthasar descends from the pulpit. And the pipes of the organ sound – short, high-pitched, anxious. For Meckius has heard the mention of fabric for new trousers and his trills are hopeful, seeming to call out: Wait, wait! – it's too soon to leave the church just yet . . . And so, moving out from under the burden of poverty and sloth, and stepping over the ditches of reluctance and stinginess, the parishioners, at first one and two at a time, then in small groups, and finally as one whole, move towards the collection box to the right of the altar. Balthasar makes his way through the crowd, encouraging them:

"Step up! Be bold! Be generous! Open your purses! When you give to the school you are giving to God!"

Someone watching the hands dropping their offerings into the slit in the padlocked collection box – the hands of farm-workers, carters, and wagon-drivers, rough from their labours; the hands of sailors and boatmen, calloused from oars and ropes; the hands of blacksmiths, peppered with bluish iron filings under the skin; the hands of stone-cutters, coarsened and permanently grey from limestone dust and red-streaked from granite dust; the hands of tanners, oak-stained, brown; the hands of shoemakers and haberdashers, their fingernails pockmarked by the awl – someone watching them all and hearing the coins clinking into the box could have composed an impossibly variegated picture of the relationship between poverty and wealth, stinginess and generosity . . .

As Balthasar is about to leave through the door at the back of the altar, he hears someone behind him call out:

"A word with you, Russow!"

Ahaa – it's not "A word with you, Pastor", nor "A word with you, Herr Balthasar" . . . He looks over his shoulder. It is Tõnis Maidel.

"I'd like a word with you."

Not that Balthasar is terribly surprised. If the man wants to have a word with him, so be it. To tell the truth, after seeing Maidel in church, Balthasar was half expecting him to make an appearance. Even if not quite so soon.

"Let us go across the yard then."

They proceed along the well-trod snowy path between the low mounds of graves. He should decide – to keep trudging on ahead like this, or to let the man pass, and walk behind him? Nooo! Best not make anything of it! Best to keep going. Who is Maidel to him anyhow?

What of it that he's an admiral to his seamen? Still, Balthsar is curious
to know what he wants.

They go into the sacristy, Balthasar still ahead. He gestures to Maidel
to take a seat and looks around: Well, everything is the way it is. The
large patch on the vaulted ceiling where the plaster has crumbled.
The chairs cracked with age, shiny from wear, dirty with use. The old
stone stove in the back wall, barely lukewarm. The housemaid has swept
the floor only so much that the tracks left on the limestone tiles by
morning visitors and the marks of the broom as well, are still visible . . .
Who was here before the sermon? Oh yes, there were several, and
then that woman from Härmapõllu, Madli by name, whose husband
had stolen the pig belonging to the night watchman of the herring
house . . . True enough, his children were starving, but that's not . . . Oh
what the hell! . . . Everything is as it is . . .

Balthasar places his Bible on the lectern and turns to Herr Maidel,
who has not taken a seat. They stand facing each other. A third party,
catching sight of them, might say: Those two men look almost friendly
all of a sudden! But he would have to know human nature well to be
able to say: Their friendliness is as different as the two men themselves.
For the genial curiosity that rises from Balthasar's reddish skipper's
beard spreads across his face, whether he is aware of it or not, to mask
the defensiveness that stems from the peasant in him. Whereas the
cordiality in Herr Maidel's gruff voice (a tone he cannot summon without a certain self-conscious effort) is meant to mask and render harm-
less his skill as a swordsman, honed over four generations of knighthood.

"Well, then . . . what is troubling you?"

Herr Maidel had already planned his chess move in church, while
he and his friend Reinhold Tisenhusen were sitting up in the choir,
listening to the shameless talk of this bumpkin, who was by no means
the first Estonian to have pulled himself up to the position of pastor
in this town. The outlying villages – those nests of vipers – had hatched

others like him. But no-one else was quite such a lout as he. And now Herr Maidel would personally sound him out.

"You know, when the plague comes so close to you and passes you by, it gives rise to certain fundamental human questions, like it or.not."

Ah. And so now it is suddenly up to a certain peasant-pastor to provide answers to the gentleman's fundamental human questions . . . ? Perhaps Balthasar feels flattered for an instant that Herr Maidel has really come to *him* with his fundamental human questions . . . ? Hardly – in any event, for no more than a quarter of an instant . . .

Knock-knock-knock-knock.

Balthasar is about to call out: Come back later, whoever you are. I'm busy. But then he swallows the words. He has no objection, in fact, to the interruption. The gentleman here has come with his questions. And others are coming with theirs. And he, Balthasar, their shepherd and teacher, will answer them one by one, as they arrive. As Solomon said: "The rich and the poor come face to face, all of them God has made . . . "

"Yes? What is it?"

"I wanted to pay the dues I owe the church . . . "

Aha . . . it's that – what was her name? – Kerstin. The liveliest little bird at the Red Cloister. The fact that we're allowing her, of all people, to interrupt the questions of our Herr Admiral may offend him . . . *Hh-hm-hm* . . . But what can the man actually do? Complain to the Town Council about our rudeness? The council would pay as much attention to a little poke in the ribs like that as would a bag of sand to the blow of a club. Or will the Herr Admiral go to the vicegerent with his complaint? Not about something so trivial. Or if he did say something, it would be in passing, the way I talked to Boissmann about my father-in-law. But it's most unlikely that Lord Leion would summon me to account for such a thing. Or will the admiral go to the king while he's in Stockholm . . . ? To compete with this little strumpet . . . ?! *Ha-ha-ha-ha!*

"As you see, a little interruption. Well then, count out your shillings.

218

If Jesus did not spurn the ointment with which that sinful woman washed his feet, then your shillings are not tainted either."

The little harlot has washed the beet juice from her cheeks and it appears that she in fact has naturally rosy cheeks. And she has put on a clean wrap for the visit to the sacristy and looks so proper now that . . . Of course Balthasar does not say: Well, you strumpet, your business should be doing quite well, eh? . . . But he cannot swear that he would hold his tongue were Herr Maidel not present . . .

The girl has dug out her shillings from a knotted rag.

"Well, be off then" – Balthasar sweeps the coins into the drawer of his lectern – "So. So you have questions? Why do you not ask them of your pastor at the Dome Church?"

Herr Maidel has not noticed that he has been slighted by Balthasar in this matter with the strumpet. Can that be? Or did he just swallow it? That would be even more surprising. He is actually taking a seat now, and calmly crosses his legs clad in high boots of pale elk skin. He replies in a businesslike manner:

"If you're referring to our bishop – Geldern just moved up to Toompea a few weeks ago – you know, he is such a great man in his own estimation that he sees only the things that please him. And that's all he talks to me about. As for his subordinates at the Dome Church, Querlemann and others, they only tell me what they think pleases me. They would not tell me the truth. Even if they knew it. And whatever you say about Geldern, these subordinates of his are too, well, let's be honest, too limited. They merely read you verses from the Gospel and attempt to apply them in one way or another to your situation. But my questions about heavenly matters are also intertwined with earthly concerns. In my questions, one cannot separate heavenly and earthly matters at all. Since you're wondering, that's why I've come to see you. Because I need a pastor who – well – who is intelligent enough to see what is happening in the world beyond the sound of his own church bells. Someone who is not dependent on me. Someone who is in effect not dependent on anyone, but consults his own conscience."

"*Mmmm.*"

Herr Maidel gets to his feet. Perhaps he is not in fact quite so self-possessed as one might suppose. Perhaps the eyes looking back at him from under the straight bushy brows – eyes that Herr Maidel would probably describe as *stupidly naïve but also stubbornly sharp* – maybe they are making him a bit uncertain. Now Herr Maidel says, in a tone vaguely menacing:

"It's understood, of course, that everything I say here is as confidential as any confession. Right?"

"*Mmmm.*"

"The punishments of the plague that the Lord inflicts on us" – Herr Maidel begins to pace back and forth in front of the lectern, pausing once in a while to look at Balthasar – "why are they inflicted on us?"

Balthasar remains silent and Herr Maidel continues:

"I think it's to make us ponder our own sins. To frighten us into abandoning them. Right?"

Herr Maidel stops in front of the lectern, pushes back his short black cloak and folds his arms across his chest. The fashionable slashed sleeves of his blue wool coat spread apart at the elbows to reveal a yellow goatskin shirt underneath.

One man wearing three coats. Four, counting his own skin.

"*Mmmm.*"

"But what about the soldier?" says Herr Maidel. "In his case it's always the same problem: he's either saint or sinner. When he fights for the side praised by God as just, he is considered blessed, he is glorified. But if not? You don't understand me? Look – a fighting man of our time, here in our land, someone like me – what is he supposed to do! You still don't understand? Five different rulers have been wrangling over our land for twelve years. We cannot know how much longer.

But we know one thing for certain: one of the five will defeat the others. One will be victorious. One of them has been chosen by God. But what could be of greater importance to the soldier than to gain foreknowledge of which one?"

Ah, so, thinks Balthasar. Somehow I have never noticed that soldiers consider this to be of great consequence.

"Why is this so very important to the soldier?"

"Because if he serves the wrong master, and let us imagine that it is for many years and with great dedication – a master whom God has not chosen, one whose banner He permits to be torn to pieces and trampled in the mud – if a soldier serves such a master, he is fighting against God's plan and will! And he would be thus engaged for years, and the more dedicated a soldier, the more fatefully he would be committing a terrible sin! Isn't that right?"

I just don't understand where he is heading, thinks Balthasar. Judging by how overwrought he is, this matter is oddly important to him. And his logic, to all appearances, seems valid. As though he had studied Aristotle. But that's not likely – I didn't manage to get to Aristotle either. I know Tõnis' logic is not worth a pup's penis . . . Because according to his reasoning, the losers always go to Hell and the winners to Heaven! Nooo . . . God would not separate His sheep from the goats in so crude a manner.

As casually as possible Balthasar says:

"So, in your opinion – and most likely you're right – Heaven has foreordained that it is not to be our King Johan, but rather, let us say, Sigismund or Ivan or Frederik . . . or perhaps Magnus, who has already come here once to test us . . . ?"

"Exactly. Our respect for the Swedish crown notwithstanding, let us look at the facts. Poland is more powerful. As is Moscow. Denmark is clever and tenacious and has longstanding claims to the territory of Estonia. We do not know what kind of pact it might make with Moscow.

Magnus is a possibility. If we take the long view, it does not count one whit that our Tallinn is, at this moment of uncertainty, in Johan's hands. And of course, you can see that in this infernal mess, even the noblest of nobles could eventually land in the same kind of situation as the leaders of our manormen."

"Why, what's going on with them?"

"You haven't heard how they're derided? Last evening, while sipping wine at Tisenhusen's, some observed that if these leaders were to take another oath, they'd have to hold up their legs and do it with their toes . . . they've already sworn fealty to someone or other with every finger of both hands. That's how it is. And I have reached the conclusion that to avoid such a state of affairs, we need to know how to see through to God's purpose. And I believe you can do that."

"*Hmmm*. You mean – which one – of the five rulers?"

"Exactly."

Why the devil is he pressing me on this . . . ? I would not tell him such a thing even if God Himself had revealed it to me in my sleep last night . . . But I have no idea. Why does this popinjay think I would know? All I know is this: the rulers who have trampled this soil come and go, together with the young squires who serve them. Jesus Christ, I have just been reading about it all . . . the Brothers of the Sword, the Danes, the Swedes, the Order (to be sure the Order's been here for three hundred years, but in the end all they leave behind is a heap of rust and the stench of cadavers . . .) But the people are still here. Still on this soil. This people, to whom I sometimes feel I no longer belong . . . and with whom, at the same time, I feel I am one . . . This people, who come from this soil and who will return to this soil and whose children will come from it . . . Damn, now this fellow is eyeing me with his eyes half-closed, trying to look amiable, but I do not trust his amiability . . . not one whit . . . He's an arrogant, impudent man . . . whenever I see him on the street he glares at me as though I should bow to him in greeting! And in the draft for his *Bauernordnung* – which his private tutor, Fabian, a friend of Annika's husband, has copied section by section – Tõnis is apparently contriving a plan to impose upon the peasants the most restrictive conditions of bondage, with no rights whatsoever . . .

"Yes, yes . . . well, look here, Herr Tõnis, I have no knowledge, either, about whom God has chosen to be our ruler. None whatsoever. And I think that the sins you commit out of ignorance will be forgiven at the Last Judgment . . ." (That's enough! Enough! Stop! . . . Ooh, I don't think I can. I just have to tell him outright . . . I know it is vanity, weakness, foolishness . . . but no-one, in the course of several hundred years, has said it to the face of anyone at the top of the knighthood . . . except perhaps some nobody bound to a whipping bench. The temptation is stronger than I am . . .) "But I do know your greatest sin, which will probably not be forgiven, even on Judgment Day."

"Really?! And that is . . . ?"

"It is this: that all of you are sucking the blood and marrow of the peasant! You are all living on his marrow. But you do not consider him human!"

"Now look here . . ."

Knock-knock-knock.

"Come in!"

On the threshold stands a small woman dressed in rags, her eyes brimming and unfocused. A woman whose audacity undermines the effect of her tears, the kind who will come back through the window if thrown out the door, and who will wail, plead and cry, tears streaming down her face, and sometimes will manage to get what she wants.

"Pastor, I have come again, on account of my man, Paap. If the Pastor would speak just once more on his behalf . . ."

It infuriates Balthasar and makes him laugh at the same time – this leap from the general to the concrete, from the injustices suffered by the people of this land to the troubles of a specific good-for-nothing peasant. And the woman with her concrete tale angers him both *a priori* and in general. So – in the contest of anger versus laughter it is two to one; in light of the accusation that he has thrown into Maidel's face, three to one, and, given Maidel's presence, four to one. Balthasar lashes out at her:

"So – it's you again, the wife of the pig-thief! Listen, I convinced the bailiff not to make you a widow! If you want me to plead further, then I have only this to say: Fifty lashes are too few for him. Too few! Understand? *Sacramentum!* If all over Livonia people started stealing pigs to feed their hungry children, we'd clear the land of pigs in one day! A hundred . . . a hundred and fifty lashes for him! . . . And you claim to be from the district of Raasiku . . . Begone!"

The woman slinks back to the threshold. Balthasar notices that she has left a thaler on the corner of the lectern. He does not take the trouble to register that she may be better off than she seems, this woman, Madli, or that she places a surprisingly high value on her thieving husband's skin . . . For some reason, Balthasar is beside himself. He does not hurl the thaler down onto the floor; he brushes it off with the back of his hand, shouting: "Begone along with your thaler!"

Madli picks up the money from the floor and flees the sacristy. Balthasar turns around, heaving a sigh – to encounter Herr Maidel's angular, mocking face.

"See now – it's clear that she isn't."

"Isn't what?"

"Human. In our sense of the word."

Balthasar does not ask himself, as he often does, what the pause in Herr Maidel's statement might mean. He does not ask how real or how false is the common bond implied by the phrase "in our sense of the word", or whether this was a test, or the offer of a footbridge. Balthasar begins in a ringing voice, true, but in measured tones, nonetheless.

Later, thinking back on what he said, he recalls that by the end he was shouting:

"Look here, Herr Maidel, you know full well that I come from the same stock. Ergo, I am not 'human' either – in your sense of the word! What confounded truth" – he smacks the lectern so hard that the small bronze crucifix on it tips over – "what confounded truth do you expect to learn from me?!"

He sets the crucifix upright with an abrupt clunk, and Herr Maidel says, equally abruptly:

"*Gut.** Let's get to the point. How you define yourself is your business. But I want to know: for whom, in our town, have you been collecting information all these many years?"

"Aha!" says Balthasar. "So that's the issue . . ." He steps up to Herr Maidel. "I can tell you that with a clear conscience." He places his hands on his hips. The two men, both about the same height, both broad-shouldered, stand facing each other, a few paces apart. Balthasar looks Herr Maidel cheerfully in the eye, and with great gusto, with a burst of expansive, all-embracing good humour – the devil knows where that came from – he replies, his voice noticeably louder than necessary:

"For myself! You understand?"

Perhaps Herr Maidel is confused for a moment, for he asks, his eyes widening in bewilderment:

"But why . . . ?"

"Out of foolish curiosity," says Balthasar.

Herr Maidel has heard enough. He cannot permit this peasant-ox to make a goose out of him for longer than five heartbeats! He turns on his heel and slams the door shut behind him.

Balthasar stands motionless for a moment. Then he folds his arms across his chest and for a little while rocks back and forth, heel to toe and back again. He pushes out his lower lip, narrows his eyes – and

* Good (German).

225

stares hard at the large masonry stove: heavens, a stone at the front edge of its flat top is moving – rising up – getting lighter in colour – becoming hairy – detaching itself – it's Märten's dishevelled head and his somewhat embarrassed, somewhat glum face!

"I'm sorry . . . I was cold . . . came in to warm up for a bit . . . and then was stupidly trapped up here when you came in . . ." He climbs down. "But shouldn't you have told him . . . ?"

"What?"

"You know, about your chronicle . . . ?"

"Are you off your head?! You can't imagine what would have happened! . . ."

"But now he still thinks you're spying for someone – who knows, whom."

"Let him think what he wants. If he doesn't know whose spy I am, it means he doesn't know whether to bite or not to bite. But, not a word – to him – about my chronicle."

Balthasar can well imagine what would have happened if he had so much as whispered a word about his work: Herr Maidel, surprised and attentive, would have raised his red-and-grey eyebrows and wrinkled his brow with an "ahaa . . ." It would probably have been quite an approving "ahaa" in fact. For Herr Maidel is not without interest in the events that have taken place in his homeland and in written accounts about them. But because of that interest, it would certainly have been a concerned and worried "ahaa". For a matter of such undeniable import as the writing of a serious chronicle (the writing of a serious chronicle, mind you, and not simply smearing pages with who-knows-what kinds of dirt) – such great responsibility should not be left wholly to a man with no knowledge or experience at all of affairs of state, no matter that he is pastor of his peasant parish, for he would not be capable of carrying it out responsibly! And especially if he has not procured the proper permission from the rulers whose affairs he is writing about. And even less, if there are no official advisers standing by his side, no judicious men with government experience and wisdom, to weigh and winnow all that he has discovered, collected and written down concerning the affairs of the land. To ensure that only kernels of truth are set down in print, after the chaff and ergot are duly discarded. And to be even more precise, after a part of the truth is also discarded. For, let us admit: from a certain perspective, everything in the world can be seen as the truth. But it would be childish, after all, to think that one should therefore set down *everything* in a serious chronicle . . . It is a deeper truth, that a serious chronicle is not a place where each and every kind of truth should be recorded . . . Oh yes, Herr Maidel is a man with a fluent tongue and flowing pen, and Balthasar can clearly imagine what else the man might have said, for example: Balthasar, let us imagine the journey of a particular land through time as the voyage of a ship across the sea, towards a specific, unknown harbour determined by God. Naturally, this journey does not take place in perpetual sunshine and fresh breezes, or over leagues of shimmering waters flowing under its keel. There are also salty swells that break over our decks and hail that beats against our faces, and at times we suffer thirst and the attacks of pirates and injustice and despair and the threat of death . . . But the author of a chronicle must be able to distinguish between the truth of the captain and that of the slaves at the oars who, in their ignorance, resort to vulgar and gross utterances. Of course, one can write about anything and everything. Why not? To a certain extent, a chronicler must do that. So as not to be unbearably bland and dull. But his work should not merely consist of complaining about God and grumbling about the masters chosen by Him. Yes indeed, the most important thing in writing a chronicle is this: it must be written with an understanding of heavenly and earthly harmony. That is the only way one can endure the writing of it. And that is why . . .

"Märten, what are you snickering about?"

He clears his throat. "I think you're probably right."

"But what are you snickering about, then?"

"I was imagining . . ."

"What?"

"What if I were to set up, in the Old Market, a wooden column three fathoms tall, and announce that I was going to carve a figure out of it like the one in Bremen – the one you told me about . . ."

"You mean the statue of Roland? Theirs is of stone."

"No matter. And if I were to announce that I would not name it Roland or Olev or Kalev – which would interest only a few councilmen or masters of the Kanuts' or Olaf's guilds – but that I planned to name it 'Livonia' . . . right away there'd be a hundred people for sure, pestering me with advice about the face I should carve."

Balthasar paced up and down between the two windows of the sacristy on this chilly, forbidding morning and smacked his lips – as if enjoying the pleasant taste of mutual understanding, a bit like the taste of a St John's carob pod.

"You know," he said, "I'd be willing to wager that even the blessed Sittow, not to mention you or me, would have caused a huge row had a foolish idea like that popped into his head: had he not decided to adopt the element of surprise – to complete his work and only then to reveal that it bore the face of the sculptor . . ."

PART TWO

PART TWO

CHAPTER SIX,

in which excavations from the well of forgetfulness bring to the surface things that never should have happened and things that perhaps never did happen, and this man whose footprints we are following is set, bewildered, upon the path of his own yesterdays and tomorrows, where he is compelled to make a seemingly hopeless effort (with which he nevertheless remarkably comes to terms) to apprehend and disavow – to disavow and, at the same time, to recognise clearly the continuity of his self from the days of his forefathers to the self of his own yesterdays and todays and tomorrows.

"In the name of the Father, the Son and the Holy Spirit, I christen you – Balthasar."

The pastor, who was the child's own father, dipped his fingers into a tiny silver bowl of holy water and sprinkled it on the little fellow's round reddish head. And even though Bishop Geldern's widow herself was holding Balthasar junior during the christening and his father was thinking elevated thoughts as he blessed the water, when the cold drops touched the infant's brow, his wails echoed throughout the great-room of the parsonage. This was apparently a sign of great vitality and a sharp mind. But, for some reason, Balthasar's thoughts turned to the first christening he had ever performed. It was – how long ago? Good Lord, fifteen years ago, on a day crowned by a strange triumph, namely, the comedy of putting fear into Herr Hasse. Afterwards, in response to Epp's curious request, he had christened her flat-faced little boy, Paavel's son, at the knee-high table in the main room of the Kurgla house.

That odd, singularly moving moment came back to him now, in part because Epp had been living under his roof for nearly a month. Balthasar had asked Aunt Kati to come and help Elsbet over the final weeks before the birth and her lying-in period afterwards, but Aunt Kati, complaining of a backache, had sent Epp in her stead – she was younger, after all, and quicker on her feet. Elsbet even seemed to prefer this arrangement. Balthasar thought he knew the reason why, although he refrained from spelling it out for himself. In brief, since Elsbet had to deal with her husband's "yokel relatives" (and to a certain extent that was unavoidable), it was preferable that it not be his aunt – to whom Balthasar would no doubt have sometimes deferred in household matters. Preferable that it not be an old peasant woman whose wishes Elsbet would have had to take into account for his sake, but rather a young woman who, though kin to his country relatives, was earning her keep in their household.

So, at this moment, Epp was standing, at Balthasar's request, behind the genteel godparents, among the genteel christening guests. And why should anyone consider her out of place? She was, after all, wearing a proper blue dress made of fabric from a shop in town, and red-tanned leather shoes, and even a necklace of small silver beads . . .

Balthasar began the hymn: "Now I have been christened and become my Father's own" – the very same that the gathered guests had sung fifteen years ago when he had christened Epp's son Tiidrik in the family room at Kurgla. To be sure, the singing here today was much more polished. For Balthasar himself had ten years of pulpit experience behind him now, as well as daily practice in singing. And the others in the room were mostly singers too. There was the bishop's wife, who, with her ringing soprano, could have held her own with the musicians of Jericho; there was Balthasar's brother-in-law with Annika, and his colleague Walther with his young wife, and *köster* Meckius with his spouse. The sonorous, beery baritone of Dehn, alderman of the Kanuts, was like the caress of a calfskin glove . . . And yet, something about the smooth, effortless sound of the singing was less than pleasing to Balthasar. Had he thought about it more deeply, it would have struck him as casual and complacent enough to deserve reproof, compared with the earnest, halting efforts of the Kurgla folk, straining to follow his lead at Tiidrik's christening long ago. And compared with the confident young voice with which he had led them.

The bishop's wife herself carried the christened infant up to the bedroom, to Elsbet, whom the midwife had instructed, in no uncertain terms, to stay in bed, no matter that a week had passed since the delivery. For young Balthasar's entry into the world had been difficult and bloody, not at all like the easy birth of the twins, Anna and Elisabet, in January of the previous year, when much greater complications might have been expected.

When the guests had congratulated Elsbet and conveyed their good wishes and returned downstairs, and when the infant had grown quiet in Elsbet's arms, she asked Balthasar for a clean rag. Not finding one in the chest, Balthasar called out to Epp, who went upstairs and immediately found what was wanted. And Balthasar junior, in fresh swaddling, began to nurse at his mother's breast.

Balthasar paused at the foot of the bed to watch, and asked Epp:

"Did you wrap him in your shift after he was born?"

"And how would . . . ?" murmured Epp. She cast a quick look at Balthasar, an indulgent smile spreading over her face, then glanced uncertainly at Elsbet and went out.

"Why should he have been wrapped in Epp's shift?" asked Elsbet from the bed.

Balthasar tried to explain, and the longer he talked the more rushed his words became, for he realised he sounded more nonsensical, strange, and foolish with every word:

"Well it's customary – it's a kind of charm, so that, as a boy grows into manhood, he'll become a strong man. The kind who'll also be pleasing to women in every way, you know ..."

Elsbet replied emphatically, with more than simple impatience at Balthasar's unseemly talk:

"You'll put a spell on him yet, with your peasant hocus-pocus!"

She clutched the babe so tightly to herself that he ceased suckling and began to wail, as though he really had cause for fear.

Balthasar laughed with exasperation, a brief, sputtering laugh. Elsbet's words were too silly to argue over; he left, closing the bedroom door behind him. Downstairs, Meckius' wife handed Balthasar a beaker of wine, which he gulped (with what might be called unseemly haste) in the company of the christening guests. Then he saw them out and bade them farewell:

Schönen dank allen dat ir gekommen seyt.
Und den ersamen Paten sonderheyt . . . *

He went upstairs to his small study and closed the door. In recent years he had learned to shake off the day's accumulation of anxieties and irritations here and to focus his mind and spirit on the subjects he had been reading or writing about. Within these plastered walls he had learned to view himself as sovereign. But now he felt dogged by unease, by the deeply disturbing feeling that this latest christening differed in some profound way from his first, which he had performed when he was virtually a boy . . .

He stood often at the narrow window to look out upon the roofs of the Almshouse and the walls of the monastery, and, above them, the ever-changing north-eastern sky (today the blue streaks in the copper-hued springtime sky seemed cold as ice). Here he had trained himself to examine things scrupulously and thoroughly – and himself as well –

* I thank you all who came today / The honoured godparents especially (Middle Low Geman).

to the extent that anyone can. He could say that when he christened Epp and Paavel's child, he had just returned from confronting an enemy face to face and, having cowed him into silence, was brimful of a young man's brash, carefree self-confidence . . . Whereas today, he was, yes, he was himself a man cowed. So that perhaps his agitation, his discomfiture, his sense of not being quite in his own skin, was not, upon closer examination, a coincidence of random and unpleasant happenings (among them, Elsbet's unsparing reference to his yokel roots); perhaps it really was, in fact, fear . . . ? But no, that was silly! Obviously silly! Considering the near-daily recurrence of events that still continued to shock and frighten, even in these years after the great siege and two outbreaks of the plague . . .

To think that the senseless, endless warring and killing and plundering continued day after day across the whole of ravaged Livonia. Beyond the protection of the town walls, not a soul could know in the morning what would become of him by evening – whether at sunset he could fold his hands in prayer and thank the Creator that he was still alive, or whether his stripped corpse would be lying in a roadside ditch as pickings for carrion crows . . . To think that in the midst of this bloody *tohuvabohu** there were those who could still hope for something – donning the hat of hope every morning as though it were a magic hat rendering the wearer invisible and invulnerable to the enemy – the more foolish ones replacing it with another from week to week . . . It all seemed to indicate nothing other than the incorrigible childishness of people . . . Heavens, in the autumn of the past year, when the Duke of Södermanland was expected to bring fresh forces to quell the Muscovite, there was much rejoicing and celebration among those who favoured this turn of events. But then he failed to appear, and the army of Swedes that he sent to Herr Åkesson amounted to a mere five thousand men (two fishes and five loaves could not have fed these

* Chaos, confusion (Hebrew: *tohu-va-bohu*, Genesis 1:2).

five thousand in hunger-stricken Tallinn). But in December, the Grand Duke himself arrived at Paide with eighty thousand men! And the Lord God decided to afflict the Swedes with such blindness that they would know nothing whatsoever about the arrival of this enormous army in Järvamaa. And on the first of January, the Grand Duke simply took the castle at Paide for himself as though it were his New Year's gift – after pounding it mercilessly, to be sure, with cannonballs. Herr Åkesson, who at the time was laying siege to Põltsamaa with five thousand men, thought, in his ignorance, that the cannons were being fired in celebration of the New Year . . . (At the same time, people said that the governor of Paide, Hans Boije – who had to be the younger brother of the Göran Boije that Balthasar knew – had been roasted alive on a spit, God help us, on the Grand Duke's orders . . .) And so it went, week after week and month after month: terrible defeat with the fall of Paide, awful betrayal at Uuemõisa manor, wretched surrender at Karksi, deplorable defeat followed by inexplicable victory at Kolovere (where a contingent of honourable men of Tallinn, including Michel Sloyer, captain of the footsoldiers, perished). Balthasar had been trying to write all this down on his grey pages, chronologically and in detail.

Be that as it may, after such horrors had become a daily occurrence it was silly to talk of fear in connection with a merely personal threat . . . And yet, God had willed that on this very morning, just before Balthasar's first son and namesake was to be christened, certain events should come to pass . . .

Balthasar had learned the previous evening that the first ship in this extraordinarily cold spring of 1573 had arrived from Germany, having battled ice floes in the bay of Tallinn, no less. Which was not surprising in a year as frigid as this, when one could travel across ice from Porkkala to the northern tip of the island of Naissaare in mid-May, and from there continue across the strait to Tallinn. Among the passengers on the ship, there were apparently a few sons of Tallinn's merchants and a few Blackhead brothers. It was rumoured that one or two of them had been in Paris the year before, during the horrors of St Bartholomew's Night, and had observed the heinous deeds of the papists with their own eyes. Balthasar, of course, had to find out immediately about all this, not to mention all the other news that the travellers might have.

That very morning at about eight, he had gone to Pikk Street, to the House of the Blackheads, to meet the new arrivals before they could wander off, as they might well have done. He walked through the lower hall, empty at this morning hour, where he had spent a few months in his youth learning the basics of swordsmanship. For some reason he thought (and immediately recognised the impropriety of his thought, given his current position and status): What a pity that I haven't acquired more skill in handling a sword, for in such times as these, I should be much more adept at it than I am . . . A manservant showed him the way to the refectory, where he found at least two of the new arrivals sitting with their beer mugs.

Salve! And *Servus!* What a surprise! For God in His mysterious way had ordained that these be men he knew! His dear schoolmate from long ago, Kaspar Buschmann, now a portly, ruddy-complexioned sea-man and merchant, in short, a friend who had sailed many a sea. And also – wonder of wonders! Balthasar's schoolmate and milk-brother, Balzer Vegesack . . . Still the same squinty-eyed, skinny malcontent. It was not only his complexion now that was greyish, but also his thinning shock of hair, and all in all he was so utterly unchanged that Balthasar instantly recalled his nickname, "Dung of the Orient" . . . He also recalled his own odd sense of godfatherly responsibility for that nick-name, blameless though he was, and, simultaneously, the stirrings of the mutual dislike he had sensed every time he came near Balzer at school.

When it came to news from abroad, Balthasar did not in fact learn much from Kaspar. Yes, Kaspar did say he had been in the kingdom of

France, right in the city of Paris, at the end of August last year. And oh, what a city! No-one who had not been there could even dream about it. He was on a small carrack from Antwerp, and they were anchored near the southern quay on that river of theirs, the Sayny, or whatever it was called, awaiting their cargo – barrels of Burgundy and other stuff – very profitable wares. Of the night of the massacre itself he had only very vague recollections, for he had lodged, as he said: "*He-he-heh* . . . not exactly with the prince and princess in their bridal bower, where the bloodbath apparently began . . . but in another house altogether, and I'm sure you know what I mean . . . Oooh! What women! I'm telling you, a man who's never had such women can't even dream about them . . . You, Balthasar – I'm talking to you, as an old school chum, isn't that so? . . . I know your pastor's ears won't hear any of it – *ha-ha-ha-hah* . . . Anyway, I imagine there were shouts and screams in the streets that night, and the clash of swords. And in the morning, when I got back to the quay – I didn't have a long way to go . . . my own *Venusberg* was right on the river – there were a few men lying about dead . . . Ah – you say it was two thousand that were killed that night in Paris? Is that so? . . . But then, what's two thousand in a city like Paris, where, they say, there are three hundred thousand people . . . ?"

But Kaspar could say nothing at all about the role played in the massacre of the Protestants by the king or his mother, or by the ignorant supporters of the papists. Just as he had been unable, long ago, to tell Master Sum who came first, the Greeks or the Romans . . . Nor could he tell Balthasar about more recent events, which Balthasar had vaguely heard about. For instance, the fact that the Dutch had worked out how to use pigeons to send messages from their cities, which were for the most part encircled by the Spaniards. Or that a Dane at the old Herrevad monastery, peering at the heavens last year, had discovered, in Cassiopeia, the brightest star ever seen . . .

Balzer Vegesack had even less to say about these things than Kaspar.

But his sour half-smirk, like the expression he had worn long ago, belied the impression that his silence stemmed from ignorance. It seemed, rather, to arise on this occasion from something that he, and he alone, knew. Was Balthasar perhaps projecting this impression upon Balzer retrospectively? No, probably not. For he had had such premonitions of impending trouble in the past.

When Balthasar had emptied his tankard and was about to depart, Balzer took him aside, out of Kasper's hearing, leaned against an elegant octagonal limestone column, and drawled:

"Balthasar, I've been wanting to ask you something for a long time, but have never found the right moment – one or the other of us has been away wandering the world – tell me, how in hell did you end up among the spokesmen for those rebel peasants in the autumn of '60?"

Balthasar felt something cold flood his insides and rise to his knees, loins, chest, and over his head – and then it began to ebb (there was actually no need to take Balzer's words so seriously). His head rose again above the icy fear, thank God, and the fear retreated downward over his pounding heart. Yes, it was in this hall that he had first practised the art of swordsmanship – how to advance, retreat, how to parry a thrust. At the same time, he recognised that something banished and buried long ago had been exhumed by Balzer's question and now assumed a fateful reality.

Balzer was not likely to have noticed that Balthasar's voice was a bit hoarse as he asked, in a tone of such genuine bewilderment that no-one could have thought it pretence:

"What are you talking about? You're saying I was with whom?"

"Stop pretending. You were with the peasants – the ones who came in the autumn of '60 to negotiate with the Town Council. You were with them! I saw you with my own eyes."

"Balzer, you were dreaming."

"I was dreaming? Standing at the door to the Council Hall?"

"What were you doing there?"

"My old man had left for the meeting that morning in a hurry and forgotten his official medallion. I remember, Mama found it hanging from a nail in his writing desk. And she sent me to the Town Hall with it. The foolishness of mamas – worrying about how Papa could sit there among all the others without his medallion. I went to the Council Hall and looked in. The old man saw me and waved me away – I wasn't to disturb them. But I saw *you* there with the peasants."

"Nonsense."

"No doubt about it. Granted, you were wearing peasant rags and you'd grown a beard, but I can swear on the Bible that it was you."

"Balzer, you're talking nonsense. I was in Germany at the time."

"I understand that you can't admit it. The leaders of the rebellion were all executed on the wheel or the gallows. Eleven men, on Jerusalem Hill. I went to see it – to see whether you had perhaps landed among them. In Kolovere and Kuressaare, others were broken on the wheel or hanged. So that I do understand – as you do, of course, even better. *Ha-ha-ha-hah*. What an uproar there would be if the story came out: Herr Pastor of Holy Ghost Church was one of the leaders of the rebels and bandits disrupting the peace of the land, a devil's-dozen years ago . . . What?! A spokesman of murderers – now in the pulpit at Tallinn! What?! Whether a spokesman of murderers or a leader, you understand, in a case like this, there's not much difference . . ."

"Stop it, Balzer. They do say blood is thicker than water but this is . . ."

"Balthasar! You sound just like my departed father! He said the same thing when I told him I had recognised you – he, of course, hadn't noticed you . . . He just said that though blood is thicker than water, he had not thought it could draw a young man of sound mind into such a morass . . ."

"Oh, so you told this nonsense to your father too . . . ? And what else did he say?"

"He? Nothing else. As you know, he wasn't one to indulge in idle talk."

Thank God! At least old Vegesack had not told his son that it was in fact Siimon Rissa who had persuaded him to arrange for safe conduct for the peasant delegation . . .

"And who else did you spout this nonsense to?"

"No-one. What do you take me for? A babbler? A prater?"

"Well, how would you describe yourself, the way you've been going on?"

"*Ha-ha-haa.* An honest man. Even if not the most appealing, to some. But that does not interest me. Do you know what would interest me?"

"*Hm?*"

"To see the expression on your face as you, a man of God, swear to the court bailiff that you were never, ever, involved with those events."

"*Ha-ha-ha-ha* . . ." Balthasar heard himself laughing louder than necessary. "And what kind of expression would you expect to see? In fact, you'd see the most ordinary expression. If, that is, the bailiff were so foolish as to ask me to swear to such a thing. Which means, if you were so foolish as to relate this rubbish to him. But go off and get a good night's sleep. You've had more ale than you can manage. After all, you've been drinking much lighter ale for some time now than Tallinn's strong brew."

"I am completely sober, Balthasar."

"No, you're not. Though I do remember that even sober, back on Munkade Street, you enjoyed spinning stupid tales."

"Is that so . . . ?"

"Yes. You'd twist and spin all kinds of rubbish together, endlessly and tediously. As though the rubbish were hemp and you the rope-maker . . . Go, sleep it off now."

"So, you won't admit it? If – as a friend, for old time's sake – you admitted it, I would not be trying to catch you out."

"Balzer, if you really believe you saw me there, I'm telling you, you were mistaken."

"You think so?"

"What do you mean, do I think so?"

"Alright. Let's assume I was mistaken. Even there, at the door of the Council Hall. That is a possibility, given your face. Among those peasants. Just a likeness, that's all. But then, explain something else to me."

"What?"

"I told you. I went to Jerusalem Hill to look around. On account of you. Not at the execution itself, but later that evening, at the corpses. Before they were shovelled into a hole. They were lying about on the ground in the alder grove behind the knoll, and the executioner's men were just then digging a grave for them. There were guards standing at the edge of the thicket to keep away the curious. The big crowd had scattered, but a few lone figures were still prowling about. I pressed a farthing into the hands of the executioner's men, and they let me get closer to the corpses. Well, you weren't among them, of course. But you can imagine – the scene was grim enough. Bloody bodies, broken limbs, blue faces, lips chewed to tatters. I felt ill. And as I crouched there under the alders, an old man came to look over the dead. He paid off the guards. I didn't see how much, but it was enough for them to stop shouting at him and to offer their help. He had them turn all the dead bodies face up and brush the hair away from their faces, and he examined each one in turn."

"And?"

"And then he crossed himself and left. He paid the guards another mark, I saw that – a whole mark, and went off with a light step. Because the man he was looking for was fortunately not there."

"And then?"

"And then! Do you know who that old man was?"

"Well . . . ?"

"It was your father."

"*Hmm . . .*"

"You tell me, who was he looking for?"

Balthasar shut his eyes tight and listened. He was straining to hear the sounds of the world outside. The footfalls of people passing in the street. The clanking of wagon wheels on cobblestones, the creaking of axles. The baying and growling of roaming dogs. People talking, indecipherable snatches of conversation. The liberating sounds of the world outside. But he could hear not a thing above the roar of his own blood. He opened his eyes and looked into Balzer's cool, narrow, expectant eyes – the eyes of an alchemist who has poured acid on iron filings and is watching intently to see what will happen in the flask. He said:

"My dear fellow, even if this were true – for I could not very well ask my father in his grave whether he was really there – but even if it were true, why do you assume it was me he was looking for? We have relatives in several districts outside the town."

"Damn right. But if I add to that the fact that a week earlier I'd seen you for myself, standing in the Council Hall amongst those ragged rebels? You see, when I set these two things side by side – your presence in the hall and your father there in the wilds, examining the faces of corpses with care and dread, I'd have to be stupid if I didn't get it. It was *you* your father was afraid of finding there. Well?"

"Well what?"

"You won't admit it?"

"Balzer, as we used to say, in the friendly old words of schoolmates: Drop your trousers and crawl up your arse."

It was from this exchange that Balthasar had come to his son's christening. And now, standing in his study, taking grey sheets of paper out of the wall recess behind the iron door and leafing through them, looking for something, his thoughts kept returning to the disagreeable conversation under the elegant vaulted ceiling of the Blackheads' house.

He knew enough about Lübeck Law and the traditional legal practices of the town to be fairly certain of one thing: even if Balzer Vegesack testified under oath, his accusation would not represent sufficient grounds to arraign him, Balthasar, on charges of disturbing the peace and engaging in plunder . . . That would be absurd . . . Or on charges of participating in murder . . . in the murder of Herr Üxkyll at Limandu, for example . . . If Balzer Vegesack were to tell his tale under oath, he would need many supporting facts (especially if the bailiff put it in writing). So many facts, that there was actually no need to worry too much . . . Herr Krumhusen of Pomerania was dead, and his son was God knows where. To be sure, bad luck could intervene: Herr Wolff might be located in Greifswald . . . and testify, if asked, that the student named Rissa or Rüsso or Ryssow – or whatever his name rightly was – of the Pedagogical Institute, was definitely not in Germany at that critical moment in the autumn of 1560, not at all, no . . . for Herr Wolff would remember it all in detail: the now-departed merchant Krumhusen, his old friend, was sending his young friend, this very Russow, off on his ship on some business, precisely at that time in late summer – early autumn – no, no, not to Tallinn, but to Narva, Narva. In any event, to Livonia, yes, that was true. And he returned from there towards the end of 1560, or even the beginning of '61. (Herr Wolff would say: Oh, *that* I remember even more precisely, for it was the start of our long and complicated financial relationship.)

Balthasar was digging the ground out from under his own feet in a fervour of alarm, wondering what would happen if such information from Herr Wolff found its way to Schröder, the Court Bailiff of Tallinn . . . And if the elaborations of that ominous redhead – Herr Antonius – were added to them . . . A man like him might well be in Mitau somewhere, idling about at the court of Duke Gotthart. Were Herr Antonius asked, he would scarcely still be worrying about the death of his mother and would recall with malicious glee how they met under the pillory on the marketplace in Tallinn, just after Balthasar emerged from the Town Hall with the peasant spokesmen . . . And this morning, Balthasar himself had put an idea in Balzer's head – that confounded buffoon – when he mentioned relatives living outside town . . . Uncle Jakob . . . he would be mute as a rock in a ploughland about his own affairs, and especially about his nephew's, even if they put him on the rack. But if all else failed, they might start harassing and investigating the Kurgla folk, who, in the course of these many years, were bound to have shared confidences from time to time . . . One could not expect them all to have the fortitude, if abused and hectored and threatened with instruments of torture, to protect themselves with a wall of disavowals and amnesia . . . Suddenly Balthasar's heart contracted, shrinking to normal size, and he felt a surge of hot blood course through his body: What about Katharina?!

No-no-no! Even if Balzer were to go personally to Riga to ask Katharina, or if the bailiff sent his officials to her, Katharina would smilingly deny that she had seen Balthasar on those days (and that he had told her whose camp he had just come from – *oooh*). She would deny it, beyond a doubt. For her own sake as well as Balthasar's. But it would be interesting to know which came first . . . ? (Oh Lord, what lamentable vanity can lie concealed in a man's breast, no matter how serious a man – a man of the Church, a man of learning, a married man – who, coming from the christening of his first-born son, and with such a vile threat hanging over him, is capable of thinking how sweet it would be to know that such a woman would lie under oath – for her own sake, to be sure, but above all, for his . . .)

Balthasar went to the window of his study and looked out over the Almshouse courtyard, at the triangular gables of the houses facing him, alternating with the upside-down triangles of the clear, cold sky. Yellow gables, blue triangles. Or – yellow hills and blue funnels of lake between them. Or – goblet-stems of stone, interspersed with goblets of blue glass without stems. Or – triangular dragons' teeth: yellow lowers, blue uppers. Clamped together. Today was the day of the dragon's bite. But today was also, after all, the christening day of his first-born son . . . On the other side of the door with its furcated iron hinges, he heard his son wailing softly and then Epp's footsteps on the stairs . . . What would Epp say if she were asked . . . ? Would she say that Balthasar had indeed stopped in Kurgla that October, dressed as a peasant . . . that he had helped them lead the farm animals into the woods . . . and slept among them that night on Hongasaare Island in a cave of fir branches, where, for some reason, they were lulled to sleep by the fragrance of birch leaves . . .

Nonsense! Epp would never tell anyone anything. Not Epp. (It would of course be ridiculous to start coaching her about it now . . .) Because no-one would be questioned about anything! Balzer, that cursed, poison-tongued snake, his classmate, milk-brother and namesake into the bargain, would sleep it off, wake up with a clear head – maybe he had already had a good sleep – and feel embarrassed at his vile, spiteful talk! The Lord could not want to – but what if He did?

Balthasar did not, of course, have thorough knowledge of either the articles of Lübeck Law or the rules of Tallinn's criminal court. And it was not at all certain that the laws were sufficiently consistent to enable anyone, even someone well versed in them, to determine whether a charge that might possibly be brought against him twelve years after the fact could be dismissed as – what was the term – *vetustate abolescendum.*[*] Or, would his case be found not to have exceeded legal time limits? Anyway, it was of no importance. For the greatest danger was not that this affair would be brought to the attention of the bailiff: rumours about it would be just as harmful. Well, not quite . . . rumours might not be as bad as a trial. Yet the difference would mean very little in relation to the Pastor of Holy Ghost Church, an honourable member

* Beyond the statue of limitations (Latin).

246

of the clergy . . . Imagine the talk in parishes, in vestries, at church doors, at the wine tables of councilmen, in the ale halls of the guilds, in workshops, in taverns, at market shops, in the homes of burghers – from kitchens to bedrooms, faces flushed with the shock and glee of the gossip: Lord! Have you heard?! That lout, that yokel, that would-be German with those goggling bull's eyes, he was apparently here during the peasant uprising – Yes! – at the uprising – the first among the murderers and marauders, the first among those setting fires . . . Good God, the leader of the villains in the forests of Läänemaa is now the Pastor of the Town Hall Chapel . . . I've been saying for some time, the man is suspect . . . Jesus Christ, if such things are possible, the end of the world must truly be at hand . . . *Hah!* It's no wonder, given what a boor and a brute he is . . .

This is how it would be . . . And, worst of all, it would be impossible to deny the kernel of truth in such tales. At least before God . . .

Ah . . . there they were – without noticing it himself, he had found and put to one side a few pages of his chronicle. These were the pages that he wanted to reread now, because of the hives that had erupted on his body after his talk with Balzer that morning.

He pushed open the window – for some reason he suddenly felt hot. He heard (and did not hear) the heavy rumbling of salt wagons as they rolled down Holy Ghost Street, and the shrill cries of schoolboys at recess, borne on the cold east wind from the monastery courtyard and up over the rooftops. He read:

LXXIX. THE PEASANT UPRISING OF 1560

That same autumn, with the country in turmoil, the peasants in the counties of Harju and Läänemaa rose up against the nobility, for although they were compelled to pay an onerous tithe and all manner of other fees and perform gruelling labour for the estates, they were given not the least protection by their lords in times of danger ... And since their defenceless situation had endured several years and was becoming more desperate by the day, and since they had learned from experience that peasants could hope for naught from the current rulers of the land, the rebellion broke out with especial fury and spread so widely from Harju and Läänemaa that even from Järvamaa and the territories under the *voevoda* of Narva, such as Ilumäe, Loobu, and others in north-west Viru, bands of armed peasants began secretly to join with the large peasant army in Läänemaa ...

Balthasar read the last long sentence with alarm, dipped his pen into the inkwell, and crossed out the words, rendering them illegible. God knows, maybe this was not necessary. But suddenly it seemed to him that it was mad and utterly reckless to keep among his own writings, in his own house, such damnably clear evidence against himself: for did not the names Narva, Ilumäe, Loobu and Läänemaa reveal quite unmistakably the route that he himself had travelled at the time ... ?

But this army gathered first of all in south and south-west Harju. And in order that it not be merely a rioting herd but that it have serious leadership, its chosen representatives assembled, one for each ten men, to that place where, more than three hundred years ago, the peasants were said to have convened their Councils of Elders (as was known from the writings of Henricus de Lettis). And there, in the village of Raikküla at Pakamäe, on a singular limestone bluff created by Our Lord, in the middle of the forest, over three hundred men raised their voices in noisy debate at sunrise. And when the sun had climbed high and was nearly overhead they acclaimed their chosen king ...

Good Lord – such details could only be known to one who had been present, or, at the very least, one who had heard them from the participants themselves . . . Meaning that anyone who knew all this was not merely a casual acquaintance, but one whom the rebels considered wholly trustworthy . . .

They chose as their king a one-foot blacksmith from the village of Alaküla, a man of keen intelligence, and placed upon his head a most unusual crown, a shaggy, double-layered hat festooned with fresh-cut oak branches . . .

Balthasar squeezed his eyes shut, musing: The king's crown was not a dream, after all, as it had begun to seem, from time to time . . . And thus neither was this king a dream, as was evident from what he had written long ago:

And the King selected twelve men with good swords to be his bodyguards, and some with shepherds' horns, to act as heralds . . . He appointed the more enterprising of the men to take command of the smaller divisions within the army and gave to each of his messengers an oak leaf for identification, with an imprint of his tiny blacksmith's tongs . . .

So, none of this was a dream . . . But he, Balthasar, dared not write about it! He had to cross it all out, render it illegible! He had to destroy it! For he could not know more about all this than was generally known . . . Those who had taken part in it and managed to stay alive were hardly going to write about it . . . Which meant that no-one would probably ever write a word about it. With the exception of someone who might want to condemn it and thus spit some ink at it in passing . . . And with the exception of some literate fool, standing more or less at a distance from the events, someone who had chanced to collect bits of information about those days . . . Indeed, did not that notary, that small-eyed, grey-complexioned man by the name of Renner, say, ten years ago, aboard ship on the River Weser in Bremen, that he had been keeping a record of events in Livonia . . . ? Perhaps he also wrote about the peasant rebellion, although he did say he had left the country before that . . . as had Balthasar, by the way! Fine! Let the notary write it all up in as much detail as he liked. But not Balthasar! Let those write about it, with the help of God, who had simply heard others tell of it! And, in the name of God, let those who actually witnessed it remain silent.

And the rebels proclaimed far and wide that they would no longer obey the nobles nor render further services to them, and that they desired to be free and liberated and to destroy the nobles and root them out.

Well, this was so widely known everywhere that there was no need to cross it out. Let Tallinn's councilmen (the selfsame ones with whom we – uh, the rebels – tried to make a pact) . . . let them keep thinking, as they did to this day, that the peasants might be capable of killing a few dozen Germans, but that they could not possibly conceive a goal as radical as rooting out the nobility as a whole . . . *Ho-ho-hoo* . . . The nobles, on the other hand, were not at all so sure about this in those days! When their neighbours groaned in pools of blood, when the waves of revolt roared over them, when their estates were plundered and their buildings burned, they were convinced that a decision had been made to eradicate them . . . Yes, those who remembered the cries of those days, the rough, raw cries of distress and astonishment and triumph; those who remembered the glittering eyes of Kulpsuu of Tõdva, those furious, unthinking, childlike, captivating eyes, round and wild with bloodlust; those who remembered hundreds of such eyes; those who had sensed thousands of them in the autumn mists and underbrush – they could only laugh at the tales told afterwards by those who had sat behind the city walls at the time, keeping their arses warm . . . But when it came to writing about it – Balthasar could do that only in the cool, general words of a detached observer . . .

> And in this way they continued their undertaking and set upon many a manor and cut down and killed several nobles whom they found at home on their estates, Jacob Üxkyll of Limandu to name one . . .

Barely perceptibly, Balthasar flinched, compressing his lips inside his russet beard into a thin groove that turned down at each corner . . . Then the corners of his mouth began to quiver slightly and turn upwards, and had it not been hidden inside the beard, one might well have described his smile as roguishly smug. He picked up his pen and crossed out the name "Limandu". In any event, this tale would have to be cut to a quarter of its length and rewritten. And so there was no need to mention Limandu by name . . . He scratched behind his right ear with his pen and wrote above the crossed-out word – God knows where he got it from – L-u-m-m-a-t . . . If anyone later should dare suggest that he had had anything to do with Limandu, he could say: Look, I do not mention such a name, for I recorded all these places according to what I heard rumoured!

> But these same peasants also sent spokesmen to Tallinn, to establish peace and friendship with the town. At the gathering with the king, they chose as their spokesmen three of the most judicious and diligent men they could find in the brief time allotted them, and, as a fourth, they designated a young man to accompany them, because of his knowledge of German—

Good Lord! He must have been utterly blind to permit himself to make such incriminating references to himself! Cross them out! Obliterate them! Relegate to the eternal darkness of ink this vain young man, this half-witted youth whose immature heedlessness goads him, even to this day, to work in puerile, stupid ways! He must reread every page with care, not just this tale of the rebellion, and eliminate, ruthlessly, every "I" wherever it appeared. And especially, of course, in accounts of the rebellion . . . those, for example, as the long, foolishly detailed story of the exchange between the spokesmen and the councilmen and their comments on it . . . Who might possibly have heard such a thing? . . . For the only record (according to Herr Topff's most reliable report), the only sheet of paper upon which Herr Loop had noted the general points of the conversation, had been torn out of the record book and burned just a week later, before the end of October 1560. Which meant that the Council had done back then exactly what Balthasar was doing right now: behaving like a fox, like old feather-tail rubbing out his tracks . . . *ha-ha-ha-hah*, except that he was now that pitiful fox whom the hunters were circling – the one whom that blackguard Balzer was stalking with his crossbow of insinuations. But at the time it had been on account of him and the others that the councilmen, tails thrashing, had scurried to cover their tracks, and, anxious and troubled though he now was, it made him laugh . . . albeit bitterly . . . Yes, but how could he possibly have known about the things he had written here?

—so that the peasant delegation decided not to make excessive demands of the Council at first, but to return to their army at Kolovere and advise their king to besiege the castle and storm it without help from Tallinn, after which, so they thought, Tallinn would listen more receptively to their goals . . .

Out, out, out! To be rubbed out with the fox-tail! And what was this?

On Herr Monninkhusen's orders the leaders of the rebellion, whom he had captured at Kolovere, nineteen men altogether, were broken on the rack immediately after the siege, but their king was transported on a sloop to Kuressaare, to Duke Magnus. There he was interrogated for five consecutive days and nights . . .

Balthasar leaned against the stone window frame and stared at the shadows on the plaster wall opposite . . . Good God – where do memories end? Where do dreams begin? Thirteen-year-old memories and the dreams dreamed during those years . . . Memories grow like plants, with their roots in the ground of one's waking life, and put forth blooms, one brighter and more luminous than the next . . . Memories flow into dreams and dreams begin to seem like memories, especially the ones that for some reason recur; and one awakens with a sigh of relief from their oppressive, elusive clarity into the safe, comforting rooms of everyday life . . . The dreams had begun to hound him after his great escape – in the bleak dormitory room in Stettin, in the dark den of the tanner Manger in Wittenberg, in Herr Puttemann's spacious house in Bremen, and had not left him in peace to this day, continuing to torment him here, in the parsonage of Holy Ghost Church. Though it was true, they rarely appeared when he was lying next to Elsbet in their marriage bed . . . And then there were the things that had actually happened . . .

The things that had happened: what probably did happen was that after the battle, at about nine in the morning on the thirteenth of October, he raced blindly through the underbrush in the direction of Haapsalu. He threw his peasant rags somewhere into a brilliant yellow birch grove and pulled out of his saddlebag the clean white shirt and black woollen suit of the departed son of Kimmelpenning, leaped again into the saddle and galloped on, and suddenly felt the king's helmet banging against his right knee. He had wanted to throw it into the withered fireweed. Then he raced across the marsh and out onto an island, dismounted under an oak seared black by lightning, and with the helmet itself dug a hole in the ground and buried it under a dead tree in a young oak grove, using his hands to fill the hole with gravel and then washing them in a spring and hurrying on. He had shaved his face with a borrowed shaving knife in a pub at Lähtru. And at three in the afternoon, crossing himself, he trotted into Haapsalu through its Tallinn Gate. In through a gate partly burned down, into a town nearly wholly consumed by fire in the course of the preceding month.

He rode through the town, past the endlessly long castle walls scarred by recent cannon-fire, past smouldering ashes of wooden houses and sooty walls of stone houses, past gaping window holes, past doorways and windows haphazardly patched, occasionally catching fleeting glimpses of faces among the ruins – some fearful, others impassive from incessant fear. Sitting in the saddle, he exchanged words with a few townsmen and realised that no-one here had heard about the battle at Kolovere. And when they asked him, worriedly, if he had encountered any peasants on the road to Tallinn and whether they might have been moving towards Haapsalu, he knew nothing about the peasant army. But at Viigisadam harbour he found, as the Lord had ordained, a gentleman with a broad nose and nervously twitching moustache, just boarding a large sloop about to set sail for Kuressaare. It was Poll, steward of the estate of Johann Yxkyll the marshal at Duke Magnus' court. He had been dispatched to the Haapsalu area to see how the estates at Läänemaa had fared after the recent plundering raids of the Muscovite, and was now hurrying back to his master to announce that the estates at Vigala and Haeska had been pillaged and burned to the ground. Judging by his questions – to which the young man from Tallinn, oddly enough, could not respond at all – it seemed that he was in great haste to leave, at least in part to escape the peasant uprising. Yet he willingly took on board this young man of Tallinnn – who was he? . . . the son of some artisan, with his cheerful talk, if not a very perceptive eye, this young scholar who, the devil knows how, came to be visiting his hometown at this chaotic time and was now heading back to his university in Germany, in Greifswald or Rostock, or somewhere. Yes, he would gladly take the young man to Saaremaa. There were sure to be ships sailing to Denmark and Germany from Kuressaare, the capital city of our young Herr Duke-and-Bishop, even at this late time of year. The somewhat rash and thoughtless young man from Tallinn sold his bay right there on the pier – the beast was noticeably overdriven but still quite serviceable – to the harbour bailiff for a proper sum and hopped aboard the low-slung vessel as it was casting off.

On the morning of the fourth day, the seventeenth of October, they sailed into Kuressaare harbour next to the castle. The young man from Tallinn raced along the gravel path, between the rusty-orange stalks of bulrushes, towards shore. He stared at the enormous castle on the other side of the wall, with its two towers, and at the Pikk Hermann Tower in the centre, and at its needle-like spire with an exceedingly long pennant of glittering yellow brass at its tip, looking as though one of the bulrushes growing at the water's edge had been put up there to turn in the wind. The young man walked and walked, his clothes wet from the autumn waves that had washed over the deck, in his body the after-effects of several sleepless nights both on land and aboard ship, and he felt as if he were half-walking in a dream. As though the great grey expanse of castle wall seemingly rising out of the sea – its brass pennant against a grey sky – were partly a dream, as though the settlement beyond the castle, with its sod and stone and straw roofs, its cobble-stone market square, its church and its muddy streets and rail fences, were all a dream, and as though he himself had mysteriously slipped out of a terrible reality that had simply ebbed away, and was now walking behind a protective, friendly dream-wall, with the carefree ease of a sleepwalker, a detached observer who neither knew nor cared what lay ahead, but knew that there was Someone who had long known . . .

And in order to have a word with that Someone, he stepped into the St Lawrence Church by the marketplace, a church that, as he had learned aboard ship, Duke Magnus had elevated to cathedral rank after the Muscovite had laid waste to Haapsalu.

The young man knelt before the altar and raised his face, reddened by sea spray and wind, to the mournful visage of the Crucified One, blackened by the smoke of burning candles. He spoke, scarcely moving his cracked lips: "Lord, You know that mortal man cannot stand before You. When I look from one perspective upon the events I have just lived through, I see an intolerable contradiction between Your Word and these events. For it was nothing but the wretched vaunting of the flesh before You. But when I look upon them, not with the eyes of reason but with those of the heart (Oh, I myself do not really know how I should look upon them), then I dare to ask: Was it not all merely an attempt by desperate people to help bring the affairs of that land – for this is what I must say, since I am across the sea – closer to the truths of Your Gospel . . . ? Even though the means necessary, yes, I must confess, at least some of the means were thrust into people's hands (mine included) as though by the Devil himself – I mean swords, clubs, scythes, burning torches, *et cetera* . . . though I do not know by what other means this thing could have been undertaken . . . In short, we mortals are not capable of understanding Your truth without Your help. But this I do understand: that You have decided to pluck me, unscathed, from the bloody affair, and for this miraculous salvation, Lord, accept the childlike gratitude of this, Your sometimes stubborn but nevertheless humble servant—"

When the young man reached this part of his prayer, he sensed something with the back of his neck – a disturbance behind him in the church. Someone had whispered something, someone had called out, and four or five people who had been standing or praying in the empty church had quickly departed. The young man followed them and saw people running in the rain across the market square, towards the castle. He joined them, for there was apparently something to be seen in that direction . . . He trotted over muddy stones with a band of village workmen and heard that the duke's commanders had sailed their sloops into harbour. That on the mainland, the peasant army had been crushed, their leaders taken prisoner and hanged or broken on the rack. But that apparently the king of the peasants had been brought to Kuressaare and was being conveyed, at that moment, from the harbour to the castle . . .

Alongside the others running through the rain, the young man reached the west corner of the outer moat, where the mercenaries and knights turned the corner and headed for the drawbridge. He shrank, startled, for he recognised an old acquaintance – Herr Christopher Monninkhusen, with his booming voice and lanky build, riding ahead with several knights in armour. He also saw the king, walking alone, flanked by guards, his hands tied behind his back. But the young man could not see his face, for the king had just turned his head to the right to look up at the forty-cubit height of the dark, wet, imposing corner tower. And then the group had passed him by. The young man tried to make his way through the crowd so that he might run after the group along the banks on the other side of the moat – from the pointless desire, the foolish urge, the inexplicable wish to *see* the king's face – but a mercenary soldier, reeking of onions, blocked his way with his halberd, shouting: "*Halt, junger Mann!*"* Not with the insolence customary in addressing the local yokels, but peremptorily enough to stop him in his tracks . . . He joined a group of curious villagers – farm-hands and saunamen in homespun woollen trousers and felted-wool coats – trailing behind the prisoners across the first bridge. Only under the echoing arch of the gate tower did he notice that the others had drifted away, that he alone had entered the outer courtyard, while the knights and their men and the prisoner had crossed the second bridge over the inner moat and disappeared beyond the inner gate. The young

* Stop, young man! (German).

man followed them. He walked across the wet, slippery log bridge over the grey water of the moat, water like wet, grey gooseflesh under the falling raindrops. If necessary, he thought, he would tell them he was looking for Marshal Yxkyll's steward, Poll, with whom he had travelled from Haapsalu. But when he entered the next gate and arrived at the inner courtyard, he thought: I'm already here, I can't turn back, and continued through the gate of the castle itself, pausing in the high-walled stone enclosure of the inner courtyard. There was no trace of the group he had been pursuing. Not a soul on the flagstone stairway, with its artfully hewn handrail, nor at any of the surrounding windows. Occasionally a lone soldier or solitary servant flitted across the rain-splattered courtyard. And when the young man turned around and started back, he noticed that two mercenaries, each with a naked sword on his hip, had positioned themselves at the cellar door to the right of the exit; both men's faces had been scarred – the one by sword, the other by smallpox.

The young man walked around the outside of the castle and wandered about in the village and along the shore among the bulrushes. He strolled through the marketplace and past the customs house and around the outer and inner harbour. His clothes were sodden to the skin from the rain, and when chills brought him to a sudden shivering awareness, he felt that there were two of him: one was wandering about in a kind of feverish half-sleep, his thoughts running about like ants vainly trying to scale an impossible glass wall, even as they fell back again and again. The other was shambling along the market square and down the quay and into the Three Seagulls tavern, to strike up conversations with sailors and seamen and skippers. And he learned that in four or five days a sloop from Kuressaare would likely be setting sail for Riga. At this, his first self entertained the most fantastical plans as he waited for the departure . . . Heavens, the thoughts that had come to one's mind thirteen years ago . . . And what about now? Could it not happen now? . . . The most fantastical plans: to lure the two scarred guards to the tavern, to ply them with drink, pick the lock on the cellar door . . . get some apple sleeping-powder (which Katharina had used to drug the coadjutor) and put the guards to sleep . . . to come to an agreement with the skipper of the sloop – the foolish, childish turmoil of desperate thoughts.

At about the hour of nine in the evening, the young man was sitting with a mug of ale in the gloom of the Three Seagulls tavern, his wet coat drying by the hearth, as he listened to the splatter of rainfall and the ale-induced droning of the locals and a couple of the castle guards. Suddenly the door opened into darkness and closed again. Someone had either arrived or departed. And along with the wet gust of wind, the same two fellows walked in, one scarred by sword, the other by small-pox, just as though the young man had magically conjured them up while staring into his dark ale.

They were fuming and cursing and had already drunk a double ration of ale with their supper, but they ordered two more tankards. It seemed they were regulars here, and other customers gathered around to listen:

"Beelzebub! Up to now we've been serving the duke in return for watery soup and piss-poor pay – which, by the way, is still owed us – so we were 'bout to stage a row . . . But as of this morning, we are to be – Guess what? The bodyguards of the peasant king! *Ho-ho-ho-ho* . . . The man's like a bull, a small bull, I say . . . I swear to God! Wearing Spanish boots – and I know what Master Schwartz stuffs into 'em . . . But he – that fool of a 'king', of course – does no more than snuffle . . . ."

Upon which the young man slapped down the next-to-last Maximilian thaler given him by Herr Kruse and ordered Rhine wine for the guards, and they continued their tale as they quaffed their second beaker:

The king had at first been put into the cellar between the gate and the

Pikk Hermann Tower, but was not kept there long before being taken straight up to the chapter hall, to the duke and his counsellors. Herr Behr and Monninkhusen and Yxkyll and Schrapfner and the others there all enjoyed a hearty laugh at the stubborn little ox with his doltish responses and stupid silences. The duke asked the king to tell them who among his men might still be at large, to which the man replied that he knew none of their names. When asked which of Tallinn's councilmen they had contacted, he answered: None of them. To the question of what they wanted from Tallinn, he answered: An alliance. When the duke asked how Tallinn had responded, he said he did not know because he had not seen his spokesmen after they left. When asked who his spokesmen were, he said again he did not know them by name. When the duke asked him to describe the purpose of the whole terrible uprising, the yokel said it was to wipe out the nobility once and for all. The duke had asked the interpreter to repeat this question, and upon receiving the same answer he drummed his fingers on the armrest of the white bishop's throne and asked: To which sovereign would you have submitted had your plan succeeded? The king's reply was: Not to any of them. At this the duke called out with a high laugh: Really?! So – that means *you* are their true king and sovereign! But then I must bow before you – at which point he stood up and made a deep bow – For I am but a duke and the son of a deceased king, whereas you are a living monarch! He had then stepped up to the yokel and with his royal hand smacked him across the face, saying, Take him away! But I alone am to touch him, I and Master Schwartz.

The king had been led away to the Sturwolt cellar and Master Schwartz immediately began to execute the third torture as commanded: thumbscrews, Spanish boots, the rack and fiery rods.

The pock-marked guard said:

"He was pale alright, standing there before they started on him. But he had grit, that man. I heard him say – so much I've learned of the local dialect on this confounded island: 'If I should make a sound, dear father, help me, that it not come from my front end . . .'"

Imagining the scene, the young man felt ants running over his back, and he wondered who the king was addressing as his father. Was it our one and only Heavenly Father? Or his mortal father – for he had one, of course. Or was it the pagan Father-of-Thunder that many of the peasants still worshipped?

The guard with the sword scars on his face muttered: "Damnation! Schwartz worked on him for an hour and a half. And when they untied him from the rack, he dropped right there, into his own filth, like a piece of limestone. But they couldn't get a word out of him. Not in the morning, not in the evening. Damn him! Anyway, tomorrow there'll be a service of thanksgiving in the town church."

Lord God, where do memories end? Where do dreams begin?

The young man had curled up on the straw in the back room of the tavern and listened to the wind howling behind the windows and whistling in the chimney when the gusts blew hard. And then the door had opened and his old acquaintance Monninkhusen stepped in and stood there before the young man, the glow from the hearth red on his hobnailed boots and around his black nostrils. He ordered the young man to get up, laid his hand familiarly on his shoulder, and said:

"Balthasar, you have been of great service to dukes and kings – to Johan, Gotthart, Erik, and to your peasant king as well – yes, I know, I know about it – you have served them well. Now – please do our poor Duke Magnus a service, too. And your peasant king at the same time. Exactly. You have had such extensive experience in translation. Come. Ask your king why he does not answer our questions."

So the young man had left the Three Seagulls with Herr Monninkhusen. The rain had stopped. The clouds had pulled away from the moon. They walked in the moonlight across an expanse of reeds the colour of liver and through several walls a fathom thick . . . and then he was standing (it seemed, at one moment, that he was with Herr Monninkhusen, at another, that he was alone) in the king's prison cell. The seams between the limestone blocks of the walls glowed in the moonlight. The young man bowed towards a dark corner, then knelt in front of the mysterious shape that could have been a person or a stone bench, and said in a half-whisper: "King, your silence does not avail you. There is no purpose in your suffering. You may talk. Yes. The only thing you need not tell them is that you know me. Not that. But otherwise, tell them everything. Everything. Why do you not speak?" To the young man's shock, the shape on the floor opened its mouth, or, if it was really just a slab of rock, then a crack opened in the stone and it spoke: "You, learned boy, is it not written in the criminal code of your emperor (why did he say 'your emperor'?), Karl the Fifth, that he who endures all and gives no evidence shall be set free?" And the young man had found himself back on the straw again, thrashing about, his soul wracked with despair and pity and rage at his own weakness and at the king's childish belief – which he had not been able to set right . . .

Where do memories end, where do dreams begin . . . ?

On Friday the eighteenth of October, the young man had been standing in the Church of St Lawrence during the service of thanksgiving, fairly close to the pulpit, listening to the sermon of Court Pastor Schrapfer. This bald, fat man in extravagant red ceremonial robes, had with peculiar zeal poured out his tirades upon the heads of the bishop's counsellors, officers, mercenary soldiers and local craftsmen in the congregation. Powerful diatribes against wolves in the grey sheep's clothing of peasants who had now, at last, been mercilessly cut down! Cut down by God's own sword in the hand of the Archangel Michael himself, who had appeared in the form of our most gracious young Duke Magnus! And about the hydra-headed criminal rebellion of yokels and how their crowned viper-king had been beheaded by our beloved young Bishop-and-Duke Magnus and by Lord Monninkhusen, for the greater glory of Our Lord Jesus Christ . . .

The young man had taken a good look at Magnus – a twenty-year-old boy who was both duke and bishop and was said to be the first Danish prince to have studied at Wittenberg. He had looked at the narrow, pale face and inflamed red lips, at the white bishop's robes flapping as Magnus approached the altar and in a high, thin voice read the prayer of thanksgiving, and later laughingly tossed a hundred marks' worth of silver shillings to the beggars in front of the church, as if he were the Roman Emperor himself . . .

That evening in the Three Seagulls tavern, the king's guards were gossiping: "Today was just like yesterday. Torture in the morning and again around sunset. But not a word out of the man." Same thing on the nineteenth. And on the twentieth. Except that on the twentieth, a Sunday, it had not been possible any longer to take him up to the Chapter Hall, because of the condition of his legs. So the duke and his counsellors had had to go downstairs. Not to the prison cell – there would have been no room for them all – but to the dungeon of Sturwolt, where Master Schwartz did his work . . .

The sloop bound for Riga had not yet loaded its cargo, and the feverish young man in the tavern tossed and turned on the straw, cursing the delay in their departure, yet, for some reason, secretly thanking God for it.

During the night before the twenty-second of October (some time ago, in his capacity as chronicler, he had taken upon himself the foolish burden of memorising dates, even those in his dreams) the young man had again made his way to the king. This time it was entirely against Lord Monninkhusen's will – who tried to hold the young man back at the door of the tavern, where they wrestled, like Jacob and the Stranger at the ford of the River Jabbok. He had pushed Herr Monninkhusen down onto an old millstone in a growth of orach bushes and fled. In the darkness he saw the drying frames for the fishermen's nets and pulled himself up onto the crossbars, running along them and along the skywalkers' rope as far as the brass weathervane, sliding down the roof of Pikk Hermann and straight through the vaulted ceiling into the king's cell. Panting, he spoke: King! Forget what I said before. I don't know what happened to me. Don't tell them anything! Not a thing! No, I'm not saying it on my own account. I'm not really sure why I'm saying it. But tell me, in God's name, tell me that you won't speak! At last the king turned to face the young man. And the young man saw to his astonishment that he did not have the face of the peasant king but that of Doctor Friesner's mute servant Paap, whom he had last seen shoving a flaming torch into Doctor Friesner's hayloft at his farm at Üksnurme, and who had later disappeared into the anonymous tumult of the great rebellion. The young man called out: By God, tell me, how can it be that it's you here all of a sudden?! Mute Paap opened his mute mouth; he looked both helpless and triumphant as he pointed to it – regretting that he could not respond to the young man, but grinning at the thought that his tormentors would get no answers out of him . . .

Before daybreak, the skipper of the sloop departing for Riga sent a cabin boy to fetch the young man, who rose from his straw pallet, still feverish, and let himself be rowed to the ship. At ten in the morning he was standing at the railing, his forehead burning. The ship was riding at anchor under a still, grey sky at the island of Laisma, awaiting a favourable wind. On the horizon, the islands of Loodenina and Roomassare and the shores of Abruka rose up high at the edge of the cold, leaden sea. Then, from a distance of half a league to the north, beyond the castle and the village, the sound of tolling bells reached them. The slow booming sounded with exceptional clarity, for the weather was such that every creak of the oarlocks and every cough could be heard across the distance of a hundred cubits. The young man noticed that the sailors on the deck interrupted their tasks and looked towards the shore, to the west of the village, and crossed themselves.

"What is that?"

"The bell at Kellamäe. They've just begun to draw and quarter the peasant king."

The young man had gone below to the forecabin and lain down upon the seal-oil barrels. It seemed to him as though the tarred hull of the ship and his own heartbeats were booming in time with the tolling bell to the point of bursting, until finally the north-east wind began to rise and blew them out to sea, thank God, and the sound of the bell was drowned out by the sound of the waves . . .

Balthasar leaned back on his shoulder blades, pushed himself away from the wall, and tilted his head back, raising his chin up and above the fog of his dreams and the events of thirteen years ago.

He squeezed his eyes shut, feeling a dark-grey, red-streaked pain throb in his eyelids. When he opened them again, he was staring at the stucco wall of his study. What was he to do? Go back to Balzer and plead with him: My dear man, be reasonable, don't talk to the bailiff or anyone else about that old business, not to anyone – because, well, you understand . . . Is this what he must do? No! Not even if he knew for sure that it would do some good. In fact, he was more or less certain that such a step would goad Balzer to action rather than restrain him. *Ergo*, what else was there for Balthasar but to do nothing at all, nothing but live from day to day and wait to see whether Schröder sent his scribe after him (he probably would not send his gaolers). When he arrived at the court, Schröder would look at him with a somewhat puzzled expression. And then – Balthasar could picture it, the thin-lipped mouth above the heavy bluish chin, mumbling something but recovering his official voice all too quickly: Herr Balthasar, I have been urged lately to look into a rather foolish tale, but the source is such that, I must say, I cannot simply dismiss it as the empty chatter of town gossips. I would like to give you the chance to disavow it under oath, and thus free us both . . .

So what was left for Balthasar to do but wait? And pray: Lord God, grant that I not be compelled to stand before that wall-eyed lump of blubber and to lay my hand on the Bible and lie under oath, and possibly be forced to leave Tallinn in disgrace despite what I have sworn, should rumours swell and grow . . . Lord God, I pray, place Your hand upon the mouth of that vile knave and wastrel that his accursed jaws remain shut . . .

As Balthasar was thus addressing his Lord, feeling entirely in command of the words he spoke, he became aware of something disquieting. He could even see how, behind his somewhat crude though honest words, there were others – shameless, even outrageous words – marching in the opposite direction, grimacing and sneering. He could see the words in the first row struggling to restrain those in the second, which broke loose and stomped past them, gloating: Even better Lord, if You would rid Your earth wholly of him – of that dung-heap, Balzer, that he no longer loaf about on your earth . . . Lord God, forgive my abominable thoughts! I cannot explain how such effrontery came to mind – the insolence of a hireling against his fellow man . . . Hah! A fellow creature round and about . . . Indeed! But tell me God, of what use is he to You? Or to anyone . . . ? Lord, Lord, I pray: with Your breath, Your spirit, cleanse my mind of such wretched chaff . . . But still, of what use is he, this "Dung of the Orient", to anyone? He's come back now for his father's property – to consume it and pass it through his miserable, puny body and turn it to dung . . . Dear God, take these cursed words from my mind. All I ask is that You prevent this Balzer Vegesack from blazoning his tales abroad. But Lord, You know that to expect miracles of You is also sinful and depraved, and I say it would indeed be a miracle if he should remain silent . . . So, would it not be better to pray that You summon him to You . . . Forgive me

Lord, somewhere in my thinking there is a deplorable sophistry . . . But see, Maret, the daughter of the miller on the millpond, died just two weeks ago of the plague, and here and there in the settlements there have been deaths occurring to this day, so that . . . But why should it necessarily be plague that takes my milk-brother . . . ? Lord! Help me banish the most foul Devil that is whispering these vile thoughts into my ear . . . No-no, I will not touch Balzer Vegesack. (I cannot very well attack him with a sword. For what would it profit me to become known for my violent heroics with a sword – how would that be any better than the notoriety I fear from his idle talk?) Lord, no, it would not even occur to me to pay some criminal to dispatch him, say, in a tavern brawl . . . I wonder, would Märten do this for me were I to ask him . . . ? You blaspheming Devil, where are you that dares to fill my mind with such foul thoughts? Where are you, that I might spit three times in your direction – *ptui! ptui! ptui!* – I'm spitting in the direction of the window, in case you're there, peering into my chamber, in that cold bluish light beyond the stone wall. I spit into the grey shadow in the corner behind my lectern, in case you're there, invisible and sneering . . .

Balthasar went down into the courtyard and plunged his hands into the dark rain barrel beneath a break in the gutter, under the overhanging stone eaves. He kept them in the icy water for a long time. He rinsed his face from brow to chin. He straightened up, feeling as though he had pulled on a pair of long iron gloves – to deliver a blow to the Devil, and as though he had pulled down an iron visor – to face the Tormentor! A visor of clarity, purity. I vow to You, Lord, I shall not raise a finger, either in thought or deed, against Balzer Vegesack, that miserable milk-brother of mine, that cursed namesake, that wretched fool! But I pray to You in the words of Your Son in the Garden of Gethsemane: Father, if it be possible, let this cup pass from me – by which I mean hold this man Balzer back, not according to my wish, but according to Your will . . .

And his prayer helped! Or perhaps not? Or did it do the reverse . . . ?

Two weeks later, on a grey and rainy Tuesday morning, fragrant, at last, of spring, and sultry as if a thunderstorm were brewing, there was a knock at the door of the sacristy. Balthasar flinched slightly. Refusing to believe, maintaining his overbearing mien, smiling to himself – but thinking, nonetheless, of Schröder's gaolers or his scribe. He called out: "Yes!" It was obviously not the bailiff's messenger who stepped across the threshold, brushing the water from his rain-streaked coat. It was Herr Joachim Walther, Balthasar's colleague from St Nicholas' Church, who had become the son-in-law of the bishop's widow the previous spring. He was a long-legged, somewhat sluggish hulk of a man with a peculiar gait and a quiet voice. For some time, since Balthasar's wedding, in fact, the man had taken pains to ingratiate himself with him. Not that his politeness could be called sycophantic. He said he had just been passing by and had come in to rest a bit and wait out the downpour and, of course, to offer his best wishes on the birth of Balthasar's son.

Joachim shook out his raincoat, the wet drops patterning the floor at the entry, and then spread the garment over the old wooden sofa. He inquired after Balthasar's health and that of the family, and when his questions had been answered – everyone was in good health, thanks be to God, and Elsbet was on her feet already, even though a little weak – Joachim pursed his lips with concern, and said:

"Let us hope that it does not mean the return of the *contagio* . . ."

"What are you referring to?"

"Balzer Vegesack, you know him – the fellow who just recently returned from abroad, a member of my congregation – he took ill on Sunday. Last night there were buboes on his body – and early this morning he gave up the ghost."

"Gave up the ghost?! Good Lord . . ."

Balthasar stood up and turned towards Joachim, intending to ask

268

him to repeat what he had said. For it was too shocking to believe upon first hearing. And he wanted to get the details . . . the details. But he fell silent. For turning towards Joachim, he happened to glance at the door leading to the courtyard. The door was recessed in a thick wall nearly three cubits deep, and on this dark, overcast day, the gloom within the cavity was dense as grey homespun. Balthasar clearly saw a small, dark-blue devil, not quite two cubits tall (half the height of Doctor Friesner, but otherwise shamelessly similar to him) jutting his pointed beard out from the shadows and bowing deeply to Balthasar, like a deferential but smirking servant.

CHAPTER SEVEN,

*in which a man (on occasion with another man by his side) travels over
land and sea and within himself, towards what a bystander might call the
fulfilment of his destiny – whilst he remains as dimly aware of his progress
as someone on a boat who can see no more from his necessarily limited
vantage point than the crests of the closest waves, and who would be able
to divine the presence of the horizon and its distant shores and the
thunderclouds overhead only if his powers of divination were given
wing to rise to the seagulls and the clouds above.*

When Balthasar thought back now, in October 1576, to his own fear at
that earlier time, it puzzled him. True enough, his milk-brother and
namesake Balzer Vegesack ("Dung of the Orient" – God have mercy on
his soul), had died suddenly of the plague, though only after the disease
had nearly run its course in town. But was this unusual, given the
hundreds of plague deaths in Tallinn in recent years? And the thousands of deaths, year after year, across the entire Christian world (not
to mention those in the pagan world) . . . Balzer had, however, gone to
his Maker not only after plague fatalities had supposedly ceased, but
just before he could pursue his fateful, foolhardy inquiries regarding
Balthasar, at the very moment when Balthasar was on the verge of
deciding whom to hire to kill Balzer . . . Childish stupidity of course, a
wretched thought like that . . . But a man can no more ward off such
thoughts than prevent a flying thrush from depositing its droppings
on his head . . . And it was just as childish to suspect that Balzer's death
was a peculiar, ill-omened "good deed" on the part of the Tempter.

Why, indeed, could it not be God's own helping hand that had been at work, especially as His hand had so clearly guided Balthasar and his compatriots' little ship through these trying times? That little ship had sailed a much more steady course than this madly lurching ketch or yawl or dandy – or whatever it was called – on which he was now sailing from the island of Prangli back to Tallinn . . .

It had by no means been a mere pleasure trip. On the contrary, Balthasar had been performing official duties: Pastor Vulpius and the elders of Prangli parish had requested that he bless their new steeple. St Lawrence Church was a small, plain structure, built in an unusual spot: a quarter of a league from the village, on the other side of a dark stand of firs, squatting at the water's edge amid the dunes and drifting sands of the seashore. The steeple had been struck by lightning and badly burned the year before last, and now a new steeple was finally in place. And since the parishioners considered Balthasar's blessing more reliable as protection against lightning than that of their own Pastor Vulpius . . . Well . . . The village blacksmith had fashioned a whimsical copper rooster with widespread wings for the steeple, where it now perched, looking out over the tops of the firs and the sandy shore and distant reefs. And on this day in church, as tufts of insulating moss quivered between the logs, and blowing sand peppered the outside walls – the sound oddly penetrating the awareness of those inside, even though muted by the roar of the sea – Balthasar spoke to them about the rooster crowing and Our Lord's words to Peter: "Before the cock crows twice, you will deny me three times." And he spoke of man's everlasting obligation to strive to be true, no matter how unexpectedly difficult it was under the weight of life's temptations and dangers to remain true to the Lord. Naturally. But not only that. To be true, as well, to the king. Of course. But more than that. To be true to one's fellow human beings. That too. But more. To be true to the wife or the husband one had been given. Absolutely. But to be true, also, to oneself. That especially. And thus also to God. So that the circle might be closed. Like the circle formed by those holding on to the Lord's left hand and right hand. God knows why he spoke of all this or how much of it they understood – these men and women whose faces were even more weathered, wooden and uncomprehending than those of the congregation he preached to daily. These people here would have understood him much better had he spoken, for example, of Peter's activities as a fisherman.

They returned to the village for the midday dinner, past low dwellings with roofs of thatch or sod, past split-rail fences with fence posts white from seagull droppings, past scattered boulders and leafless brown sweetbriar bushes, their light-red berries bobbing in the wind. The dinner was served at the home of hoarse old Vulpius: spit-roasted pike with an egg sauce. During the meal, they related how the people of the island had first met the pastor of Tallinn's Holy Ghost Church. And it was agreed that it all began with the Moses carved by the pastor's friend, the bell-ringer Märten Bergkam. That carved pillar had been holding up the north-western corner of the pulpit in the Prangli church for three years now. Hearing this, the bell-ringer–woodcarver, sitting at the foot of the table, wrinkled his brow and coughed three times into his empty tankard.

As twilight fell, tallow candles were brought into the room. Balthasar spoke to the dinner guests of the great example God had made to all Christians everywhere, of the city of Tallinn, by mortifying it with war and plague, trampling it to dust and ashes, and then miraculously coming to its rescue at its moment of greatest hopelessness and deepest despair. The islanders here had fortunately been spared such calamities, he added, especially since, under the Swedish kings, Prangli Island had not fallen victim to pirate attacks. But the islanders were not to indulge in pride on that account. Finally, they sang, by flickering candlelight, "A mighty fortress is our God" – a bit unevenly and haltingly at first, but towards the end, with confidence and zeal, and after that, Pastor Vulpius' guests went on their way.

Balthasar stepped outside, too. He heard the gravel crunch under his feet and the thorns of sweetbriar bushes scrape his boots. On impulse, he headed towards what he surmised to be a good-sized boulder, where he sat down and listened to the darkness.

The wind had subsided. The sea on the eastern shore was no doubt still murmuring, but the sound did not carry through the nearby grove of firs. To the west, the water between the islands was soundless and still. Balthasar rested his hand against the cool, rough stone for support in the dark, and let his thoughts wander. Was it really true, this story he had told them there, in that room, about God's great mercy as demonstrated by the fate of Tallinn? Was the great salvation of the town, as he had called it, really so praiseworthy and miraculous a thing, considering that it had come at such enormous cost: thousands of deaths resulting from plague and war, mountains of ash and ruins at the town walls, a devastated countryside? Moreover, such little islands as the one where he was standing, even if godforsaken, were the real miracles. He felt the immeasurable silence of this small, insignificant place and the deep darkness of the October night begin to expand and grow in concert, as if swallowing him, becoming so immense that, in a slightly intoxicating mixture of pleasure and trepidation, he addressed God: Lord, in this boundless darkness and silence, such as one never finds within the walls of a town, grant me a sign . . . that You will keep Your hand over this land and over me, and that what I have believed and spoken is the truth . . . (The last lights in the village – extinguished. The frosted grass – silent. Not a glimmer of light, not a sound . . .) And then a murmur. From the north-east. Up high, beneath the dark sky. The sound of angels' wings. Approaching. Growing louder. Growing so palpable that the air set in motion by their wings seemed to touch Balthasar's forehead . . . And in the next moment,

Balthasar realised it was a flock of brent geese in flight, coming across the sea from Finland or some eastward islands, fearless in the dark, flying with the courage of God's birds . . . A flock of brent geese on their way to the islands west of this one. But it was a sign as well. And so clear, it would be hard to imagine one clearer. At least to a man whom we may assume to be familiar with Holy Writ. After all, it is written in the Book of Isaiah, chapter 31, verse 5: "As birds flying, so will the Lord of hosts defend Jerusalem; defending he will deliver it; and passing over he will preserve it."

By the early light of day they sailed out of the Mustkoopa Inlet on the southern shore of Prangli Island, and now they could hope that if the strong north-west wind held, they would reach Tallinn before dark. Especially since they had already passed through Aegna Strait by midday and were rounding the western tip of Kräksuli Island and heading south. And then the bay of Tallinn spread before them, and the sight of the great expanse of black water – choppy, with cresting, foaming waves like white rabbits bounding over a dark field – filled them with apprehension. At the same time, much to their relief, the needle-like spire of St Olaf's Church came into view on the distant shore where the bay narrowed.

The little ship ploughed its tarred bow down into the waves, as low as deck level at times, though given the many storms of that autumn, the swell was fairly temperate, and the sky above, blue in patches. The three Prangli men at the rudder and the sails were silent, not because of the requirements of their task but out of respect for the pastor. Märten was silent from long habit. The sea soughed. The patched sail swelled and flapped with loud retorts. Seagulls screeched. Balthasar was sitting on a seal-oil barrel, his back against the foremast, his clothes splashed wet, feeling that the lurching of the ship, noticeably more severe since entering open water, was no longer frightening but beginning to seem normal. The alternation between the hopeful rise to the top of the swells and the plunge to the trough – which left his insides hollow – called to mind the dangerous upheavals of recent times which had begun to seem, God forbid, like ordinary events: the endless bloody chaos that had washed over this luckless land year after year – Muscovites, Tatars, Poles, Swedes, Scots, manormen, bandits, plunderers – its breaking waves crashing at the town walls again and again, when hordes of Tatars and Muscovites (at times armies of more than ten thousand men) brazenly forced their way into the settlements at the outskirts of town. So that Tallinn, especially since spring, was overflowing with refugees from the countryside, and the value of the mark had fallen to a twelfth of the thaler, lower than ever before, and if this very rising–falling seaway along which they were sailing towards Tallinn had not sustained and fed the town, the pastors would long have been burying people dead of starvation, and the Town Council would by now have been prepared to surrender to just about anyone.

Lulled by the rocking of the ship, Balthasar had briefly dozed off. For when he next looked around, the cold clouds above the island of Paljasaare were ablaze in the setting sun, the whitecaps blood-red in the rising wind; and the Gothic windows of Pirita Convent, those that had not been destroyed on the Ash Wednesday assault the previous year, glowed as though on fire. It was no more than a quarter of a league to the breakwater and the harbour and its ships and toll houses. If the distance had been much greater, they would have been caught in the storm. For the north-west wind had risen considerably and grown quite strong. All the more comforting was it to see the town draw near – his beloved town, resolute and unshakeable, its walls brightening in the clear evening light, its church windows blazing. By God, it felt safe to be returning here from the free-wheeling seagull-life of the islanders, back to this solid stone nest with its bold, proud, impudent towers (and that of Holy Ghost Church not least among them). And there, under the steeple of God's house was his own home, his own nest of stone. In the midst of all the awful turmoil and dangers of the world. Elsbet and his little ones would be waiting for him and the table would be set . . .

"Märten!"

Märten scrambled over the barrels of oil to get to Balthasar.

"Märten, do you think Uncle Jakob thought to heat up the sauna?"

"Why, I should think so . . . By the way, Bal, I forgot to tell you in our rush to get ready for the trip to the island: Friday night, while you were at Schenckenberg's place, there was a young fellow come to see you."

"Who was it?"

"Slahter."

"Which Slahter?"

"Mihkel. You know, that baker fellow. He's back from Germany."

"Oho . . . Then we'll get to hear news from abroad. And right away, God willing."

Balthasar did not need to go out that evening into the rising storm winds to look for Mihkel. When he and Märten walked in through the door, Mihkel was already there, sitting in the great-room, his legs in their high boots crossed, conversing with Elsbet. As Balthasar entered, Mihkel sprang to his feet and came respectfully to greet him, displaying the courtesy of a much younger man and, at the same time, the easy affability of a colleague. For the young man was indeed now a colleague, or at least an aspiring candidate after completing his studies at the university in Rostock.

"Well, well . . . what a *gentleman* . . ." Balthasar said, taking pleasure in both teasing him a bit and acknowledging his status, after looking him over from head to toe. From the grimy-faced little street urchin of Rüütli Street, whom Balthasar barely remembered, and the skinny *primaner** in the Trivium School, whom he clearly recalled, Mihkel had grown up to be a very refined young gentleman. A tall, straight-backed

* Boy in the graduating class (German).

fellow, in his black coat of respectable, medium-priced wool. Light hair, a friendly face, blue eyes. A heavy silver signet ring on his finger. And through the smells of the sea and of fish and seal oil clinging to himself and Märten, Balthasar caught the scent of fine German soap.

"You and Märten will surely want to go to the sauna now," Elsbet said, and it was apparent from both her pink glowing face and Epp's that the women had taken their turn.

"Absolutely. Especially after the salt-water baptism we just had. Just one moment."

He ushered Mihkel into the sacristy, closed the door, and motioned for him to take a seat on the bench, while he himself remained standing at his lectern:

"We'll discuss everything – how you'll set up your everyday living now and get a start – we'll talk all that over, as I promised your father. Did you get the letter I sent to Rostock?"

"Yes, I did."

"Then you know that I am holding five hundred marks of your inheritance, which you will naturally get right away, whenever you need it. Not tomorrow, but—"

"Herr Balthasar, let's not talk about that . . . It's . . ."

"And why should we avoid it . . . ? A debt is a debt. And there's nothing more to be said about it. Let's go to the sauna now."

Yes, Balthasar insisted on dragging Mihkel with him to the sauna:

"For how can we deny the man that pleasure! And how would I find the patience to wait until *after* a proper sauna to hear his tales . . . hah-hah-hah!"

In the dark and sooty sauna, by the light of a stubby candle set inside a storm lantern, and interrupted by the hiss of water exploding into steam as it hit the red-hot rocks on the sauna stove, Balthasar plied Mihkel with questions. First of all, where was he staying in Tallinn? On

Toompea? *Ah-hah*. Oh, at the Tisenhusen residence, the old Reinhold house? Oh yes. He had landed in a very fine establishment! Oh, so he had travelled with the young gentleman Tisenhusen, Wolter, that is, from Rostock. And they had studied together as well, Wolter, concentrating on *iuris disciplina** . . . *Ah-hah* . . . *ah-hah* . . . Well, would Mihkel like to be properly swatted with juniper branches? Or just a few gentle strokes with the birch bundle? He would like to try it? Good, they would give it a try . . .

Balthasar pulled the bundle of juniper branches out of a bucket of hot water and the three men – Märten, Balthasar, Mihkel – took turns swatting each other so energetically that the sauna echoed with the sound of wet leaves slapping bare backs. Balthasar urged Mihkel on: "Don't just be rustling the thing! Go to it – make him feel it – or there's no pleasure in it!" But he did not need to say a thing when Märten set to work on *his* back. Märten knew just how vigorously to wield the bundle of branches. Balthasar himself, actively and energetically, did his best to provide Mihkel with a satisfying sauna session. Only when he noticed Mihkel grimace did Balthasar realise that swatting the bare back of this baker's son, this aspiring young pastor – was providing him, Balthasar – *he-he-he* – with just a little bit of wicked satisfaction . . .

"Well, that should do it. Your back's got a good red glow to it."

But then, when they were sitting, panting on the sauna platform, with the sweat coursing down their bodies, and Mihkel poured a bucket of cold water over his head so that he could give Balthasar clear answers to his questions, Balthasar quickly realised that, when it came to expounding on life abroad, Mihkel was no simpleton, nothing like Kaspar Buschmann. Mihkel had even managed to study the complete, recently published *Magdeburg Centuries* by Flacius! (Incidentally, when Balthasar observed that it was unbelievable that a yammering loudmouth like Flacius, whom he himself had seen behaving as such,

* Study of the law (Latin).

had managed to write a serious book, Mihkel said not a word. And Balthasar said to himself: See now. A discreet and serious fellow. In no rush to agree with me, the way some eager-to-please greenhorn would have been . . .) Mihkel was able to tell him about the ailing Emperor Maximilian and his son Rudolf. In his view, if the latter were to become emperor, which seemed likely, Livonia could expect even less help and support from Vienna or Prague than it had received until now. For a law student from Prague, enrolled at Rostock last year, whose papa had close connections with the nobility of Hradčany, knew enough about it to say that the future emperor was interested only in hunkering down in the dust of his library and art gallery, and conferring with astrologers and alchemists about the secrets of the macro- and microcosm. In fact, he had apparently not set foot outside his castle for several years . . . But Stephen – the Prince of Transylvania, who had been crowned King of Poland in Cracow last year and was thus also sovereign over southern Livonia and Riga – was said to be a mighty warrior, true enough, and a Catholic of course, but of even greater concern to the poor Livonians was this: he was a friend and protector of the Jesuits. Consequently, the Lutheran Church of Polish Livonia had difficult days ahead if religious conflicts were added to all the current calamities of war and destruction. Balthasar learned something else, after they had doused themselves with cold water from the barrel behind the pastor's house and were putting on clean shirts in the changing room: in France, the son of the famous Nostradamus had apparently been put to death by the sword the year before. And he was fortunate that it was by the sword, for his punishment was in retribution for a heretofore unheard-of act. He had reportedly prophesied, by reading the stars, that the town of Salon would burn on a particular day in March. And when that did not come to pass, he had set fire to the town himself, burning down nearly half of it. Merely to fulfil the prophecy . . .

Later they sat around the table, refreshed, clean, tired, and feeling newly born, Elsbet next to Balthasar (the little ones upstairs in their beds). Epp served them salted meat, which was quite palatable after a lengthy soaking. At this wretched time, after all, fresh meat was available only for an exorbitant price. In honour of their special guest, Balthasar asked for a small keg of Rhine wine to be opened. And then they listened with interest to their visitor's stories about the town of Rostock and took pleasure in the tales of his own adventures as a scholar. Especially since he had a talent for storytelling, pausing only briefly now and then to listen to a sound that his tablemates had noted some time earlier, even above his strong voice, a sound that had been growing ever louder during the pauses in talk: the north-east wind, which had swollen into a storm. They heard it howl around the church, heard it gust and squall over the rooftops and down into the courtyard, heard it hurl soil from the cemetery against the west-facing windows of the pastor's house. They heard the weathervanes creak and clang in the roar of the wind, heard the lead frames of the great-room windows rattle . . .

But Mihkel talked on, telling Balthasar the whole story of the great battle in the town of Rostock against the duke of Mecklenburg and the king of Denmark, and the siege of the town and the final surrender the year before last. And he added – who knows, perhaps to console himself – since he had returned to a deeply suffering Livonia:

"So people here should not think that riot and rebellion and war are happening only around these walls and that elsewhere in the world all is peace and blessed serenity. Right now the town of Rostock is so deeply in debt to Duke Mecklenburg – there's talk of a hundred thousand gold coins – that the situation there is no rosier than here. Despite the fact that the Latin name for Rostock is *Rosanum urbs*."[*]

Balthasar smiled at that, saying:

* City of Roses (Latin).

"Let your story then be a consolation to us. Especially since I recently heard a learned man voice the opinion that Reval comes from a word in country-tongue, räbal.* Let us then agree that life in Rostock is not all rosy, nor is it all wretched in Reval."

Naturally, Mihkel also told Balthasar about the lectures on theology and the Latin language by the brothers Chyträus, and the outpouring of Greek thought and learning from the famous Caselius. To Elsbet he described how the more genteel students would hire musicians for a little night music under the windows of pretty burgher maidens. And how it sometimes happened that one suitor's players and another's would come to fisticuffs right there on the street, and by God, the musicians would have at each other with their violins, and the suitors with their swords.

"And of course, right under the windows of the most beautiful maidens..." Mihkel smiled brightly at both Elsbet and Balthasar across the pewter plates, goblets and candelabras, adding: "So it is most fortunate that we have no such customs here in Tallinn. Or otherwise Rataskaevu Street in front of Herr Gandersen's house would have been constantly stained with spattered blood and littered with pieces of violins."

Elsbet remained silent, demurely lowering her eyes, and the howl of the wind sounded long and loud in the room before Balthasar burst out laughing:

"Well now, see how they learn to pay compliments in the *Rosanum urbs* . . . Just like in that game with sticks – remember? You have to make the stick fly, but you're not allowed to touch it. *Ha-ha-ha-hah*."

But Mihkel had turned to Märten and was praising the extraordinary qualities of Rostock ale to him: how strong and dark and good it was and how it was transported everywhere, all the way to Denmark, and how many years it stayed fresh under proper conditions.

* Wretched (Estonian).

At about nine o'clock, they rose from the table and Balthasar suggested that Mihkel stay the night – why go trudging back up Toompea Hill in this storm? Mihkel countered that he would set out with God's help – what could this storm do to a young man here, inside the town walls? Balthasar demurred – of course, whatever he wished. As long as he agreed to return in the morning to discuss his plans for the future. And on condition that Päärn, son of Traani-Andres, accompany him home with a lantern.

Päärn was back in half an hour and reported that he had handed their guest over to the servant at the threshold of Tisenhusen's house. But the wind had blown out his lantern on Toompea and he had made his way back, battling the storm – groping his way along the walls and stumbling over fallen roof tiles lying in the streets.

Balthasar took a candle and went up into his study. His mind was clear and alert – invigorated by the sauna, half a beaker of Rhine wine, and all that he had heard of the thought-provoking, engrossing news of the world. He took out his grey manuscript pages. He eyed the candle flame guttering in the gusts of wind that blew through the cracks around the window frames. He read his most recent notation:

Since the Russians and Tatars were ceaselessly pillaging and plundering in Järvamaa, Harjumaa and the lands outside Tallinn, deporting scores of people and creating chaos day and night at the city walls, so that alarm bells boomed without cease and peasants from all across the land fled with entire families and none of their possessions to the security of the town, with the result that every garden plot and barn and nook teemed with peasants and great hardship and hunger began to oppress them, the Swedish governors at the castle in Tallinn decided to permit the peasants to loot all Russian lands everywhere in Livonia. And Ivo Schenkenberg, a journeyman minter, was appointed their captain.

The previous Friday, before the trip to the island of Prangli, Balthasar had gone to see Ivo Schenkenberg at his home in Karja Street, having heard that Ivo had arrived in Tallinn ahead of his company. But there was no sign of him, and his wife had apparently left to see her husband's stepfather, Gulden the Minter. Hoping to hear more about Ivo's activities and about his comings and goings, Balthasar thus headed that way as well, to Kannuvalajate Street. And there he did hear about Ivo – if not about his arrival in Tallinn, at least about his activities.

Ha-ha-ha-hah! For several months now, ever since his stepson Ivo had been appointed captain of the peasants who had fled their farms to take refuge in town, old Paul Gulden had been treating the "knave and laggard" with new-found respect. Before that he had been heard to complain quite frequently about the "loudmouthed good-for-nothing" he had had to take on when he married Gertke. But now the old man told his buxom daughter-in-law to bring two mugs of ale to the table (it was apparent that he himself had already been partaking of it). He was worried and dignified as he spoke:

"He left with his men for Järvamaa last week. But since then, we've unfortunately had no news of our young captain."

He swallowed some ale and, as the little wart resembling a tiny cauliflower twitched on his thick nose, related with satisfaction:

"On his two previous forays – playing with death, you know – imagine what booty he took! Rings, silver dishes, silk kaftans . . . You know, he's managed to cobble together quite a respectable company out of those oafish peasants."

Then he gulped down another draught of ale and concluded angrily:

"But those infernal tin-pants up on Toompea – the knights, that's who – I won't forgive them—"

"What won't you forgive?"

"That they mock Ivo! It's out of sheer jealousy, of course, the snot-noses."

"How do they mock him?"

"You mean you haven't heard the name they've given him?"

"No."

"The 'Hannibal of the Greys' . . ."

Hm. But in order to understand this Hannibal of the Greys, the lanky fellow with his clipped reddish moustache and slightly protuberant eyes, in order to write about him in the pages of the chronicle, with an understanding of who he really was – whether a captain or an adventurer or a common bandit on a slightly larger scale than usual (or how much difference there in fact was between the three) – for that, Balthasar would need to talk to the man himself. And presumably to wait and see what direction his and the peasants' activities took . . . But this evening, Balthasar wanted something else . . .

Something else . . . Here, in this thick-walled chamber, with his back against the warm, green-tiled stove built just the previous year, the autumn storm on the other side of the windows – probably the most severe of this year's days of the dead – gave him a pronounced sense of the house and the hearth, a *sense of home* that, after the day's successful sea voyage, was particularly pleasurable and comforting.

Balthasar returned his sheets of paper to their place in the niche in the wall and walked across the dark landing to the bedroom.

Elsbet was sitting on a stool at a little table against the whitewashed wall between the children's beds, Balthasar junior to her left and the girls to her right. She had placed a short candle on a tin saucer and a prayer book in front of it to keep the light out of the children's eyes. Her lovely, clear profile – pensive, melancholy, content – her face in the candlelight above the shadow of the prayer book, her every eyelash familiar to him, and the greenish candle glow circling her thick, dark hair – loose, freed from its binding ribbons. She turned and looked over her left shoulder and smiled at him. Balthasar went to her, stood behind her, buried his hands in her hair, then placed his palms on her shoulders, feeling her cascading locks tickle the backs of his hands. His thumbs stroked the smooth warmth of her skin under the neck opening of her nightshirt, and his fingers felt, under the coarse fabric, the resilience of her collarbone, fragile as a bird's bones. Elsbet stood up to face her husband, her right hand pulling the blanket up higher over little Balthasar as she did so. She looked up at him, a gleam of light on her half-open lips, on her questioning, knowing smile.

Balthasar wanted to say something good to his wife, something unequivocally, comprehensively good, something that would bring them close, create complete trust between them . . . For he was truly happy with his Elsbet. He was . . . He put his arms around her. He looked into her dark oval eyes, at the point of light in each one, and then at the children to her left and right, sleeping in the wavering shadow of the prayerbook . . . And he said:

"This bringing of children into the world must be very difficult and painful . . ."

"Yes, it is difficult . . ." Elsbet answered in a whisper (and Balthasar saw how the little points of light in her eyes grew larger with gratitude), "but there's also joy in the pain. Once they've been brought into the world."

"Wait here —" Balthasar went to his study, fished out the key hanging on a string around his neck, under his shirt, and unlocked the familiar iron door of the wall-cupboard. From behind the loose sheets and rolled pages of his manuscript, he took a notebook with wooden covers and leather spine, in double-octavo format. This is where he had copied the carefully selected contents of his manuscript sheets, in revised, edited and emended form. He returned with it to the bedroom, pulling Elsbet down beside him onto the dogskin coverlet of the bed. He put a candle on the bedside table and placed the notebook on her lap:

"Look, this is what I have been working on these past years – this effort, for me, has also been both painful and joyful."

He watched over her shoulder as she opened the cover, the candle-light flickering on the first page in the draught from the window. To be sure, he had to admit that he would never manage to be a real copyist, not to mention an illuminator . . . On the other hand, the angular, barbed letters on that opening page clearly evinced his effort to copy the capital letters of printers.

CHRONICA DER PROUINTZ LYFLANDT/
DARINNE VORMELDET WERDT . . .*

Elsbet turned the pages.

"And you are writing this . . . ?"

"As you see . . ."

"And why *you* . . . ?"

"No-one else has undertaken it . . ." Balthasar said, a little uncertainly, and then realised he had raised one shoulder as he said it, exactly as he had done at the town school on Munkade Street, with Herr Frolink (who at that time was not yet "Meus") when, instead of answering the teacher forthrightly and directly, he had muttered a vague response . . .

"And what is your reason for writing this . . . ?"

"Well . . . it's . . . how should I put it . . . ?"

Elsbet continued to leaf through the pages. Balthasar saw the last few chapter titles flash by under her fingers: Magnus' Wedding in 1573 . . . The Vain Hopes of the Livonians . . . The Latest Plots against Tallinn . . . He suddenly felt somewhat disconcerted at having to clarify just what he had hoped to achieve . . . Good Lord, how could he actually know what kind of wedding it had been or what the Livonians *summa summarum*† had hoped for, or what kinds of plots had been devised

---

* The Chronicle of the Province of Livonia, in which will be recounted . . . (Middle Low German).

† On the whole, taken all together (Latin).

against Tallinn? And it seemed foolish, particularly with regard to recent events, to say what his intention was (whatever the case with the older tales, which had faded from everyone's memory). But he swallowed and replied anyway:

"Well, in order that the truth of the things that have happened survive."

As soon as he had uttered the words, he recognised his own arrogance. (Lord, if Our Saviour refused to answer Pilate, how then could *he* know what the Truth is . . .) And yet, and yet . . . He was looking for a way to continue, a way to moderate his arrogance. He said:

"Yes . . . so that it . . . would be available . . . to weigh and mull over, in the future . . ." He motioned with his chin towards the children's beds, concluding with a somewhat forced, doubtful smile . . . "for . . . them . . . the little ones . . . and for others, who will come after us . . ."

Elsbet raised her eyes from the book: "But . . . isn't it dangerous . . . this work you're doing?"

"Why dangerous?!"

As he said this, Balthasar raised his eyebrows as though the idea of danger had never occurred to him. God knows, women have an uncanny intuition about such things, no matter how limited their grasp of one's work and activities might be in other respects. The writing of the chronicle was, of course, a risky business. Why else would he carry the key to his wall-cupboard around his neck? Why else had he been telling curious questioners, for years now, that he was studying the history of Livonia purely for his own amusement, out of boredom? And explaining that only very rarely was he curious about last year's or yesterday's events. Like anyone else . . .

"I don't know, of course . . ." Elsbet said, uncertainly, "but when you say that your writing should preserve the truth . . . well, that wouldn't necessarily be pleasing to everyone in power, would it . . . ?"

Balthasar listened to the wind rattling the graveyard gate near Holy

Ghost Church – *Clunk-clunk-clunk! Clatter-clatter-clatter!* His parishioners, half or three-quarters of whom were superstitious, would probably have said that the ghosts of the town were somehow trying to break into the churchyard. When the clanking and rattling had continued for a long time, Balthasar said:

"My dear Elsbet, what does it mean – 'it wouldn't necessarily be pleasing to everyone'? Not everyone finds our faces pleasing either – when the face is our own, and not a carnival mask that we change depending on who it is we're turning to. And it's not worth worrying because of some petty intrigue that someone or other might concoct against me on account of this work. At least not so long as no-one knows I'm writing this chronicle. No-one but you and a few of my closest friends."

He picked up the book, returned it to the cupboard in his study, and locked the heavy iron door. Then he went back to the bedroom and lifted Elsbet up in his arms, turning down the dogskin coverlet on the bed with one hand.

"I have to make sure the children are covered – it's such a windy night," exclaimed Elsbet.

Balthasar continued holding her, looking at her, his eyes round, reflecting the candlelight:

"I'll do it."

He laid her down on the bed and drew the covers over her. Then he pulled the blankets on Balzer and the girls up to their chins. His hand stroked three silky little heads and touched three warm, damp noses. He went to the bed and gazed into his wife's black eyes, where candle flames flickered. God Almighty, there were outbreaks of plague in town and enemies outside its walls (he blew out the candle and took off his jerkin); there was doubt and superstition among the congregation; the writing of his chronicle was beset with difficulty and dangers – heaven knows what kind of intrigues there might be . . . But here he was, with his quiet and inscrutable and wonderful wife – and he was happy. He was! He was. Wasn't he . . . ? Absolutely.

But in the matter of the possibility, or even the reality of intrigues, and not merely in connection with his aspirations as a chronicler, Balthasar erred far less than he probably assumed – or perhaps he erred far more.

An hour earlier, Päärn, son of Traani-Andres, had left Mihkel Slahter in the care of the retainer, on the stoop of the Tisenhusen residence behind the cathedral on Toompea. And Mihkel had dashed up the stairs so cheerfully and energetically that the servant did not venture to follow him with his candle, thinking to himself: he might be a pal of young Herr Wolter, but I knew his father at a time when he couldn't even say the words "Schwein" and "Wein"* correctly, saying "weyn" for both – it was all the same to him. So I'm not going to shuffle up the stairs on account of the young slacker – not with this aching back of mine . . . And as Mihkel sprinted up the stairs, he was indeed full of energy and in high spirits – partly from battling the exciting storm that here, between the town walls, was not at all dangerous, but which had nonetheless threatened to carry him off on the corner of Nunna Street down below, and again on Castle Square above.

Mihkel entered the guest chamber, which had been put at his disposal at the Tisenhusen house. Groping around in the dark, he found the flint and steel and lit a candle. The low bed and the little table and his chest at the head of the bed swam out of the darkness into view. And even the garlands painted on the whitewashed vaulted ceiling burst into bloom in the dusky light here and there, putting forth red blossoms. Mihkel tossed the beret he had been clutching with one hand, onto the moose-antler hat-rack and came to a standstill in the middle of the room. Apparently his lungs were still so full of the salty

* Pig and wine (German).

wind that had whipped along Pikk Jalg Street and across Castle Square, that it could not be exhaled in silence, but became a melodic hum.

"Aha," said a voice behind his back.

Mihkel turned around and saw Wolter leaning against the doorpost.

"It's understandable," Wolter drawled, a smug grin on his lean and angular, man-about-town face.

"What's understandable?"

"That you're humming a song like that."

"Like what?"

"You weren't aware of what you were humming?"

"No . . . "

"Well, this one—"

Yk spreke und rade in minen mud:
Man kan teyne ovelle lyden
Umme eyn gud . . . *

"And what of it?"

"Well, haven't you just come from that man *Russow's* place?"

"And?"

"And Russow has a beautiful young wife. It's understandable, as I said."

Mihkel turned to face Wolter and laughed, a bit too quickly, a bit abashedly. It was the laugh of a callow youth whose earnest self is embarrassed at being associated with a certain woman, but whose vanity is greatly flattered.

The next morning, when Mihkel was summoned for breakfast with the gentlefolk of the Tisenhusen household, he planned to eat his slice of rye bread and piece of meat and drink his ale quickly, in order to head straight down to Herr Balthasar's place in the lower town, to

---

* I tell myself within my mind: / one can endure ten evils / for the sake of one good (Middle Low German).

discuss his plans for the future. But shocking, unthinkable news had already reached the Tisenhusen house.

By now, eight o'clock, the tempest had spent half its fury. But at two o'clock in the middle of the night, at the height of the storm, men on horseback had ridden from the harbour up to Toompea, to inform Tõnis Maidel that the storm had ripped the bulwark loose and carried it away! It was true! The pride of Tallinners from time immemorial, their indestructible bulwark, one hundred and fifty fathoms long, their gate to the sea that could never be blockaded, had been swallowed up by that very sea, as though it had never existed . . .

When Mihkel arrived at the parsonage, Balthasar had just returned from the harbour. Indeed, the section of the sea wall constructed of logs was gone, along with the harbour watchman's house. Thank God, that the fleet of warships assigned to protect the town in case of necessity – two ships armed with cannon and one island-galley – had, upon Tõnis Maidel's orders, been moved into the inner harbour at the onset of the storm and thus been spared. A ship from Stockholm carrying provisions had sunk in the bay, along with the sea wall. Two of Rosenborg's merchant ships had been torn loose and thrown up onto shore near Ristimäe Hill. And then the news had reached the harbour: a quarter of the breakwater, together with the watchman's house, had washed up on low ground at Lillepi, near the farm of the town's fence-maker, south of the Pirita estuary. Three harbour guards had been swept out to sea from the watchman's house and drowned, but two had tied themselves to the roof with ropes and were alive, if only barely . . .

Nearly thirty harbour guards and seamen drowned in the great disaster, and losses of goods from the ships, smaller vessels, sloops and barges amounted to several thousands of marks, but the reconstruction of the bulwark would cost tens of thousands, even though, in the weeks following, the sea tossed most of the logs up onto the shores of Viimsi peninsula, and they were hauled back to town to be used in the rebuilding.

In the next few weeks, severe storms alternated with uncommonly fierce blizzards. The steeple of the Almshouse Church was blown off its base, and on the Thursday before St Martin's Day, so much snow fell in the course of a few hours in Tallinn and the surrounding country-side, that hundreds of sleighs got stuck in snowbanks, and vulnerable infants being brought to town to be christened died of the cold. But over all these singular calamities loomed the inexplicable, frightening omen of the loss of the bulwark. Those who attended church services during these weeks noticed that the same message was heard from all the pulpits: Take note, the Lord God has not yet meted out sufficient punishment for the arrogance and profligacy of this town! Take note, we in our mortal wisdom thought that whatever might happen, our grand bulwark was indestructible and no blockade could break us! But the Lord said unto us: "And I will take from you your last consolation and hope and support, that your hard hearts might become soft . . ." All the pastors were saying the same thing – Querlemann of the Dome Church, Elard of St Michael's, Gerstenberg of St Nicholas', Schroeder of St Olaf's and Bushover of the Almshouse Church. And, truth be told, Balthasar of Holy Ghost was saying the same thing as well. Only those few who listened to him attentively (if in fact there were any such) noticed that he elaborated a little on the common theme: "Yes, God has taken from us our grand bulwark, built of the straightest pine logs from the island of Naissaare, the bridge from our troubles here to the outside world, whence comes our earthly help. God has taken from us that which has consoled us, encouraged us. But pay heed: God Himself is still with us. And He says: if we are honourable and hard-working and worthy, He will protect us!"

And by the way, only the Lord God Himself knew whether Balthasar was saying this because of his strong faith in God or because of his profound love of life or because of his great love of humanity. Or, perhaps even more, because of his woeful stubbornness in the face of his own fears and frailties of spirit.

For there was reason enough, that winter in Tallinn, to be plagued by fears and to lose heart. Just when the shipload of provisions from Stockholm, with its cargo of gunpowder and lead, sank and was lost, just when news arrived that the mercenaries hired from Danzig would not arrive, because war had broken out with the Polish king, and those hired from Lübeck were not coming either, because of the raging storms on the Baltic Sea – just then, the town learned that nothing would deter the forces of the Grand Duke . . .

And so it was to some extent only natural that the people of the town drew closer to one another, for this is what generally happens in times of trouble. At least it was the case with thoughtful people concerned with the general welfare, whereas those by nature more shortsighted and self-centred began to express greater intolerance towards one another. As always. In any case, Mihkel, as a young man without family or kinsfolk in his hometown, was included in Balthasar's household as a matter of course. Not to mention that Balthasar had both a debt to repay to Mihkel and a pledge to fulfil. And regardless of the fact that Balthasar harboured – how to put it – a dispiriting recollection from the very first days after Mihkel's arrival. For which Mihkel himself bore no responsibility whatsoever.

It had happened early one morning, a week after the great disaster of the bulwark, when Balthasar and Mihkel were sitting in the sacristy in the dusky light of dawn. Elsbet brought in a couple of mugs of ale and left, and they had just broached the subject of Mihkel's future plans. Balthasar said that at the moment there was no pastoral position available in Tallinn or anywhere at all in the surrounding area. Especially since five or six pastors from Harju county had taken refuge inside the town walls in the last month, to escape the endless daily looting in the open countryside. And suddenly, as if to underscore their discussion – the way a coloured woodcut serves to illustrate a text – the bells of St Anthony's Chapel on Tõnismäe Hill began to peal, and from the city walls to the south, apparently from Zeghen and Assauwe towers, came explosions of gunfire.

The two men went out onto Apteegi Street and met Märten on the steps of the Apothecary. He had already heard from witnesses running past that a mounted band of robbers had managed to reach the rondel at the Karja Gate and, right there, had been harassing people going in and out. The gunfire had scared them off, but a number of the wounded had been carried into town. Balthasar and Mihkel had gone back to the sacristy to discuss the possibilities for Mihkel's future and had just sat down when Gandersen's journeyman, Peeter, charged into the room, his face pale with fear and red-splotched from running: his master was urgently summoning his son-in-law! Three of his workmen had fallen victim to the highwaymen and one was near death . . .

Balthasar motioned for Mihkel to come along with him:

"Let's go! Do you know my father-in-law?"

"I do. From a long time ago. I grew up in Rataskaevu Street . . ."

They wrapped their dogskin-lined cloaks about them. It must be said, not only had Mihkel's lining obviously come from a better-fed dog than Balthasar's, but the cloak itself was also of finer, smoother fabric. The men themselves were in too great a hurry to notice. They followed Peeter along the slushy streets, to the furrier's house. Balthasar led the way through the workshop to Gandersen's private workroom, knocked on the familiar door, and entered:

"Greetings!"

To tell the truth, ever since the somewhat embarrassing incident of Elsbet's jewellery case several years earlier, Balthasar and his father-in-law had maintained a truce. It was a constrained, cool peace, to be sure, but the grass of mutual respect had nevertheless slowly begun to sprout in the cracks of its stone floor. And if Balthasar had taken the trouble to notice, he would have become aware of signs of a growing warmth in Gandersen, or at least of a greater acceptance of him, especially after the furrier's other son-in-law, Godert, had been summoned to the Council and publicly chastised for beating his wife. Under the influence of drink, such things happened in many households more respectable than that of a boozing, brawling master baker. But still, the story of Godert and Agnes was bandied about for some time in the artisan community, lamented by some and lampooned by others. At least the Master's other son-in-law, the peasant-pastor, had the reputation of treating his wife decently, whatever else he might do. And thus, Master Gandersen responded entirely amicably:

"*Tag*, Balthasar."

"Where are the wounded men?"

"Over there, across the courtyard. Peeter will show you."

"Look here – I brought you a visitor." Balthasar stepped away from the door and pulled Mihkel out of the shadows into the room.

Gandersen's black, slanted eyes stared for a moment at Mihkel's beaming face, and suddenly the old man's expression reflected the other's smile:

"What a surprise! Young Slahter has come home . . . !"

He rose from behind the table piled high with wolf pelts to greet Mihkel with outstretched arms. Chuckling, Balthasar returned to the workshop, closing the door behind him, and followed Peeter across the courtyard to the vaulted cellar where the wounded men lay. What he learned in his brief talk with them was so instructive and raised so many conflicting questions in his mind, that it erased all thought of Mihkel for a while.

Three men with bloody bandages were lying on straw in the low cellar, two with knife and sword wounds. The third, with a severe head wound – probably the result of a halberd blow – turned with a groan towards the door as it creaked open. Balthasar saw immediately that even the last man was not, at least not yet, in need of a clergyman, and that Gandersen, or more likely his housekeeper Maijke, had summoned their family pastor somewhat prematurely in their initial fright. For even the man with the head injury appeared vigorous enough – he was anticipating the arrival of the barber, who was to dress and bandage their wounds properly, and he provided the most thorough answers to Balthasar's queries:

"No way could we tell who they were – 'twas half dark and the snow coming down thick . . ."

"I saw a fur hat and slanted eyebrows . . . Tatars no doubt . . . or maybe Russians . . ."

"But there were German manormen – the scoundrels – amongst them too. I heard a number of *deyvels** clear as can be . . ."

"And there was a redbeard, with a knife in his fist, letting loose with those *gohddammitz*, or whatever the word is. It's what those Scotsmen, the swine, used to say when they were strutting about here year before last . . ."

"True – not all of them were done in at Rakvere. Some of them fled into the brush, and now they're looting and plundering . . ."

"And I think there were some of our old Jenses† in the pack too . . . deserters or such. There's all sorts here, after all . . ."

"Oh, I don't know there were any Swedes . . ."

"Bah – they're all the same!"

"And the two that grabbed our money pouches, they were Poles . . ."

"Maybe so. Though their leader was cursing in pure country-tongue, asking why the devil we didn't have anything on us but a few mangy calfskins . . . ! We'd been out buying calfskins for Master Gandersen

* Devils (Middle Low German).
† Plural of the Swedish name Jens, refers to Swedes in general.

and were returning with no money . . . That made 'em so mad, they set to beating the tar out of us . . ."

"So it seemed that our local tribes had all banded together?" Balthasar asked.

"Seems that way . . ."

"Or were the ruffians merely throwing around foreign words here and there, and were they perhaps all our own peasants . . . ?"

"Could be, of course . . ."

Thinking back over this story at home afterwards, Balthasar realised, to his chagrin, that there was something in this undeniably dismal tale, in this basically infernal mess, that made the corners of his mouth twitch, in spite of himself. He pursed his lips to suppress an unseemly urge to smile and focused on calling to mind the dreadful implications of the incident: the appalling conditions that had become the reality of daily life in the countryside and made such events possible! What a great temptation it must be for the entire unfortunate peasantry to blame God for permitting all kinds of peoples, invited and uninvited, to come here to rob and plunder . . . And what a devilish allegory lay in his question and in the answer he had anticipated from the wounded men. "Or were the ruffians perhaps all from our own villages . . . ?" The answer that had come from the heap of bloody rags on the dirty straw was matter-of-fact, conveying not the least hint of surprise: "Could be, of course." A sense of pitiful–damnable pride tugged at the corners of Balthasar's mouth: see, in spite of everything, they're still strong enough to be capable of robbing themselves . . .

Balthasar did not know whether his next thought was sent by the Devil to torment him, or by God to spur him into checking his scornful, judgmental arrogance, the way a goad prods a stubborn beast to move. He paused in the sacristy behind the little maple table, worn black with use, where he and Mihkel had been sitting an hour earlier when the bells sounded the alarm. Their two clay mugs were still there, his own empty and Mihkel's two-thirds full. His father-in-law's yellowish face came to mind – the change in its expression when Balthasar pushed Mihkel into the room. A face always closed to his son-in-law had suddenly lit up at the sight of Mihkel. His black eyes, usually guarded, wary (preparing for a defensive strike), had glowed with pleasure. He had extended his tannin-stained hands, spreading wide his usually stiff and bent fingers, to welcome this son of a German master craftsman, this neighbourhood boy, from their part of town . . .

But it was in no way Mihkel's fault that Balthasar felt an odd prickling in his throat as the old man's face rose now before his mind's eye, a feeling that he had to acknowledge as jealousy, foolish though it was – or, at least, as surprisingly deep bitterness. Not because of Gandersen's warm, welcoming reception of Mihkel. (God, why not? He was, after all, from the same neighbourhood, a nice young man who had returned after many years abroad, at a time when there were con-siderably more people departing than arriving.) Not because of that. But because of the natural, easy, unequivocal embrace of Mihkel as "one of us"– an acknowledgement not ever, in all these years, extended to Balthasar, despite the aforementioned grass of mutual respect pushing up through the cracks in the stone floor of domestic harmony.

No, Mihkel was in no way at fault. Perhaps Balthasar's need to underline Mihkel's blamelessness, or maybe his need to compete with his father-in-law in his embrace of the young man – perhaps all this induced him to show greater amicability towards Mihkel on future occasions than he might otherwise have done. On many a winter evening, in November and December of 1576, with snowstorms swirling outside, Mihkel sat in the parsonage with them as if he belonged there, talking and sharing their oatmeal porridge and scant pieces of meat. He told Elsbet that the Spanish fashion in dress was becoming increasingly popular in Germany, especially with the gentry. Among the councilmen and administrators in Rostock, for example, only very tight, stiff, raven-black attire was worn on festive occasions. And women's necklines had risen all the way to their chins . . .

"Which has fortunately not yet occurred here, in this land," he added, his grey eyes smiling, darting a glance at Elsbet's low, straight neckline. Only after the fact did he blush, recalling the glance as he raised his mug of ale to his lips, the mug serving to conceal his red face from the others.

On many of these evenings, Balthasar discussed the fate of the town with Mihkel. For the issues concerning it were becoming ever more complex on account of the expected arrival of the Muscovites. Or, at other times, they reminisced about the Trivium School – both having been schoolboys there. Especially about the one close encounter between them.

"It was in the spring of '63, remember? I'd just come back from Germany and was looking for a position, and you were – how much younger are you than I? Twelve years – you've been roaming around Germany for so long now that the age difference seems much greater – but at that time, you were already in the advanced *secunda*. And you had a better command of Latin than most of the boys in *prima*. And you were quite a spruce-and-ready fellow. Balder chose you for the role of Callicles in *Trinummus*. Remember?"

"How could I forget!"

"Let's drink to that!"

They drank ale, recalling smells and faces from their distant school-days. The fire roared in the tall fireplace at the back of the great-room. The logs that old Jakob chose always burned as though they had a core of pure sap. Especially in this kind of weather, with the wind rushing down the chimney as if to suck up fire and logs along with smoke and sparks . . . And so the men drank their ale, and Elsbet, sitting on a bench a little closer to the fire, took a sip once in a while, too, and listened to the men's talk. A costly cape of fine fur, light and warm – a gift from her father on her last birthday – helped ward off the chill of the room. As she listened, she was practising a new and intricate craft – brought back from Germany by a councilman's wife, Brigitte Holthusen, who had taught it to her friends. With thin wooden sticks that Märten had cut for her from wild apple trees and polished smooth with ashes, she was trying to knit a sock of soft grey wool for little Balthasar.

"How could I forget!" Mihkel said. You played Megaronides and I was Callicles. *Ha-ha-ha*. All the members of the Town Council were there with their wives. And the gentlemen of the Council of Clergy and the guilds. Herr Holthusen was just telling me the other day that he remembered me from that time . . ."

"And Herr Balder – remember? – was Charmides," Balthasar said. "He was a lazy one, saying he couldn't possibly cram all those lines into any one of his boys, and better that he take on the role himself . . ."

"And Ivo Schenkenberg, he was barely fifteen at the time, played Sycophant, the swindler. Remember that?"

"As if it were yesterday . . ."

"The year Ivo graduated we put on *Miles Gloriosus*. I was Pleusicles and he was Bramarbas, the braggart. *Ha-ha-ha-ha*. Sometimes there are omens in chance events, don't you think?"

"For example?"

"Well, from what I've heard, Ivo is still playing the swaggering Bramarbas with his exploits as leader of the looters and marauders . . ."

What a clever fellow, thought Balthsasar. But he said:

"*Ha-ha-ha-haa* . . . that could be . . . Time will tell what game he's playing . . . Do you remember the time we were standing in the great hall? "

"Behind the partition—"

"Yes, they'd set up a partition at the back of the hall—"

"It was a painted to depict a street scene in Athens. Well, one might say, it was dabbed on rather than painted," Mihkel added with a touch of condescension. "One of Master Krafft's pupils did it for Herr Balder, in return for a mug of ale."

"Well, at the time we thought it was rather grand – all those white walls and white columns. And you and I were standing behind the partition, waiting for the play to begin. Remember? We peeked through the cracks at the audience. With the strong, foul smell of hempseed oil burning our throats – the stink of that same white paint . . ."

"Now that's something I don't remember," Mihkel said. "But we were wearing some kind of white togas."

"Exactly. Annika sewed them for us – my sister, Annika. Herr Balder asked her to do it in Meus' – I mean, Herr Frolink's – memory. And then Annika stitched together the togas out of the linen that had been part of her dowry. Afterwards she took out the stitches, of course, and the fabric was put back into her chest."

"And on our feet we wore something really strange, remember?"

"Buskins – of course I remember! Märten made them for us out of birch, at my request, and I nailed on the leather straps. And that's what we were wearing as we waited for the signal from Herr Balder . . ."

"And then he signalled to us and we went clomping out into the streets of Athens, and you began reciting – I don't remember exactly how it went . . ."

But Balthasar remembered. He did not stand up nor place one foot in front of the other, but he listened for a moment to the whine of the wind, glanced at the flickering flames, furrowing his brow at Mihkel, and thundered:

Nae amicum castigare ob meritum noxiam
Immoene est facinus, verum in aetate utile
Et conducibile. Nam ego amicum hodie meum
Concastigabo pro commerita noxia

Invitus, ni id me invitet ut faciam fides.
Nam hic nimium morbus mores invasit bonos:
Ita plerique omnes iam sunt intermortui.
Sed, dum illi aegrotant, interim mores mali,
Quasi herba inrigua . . .

"And so forth."

"And what does it mean?" Elsbet asked. Her sticks of wild apple-wood had stopped moving. She adjusted her fur cape, pulling it more closely around her shoulders, her almond-shaped eyes fixed on Balthasar.

"Well, it goes something like this." Balthasar translated haltingly: "It is a lamentable thing to condemn a friend for a transgression he has committed, but, at the proper moment, it could nevertheless be salutary and beneficial, and therefore, today I will condemn my friend for his serious transgression, and although it goes against my grain, I must do it for the sake of our friendship . . ."

"And what is this transgression?" Elsbet asked.

"Well," Balthasar said, "Megaronides thinks that Callicles has gone behind his friend's back and gained his house for himself by devious means . . ." Balthasar reached across the table to grab Mihkel by the shoulder, shaking him and laughing hard:

"Hey there, Callicles! It's a damn good thing that you were such an honest fellow! Let's drink to that!"

When they had clinked their cups together, Balthasar stood up.

"Fine. There's some work I still want to do tonight."

He took one of the three candles burning on the table, nodded to Elsbet and Mihkel, and went upstairs. She watched him leave, and as she looked at Mihkel, the unwonted expression on her face did not in any way reflect apprehension. (Apprehension, at being left alone with Mihkel in the great-room, which was inhospitable in spite of the fire in the hearth – after all, she had known him since childhood and in recent days had had several one-to-one conversations with him.) Her strange *help-me-no!-don't-notice-me* expression derived from a shock she had just experienced from thoughts that had been stirring almost imperceptibly in her mind and of which she now suddenly became aware: compared to Mihkel, her Balthsasar appeared rougher, cruder, less cultivated. It could not be helped. Even when it came to God, Balthasar displayed less reverence. When Balthasar said grace at the supper table, Elsbet had noticed (and tonight was not the first time) just how fervent and respectful Mihkel looked as he whispered the words of the prayer, even as Balthasar mumbled the words as though – had they not been in German – he were talking with his uncle Jakob about how to clear away the snowdrifts from the church entrance. No, not that he could be described as a yokel, in the common sense of the word. Her father's animus, the resentment of an old man, was unfair . . . this had been apparent a couple of days ago, when on a visit he remarked to her: "That Mihkel is an indescribably nice young man, he even talks about your yokel husband with such respect, that . . ." Which was exactly how the nice young man ought to talk of her husband – with respect. And how he ought to think about him, too. If anyone had something to reproach Balthasar for, then in any event . . . Oh Lord . . .

The nice young man cleared his throat and gestured towards the stairs leading to the second storey, his silver ring flashing on his hand, and said:

"Is Herr Balthasar working on his sermon for Sunday?"

Elsbet looked into his light-grey eyes and thought with an excess of fervour: He must respect him! And hold him in esteem! In the highest esteem! She answered ardently, enthusiastically, glad that she could enlighten him:

"No . . . He is writing a great work – a chronicle of Livonia. He has been working on it for a number of years. It will soon be finished."

Mihkel looked truly astonished and observed, with sincere admiration (just as Elsbet had hoped), that God's Grace was indeed abundant in that Balthasar had been able to bring such a work as that to near completion – in spite of times like these and the innumerable, untold hardships endured by this country and many another . . .

Later, Mihkel knocked on the door of Balthasar's study and entered to bid him goodnight:

"By the way," he said, "your wife told me about your great undertaking . . . I want to wish you success with it! A serious chronicle – why that's something of incalculable importance . . . And I hope that . . . that I will be permitted to take a look at it, before you . . ."

Balthasar looked down at the lines he had just copied into his bound notebook from his loose sheets of notes:

In the year 1576 three nobles from Kuramaa launched a surprise attack on the castle of Amboten, which belonged to Duke Magnus of Holstein. The castellan was abroad at the time, and these three, having convinced the wife that they were friends and relatives of her husband, gained entry to the castle and took possession of it.

He raised his eyes and his somewhat dour expression began to soften as his eyes met Mihkel's. Perhaps he recalled old Gandersen's expression at the sight of this tall young man, his face visibly brightening, acknowledging Mihkel as one of them, and perhaps he remembered being stung by that look. Perhaps some inner lamp behind his bushy, reddish eyebrows wanted to glow even more brightly . . . In any event, Balthasar responded most genially:

"You? Of course you may take a look at it. Maybe I'll even ask you to copy parts of it for me. How about it?"

"Herr Balthasar – that would truly be – a very great honour . . ."

*

Looking back across the many years that separate us from these events that we are attempting to recount, it is unfortunately not possible to say whether or to what extent the Devil himself enjoyed acting as stage manager for what followed. We cannot say with certainty whether he arranged the meeting between Mihkel and certain prominent worthies up at Tisenhusen's high-gabled house for a mere half-hour after Mihkel had left the parsonage, on that very same stormy evening, or for a few days later, or not until a bone-chilling day in January of 1577. But one thing is certain: the meeting did happen. On a bitterly cold winter evening, Wolter summoned Mihkel downstairs:

"Come. Father wants to talk to you."

When Mihkel entered the great-room, he found two men at the round table, each with a goblet of wine. In addition to Wolter's father, a man with fish eyes and a protuberant nose, there was also a kinsman – Mihkel did not know how they were related, but he had seen him a couple of times at the house. It was Admiral Maidel, tall and lanky, his complexion reddened by exposure to the elements. Wolter himself, having led Mihkel to the room, disappeared. Mihkel scarcely noticed him leave. The gentlemen offered him a seat at the table and pushed a third goblet towards him, and he was so overcome with deferential astonishment that he only half-sat on his stool.

Herr Tisenhusen looked at him, his fish eyes bulging amiably beneath their freckled lids, and said:

"Michel,* my friend Tõnis and I were just talking about setting you up in a pulpit somewhere. But now, with all signs indicating that the Muscovite is hatching another plan to attack our town, we will have to postpone the matter until better days return. But be assured, we will take care of you."

Mihkel started in alarm. Did this not mean that he would be consigned to the streets until "better days" arrived? He replied:

* Michel is the German name for the Estonian Mihkel.

305

"Gentlemen, my esteemed benefactors, I am most grateful to you. I know not in what way I could possibly . . . But I give you my word that when I do assume a position as pastor I will do so by fulfilling my obligations responsibly, with utmost care . . ."

"Indeed, indeed . . . that is what we too anticipate . . ." interjected the thin-lipped admiral. "And in this spirit, we would like to request that you do us a few small favours even before that time."

By all means. He had, after all, been living here under Herr Tisenhusen's roof and eating at his table for two or three months already without paying a penny, without any obligations. He had already told Wolter on a few occasions that he could not continue to accept this hospitality. So:

"With utmost pleasure!"

"Well then," said Herr Maidel. "But let us agree on one thing: everything we discuss here today and in the future remains in this room. Agreed?"

"Agreed."

"*Gut*. And to ensure that this not be forgotten . . . " Herr Maidel – he seemed to be the one in charge here – signalled with a tilt of his heavy chin to Herr Tisenhusen, who clapped his hands. A rheumatic servant emerged inexplicably quickly from the darkness into the circle of candlelight, and the master of the house whispered something in his dusty ear. The servant hobbled away, soon returning with a volume bound in light parchment, which he placed on the table.

Let us recall that when Doctor Friesner sent the young Balthasar to Turku, to see Duke Johan nineteen years ago, he said, knowing the world and knowing people as he did, and sounding almost like a heretic: "I won't ask you to take an oath of silence on the Bible. Every intelligent person knows that God is everywhere." But here, today, it was different. Not that the business conducted in the Tisenhusen house was of greater import or significance – at least not from the perspective of the world at large – than the affairs of the Doctor. Nor did it mean that Christian customs were now held in greater esteem than they had been two decades earlier. If the little ceremony that followed meant anything at all, it was this: up here on Toompea, in this eyrie of stone where tradition ruled, a ceremonial oath of silence was held to be more binding than an ordinary oath. Or, who knows, perhaps these gentlemen – who did not, of course, lack for experience of their own – had reached the conclusion that this one-time baker's boy before them would be more firmly bound by taking a ceremonial oath than otherwise. Something Doctor Friesner apparently had not held to be the case with regard to Bal.

When Herr Tisenhusen pushed the Bible in front of Mihkel and opened the bronze clasps to show him that it was a volume printed in Wittenberg by the famous Lufft, Mihkel realised that on an occasion such as this it behoved him to rise to his feet. And so, left hand resting on the cool parchment, right hand raised, with its somewhat nervously trembling fingers pointing towards the dark log ceiling, towards the bull on the Tisenhusen coat of arms carved into the stone walls, Mihkel repeated earnestly:

"I swear on the Holy Bible that everything that my lords and masters discuss with me here" – at the same time he wondered just what they could want to discuss with him . . . nothing dishonourable, of course not . . . not these respectable and benevolent gentlemen – "shall remain within these walls. Amen." (And if he happened to break his vow, that bull there on the wall would come down and gore him . . .)

More quickly than he had anticipated, he learned what they wanted to discuss with him – and what a thorny business it would be. Scarcely had he managed to lower himself back to his half-perch on the stool than Admiral Maidel threw his cards on the table:

"Michel, you are a frequent visitor at the home of Holy Ghost Pastor Russow, is that not so?"

"Ye . . . yes . . . I . . ."

"Consequently, you have no doubt noticed that he's a – well – a man of extraordinary curiosity."

"I'm not certain . . . It could be, of course . . ."

"Well, yes. We are aware that he's been gathering all manner of facts and information on the town of Tallinn, as well as the entire province. At times, casually, at times, quite aggressively. For several years already. I know that he is your pastor. But right now we are under threat, each and every day, of another siege by the Muscovite. And at such a moment, you, as a German, must rise to your obligations. Don't misunderstand: we do not suspect him of, let us say, being another Heinrich Boissmann, disguised in clerical robes within our walls here. But we do not know for whom he is working. He socialises with all the councilmen. Since you were gone for many years in Germany, you might not be aware of the divisions that have formed in the Council . . . And he visits them all: the Swedish, Polish and Danish councilmen, and those of Magnus – Muscovy, that is. Johann Boissmann is apparently an old friend of his. And since the time that the Horns established themselves on Toompea, he has been a guest at their house as well. It seems they're friends of even longer standing. And whenever there are ships arriving from abroad, he hastens down to the harbour. And he's round and about the taverns and pubs and at the house of the Blackheads. We have to find out, quietly, without making any noise about it, just whose man he is."

When Herr Maidel laid Balthasar's name on the table, Mihkel's heart filled to the brim with incredulity and shock, and then with burning anger. But almost immediately he understood these lords' fatal error. And his conviction lent him such confidence that, although he spoke mildly, his tone was almost mocking:

"You want to know whose man he is – what you mean is whose spy, isn't it?"

As soon as he had said this, his courage and relief and sense of release grew so great that he burst into laughter:

"*Ha-ha-ha-ha!* No, my esteemed benefactors! Herr Balthasar is no-one's spy. He is collecting information only for himself."

"Can he think that we – or you – would believe such nonsense?"

Mihkel was so full of cheerful self-confidence that he would not permit the admiral to interrupt him (which was unprecedented).

"But it's true!" he cried. "Herr Balthasar is writing a great work – a chronicle of Livonia!" He added, into the silence that followed, "And if God so wills, it will soon be completed."

In the quiet that once again settled upon the room, Mihkel noted that his benefactors did not seem to share his delight in this news at all. On the contrary, Herr Tisenhusen put his wine goblet down on the table with a clunk, and Herr Maidel whistled through his teeth, as though a gust of wind had at last found a crack through which to enter the room.

"A chronicle could be a worse enemy than a spy. A spy is active only as long as he lives. And he often comes to a sudden end . . ." He pulled one of the four candlesticks on the table towards himself and blew out the flame. "But a chronicle, especially if it is published, will live on."

"And what's wrong with that? If it tells the truth?" Mihkel asked, not without pride in being able to come to the defence of his esteemed teacher.

"You see?" Herr Maidel said, hard as iron, "we come back to the same thing: whose truth?"

"But that's obvious – if it comes from Herr Balthasar's pen. It is the truth of our Christian Gospel. The truth of His Majesty, the Swedish King. The truth of the lords of the land in Livonia."

"And that is a simple matter, in your opinion? You're absolutely certain?" asked Herr Maidel, with a scornful glint in his eye, which

Mihkel, in his excitement, did not notice. (But who knows whether he would have noticed, in any event.)

"I'm absolutely certain."

"So you've read his manuscript?"

"We-e-l . . . l . . . unfortunately I can't say that I have," and in fact he was deeply embarrassed, in spite of his *bona fide* conviction that he had so expansively spoken about a work which he now had to admit he had not even seen. Because of that, and also because of an unfortunate stubbornness in his nature, and because of a certain vanity fed by the sense of being in the know, and, of course, because of his eagerness to defend his esteemed teacher, he said:

"But Herr Balthasar promised to let me read it! Even before it is completed!"

"I see," said Herr Maidel, his voice lower than it had sounded until now. "That simplifies things considerably. You will read the chronicle and report to us on it."

"I . . . well . . . alright . . ."

Herr Tisenhusen nudged the wine goblet closer to Mihkel and added, so genially that the admiral's excessively peremptory tone (he had, after all, been addressing a soon-to-be cleric, if God so willed it – and if these same gentlemen helped . . .) – so genially, yes, that that tone simply faded away.

"Herr Slachter, I'm sure you understand, it's possible that we have no cause to doubt Herr Balthasar. But the leaders of the knighthood still need to know – at least in general – what is being written about Livonia for the world to read. All the more so, since we are not aware that Herr Balthasar has requested permission of any official authority for his work. We believe that you are not mistaken in the matter of the chronicle. But belief is merely resolute hope, as is written in Doctor Luther's catechism. We, however, need certainty. And furthermore, this will be of no less benefit to Herr Russow than to us. So, let us empty our goblets to that!'"

"Yes . . . I understand entirely . . ." Mihkel said earnestly. And sipping his wine, he thought: What he means is that they don't want to ask Herr Balthasar themselves. He could let them see it, and why not . . . ? But as far as I know him, he might also tell them to go to the Devil. And since I will be reading the chronicle with his permission and at his request, why shouldn't I be the one to tell them that it is an impressive and factual work? Actually, it is my duty in a case such as this! And if these gentlemen do not wish me to inform Herr Balthasar of this, so be it. No doubt they have their reasons – prominent, venerable gentlemen that they are. And in addition, they are to some extent in control of my future . . .

As if completing Mihkel's thoughts, Herr Maidel asked:

"By the way, if we succeed in creating a position for another deacon at the Royal Garrison Church here in Tallinn – I assume that that would be acceptable as a start . . . ?"

"Good Lord . . . Would it be *acceptable* . . . ?" Mihkel even sprang to his feet – as he had for the oath, and began:

"My superiors and benefactors . . . I do not know what I have done to earn such good fortune—"

"Actually you have not yet earned it," Herr Maidel said drily, "but I believe you will manage to do so."

That night, Mihkel Slahter was kneeling on the stone steps of a stairway in a place he did not recognise. At one moment, it seemed to him that he was under the soaring grey arches of the Notre Dame Church in Rostock and that what he heard above him were the quiet, high strains of organ music. And then it seemed that he was under a low grey sky, kneeling at the foot of a steep and unfamiliar hill, possibly even Lühike Jalg Street leading up to Toompea, on the corner of Rataskaevu Street, but there were no real stairs there. And what he had thought was organ music was actually a flock of jackdaws, or perhaps the autumn wind. Standing above him on the stairs stood a woman, her back to him. He could not tell whether it was Magdalena, the daughter of Rostock Professor Chytreus, a girl with splendid dark locks, whom he had been pining after for several years. Or Marta, a girl from a tavern behind Munkade Gate in the same town, in whose embrace he had sought sinful consolation for the loneliness of body and soul – either Magdalena or Marta, one or the other – but he knew something about this woman, and he stretched out his hand and wanted to say it, but suddenly he could not remember what it was . . . And then the woman on the stairs turned around and he saw that it was Elsbet Russow. And Mihkel realised that he had known this all along, and wanted to say – Elsbet Russow, Elsbet Gandersen – the little girl from Rataskaevu Street – quiet, dark-haired, proud and elusive, who had nonetheless joined the boys in snowball fights, squealing with delight at the height of battle . . . now grown and blooming like an olive branch – blooming and scattering her petals . . . as . . . as it says . . . where? . . . as it says in . . . perhaps in the Book of Job . . . ? Mihkel took Elsbet's hand and raised it to his lips, his mouth moving along each finger, her index finger, her middle finger, towards the ring finger, and he felt, Oh Lord God, his lips graze her wedding band, and the shock of it made his body break out in a sweat. Over the back of her hand to the wrist, his lips now kissing her arm, moving ever upward. And he was thinking: Oh God, this is how I want to arrive, always, always like this, and this is how I will at last arrive . . . He woke up on his low plank bed in the guest room of the Tisenhusen house, a snowstorm behind his icy window whooshing over the rooftops on Toompea Hill . . .

He awoke in a sweat, alarmed and euphoric, and lay in the dark, listening to the wind. Lord, I thank You that You have arranged it all so well that I may do the bidding of the high-born gentlemen and at the same time fulfil my obligations to Herr Balthasar (these grandees refer to him as "that Russow" and not with affection, it seems). And as far as his wife, as far as Elsbet is concerned – Lord, it is more wonderful than a wonder . . . the way her name has become fragrant and sweet and strong in me like the Christmas mead of my childhood – can it be anything other than Your will, O Lord?

CHAPTER EIGHT,

in which we continue along the rough terrain of one man's life and character, arriving at a barren limestone landscape where boulders and large stone slabs – grey and black and rust-streaked – have rumbled down and suddenly rise up on the path in such high heaps that one could easily break a leg, and it seems that not even the tiniest shoot could possibly sprout there. We arrive, incidentally, at an hour when not only are low clouds blanketing the ground with a fury of white hailstones, but cannonballs still trailing smoke are crashing down upon the gravelly ground – and yet, we find a little sprout of a healing herb, unaware of itself, growing in a rocky crevice and see that its roots have managed to split the stone slab. Still, we hesitate, uncertain whether to clap our hands in amazement and exclaim: Lord, what a miraculous plant! Or to heave a sigh and lament: Heavens, what a dreadful time and desolate land . . .

So, six years already. Six and a half. Soon, God willing, a full seven . . .

The subject had come up three days earlier, on St Anthony's Day,* in the course of conversation at the wedding of Arent Schulz, a scribe at the Treasury. The wedding was held in haste, lest the arrival of the advancing Muscovite at the town walls require that it be postponed. Furthermore, the occasion offered an opportunity to underscore and affirm the efforts of the townspeople towards realising a sense of their common bond as Christians (a bribe offered to God in the face of trials certain to come). The very fact that the Great Guild was made available for the wedding of a simple Town Hall clerk served the same purpose

* January 17.

as the appearance of several councilmen as wedding guests, including Wangersen, Wilber, Schröder, and so on. It demonstrated that "all of us" – from patricians to simple craftsmen to mercenary ensigns – were but one family in the sight of God, as well as in the line of fire from Muscovite cannons. At the banquet table, old Wilber, his pendulous cheeks trembling, had proclaimed after his third goblet of wine, that once a wedding mill was successfully set in motion, it generally ran for the first six years without a problem. If it was destined to get clogged, that would usually not happen until the seventh year . . . But the talk had then veered to more painful topics – to a situation that would render the town especially vulnerable upon the arrival of the Muscovite: it was now known that two traitors, two manormen named Muntzard and Kock, had gone over to the Muscovite a few weeks earlier and disclosed the strengths and weaknesses of Tallinn's defences . . .

This morning at breakfast, Balthasar recalled old Wilber's remarks about the seventh year of marriage. Old Wilber, though bow-legged and tending to drool a bit, possessed years of accumulated wisdom. It was but seven o'clock, the light still dim, and candles burned on the long table in the great-room, where Balthasar was having his breakfast of oatmeal fried in bacon fat, and washing it down with ale. He was reviewing his schedule for the day: he would finish reading Eucaedius up in his study by nine o'clock. At nine, there would be the christening in the sacristy of the twin girls of Kulli Toomas (who lived in the monastery courtyard). At ten, Mihkel would arrive with his copies of the new chapters. At about two, he would visit Topff, and so on . . . Surveying his family and other members of his household, studying them over his juniper-wood tankard and large tin spoon, he mused on Wilber's comment. He himself, at the head of the table; the hearth of the great hooded fireplace behind his back; to his left, Märten, Päärn, the son of Traani-Andres, Epp, and little Balzer; to his right, Jakob, Aunt Kati and that youth Tiidrik. And then his own little girls, Elisabet and

Anna; and across from him, Elsbet. The table, scrubbed white, was like a long axle, or a capstan, or the shaft of a mill-wheel, extending from him to Elsbet and from her to him, around which the life of their household had been revolving for nearly seven years. There was Märten, with his sharp chin and sparse, pale beard – his proud, taciturn old friend, whose pointed remarks he had to tolerate because Märten was part of himself. And Päärn, with his genial, broad face and russet beard, always humming a tune, a bit slow for his duties as sexton but ever ready to set out with his long stride when there was an errand to be run. And there was Epp (who had now been living here, under Balthasar's roof, for half a year or longer, ever since Kurgla was burned down last spring). Heavens, Epp would soon be forty, and that was no longer young for a widow and peasant woman, but still, next to others of her age at the table, she seemed least affected by the passage of years. Her small compact face still had a rosy glow, though perhaps reddened a bit by the chill autumn air, and her eyes were still a clear blue . . . And then Balzer, *Balthasarius minissimus,*[*] a little rascal, a pug-nosed little lad almost four years old, wearing a funny, sparrow-grey woollen jacket that Elsbet had knitted for him. On Elsbet's left, the twins, Anna and Elisabet, just turned five last week, a bit anaemic, a little sickly with colds, but generally loveable little creatures. And that Tiidrik there, who did not really belong to this household, the tall, lanky son of Epp and her late husband Paavel, already twenty years old. Truth be told, he had an unusually straight back and good head for a peasant boy and was even a little taller than Balthasar. He knew how to read, and to write with a quill, no less, and had been working until recently as assistant to the storehouse keeper at Raasiku manor. He had now joined Ivo Schenkenberg and his men. He was being trained along with Ivo's band of partisans, in the arts of defending the town. Next to him, Aunt Kati and Uncle Jakob, also here since Kurgla burned down, both in their

* Little Balthasar (Latin).

316

worn church clothes ("for 'twouldn't do to appear 'mong fine folk in our old country rags"), both somewhat wizened now, yet still quite vigorous. Uncle Jakob had been seated, despite burgher custom, on Balthasar's right – no doubt in memory of Siimon, and as compensation for something, and to bribe someone, of course . . . Across from Balthasar sat Elsbet. Behind her, the window of the great-room, patches of snow stuck to its tiny panes and the lower panes buried in it, with nothing but darkness, darkness, darkness behind them. The upper panes were a row of dim, pale-grey circles of pre-dawn light. Elsbet, wiping the children's noses; Elsbet, asking Epp to bring the rest of the porridge to the table; Elsbet, announcing with regret and satisfaction that they had finished the cracklings for that morning; Elsbet, sending Päärn to the pantry with empty pitchers for more ale; Elsbet, in the uncertain, flickering candlelight. Heavens, seven years! In Balthasar's coarse, red-brown beard the fragrance of Elsbet's warm, thyme-scented body lingered still from their pre-dawn moments of intimacy. Except at such moments, of course, two people were never wholly one. And yet, for seven years, Balthasar's life with Elsbet had been utterly serene. If anything had cast a shadow over their lives (other than the enormous black clouds of war and plague and want, which the Lord had sent and continued to hold over them and half the world), it was just one thing, and it was something very, very small. It came up infrequently and was of no importance. So infrequently, that Balthasar had not taken the trouble to keep count . . . The one thing was this: in the opinion of his father-in-law and of the entire Gandersen clan and their social circles, both near and far – in the opinion of the entire German citizenry of Tallinn, in fact – he was not the man who should by rights have been at Elsbet's side . . . Certainly not. Despite his honourable and respected position and, well, in spite of his serious, resolute demeanour – for one had to admit, there was nothing wrong with him. And yet . . . he did not come from where he should have: that is, from a respectable house – even if poor and rundown but at least a German house! Instead, he hailed from a dung heap, from a race of slaves who could be traded for hunting dogs and farm animals. (There were many in town who had said such things behind his back, and their words had reached his ears.) Never mind that he had arrived at his position by way of Tallinn and Bremen and Wittenberg. One might easily forget where his roots were – if only he made the least effort to conceal them! If only he did not – for God's sake – almost flaunt them . . . But what the devil was he supposed to do, eh?! Lock the door of the parsonage to Aunt Kati and Uncle Jakob and Epp, ah?! Leave them to fend for themselves? Not let them be his concern? Or perhaps he should have sent them (since he had taken them in without due reflection) across the yard, to live in the front room of the sauna, with nothing but soured oatmeal to eat? But no, Elsbet had never made any such suggestion. Nor had she in any way intimated such a thing. Not even by alluding to townspeople who had behaved in such ways themselves, and there were several who could have been named . . . people like the baker, Leveken, who had instructed his journeymen to turn away his great-uncle along with his entire family when they arrived at his doorstep after fleeing their farm in Jõelahtme: Let him be off, that dried-up old bumpkin, and he'd better not go spreading his idiotic stories around . . . claiming that Leveken was . . . what was it? . . . his brother's grandson . . . No, no, Elsbet had not so much as given Balthasar a quizzical look when he seated his Kurgla relatives at the table. But then, he was not certain whether she would have objected if, to test his wife, he had had them relegated to the sauna room . . . For in this matter, tiny, unforesee-able warts had in fact appeared on the otherwise smooth surface of their mutual understanding . . . Take, for example, the day before yesterday, when Mihkel stopped by, as the bells for vespers were ringing.

Mihkel entered the great-room with his energetic, youthful stride, his cheeks red and wet snow on his lashes. He shook the snow off his earflap hat and stepped forward, extending his hand to the lady of the house:

"Good evening, dear Frau Elsbet! What a pleasure to come into the warmth of your home from the icy teeth of this winter storm." He then turned from Elsbet, at the hearth, towards Balthasar, seated next to the stairway:

"Good evening, Herr Balthasar. What a winter the good Lord has sent us this year!"

At that moment little Balzer, the little beetle, *Balthasarius minissimus*, came tottering over to Mihkel, stopping directly in his path:

"Unca, did you bwing me tweets today?"

"Now . . . what do you think? Of course I did!" Mihkel dug around in his coat pocket and held out the golden, spicy sweets, wrapped in a piece of cloth.

"Well now, give Uncle a hand-pat!" Balthasar said.

The little boy looked around for a place to put down his sweets, wrapped them up again in the cloth, and took the twisted ends in his teeth. With evident delight he patted the palms of his hands against Mihkel's – *pat-pat-pat* – thanking the friendly, smiling "uncle", and then added a few more pats for good measure.

"But Balzer," Elsbet said, standing at the hearth, watching Epp stir a pot of hops. "Haven't I told you," she said, in a voice gentle and motherly and all the more disapproving because of its gentleness, "that it isn't proper to give hand-pats like that to anyone but your father? And only when you're alone!"

"And Unca Jakob, too!" cried Balzer.

"And to Uncle Jakob," his mother agreed.

"And Auntie Kati, too," Balzer said.

"Auntie Kati too."

"And Epp."

"Her too. But not to anyone else. Remember that."

"And not to the *köster*? Or his wife?"

"No-no-no!"

"But to Märten . . . it's alwight?"

"That's enough. Go and ride your wooden horse now."

Sucking a sweet, Balzer ran off to the passageway behind the hearth, where, under its vaulted ceiling, he would mount his wooden horse and enact knights' tournaments and the exciting travels of merchants and their journeymen. Sometimes he would groan under the weight of the heavy cargo he had to heave onto his wagon, and shout to his team in a gruff voice, and work so hard and with such zeal at helping to free wagon wheels from the ruts of a muddy road that he would forget to breathe – the way his father had helped Balzer's grandfather when he was a boy. And once, he had been surrounded for several hours by wolves on the three stone steps leading to the pantry. Just like Uncle Tiidrik, who, two years ago in early winter, had been surrounded by a pack of wolves in the woods between Kurgla and Raasiku and escaped only because he managed to race to a giant sacrificial boulder, over five cubits high, and scrambled to the top of it. There Tiidrik had had to wait, staring at the green eyes of two dozen wolves as they growled and whined and pawed at the boulder, until Uncle Jakob, with other villagers and dogs, found him, having followed his tracks in the snow . . .

Balthasar and Mihkel went up the stairs of the great-room and into Balthasar's study, where he pushed a three-legged stool towards Mihkel and sat on another. Glancing at Mihkel from the corner of his eye, as he took the man's measure, and smiling a little with the corner of his mouth, as he simulated an apology, Balthasar said:

"I was of the opinion that it was quite proper for Balzer to give you hand-pats. Since you are, in point of fact, a peasant as well."

". . . Who told you that?"

Mihkel's question came after such a long pause that Balthasar had begun to think he would not respond at all. But his tone of voice, though exceedingly polite, conveyed his intention to contradict Balthasar.

"Your own father."

"On what occasion?" Mihkel asked, as though he did not quite believe Balthasar. Balthasar realised that Mihkel was planning to explain away his father's words as a jest of some kind.

"On his deathbed," said Balthasar.

But no, to this Mihkel offered no argument. Nor did he try to explain it away as a jest. He was silent. He crossed his right leg over his left and drew circles on his right knee, and said, smiling:

"Didn't the Apostle say there is no difference between a Jew and a Greek . . . ? And what does it matter to us, anyway, since we've got Wittenberg and Rostock in our past?"

"But as it turns out, it does matter," Balthasar said slowly, with a wry smile. And as a perceptive observer would have noted, there was in his response both an insistence on the truth and a touch of smug provocation. "As it turns out, it does . . . Or why else would some Jews want so very much to be Greeks . . . ?!"

"Who, for example . . . ?"

"There are many . . . Old Maidel, for example. His forebears all come from pure peasant stock. But just try to tell that to Admiral Maidel . . . At the same time, he considers the question of his family background a point of honour, to the extent that he constantly lectures his sons about it. (I hear a thing or two about what goes on in that house.) There are several generations of Germans on their mother's side, of course. And yet, they're all descended from Ville, a butcher from Luts Street. *Ha-ha-ha-ha*. But in front of his sons, the admiral simply glosses over these humble origins with a lie, claiming that the Maidels are from Westphalia. If the bastards at least had a German name, like yours or mine! But you can see on their coat of arms what kind of men they are: three little gudgeons, or baby *maidel*s, in a row."

As Mihkel did not respond, Balthasar took the most recent chapters of his chronicle from his wall-cupboard.

"Well then, copy these into the book here," handing him the quarto volume, "while I hold the evening service . . ."

That was the day before yesterday. And the same today. The only difference being that today Balthasar had not gone to church to preside at a service, but to Herr Topff's place to hear the latest Council news. On the way, as he manoeuvred around and over snowdrifts in the cemetery and along Saiakang Way and across Town Hall Square, he was deep in thought:

What, he wondered, was the state of his and Elsbet's "marriage mill" – after turning now for nearly seven years – in light of old Wilber's remarks on St Anthony's Day? By God, there was no sign that the works were becoming clogged or stuck . . . if one might pursue the metaphor, there was no less water now in the pools under the dam – no less water to turn the millstones – than at the beginning . . . True, once in a while Elsbet looked a little weary, her expression somewhat wooden and strained, what with overseeing noisy children and household tasks and tending to sick and destitute members of the parish every day, as well as managing with a shortage of money, which did indeed affect the Pastor's family at a time like this, with prices shamelessly high and his income wretchedly low . . . A somewhat wooden expression . . . But then Balthasar himself had occasionally been more stern and severe than he meant to be. He had, at times, briefly compared his wife with others and with past sinful pleasures . . . and even, in a moment of pique, found that Katharina (God, forgive him!) was more skilled in certain ways, and her unforgettable, spicy carnation scent, more enticing . . . Also, at certain odd, early-morning moments, as he hovered between sleep and wakefulness – more asleep than awake – it perhaps occurred to Bal that though he had been but a boy, impatient and heedless, and though his memories of the blazing fire and the smells of that distant morning in Lammassaare were fleeting and fragmentary, what had happened there was so extraordinary that nothing would ever compare with it, that the touch of Epp's burning cheek and the taste of birch-brew and the smell of the earth under Epp's head and the fragrance of the "keys-of-heaven" in her hair – all of it belonged to another, and a better, world ...

Herr Topff had no news of particular import to convey, nothing but ever more heated accounts of the imminent arrival of the Muscovite. And tales of the Muscovite amassing forces at Rakvere had been heard so often that the news no longer jolted people, although hearing these stories again from the latest sources did not, of course, allay the anxiety they had already engendered.

Mihkel had been working in Balthasar's study until midday, and after dinner (bean broth with salted-pork cracklings) he brought his work downstairs. They sat in front of the hearth – Elsbet with a ball of yarn and knitting needles and half-finished socks for the girls, and Balthasar leafing with pleasure through the pages of his manuscript, which Mihkel had just completed copying in his fine calligraphy.

"Well, well, all eight chapters. So, what do you think of them?"

Out of his pocket Balthasar took a carrot that Epp had brought up from the box of sand in the cellar and rinsed for him. He was eager to bite into it, to savour the fresh, juicy, earthy taste, but he postponed the pleasure to listen to Mihkel's response.

"They're wonderfully fluent!" Mihkel said, his blue eyes glowing with admiration as he looked at Balthasar. It was impossible to interpret his enthusiasm as anything but thoroughly sincere, even though Balthasar was generally wary of praise.

"Wonderfully fluent," Mihkel repeated. "And there is nothing whatsoever questionable in it, not in the least. In my opinion."

Balthasar was about to bite into the carrot, but now he took it out it of his mouth:

"And in whose opinion might there be something questionable?"

323

Mihkel looked down at the table and then directly at Balthasar:

"Well, who knows what some might think? You yourself can't assume that everyone who reads it will agree with every last word . . . Even in my opinion . . ."

"Even in your opinion . . . ?"

"There are some things, perhaps, that could be said . . . well . . . more prudently."

Balthasar noticed that Mihkel looked to Elsbet, as if for help, and that Elsbet looked up from her knitting and nodded.

"Don't misunderstand me, Herr Balthasar," Mihkel said. "I merely think that . . . in a word . . . there'd be an outcry about any serious work of history. That's unavoidable. But we can foresee and perhaps prevent an unnecessarily large outcry – without compromising the truth . . ."

"*Hmm* . . ."

Balthasar wanted to say: My dear boy, it is not my goal to cause an uproar. But I am not going to worry too much if it does occur (and, as you say, it will occur in any case). Let me tell you what I do want. I want to go to the furthest possible limit with this thing . . . to take it to the furthest limit that the world will tolerate before it breaks my neck. I can well imagine that the loudest outcry about my picture of old Livonia will come from the nobility. For that picture includes the fathers of our current masters. And even the current masters themselves. For if anything in their manner of living has improved, it is not because they have become more virtuous, but because they have become less prosperous. Our spiritual masters will also kick up a furore. For it will be clear to everyone that what I say about the festering ulcers of the Catholic era applies to the ulcers in our own time as well, wherever they are to be found. Not to mention the ire that will be aroused by my remarks about our Lutheran pastors. The manor lords will howl because I dare to call their swinish deeds by name, and because here and there I speak of the peasants as human beings. I know too that my acknowledgement of the town Greys will not be at all to the liking of the patricians. Nor the fact that I sing insufficient "hosannas" to the wisdom of the Town Council. And finally, they might all curse me together (grudge-bearers seem to find it easy to join forces) – the nobility, the town and even the peasants, right behind them – because I rebuke them all too severely *in moribus.** Ha-ha-ha-ha!* In the first place, I do it with complete conviction. That is an absolute necessity. If one believes at all in people's ability to change for the better. And in the second place, there is a certain subtlety in my scolding. For in the name of Christian ideals it is possible to speak out about many things that in another context would create considerable ill-will. One who complains or makes light of the demands of God's Kingdom is forgiven. But just try to say something about an earthly kingdom . . . Its king will not be appeased no matter how high your praise, and all the rest will snarl at your heels and sink their teeth into your calves . . . Ooh . . . As if I haven't thought enough about all of this . . . But to set out and then to turn back before reaching that final destination – why, that would be like doing my business and then not managing to pull my trousers back up . . . Naturally, in determining exactly where that boundary lies, every man can rely only on his own life experience. But to me it seems that, first of all . . .

"*Mmmm.*"

Balthasar did not say a word. He bit into the carrot, breaking off at least a third of it and, crunching on it loudly, asked:

"Elsbet, does it seem to you, too, that some things should be more prudently worded?"

"I've only read a few parts of it," Elsbet said very quietly, "and how much do I know about these things anyway? But since you ask – yes, Balthasar, it does."

"*Mmmm.*" He turned again to Mihkel:

* About mores, customs, habits (Latin).

"But you don't think there's anything dubious in it?"

Someone who knew Balthasar (Elsbet, for example) would not have ventured to take the question entirely seriously, suspecting a bit of mockery in it perhaps . . . ? But Mihkel replied in all earnestness:

"No, not at all. Nothing at all dubious."

"*Mmmm.* Then what do you mean by dubious? If, in fact, you do think that it's offensively blunt?"

The ball of yarn slipped off Elsbet's lap and rolled past the men's feet. When Mihkel sprang to pick it up, Balthasar thought: See now, that's how a well-brought-up young man reacts! Or is he just stalling for time before answering? And suddenly Balthsar realised with surprise that his thought was accompanied by a certain dislike. The idea of picking up the ball of yarn himself came to him so late that his tardy response brought a brief, self-deprecating smile to his lips, and he acknowledged to himself that Elsbet would have every right to consider him a boor . . . and that at such a stupid moment as this, she probably did think him boorish . . . But Balthasar's smile left the impression that he was smirking at Mihkel's ready response:

"I'm referring to arousing suspicion in the matter of the Augsburg Confession and the *Formula concordiae*. Especially in view of the most recent edition from Torgau."

"Wait, wait, wait," said Balthasar, still smiling, his expression unchanged. "I'm not writing a dogmatic treatise here, so what I've written cannot arouse suspicion concerning *those matters*. To tell you the truth . . ." (his expression was becoming more serious now, but a faint smile continued to hover behind the first words) ". . . when I think of my own position with respect to the quarrels between the followers of Melanchthon and Flacius, I have been unable, for some time, to determine where the truth lies. By God. In Stettin we were told that Melanchthon defended free will. And that was right, in my view. But now, the Melanchthonites have joined with the Calvinists and are sunk up to their ears in the bog of predestination. Ever since Wittenberg and Magdeburg, I've had an unfavourable impression of Flacius – a most disagreeable man and an empty-headed prattler. That's the truth. And noisy – like a clacker attached to Luther's shadow. But now, most of Protestant Germany is of a mind with him. And I must say, some of Flacius' strictures are even to my liking, considering the needs of our church here in Livonia. But I am still caught between two great warring camps, just like Buridan's ass. And in my asinine confusion I've begun – you know what? – to consider all those to be asses who bray the words of their *Formula*s and *Concordia*s. And I do not trust what they say any more – not one whit."

Balthasar saw Mihkel's expression alternate awkwardly between amusement and alarm, but he was not concerned about the young man's bewilderment and in one rush pursued his train of thought to its conclusion: "I do not believe anything anymore but Holy Writ, as I myself understand it – and my own conscience. And you know, when it comes to the matter of *bona opera*,* I lean towards the Catholics. Really. For Amsdorf, in my opinion, is talking nonsense when he claims that *bona opera* are actually a bad thing. No! Good works are necessary, both for those who perform them and those who benefit from them. Not, of course, deeds that are performed for the sake of foul indulgences. But those that are truly and clearly of benefit to people. And *inter alia*,† I consider the writing of my chronicle, too, to be a good deed. There you have it. Now I have to go to Kalamaja to bless the shack that Peeter of Hobusepea has built at Hundimäe. He asked me to come when it was completed. And now at last, it is. Though I'm afraid that he'll be ordered to tear it down tomorrow on account of fear of the Muscovite." Balthasar was at the door, already getting into his old calfskin coat. "And I think that if all goes well with this

* Good works (Latin).
† Incidentally; among other things (Latin).

blessing, it too could be considered a *bonum opus* – even if the cabin is torn down."

Märten was already waiting on the stoop, the pastor's chest on a strap over his shoulder. Adjusting his coat, Balthasar walked quickly towards Elsbet, managing to get his hand through the reddish-brown cuff of his sleeve. He turned his wife's face to him, and with two fingers tapped her cheek, her forehead, the other cheek – in such a way that it was not at all clear what it meant – whether those taps were playful little slaps or caresses – or a casually made and only vaguely identifiable shape of the cross.

An imaginative observer might indeed have seen the taps as indicating a cross. As for Elsbet, she would readily have interpreted her husband's touch, had it occurred in private, as a gesture of affection. A kind of simple, slightly awkward playfulness, which would perhaps have annoyed her a little but also pleased her in the bedroom . . . Annoyed because of its lack of finesse, and pleased because of its sincerity. But here in the great-room, in the presence of this stranger, this well-brought-up young man (a childhood neighbour, no less!), it was out of place and irritating and even a little condescending . . . But of course Balthasar would not understand that . . .

Balthasar and Märten had left. Their hurried footfalls squeaking on the snow had faded as they rounded the corner of the church. The fire flared on the hearth and, over the roar of the flames, from the passageway behind the kitchen, little Balzer's voice rose in playful shouts:

"Gid-yup! Gid-yup! You dam' nag! The sweigh go in the dwift again!"

*"Balzer! Lat dock dat dumme spel!"**

Elsbet realised that her voice was more shrill than she wanted it to be in Mihkel's presence. But this was yet again the silly wagon-driver

* Stop playing that silly game! (Middle Low German).

game that was like a thorn in her heart. In spite of all the ways in which she tried to reassure herself, it seemed like a curse that her little Balzer always reverted to the game of playing his peasant grandfather – whom he had never even seen, whom even Elsbet had never seen (and who might be best forgotten!). But Balthasar had obviously told the boy more than he needed to know about the old man's hardened hands and crude humour, and about his life as a wagoner . . . And who knows . . . perhaps Balzer was in fact playing his father more than his grandfather. For his father had been by the grandfather's side as a young boy and had lived the life of a wagoner's son among the farm-hands . . . And now, because they had had to flee to town, Balthasar's country relatives were here in their house, and thus the whole legacy of Balthasar's peasant roots had made its way into their daily lives. And the alien smell – of smoky peasant huts and of horses and of the soil and granary bins – a smell for which, in Balthasar's case, Elsbet had at one time developed an affection (and later had no longer noticed it), and which now seemed to be exuding from the very walls of their house . . . Elsbet had wanted, from time to time, to talk to someone about it . . . But to whom? Birgit, the tanner's daughter from Pikk Street, a chatterer to be sure, but still her bosom friend from childhood and even into her first years of womanhood – Birgit was far away. Two years ago she had married a Swedish lieutenant and moved to Stockholm. Elsbet's sister Agnes? . . . Oh no! Living alongside that violent, heartless Godert, her married life, to tell the truth, was unhappy, but in recent years they had presented a façade of civility to the outside world. And in her unhappiness, as a kind of shield in defence of her dignity and worth, Agnes had held up, in a deplorable manner, the *pure Germanness* of her husband and family and household – especially to Elsbet . . . What about Father? Good Lord, no! Her father was the last person she would go to with worries about her husband's peasant background . . . Actually, it was not at all a need to complain that Elsbet felt from time to time. It was, rather, a desire to diminish certain doubts by talking about them. And – had there been a trusted soul close by – to seek advice as to how she might gradually learn to overcome those doubts.

"My dear Frau Elsbet, tell me, what is troubling you?"

Heavens . . . this . . . Mihkel . . . has posed a question to her as if she were made of glass, as if he could see right through her! Elsbet looks at him in stunned surprise and wants to avoid his glance, but she cannot turn away from his probing, light-blue eyes. For there is nothing at all untoward in those eyes, nothing but a serious, sympathetic query:

"I see that it is not only the general dread that weighs upon our whole town at this time. Is it a domestic worry? Do not be offended that I ask . . . we did grow up on the same street, after all—"

"Oh God . . . of course, it is partly the general worry, too . . ."

Elsbet looks at Mihkel's large, square hand resting on the edge of the bench. It is not an excessively large hand, nor covered with a growth of reddish hair. There are just a few fair hairs on this hand and a silver signet ring on the middle finger. She suddenly feels that if he were wearing a gold ring, it would be too showy and grand, and it would be off-putting, but she finds in this wide and simple but expensive silver ring, in a remarkable way, an affirmation of friendship and trustworthiness. Who knows why. Perhaps it reminds her of something of her mother's or her father's, seen in childhood, something she cannot even recall through the fog of the past – an affirmation of friendship and trustworthiness that God Himself has placed before her, and in response to which God Himself opens her heart, so that she suddenly surmounts her reticence and asks, somewhat startled at the sound of her own husky, agitated voice:

"Mihkel, you are – my friend, are you not? And Balthasar's friend?"

"Without question – Frau Elsbet – you are, in my opinion—" Mihkel cannot put into words just then what he wants to say, in spite of his facility with words, and he changes course. "And Herr Balthasar is – the most admirable man in this town . . ."

"Yes . . . but since you asked me what is troubling me . . . It is this: Balthasar is, after all – and there's nothing he can do about it – and I mention it only because he says it about himself – he is still – a non-German – he is a peasant . . ."

"Well, true – but Frau Elsbet—"

"No, no. That's how it is. The whole town knows it. And we have lived in this house a long time ago with Estonians. Märten and Traani-Andres and his family . . . And now our house is full of our peasant relatives from the countryside. You can see for yourself. There's more country-tongue spoken here than German . . . customs and foods and clothing and smells are entirely mixed up here . . . and if it continues much longer like this . . . if things go on like this, I'll be asking myself with some dismay: what will our children grow up to be – with respect to their customs and language? You heard how Balzer plays at being an Estonian wagoner. And yesterday, Anna and Elisabet came to me and asked me to bake them *rakatist*! When I asked them what that was, they said they wanted *lätakaid*! When I didn't understand them and was shocked because I thought they were asking for cow patties, they told me I was German and stupid – yes indeed. And that Epp or Auntie Kati would make *lätakaid* for them right away . . . Apparently they're some kind of peasant pancakes . . ."

"My dear Frau Elsbet," Mihkel says calmly, "permit me to say that you have no cause for worry. This wave of peasants in town and in your house will subside. Herr Balthasar is, of course . . . I understand. But believe me, in the end, school and life itself will make of your children such pure Germans that they will not have the slightest whiff of the countryside about them. And your home will influence them too. For how children turn out depends above all on their mother. On the mistress of the household. Elsbet, you are an intelligent woman – you should exert your influence more in this house, on the spirit of the house. And also . . . also with respect to Herr Balthasar. I'm thinking of his work . . ."

"In what sense . . . ?"

"So that the judgments he voices in some parts of his chronicle might be temperately expressed. The things we talked about. And that he be more respectful towards the *formulas* of the Church. It would be to his benefit."

"Oh, I don't understand anything about that . . ."

"But if you seek guidance from God. And from your own heart as well . . ."

Elsbet looks again into Mihkel's blue eyes. She sees reflected in them the white glow of the snowstorm beyond the windows and the red glow of the hearth. And the name of God, just spoken, hovers in the air and makes all words pure . . .

"And may I ask you, too . . . ? You will help me, Mihkel . . . ?"

"Always! At any time! With anything!"

With what astonishing ardour the young man speaks – as though taking an oath – this boy from Rataskaevu Street . . . And then he stands up. He grasps Elsbet's hand and presses it to his burning lips and his rough fair moustache, and he kisses it . . . Lord God . . . hard and long – as though he wanted in this way to keep from uttering something . . . Then he frees her hand and says hurriedly:

"But now I must go." He puts on his coat and is gone before Elsbet can think of a reply.

Elsbet would not have known, even by evening, how to respond to his unexpected ardour, nor whether she had found it unsettling or pleasing . . .

She looked at her sleeping children. She bent over their beds. She inhaled, one by one, the dense scent of her little nestlings' hair. She blew out the candle and went to bed to await Balthasar's return, thinking worriedly: perhaps he would in the end really bring misfortune upon himself and his household with the crude excesses of his unfortunate chronicle . . . ? The things he had said to Mihkel about viewing wise theologians as "asses" made her shudder in this chill room, between the cold sheets, under the thin, doghide blanket . . . But one thing was certain: Mihkel was ready to advise her and help her. ("Always! At any time! With anything!") Good or bad . . . What?! Only good, of course! . . . Only good . . . With protecting her children from the influence of their peasant relatives. With protecting Balthasar from his own – well, yes – his own coarseness . . . Elsbet, lying in the chill, dark bedchamber, burdened by the fears of the town as a whole as well as her own personal cares, was consoled by that thought, as though she had sipped some clove-spiced red wine that warmed her deep inside, even as her teeth were chattering with the cold.

When Balthasar left his study and climbed into bed beside Elsbet, she was fast asleep. He felt slightly guilty at arriving so late. He felt his wife's loose hair tickle his cheek. He passed his hand lightly over her cool back but did not try to awaken her. He stared into the darkness. The moon had to be somewhere beyond the snowstorm and clouds, for he could just make out the dim, bluish square of the frosted window. Its barely perceptible glow and the sound of the wind outside brought to mind his long-standing worries about the town out there in its restless, uneasy sleep, heading towards an unknowable fate. Perhaps Balthasar had dozed off. In any case, it seemed to him that he had just seen a snowy field teeming with stars – stars with tails, running and gliding over the snowdrifts, their tails trailing behind them – and, sitting up in the sky, an enormous, bluish wolf holding a blood-red moon in its left front paw, just like an emperor with his imperial ball, symbol of power . . . His mouth was dry and his body damp with sweat, as though he were hot. He set his bare feet on the stone floor and lit a candle. Pulling on a cloak, his let his eyes glide over Elsbet's dark mass of hair, and, candle in hand, left the bedchamber.

He went downstairs and through the great-room, towards the kitchen area in its northern part, and into the passage behind the hearth. Five paces from the steps leading to the pantry, he stopped. For he saw Epp there, rising onto her elbow from her straw mattress on a low rope-cot . . . Right . . . He had forgotten directing her to set up her bed there in the evenings. She removed it every morning, so that it would not obstruct the way to the pantry. As it did now – Balthasar had come to get something to quench his thirst.

"Oh . . . it's you," Balthasar said, looking into Epp's eyes glimmering in the candlelight. "Why aren't you asleep?"

Epp did not answer.

"Pour me a tankard of ale."

Epp slipped out from under the striped bedcovers. She was wearing a nightdress that reached halfway down her calves. Taking a juniper-wood tankard from a shelf above the hearth, she said, addressing him formally:

"If I may have the candle, Herr Pastor . . ."

Six months ago, when his people from Kurgla moved in with them and started calling him "Herr Pastor" and using the formal form of address, he asked them all to use the familiar "you". Admittedly, he had to overcome some resistance in himself, to convince himself that the spirit of Christian fairness and humility would permit nothing less. There was also the fact that Huhn, as everyone knew, had asked all his relatives from Vaskjala to use the familiar "you" in addressing him. But Harder, on the other hand, had forgotten both his mother-tongue and his heritage and had insisted that his brothers learn German, not so as to educate themselves, but in order that they not embarrass him, their pastor-brother – this Harder, nicknamed Mündrik, had always seemed to Balthasar to be crippled in some way . . .

334

"You're doing it again!" Balthasar said. What kind of a 'Herr' am I to you?"

"Fine, hand me the candle then," she replied, and taking the candle went as lightly and nimbly as a young girl up the three high stone steps to the pantry. Balthasar caught himself thinking: her calves – still as firm and shapely as ever – the same calves that had caught his eye on that dreamlike spring day long, long ago, in the farmyard at Kurgla . . .

She returned with the candle and the foaming tankard of ale and stopped in front of Balthasar. She was about to hand it to him, but suddenly said:

"Wait."

"What is it?"

"I'll pour it into something else."

"Into what?"

"Well . . . into something finer."

She was standing in front of Balthasar, holding the tankard and the candle. The candle was at chest level and she was looking up at Balthasar, her neck smooth and chin rosy by candlelight, her mouth – hard to tell – perhaps in a faint smile, a deep shadow on her cheek, eyes glimmering below the bright ridge of her eyebrows . . . And Balthasar recalled a distant, sweet and guilty moment. Perhaps for the duration of a heartbeat, he even expected Epp to blow out the candle, as Katharina had done that other time, on other stairs, facing a certain youth holding a pitcher of wine in each hand . . . But then he realised that Epp would of course not do that, nor would he blow out the candle flickering in the air stirred by their breath . . . He muttered:

"Stop . . ."

He folded his left hand over Epp's thick, fair braid at the nape of her neck, and took the tankard into his right hand:

"Do you want some ale?"

Epp did not answer, but it seemed to Balthasar that the braid he was holding moved a little at the slight nod of her head. He raised the old juniper-wood tankard to her lips, and felt some of the ale splash onto the stone floor near their feet. (Perhaps we should note that only God knows whether this happened entirely by accident. Which it is reasonable to assume. Since that is all we ought to assume. For it would be absurd to think that he spilt the ale intentionally . . . For in that case – Good Lord! – it would mean that he, a Christian shepherd of souls, poured a libation . . . to whom? – To Satan?! . . . No-no, why, would he do that? Not at all. It had to be to the guardian spirit of the house, to the earth-god – who had been forgotten, to be sure, but who existed nonetheless. For Balthasar had seen him – though it was long ago – with his own eyes. On the morning of the day when this very woman, this very girl, became his amidst the blooming keys-of-heaven on that small flowering knoll under the birches, by the blazing flames of the clearing. And none of it concerns life on this side of the town walls, none of it is a matter for the Council of Clergy or the Church or the Jehovah of the pulpits . . . Well, actually, it is a matter for Jehovah . . . As everything is . . . Granted . . . But . . . for a distant and indulgent Jehovah who forgives and thereby recognises the earth-god as one's heritage . . . at least in the case of those who have themselves seen the earth-god . . . No-no, not at all a matter for Jehovah . . . !)

"Drink!"

Epp swallowed a deep draught. Balthasar raised the tankard to his lips and drank. He paused, peering into the darkness over Epp's head (an observer might have concluded that he was imparting a secret, special significance to his first draught), and in two big gulps, emptied the vessel.

"Goodnight."

He let go of Epp's braid, took the candle from her, and walked away with a heavy, hurried tread, without looking back, his shadow bobbing along the walls of the great-room and up the stairs. Not until he reached the halfway mark – where the log ceiling and the huge hooded fireplace chimney had already come between himself and Epp – did he stop and think: Well, God did not strike me down for my libation to the earth-god (for that's what it was) . . . His lightning bolt did not strike me down into that puddle of ale . . .

Perhaps Balthasar escaped God's punishment because He had determined that the town as a whole would undergo a trial, though a few frivolous souls had already begun to harbour doubts about new ordeals.

On 22 January, 1577, at nine o'clock in the evening, as the bell of Holy Ghost Church boomed in the blowing snow, the market square below already teemed with people who had rushed there from all parts of town. Storm lanterns were coated with sticky snow and flaming torches flared in the wind.

Balthasar was standing on the steps of the Apothecary along with Märten, *köster* Meckius and apothecary Paduel with his journeyman, Suirke. At Märten's summons from the door of the church, Meckius had hurriedly grabbed a grey woollen blanket and thrown it over his head and shoulders and was peering out from under it like a frightened porcupine. Paduel, the former barber, now proprietor of the Apothecary, was wearing a fur coat, its high hood edged with wolf hide, as though he were planning to stand guard on his doorstep for half the night. Suirke was holding a lantern for his master and passing it from one hand to the other on account of the cold, for he had rushed outside without gloves . . . Soon they saw a militiaman running through the crowd towards them and disappearing around the corner of Saiakāng Way, delivering a message to the bell-ringer in the church, of course. A moment later the bell booming above them in the dark night fell silent. Päärn, son of Traani-Andres, had stopped ringing it. Just then several figures with lanterns appeared at the doors of the Town Hall across the square. Balthasar joined the crowd streaming in that direction. Pushing back anyone who came too close, a couple of men from the Town Hall were rolling two empty seal-oil barrels over the snow, towards the centre of the square, as Burgomasters Sandstede and Korbmacher, alongside the lantern bearers, kept pace with the barrels. They needed something to stand on to deliver the news to the townspeople – it would have been inappropriate to address them from the base of the scaffold. Two footstools were placed next to the barrels. Burgomaster Sandstede (who had already donned a helmet) bounded onto the barrel with the agility of an experienced soldier. Burgomaster Korbmacher had to be boosted up. Then Sandstede clapped his hands and the buzzing, questioning, anxious square fell silent. His voice rang out into the whirling snow and the smoke from burning torches.

"People of Tallinn. It is upon us . . ."

Everyone, of course, already knew what that meant. What they wanted to hear about were the details known to the Council and the instructions the burgomasters had for them.

Herr Sandstede took the lantern from a town official, who was holding it high in the air, and raised it close to his mouth, almost as though he expected the glow of the flame to magnify his voice.

"Fellow citizens! Brothers! The Muscovite arrived two hours ago, with a force of untold size, at the church at Jõelahtme and set up camp there. Tomorrow we can expect him at our walls, and he will direct his barking cannons at us. This should not cause us excessive anxiety, for we have lived through it before. But we must recognise the gravity of the situation, and we must be prudent. According to our messengers, the enemy is especially well-equipped with artillery this time. So, go home and clear out your attics. First of all, remove all inflammable items. Stock your attics with sand and water. Second, those of you that have gardens and sheds and huts outside the city walls, go out at dawn tomorrow and demolish everything – all buildings and fences. Anyone whose structures are still standing at noon tomorrow will be fined twenty marks. And all boards, posts and planks from the buildings must be hauled into town. We are already short of firewood in this cold season. None of this is anything new for us, of course. Third, all arms-bearing men of the town: sharpen your swords! And whosoever has armour lying about from '70, polish it up! Examine your bowstrings and firearms! And go to the Town Hall tomorrow and see Claus Holste to sign up with a company. In order that every man know his superiors and his duties."

The people in the crowded square wheezed and sighed and snuffled at all this, but so quietly that the blowing snow and crackling torches remained clearly audible above the murmur of the crowd.

From atop the second barrel, Herr Korbmacher then spoke of the need to be moderate in the consumption of food supplies. As he said, no-one could know just how long the Lord planned to test the town with this siege, even though the town, thanks to the foresight of the burgomasters and the Council, was particularly well supplied this time with salted meat and grain. Herr Korbmacher vowed, too, that the Council would keep an eye on the butchers, grain merchants and bakers, and would appeal to them to maintain their prices at Christian levels.

"Furthermore, my dear fellow Tallinners! Burghers! Brothers! In time of war it is wise to recognise that moderate fasting does not harm one's health, and it keeps swords sharp! And now, I wish for one and all a courageous heart, and may the Lord protect us from the enemy . . ." Instead of thinking seriously about the decisive days or weeks or even months to come, Balthasar was struck by a sudden impish thought: What a damnable irony it is, that it's the men with the biggest paunches who talk most about the benefits of fasting, and they're more in the right than those who are skin and bones.

Here and there, men more anxious or more brazen than the rest tossed questions to the burgomasters:

"But if we're to break down our barns and haul the lumber to town, where do we get horses for that? Will the town stables provide them?"

"But I have a house full of refugees – will flour be distributed to the larger households?"

"I have a stiff knee. Everyone knows that. How am I supposed to—?"

The burgomasters clapped their hands and replied that everything would be explained and taken care of at the proper time. But for now, they were all to go their separate ways and, with the help of God, uphold the honour of the citizens of Tallinn!

As the crowd dispersed that winter night, snow crunching underfoot, the creaking and banging of gates and doors spread apprehension and anxiety about war through the entire town. It was now certain, unavoidable: what people had long foreseen as inevitable was finally at hand.

And it was indeed at hand – after a week or two, with full fury: The first continuous bombardment of the town from thirty cannons spewing up to fifty-five-pound cannonballs. The first bombardment by exploding shells shot from mortars. The first outbreak of fires in town. Half the new Almshouse destroyed by fire. A cannonball shot through a window of St Nicholas' Church during services (by the miraculous will of God, wounding only one man in a church overflowing with worshippers . . .) In the meantime, city-wide shock at the plundering and ravaging of Pirita Convent. And then, early in February, daily skirmishes again and exchange of fire. Daily questions put to the captains and quartermasters and foot-soldiers. Every day, clambering up into the towers and walkways on the walls, to survey the scene from various vantage points. To get as clear a picture as possible, of course, of the state of the siege.

Outside the town walls, five enemy camps on the snow-covered fields: on Lasnamäe Hill, in the quarries, on the Sandhills, behind

Tõnismäe Hill and near the lime kiln. Around the camps, insect-like shapes moving about, out of range of cannon-fire from town and castle. Closer to town, defensive enemy emplacements: redoubts of gabions and block-houses of logs that seemed to rise like mushrooms from the ground by night, and had by the first light of day moved nearer town. Beyond the strongholds near Tõnismäe Hill and the River Mustjõe, troops of horsemen with conical helmets, armed with arquebuses or crossbows, shouting as they galloped back and forth. Across the wintry grey sky, flying fireballs like comets trailing smoke. Beneath snowflakes floating or drifting or whirling in a blinding blizzard, the constant back and forth of barking cannon: gunfire from town moving along its walls and ramparts and towers, fading at times, then resuming its yelping from tower to tower: from Paks Margareeta to Vanakuradi Vanaema to Pikk Hermann, and gunfire from the besiegers, moving along the fortifications from Härmapõllu to Toomkoppel . . . But inside the town walls – on squares, on streets, in front of churches – a more ordinary scene: the urgent comings and goings of daily life, continuing despite roaring cannons beyond the walls and whistling cannonballs overhead – people having become either brave, or careless, or just accustomed to it all. Townspeople hurrying along in brisk, measured steps, and, at particularly ominous rumblings from the cannons, pulling their heads down into the collars of their winter coats, or peering up at the sky, or keeping closer to the walls of buildings. Groups of armed burghers marching to their watchposts on the ramparts. Noisy, colourful mercenary guardsmen and their captains in plumed hats, swearing and rubbing their ears stinging from the cold . . . Look – a cart without wheels being carried down Karja Street and across Market Square and past the weigh house, with a man inside, bleeding. It is Kollon, a captain of the castle soldiers, wounded during an assault on the stronghold at Tõnismäe Hill. Those of his men who survived, about half in all, are following, dragging a captured fieldpiece. The cannon rolls along on wooden wheels, creaking in the cold as it bumps over mounds of frozen manure and rubbish. As the wounded captain sways on his stretcher, still thoroughly drunk and droning a tune, his life-blood trickling from him, the townspeople gasp at the sight as he is carried past them . . . Over there – guards, with drawn swords on either side of two captured boyars from Muscovy, prodding them from behind with the shafts of their halberds – the captives with icicles in their russet beards, wearing fur coats that no-one has yet had the opportunity to pull off their backs . . . And then, *shuffle-shuffle-shuffle*, making their way through the crowds, Hannibal's contingent of Greys, dragging their feet and hauling their fire rakes and hooks and buckets: "Hey! Look out! Make way for the fire brigade!"

Balthasar did not, of course, see all this for himself. But he heard a good deal at their table every day from Tiidrik, for the young man managed to join them for at least one meal most days – when he could find a little time, that is, between his urgent duties combating fires with Schenkenberg's company of peasants, who had been designated the town's firefighters. Tiidrik, as head of a group of four men, spent most days rushing in all directions across town with them, quenching flames from morning till night and often well into the night – from Hobuveski to Bolemann's sauna and from Karja to Nunna gates – extinguishing fireballs on the streets, hurling them down from attics when they crashed through roofs, smothering flames in the rafters or roof trusses or spaces above the ceilings where fires had started from burning sulphur and rosin.

Balthasar found his conversations with Tiidrik most interesting. For the young man described everything he saw and heard in town, not only with pleasure and enthusiasm, but with precision. And the sulphurous smells of the fires he had put out, and the stink of the wet cattle-skins he had used to smother them clung to him and to his tales. But Tiidrik had not yet participated in the sorties beyond the town walls that Ivo and his company had reportedly been aggressively mounting.

"Why not?"

Balthasar posed the question one unpleasantly cold morning in candle-month, having just returned from serving communion to wounded peasants at the Almshouse. He had hurriedly left the house that morning, without breakfast, and was now slurping down the flour broth Epp served him – broth that had become notably more watery than usual over the past several days. Tiidrik, just returned from his night watch, tired, his face sooty, was eating as well. At Balthasar's question he paused, tin spoon suspended for a moment, saying nothing, merely shrugging his right shoulder. Balthasar found the gesture irritatingly stubborn; at the same time, there was something familiar about it. A hot gust of recognition blew through him: it was his own self that he recognised. Himself as a young boy, and later, not so young, standing before any number of tedious superiors who did not understand him (an Antonius or a Balder or a Friesner or a Wolff), trying to sidestep their questions . . . Balthasar softened a bit at this recognition and then was doubly annoyed with himself. His tone was slightly reproachful, perhaps, as he asked:

"Are you one of those who's protecting his own skin?"

"No . . ."

"Then why haven't you picked up a sword in addition to your fire rakes and hooks? From what I've heard, Hannibal's men are quite adept with their swords."

"Because . . . I've been thinking . . ."

"About what?"

Tiidrik looked him straight in the eye with his very dark-grey eyes. There was a streak of soot across the light facial hair on his right cheek and his forehead was singed above the left eyebrow.

"What I've been wondering is whether the Commandment is now null and void . . ."

"What commandment?"

"You shall not kill."

So . . . this son of a farmhand, this son of flat-faced Paavel and unfortunately of Epp as well, this youth more than three cubits tall, who has learned to read and write, God knows where, and has become part of Balthasar's household on account of his mother, and who eats at this table day after day as the broth gets thinner and thinner (they were about to run out of flour in town) – with his question, the boy thrusts the very sword that he does not want to wield against the enemy in defence of the town – well, at least the shadow of that sword, transparent and so very sharp that one barely feels it – he thrusts it into Balthasar's bosom with his question and turns it, looking anxiously into his eyes . . .

Truly, is it not blasphemous – at this time, in this town where hour after hour God is implored to grant victory in battle – to invoke, with malicious glee, His Commandment against killing? Is it not? . . . Or do only very young men (by no means all, but some young men) dare ask such questions of themselves and of the world? Questions that Balthasar himself had asked twenty years before, on a hot day heavy with violet-grey fog, a day unforgettable for some reason, as he hurried through the not-yet-destroyed Rose Garden, towards the harbour: What about all the battles commanded by God in the Old Testament and all the slaughters blessed in recent times – what are they? An abyss between words and deeds, an abyss within words and deeds . . . Yes. And even some of those questioning young men seek to rein themselves in . . . As he himself had sought to do on that memorable day, staring out to sea from the wall of the Rose Garden. Alright, fine. So much for philosophising. It is pointless to try to philosophise everything to the end. For in the end it still comes down to one thing: kill or be killed.

Yes . . . And when these same young men mature a little, they will still reach – even if out of sheer curiosity – for the sword. Even if, because of their vaunting of the flesh, their hearts quail for a moment before God. And when they finally become grown men and citizens and fathers and civil servants – then, though their calling be to preach the Gospel – they no longer question the widening of the appalling chasm within themselves between life and the Word. Instead, they descend from the pulpit where they have intoned, in the name of Jesus Christ: "But I say unto you, love your enemies . . ." and go to their study and set down words on grey pages:

> And then there were musketeers and cannoneers upon all the
> rondels and towers and walls, shooting in concert at the enemy
> in a magnificent burst of gunfire and it was sheer delight to
> watch how they staggered across the snow and fell down dead . . .

And the man himself is not even aware of how the spring of his youthful scepticism has been overgrown by green algae (light-green, the colour of hope, the colour of his altar cloth – ever in the benighted hope that many behave even worse, and that forgiveness will, after all, be granted) . . . The man does not notice how sludge gradually clogs the wellspring . . . Until a youth like this one comes along, and with that sudden, impertinent shrug of his shoulder (and with a resemblance to his mother that Balthasar finds affecting) thrusts his question like a sword into the sludge of Balthasar's hopeful rationalisations, and brings its black depths to the surface . . .

"The work you're doing in firefighting is also valuable, of course, but doesn't it seem to you" – Balthasar's voice was so low that in mid-sentence he raised it, speaking louder than he had intended – "that refusing the sword or musket at this time smells of treason . . . ?"

Tiidrik's soup bowl was empty. He folded his hands briefly in prayer. Now he stood on the other side of the table and rested his large hands, singed and streaked, on the edge of the table:

"So – the Gospel teaches treason?"

Good Lord, how did this peasant boy come by his infernal logic? And the insolence to turn things on their head like this? (Or to speak the truth about them?!) . . .

"Tiidrik—"

"Herr Pastor, it would be good if you did not shout at me. Schenkenberg does it more than enough. I merely ask questions. And now I am asking you. Half of our company is going tonight to fight at Jaani Bridge. Do you think I should go along with them?"

Balthasar could almost hear the foreboding whisper in his ear: If this boy goes, he will be killed this night by an bolt from a crossbow. If that were to happen and he fell (as happened two nights ago, when eight of them fell, and last week, twenty-three), how could I face Epp? But Lord, of what importance is the death of one man when they are dying by the tens, by the hundreds? Thousands, if one counts the enemy – and why should they not be counted? They are people like us, after all. (*Ha-ha-haa* – As if we need to justify ourselves by acknowledging their humanity . . .) – Lord, it is not easy to answer this boy. Balthasar said:

"You were on watch all night. Go and rest. We'll talk in the evening."

Afterwards, it seemed to Balthasar that the knock came on the door of the great-room that very morning, right after their conversation. When he had called out "Come in!" and turned towards the door, it was Mihkel, who entered in a white cloud of frosty air, with a bag and a travel chest, putting them down right there on the floor, saying:

"May God bless this house. I have left the Tisenhusens up on the hill. Food is in short supply. Even in their house. It was embarrassing for me."

Whether the course of events was decided by the five hundred marks

(Mihkel's inheritance) that Balthasar still owed him, or by old Slahter's deathbed plea that Balthasar aid and support Mihkel, or by the spirit of Christian charity in general (most likely by all these combined) – there was no discussion about it. Balthasar said simply:

"Of course. You will live under my roof." God knows, perhaps someone with greater insight into human motives would have concluded that, to some extent, his conversation with Tiidrik influenced this decision – his impatience with Tiidrik's impertinence, and his own indecisiveness regarding the youth's question . . . For everyone wants to be patient and decisive. In any event, Balthasar added:

"My brother-in-law Godert – the baker Horstmann, you know him – has been selling us flour from his supplies. For a king's ransom, to be sure, but so be it. And Elsbet still has some peas and beans at the bottom of the barrel. And we get a little milk from our cow every day. And in general, there are so many of us in the house – think, nine people around the table – that one more will not even be noticed."

Balthasar called Elsbet away from the hearth:

"Come, welcome our guest. Mihkel will be staying with us."

They decided right then to lodge him in the second-storey room on the side of the house facing the Apothecary. Balthasar's small positiv organ was in that room, more an item of pride, or of promise, than of usefulness. He had not played it in a long time, even though he had thrown away a full hundred and fifty marks for it at a frivolous moment as a newlywed, in hopes of finding time to play it. But as for housing Mihkel in a room on the top floor of the house, it was nothing unusual. Until now there had only been a couple of instances of stone cannonballs breaking through a strong ceiling that was covered by a sod roof and limestone-slab insulation – and then only balls from the largest mortars. One could certainly hope that God would not permit such a thing to happen to the home of the pastor of Holy Ghost Church. Elsbet had concluded that, in spite of the bombing, even she and the children should continue to sleep on the upper storey. For she firmly believed, as she had during the months of plague, that if God chose them as targets for misfortune, they would be struck no matter what precautions they took. In any case, the bombardment from the great mortars had until now occurred only in daytime.

Balthasar asked Uncle Jakob to saw a set of supports for a plank bed and hammer together pine boards for the base. Up in the hayloft, Märten stuffed a burlap sack with chaff. Epp was instructed to take two heavy woollen blankets up to the organ room, where there was no source of heat. Finally, Elsbet, as mistress of the house, surveyed the room and was dusting the cover of the organ when Mihkel entered with his bag and chest, still wearing his fur coat. He put his things down on the floor.

"My dear Frau Elsbet! My heartfelt gratitude to you for taking me into your home at this difficult time. God will not forget such a deeply Christian act."

Elsbet stepped closer to the door, backing past Mihkel. She glanced at him fleetingly and murmured with an embarrassed smile:

"How could we have done otherwise? I hope you'll manage under our roof . . . even though this room is quite cold. Keep your door open – that way you'll get the warmth from the hearth down below . . ."

The chest that Mihkel had put on the floor blocked Elsbet's path. She had no recourse but to pass so close by him that, as she went out of the door, her hair brushed his face. At least he imagined that it did. A moment later, when she was already on the landing, he touched his face, stared at his palm in wonder and, still wearing his coat, dropped onto the organ bench, lost in thought. Elsbet had descended from the landing and was halfway down the stairs when she paused; she felt her body grow suddenly hot as she caught herself thinking in alarm: Ah, God will not forget this . . . Perhaps. I don't know. But is it not the Other One who will keep it even more firmly in mind . . . ?

The Other One would indeed have had cause to open his record books . . . or perhaps merely to raise an eyebrow and follow the course of events with interest, to see what happened next . . . Now that this girl and this boy, who had both once lived on Rataskaevu Street, had so neatly been brought together under one roof, this young woman of German stock and the young man of who-knows-what stock. She, with her fears for her children, her fears of peasant influence – present and palpable to her – threatening to coarsen them, make country bumpkins of them (and with her unacknowledged sense of guilt with regard to her father, for having given him an unsuitable son-in-law, and her half-conscious sense of guilt towards her husband, whom she made an effort to serve well with her body, but, God forgive her, from whom she was in her heart more distant than she ought to be). And he, this young German, with his fine education and refined manners and silver signet ring and readiness to advise her in matters good or bad (and the indescribable, sweet hollow between her heart and stomach, suspended between a longing for virtue and fear of sinning, between hope of eternal life and dread of Judgment Day) . . . And, at the same time, the master of the house was roaming about, heaven knows where – in the pulpit and the Almshouse sickbay, among those dying and those just born, at the Town Hall with Herr Sandstede, and up on Toompea with the Horns, father and son (both of them now serving the king as governors), or up on the town walls and towers that shook and rumbled as though in the throes of fever, from the cannon-balls fired from them and those fired at them . . .

On this afternoon there was a lull in the firing and Elsbet set out, for the first time in several weeks, to visit her family. Her father was not at home. She was not overly disappointed. She walked through the empty workshop (all three journeymen had been summoned to defend the town), and simply sat in her old room upstairs for half an hour. She stroked the coverlet on her childhood bed and looked at her reflection in a cracked, palm-sized mirror, which, because of the crack, she had decided not to take to her new home.

She stepped out onto the street and walked in the crunching snow towards Zeghen Tower, simply to smell the first intimations of spring – stirring and unsettling in the clear, now slightly milder, winter air.

Some of the passers-by greeted her. Possibly because they recognised her, possibly because of her attire. For, in spite of his cantankerous stinginess, old Gandersen had an open hand when it came to his daughter. He took special care that Elsbet not lack for furs (partly to uphold the reputation of his business, but perhaps also to rub his son-in-law's nose in it). Such good care that Elsbet was somewhat embarrassed by her ermine muff and otter coat, which were almost a sinful reminder – given the current deprivations and poverty and near-famine – of the former extravagances of peacetime.

After fewer than a hundred paces, Elsbet came to a standstill. In a small snowed-in square, its southern side walled by a row of miserably rundown shacks, a dozen children were loudly, noisily playing. A high snow fort had been built against a wall, and defending it were six or seven boys – grey, shapeless bundles of clothing (one might have been a girl). A similar army was about to attack. Their faces, pale after the long winter, glowed, their little noses were damp with excitement, and their eyes round as saucers. Some of them had thrown their mittens onto the snow, their hands now blue from the cold. The air was thick with shrill cries and snowballs crumbling in the dry, frosty atmosphere.

From the walls: "Give it to the Ivans – right in the face! Knock out the Tatars' teeth!" And from below: "Get out of town, Jenses! Shove the muck down their collars!"

Elsbet watched the children for a moment, feeling slightly ambivalent. The mother in her smiled disapprovingly: what else can children

350

to do but mirror their elders' foolishness? The young girl in her drew a deep breath of the spring-like winter air, longing for something nearly, but not entirely, forgotten . . .

"Frau Elsbet – do you remember—?"

Elsbet turned around, to encounter Mihkel's smiling eyes.

"Do you remember our snowball fights? The Order's forces were still in town at the time. You were seven, I was twelve. And your job was shaping the snowballs in our fort. Do you remember? And then Maijke took you home so your hands wouldn't freeze." He noticed Elsbet's bare hands. "Oh, aren't your hands cold now?" And he took them between his own. "Do you remember?"

"I remember," she said quietly and freed her hands, putting them into her ermine muff. Only then did it occur to her, surprising her, that the word which had come to mind as Mihkel held her hands in his was not "improper". She had not given a thought to propriety. "Ill-advised" was what she had said to herself as she thought about passers-by and windows . . .

Ill-advised is what Elsbeth thought of their walk home, as Mihkel animatedly recalled tales from their shared past on Rataskaevu Street and followed so close behind her that from time to time she could feel his breath on the back of her neck. But they were no longer on Rataskaevu Street. For Elsbet did not want to walk past her father's windows in Mihkel's company. Instead, they walked along Rüütli Street and then down Harju Street and back to the centre of town. At the corner of Luts Street, Mihkel recalled: "You know, at New Year's, my father used to send saffron raisin bread to Apothecary Dyck, and he would send us little marzipan sweets in return . . ." And at the corner of Kuninga Street: "Do you remember how your father and Maijke and Agnes and you would come to our home?". . . And between the pillory and the weigh house: "And I, stupid as I was, offered sweets only to your sister Agnes, for she was about my age, but you were only five, and ten-year-old boys have no idea of the kind of flower that a mere bud of a little girl can blossom into."

Elsbet did not seem to notice that she had steadily been quickening her pace, so that by the time they arrived at the marketplace, they were almost running towards Saiakang Way. An attentive bystander might well have wondered: what is she running from? Or perhaps: what is she rushing towards? The peculiar feeling that she was about to plunge into something inevitable and most likely something wicked had been with her since the snowball fight at the children's fort. But she had not managed to acknowledge it fully, for she felt the need to keep asking herself ever more insistently: what is there so very ill-advised in my walking through town in Mihkel's company – especially since Mihkel has been invited by Balthasar to live at our house, and since he just happened, like me, to be walking on the street where he'd lived as a child . . . ?

When Balthasar greeted them, it was apparent from his expression that something had happened. And although not happy, Elsbet was relieved – may God forgive her – at having been spared something worse, when Balthasar told them:

"Hannibal's provost just brought news of a death. Tiidrik, Epp's son, has fallen."

Yes. Tiidrik had decided, after all, to join Hannibal's men on their raid the night before last. He had not returned to discuss the matter with Balthasar, and Balthasar had forgotten to talk to him about it. Forgotten, because he had been summoned to a most important meeting that afternoon: the entire Council of Clergy had received orders to appear at the castle. And there, in the vicegerent's official chamber, festooned with Vasa coats of arms, the eleven shepherds of souls had listened to Herr Horn's instructive speech. The pastors were to admonish the townspeople: first, to reject the nonsensical talk about the enemy digging under the town walls and planting mines ready to explode at any moment, who knows where; and second, to counter rumours that the food supplies of both town and garrison had been sorely depleted. For even if the enemy could destroy every last ship trapped in the frozen harbour, that in itself would not be a calamity – the ships could not have delivered provisions to the town at this time anyway, and by the time the ice melted the enemy would be long gone. And finally, the pastors were to reassure their congregations that the vicegerent had been informed of unmistakable signs that the Muscovite was preparing to depart.

The pastor of St Olaf's Church, a man with tiny eyes and a face like a duck's, felt it incumbent upon himself to deliver a very brief, as he put it, "thank-you" speech to Herr Horn, conveying how very grateful the town was to him and his son for their care, and how very impressed it was with the two men's personal courage! And just how deeply concerned they all were that such high-ranking personages should repeatedly put themselves in harm's way on the walls of the town, even undertaking to aim the cannons with their very own hands! (It was bruited about that they had indeed done so.) And how very gratefully, as a result, the entire Town Council and Council of Clergy and citizenry of the town would take to heart Herr Vicegerent's words and carry out his directives without delay. *Et cetera*. The speech was three times as long as Herr Horn's. Balthasar had plenty of time to look around and note the others present: there was young Karl Henriksson, whom he had never before seen at such close range – with his oddly close-cropped round head and wispy reddish moustache. He seemed bright and lively enough, but already, at the age of twenty-five or -six, appeared to be growing a paunch. His father had hardly changed at all, except that his face and hair had both turned grey during the years that he was in disgrace. For just a moment, it seemed to Balthasar that the contours of old Herr Horn's countenance sagged a little, losing defini-tion – something he had on several occasions noticed in people who died soon thereafter . . . But Herr Horn, though over sixty, was as quick to act as ever, and simply cut off Pastor Schroeder in mid-speech when the latter paused for breath. Horn then thanked him for his words and dismissed the assembled pastors, shaking each one's hand and uttering a few appropriate words. When he came to Balthasar, he spoke loudly enough that at least some of those standing nearby no doubt overheard:

"But I know Herr Balthasar from long ago, longer than anyone else in this pastoral council."

The pastors, bundled in fur coats and hoods and earflap hats, followed the torch-bearers tasked with accompanying them through the snowbanks, towards Lühike Jalg Gate. Perhaps it was on account of Herr Horn's parting remarks, that Elard of St Michael's and Cothenius of St Olaf's and even portly Gerstenberger of St Nicholas' Church were so eager to tell Balthasar, as they plodded through the snow in the shadows behind the torch-bearers, just how splendid, how valiant, were the vicegerents in Tallinn, both the elder Herr Horn and the younger, in the service of His Majesty, the Swedish king . . .

Perhaps this conversation was in part the reason that Balthasar had forgotten to speak to Tiidrik that evening. Or the reason that he had decided to forget. Maybe he worried that his visit to the castle and all the talk of "the last successful effort in defence of the town" and of the courage of its defenders might nudge him to say to Tiidrik: Go! Why are you of so little faith, when both Herr Horn and his son and everyone else is so certain of both victory and forgiveness . . . ? Perhaps Balthasar realised then that if he spoke thus to Tiidrik and harm befell him, it would be all the more painful to bear. . .

For now too he felt a heaviness of heart he had not anticipated. He had of course pressed Epp's hand and made the sign of the cross on her forehead and consoled her in the words of Jeremiah: "See, Rachel weeps for her children and does not permit herself to be comforted, because they are no more," but Jehovah says: "Do not permit your voice to weep or your eyes to shed tears, for they shall return from the land of the enemy" . . . Balthasar had added: "If not in body then in spirit . . ." But Epp, her eyes brimming with tears, had looked at him so reproachfully that he had said no more. He had been avoiding her eyes for several days now, and in a way that he could not shrug off, he felt responsible for Tiidrik's death. Responsible, too, that it had not been possible to retrieve Tiidrik's body from the battle site at Jaani Bridge, where fierce fighting continued. Not only did Balthasar feel contrite before Tiidrik's soul and distressed before Epp and displeased with himself, he was also bitterly sorry about the death of this bright and spirited youth with his naively rigid ideas – perhaps because he was slightly envious of the elusive iota by which this youth was closer to God than any of them . . .

On a Thursday morning in early March, the enemy's cannons started firing before dawn, striking the outer wall of Karja Gate in a couple of fierce volleys, before falling silent. At nine o'clock, Elsbet came up the stairs, dressed in her fur coat, and asked whether Balthasar would go with her to St Nicholas' Church. She said she wanted to hear Master Sunschein's sermon. Balthasar, bent over his papers, mumbled that he, unfortunately, could not go. But he would not prevent her from going. He tore himself away from his manuscript pages and looked at his wife with a mischievous, teasing pleasure that always (lately, at least) irritated her.

"You go on," he said. "I have to go to see the watchman at Hellemann's Tower, and afterwards to Toompea to see Annika. But don't go alone. The shooting might start again. Ask someone to accompany you. Märten. Or Jakob. Or Mihkel."

But Märten had gone to a rope-maker to see about replaiting the bellropes. And old Jakob had harnessed the horse to the sleigh and was already in his dogskin jerkin, about to leave for the vicinity of Renten

Tower. He planned to see a merchant there from whom Balthasar had once been able to buy firewood – they needed to replenish their dwindling supply. So Mihkel, who happened to be coming down the stairs when he heard Elsbet in the great-room, looking for someone to accompany her to church, raced back upstairs to get his coat, delighted to escort her.

For a service held during the siege, there were not many people in attendance. The glass in the pointed arch of the middle window on the right, where a cannonball had crashed through six weeks earlier, was still shattered. Through the hole – about the size of an ox-hide – in the stone frame and stained glass, snow was drifting down into the church. Elsbet knelt on the cold stone floor and prayed: ". . . *und führe uns nit in Versuchung sondern erlöse uns vom Übel*".* She felt Mihkel's breath on the hair at the back of her neck, as he knelt behind her.

Master Sunschein, the fat Gerstenberger's adjunct, had been summoned from Tartu the previous year. He was a swarthy man with a sonorous voice and mobile eyebrows, whom the more prominent burghers (and not only their wives, by any means) had begun to view as a serious man of faith. On this day, he was repeating a sermon that he had delivered on the eighth Sunday before the celebration of the Resurrection, on the theme of the errant and the virtuous among those listening to the Word of God.

The errant and the virtuous in their fur coats and jerkins – their hands in gloves and muffs and sleeves because of the cold, their heads pulled down between their shoulders, their collars raised – sat in clouds of steamy breath, some of them on benches (nicked and dented here and there by shards of broken stone). Others were crowded together in front of the pulpit, around a hole four cubits across and half a cubit deep, covered by boards. It seemed to Elsbet as though they were waiting for the next cannonball to fall into the same

* And lead us not into temptation, but deliver us from evil (German).

hole, although the departed Tiidrik had said that that never happened.

Master Sunschein spoke from the pulpit above them:

"The unhappiest among those who have strayed from virtue are they whose hearts are as the ground whereon a seed may fall, but where heedlessness tramples it underfoot before it can sprout. That seed can be trampled by the cares of our daily lives – both small cares and great – and our greatest care at this moment is fear for the fate of our town, fear that should not, however, become more important than mindfulness of the Word of God within us . . ."

That most unhappy of souls is who I am, thought Elsbet with a shock of recognition. These are my worries that he is talking about – my worries about food at this wretched time . . . and about bedding and pillows and shirts and coats, Oh Lord. And of course, about the town – that the enemy not swallow us up . . . And about the children – that they grow up to be respected people here, in a secure town, and that they not go astray among the peasant masses – as has happened here, even with children of the nobles . . . And my sense of helplessness and weariness next to my husband, who seems to be living past me some-how . . . for on good days he plays with me as though I were a tamed oriole, but on bad days he is not always aware of me . . . Nor of my flinching when the cannons roar . . . Oh Lord, they're starting again . . .

And so they were. From the fortress behind Tõnismäe Hill they were again firing at the town, and, somewhere to the south, cannonballs could be heard pounding the town walls. Where could that be? Every-one after all, claimed it was impossible to hit Tallinn's walls because the earthworks had so ingeniously been constructed to protect them.

But then again, I am not the worst of those who have strayed, for I know that the things I worry about have been willed by God! And the greater those things are, the clearer it is that God has willed them. Sometimes it even seems to me that the heavier my burden of care, the more easily I bear it . . .

"But the worst among those who have strayed from virtue," continued Master Sunschein above the thundering cannons, "is one who, though his heart is by nature as a ploughed field ready for seeds, worries about the great difficulties of bearing fruit and even rejoices when he sees the many-coloured, chirping birds descend and peck at the sown seed before it has a chance to sprout. And these birds are vanity, pride, self-righteousness and sinful, secret desires . . ."

Now he is surely talking about me, Elsbet thought with a start, and she felt as though Sunschein's words had pushed her down a steep flight of stairs. Vanity – yes, yes, that is what I am – with all my lamentable aspirations to being seen as a woman of stature . . . instead of . . . Pride – that defines me as well . . . Self-righteousness – what was I doing just now? And sinful, secret desires – Oh God . . . She buried her face deep in the collar of her otter-fur coat, so that Mihkel, who had moved to sit beside her, would not see her sudden blush. And now her inner turmoil so overwhelmed her that she no longer heard the words of the sermon, nor the increasing frequency of the cannon-fire. Though perhaps it was fear of the cannons that galvanised her into action. She stood up and fled from the church. She did not look towards Mihkel, but she knew he had come after her. She felt his hand grasp hers . . . I must free myself, but I cannot . . . She noticed that they had left the church by way of St Anthony's Chapel. Right – for her first impulse had been to run to her father's house nearby, to escape the church and the roaring cannons, and to go to her children, who had been taken there two days ago. (Anna and Elisabet had been so eager to rummage through his bags of fur remnants.) But then it occurred to Elsbet that it would not be seemly to go to her father's house in Mihkel's company, and she turned right. Beyond the partly burnt roof of the Almshouse and the buildings of the transport yard, cannonballs were crashing against the town walls, which had been said to be beyond the enemy's reach . . . Elsbet heard Mihkel say:

"They're firing at the upper levels of Kiek in de Kök Tower." She recognised the small, snowbound square south of the church, surrounded by a jumble of houses, and the children's snow fort against the wall where a dozen urchins had had their snowball fight just a few days ago. Now it was empty, its walls trampled down. Elsbet heard Mihkel whisper:

"Elsbet . . . look . . . the fortress has fallen . . ."

There was something frightening in his whispered words – she felt they meant something else. They pertained neither to the children's fallen snow fortress, nor to their own fortified town presently under siege . . . She said in dismay, panting, between two bursts of cannonfire:

"But that is not supposed to happen . . ." And she realised that her words, too, meant something else . . .

They ran through the narrow Nõelasilm Passage to Harju Street and turned towards the market. Elsbet listened to Mihkel's hurried comment:

"But Elsbet . . . what if . . . this is God's will . . . ? Listen . . . how furiously . . . the cannons . . ."

Elsbet turned her head. She could see, next to her shamelessly luxurious mink hat, past a shock of hair close to her cheek, Mihkel's ardent, flushed face, eyes glowing – the face of the Archangel Michael:

"Elsbet . . . I know . . . that this is God's will!"

Just then, from the grey snow cloud above them, came a low, but piercing whistle. The thought flashed through her mind: Why should I worry about the things God has willed? And then, a thunderous crash, as a mortar bomb tore through the stone roof of a house on the corner of Kuninga Street, so close that shards of roof tiles flew down onto the snow at their feet. Desperate cries sounded from inside the house. Behind them cannons thundered ever more fiercely, and when Elsbet looked back over her shoulder, she saw puffs of stone dust and smoke rising from the now flat, bare, cobblestone head of the Kiek in de Kök Tower, bereft of its cone-shaped "hat". Somewhere ahead of them, in the vicinity of the Great Guild, another mortar bomb crashed through a roof.

"Mihkel . . . I'm frightened."

"Don't be frightened, Elsbet! I know – it is God's will!"

They ran around the corner of the Apothecary and arrived at the gate to the churchyard. The roof of the parsonage had been hit on its south-east side. Broken tiles had fallen onto the snow alongside the house. There was a black hole in the roof, four cubits across, revealing the broken ends of rafters and beams. Elsbet heard someone calling to her from a window in the apothecary's house, but could not hear what was said. She saw people moving about between the stables and the rear gate and coming out of the side door of the church into the yard, but did not recognise anyone. She felt someone squeeze her hand – Mihkel – he was saying something. She could not hear what. She ran to the door of the house and·was about to shake the handle, but the door was open and she rushed inside.

In the great-room, the middle of the log ceiling sagged, hanging about a cubit and a half below the rest. On the floor lay a heap of dirt and shattered roof tiles. Through a gap between the logs and the holes in the damaged ceiling of the upper storey and roof shone a strip of bright sky. Elsbet felt Mihkel take her by the shoulders and turn her to face him. She looked into his glowing eyes and heard him speak:

"Elsbet . . . this is the finger of God . . . It is all falling apart . . . walls . . . vaulted ceilings . . . vows . . . Elsbet . . ."

Elsbet did not hear him, lost as she was in her own thoughts: Did I really determine to heed this sign? Did I really say to myself that if our house were hit, it would be a sign that God considered my life under its roof to be a lie and in that case I could . . . I would be permitted to . . . ? No! Impossible! Or . . . perhaps not? Just then she felt Mihkel press her hand again and heard what he was saying:

"Elsbet . . . as Mary in Bethany dried our Saviour's feet with her hair – that is how I want to – anywhere, always—" And then she felt Mihkel's lips on hers – his fiery, smothering kisses – Oh God, God . . . why did his kiss not taste at all like the evil mandrake root?! God – why was it . . . not at all . . . displeasing . . . ?

After the third, fourth, fifth heartbeat, she tore herself from Mihkel's arms:

"I must go to the children!"

Her voice was muted, yet sounded almost like a cry. She ran out of the great-room, Mihkel at her heels.

A handful of dirt drifted down from the gap between the ceiling logs. Not because Mihkel had slammed the door shut behind him, but because someone was moving about on the damaged floor above.

It was Märten, straightening himself up from the edge of the depression where the cannonball lay. For a moment he just stood there, in the middle of Balthasar and Elsbet's bedroom, at the foot of the bed flung out of place by the force of the impact. His worn dogskin hat was askew on his head; his belt, which he had used to measure the cannonball, hung from his hand, its other end hitting the broken footboard of the bed. His shoulders were slightly hunched, his narrow face expressionless, wooden. In the light entering from the hole above his head, he looked for a moment like an old man. But even when he had put his belt around his waist and fastened its buckle and stepped out onto the landing, his step lacked its usual youthful spring.

He came down the stairs. He walked to the centre of the great-room, put his hands on his hips, examined the sagging ceiling and snorted.

Hearing steps, he turned around. It was Balthasar, rushing in from the storm porch, talking as he came:

". . . So they walloped us after all! I've already heard that no-one was hurt. Were you at home when it hit?"

"No, I got here just an instant later . . . there was no-one in the house at that moment."

"I'll go and see what things are like upstairs," said Balthasar and was already halfway up.

"Wait, Balthasar . . ."   Should I tell him? Or be silent? Tell him? Be silent? Tell him? Be silent? Oh, what the devil . . . I'll decide later!

"Balthasar – this cannonball – it was probably a four hundred-pounder . . . "

"Don't be silly," said Balthasar from the landing above. "They don't have anything larger than two hundred and twenty-five-pounders."

CHAPTER NINE,

in which a man who is fortunate in that he and his household
have survived the perils of both war and plague, treads unawares amongst
dangers no less dire, dangers that he miraculously manages to evade.
He has not an inkling, however, of the providential events that ultimately
enable him to say about his great work (or his great folly): At last the
grain has been separated from the chaff, and although I fear that it
remains rife with sprouting weeds and worry that I have had to sift
out good grain along with the chaff, still – I have now scattered it
to God's winds, that it might land on fertile ground and yield the
harvest of which I have dreamed.

Viewed from atop the roof ridge of the parsonage, the sea on this day in early spring was already free of ice all the way to the horizon. Its blue waters were visible, framed by the northern edge of the church roof and the gables of St Kanut's Guild, and the towers of Lippe and Kõismäe. And the smoke rising towards the grey sky from soot-blackened and white-plastered chimneys danced so lightly in the wind above the red-tiled roofs, that it seemed as though shortage of firewood and gnawing anxiety about the siege and other perils had burdened neither hearths nor hearts in this town.

Märten screwed up his eyes, in the manner of the ship's lookout that he had once been. From his vantage point he could see the many signs of damage and repair in the town's red roofs, even though more than a year had passed since the siege. The hole made by a cannonball in the Pastor's roof was still partly patched by boards, and only now were the monk-and-nun tiles being replaced. That is why Märten was sitting on this perch between heaven and earth.

Yes. Over a year had passed since the siege. The Grand Duke's forces had departed in March the previous year, after a frightful seven-week cannon assault. (Balthasar had read to Märten from his notebook, how many field culverins and half-culverins, cannons and mortars had spat out their fire upon the town, and how much stone and iron spittle each piece had had in reserve – and anyone who thinks that knowing such numbers will make a man wiser can ask Balthasar for the full tally.) The enemy had departed, true, yet a louring thunderhead threatening new dangers continued to loom over the town. Given the times, it would have been naïve to expect anything else. During the weeks of Lent, a new trial was visited upon the populace in the form of a peculiar, sudden and severe chest ailment that carried off large numbers of people. The epidemic was not as widespread as the plague, yet its effects were sinister enough. Even in the course of a service marking the end of the siege, as the congregation was singing a resounding hymn of thanksgiving ("As fathers have mercy on their little children . . .") a young boy in the church choir was overcome by a fit of coughing brought on by the disease, and choked to death . . . as though Satan himself had been granted the power to sink his claws into the boy's throat for daring to sing in praise of the Lord God . . . Then, at the start of summer, alarming news again reached town: the Grand Duke was preparing a fresh attack with new forces from the town of Pskov. Crossing itself, Tallinn had began to prepare for a terrible trial once again, but then learned that the scourge of war would pass it by after all. The Grand Duke had turned his enormous army towards the fortress towns of Latvian Livonia this time. And from there, rumours of untold horrors continued until autumn, when an unprecedented act of suicide occurred: Heinrich Boissmann and three hundred Võnnu residents blew up a powder magazine and themselves along with it . . .

But then, where, in any catechism was it written that the world had to be a better place than it actually was?!

Märten was sitting on the roof ridge – at one time plastered white, now grey with time and age – slightly above the hole made by the cannonball. As a precaution he had tied a rope around his waist and attached the other end to a rafter, and was now laying new red tiles next to the old white and grey and greenish ones, on a new roof batten extending over the yawning hole above the attic. The pail of mortar and the tiles were within reach, on a rack propped up on the ridge. Päärn, son of Traani-Andres, was climbing up three ladders fastened end to end – on his back, another rack with more tiles.

Yes, indeed . . . perhaps in the kind of acceptance of the world that actually indicated indifference, there was a certain defiance of God . . . It almost seemed that way to Märten. But the feeling did not trouble him. And why should it? For his defiance was no doubt so insignificant a thing that God would not punish him. Not any more than He had already chastened him over the past fifty years – him, a half-homeless, half-alcoholic, one-quarter wood-carver, three-quarters bell-ringer . . . whom He had seen fit to afflict with the plague and then miraculously cured (many thanks for that, of course) . . . But the fact that he himself had been saved did not mean that the whole world had thereby been healed of its real and figurative boils and blains. And just why was it that all these afflictions continued in the world – the bloodbaths, the plagues, the crop failures, the injustices, the thriving of thieves and the languishing of honest men? How could a man like him, a mere three-quarters bell-ringer, know the answer to that? The wisest men in the world could not answer such a question. Of course not. And that included Balthasar. In spite of all his years in Stettin and Wittenberg, in spite of his books and manuscripts. And in spite of the fact that Balthasar, with all his wisdom and his rise to prominence, was still more or less the same old friend and kinsman to Märten that he had been in their boyhood. More or less. To the extent that their difference in status permitted.

Nor did his old friend, Balthasar, that is, have it easy in this town still bearing the scars of war, under this roof not yet wholly patched . . . And not only because contributions from the congregation were lagging and debts for communion wine were mounting again, and the lords of the Church Treasury were even slower to pay the pastor of Holy Ghost than the pastors of St Olaf's and St Nicholas' and St Michael's churches (he was, after all, merely pastor to the Greys). Not only because of all this. But who knows whether he had even noticed anything else awry . . . For it is often the case that thoughtful men see most clearly the things that are furthest removed from them. And sometimes they don't notice at all what is happening right under their noses. Take, for example, the Dane that Balthasar spoke of with such enthusiasm – Brahe, or whatever his name was. He was said to be as familiar with the zodiac as any farmer with his own barn, but utterly unaware of how the state councillors mocked him behind the king's back. It was much the same with Balthasar. He understood extraordinarily well the Dane's inquiries into the stars, and grasped better than anyone the intrigues of Livonia's neighbouring princes. But the way that that sly Mihkel was quietly making up to Balthasar's own wife in his own house . . . that he could not see. And even though they both grew up in Kalamaja (so that thirty years ago he, Märten, would naturally have told Balthasar if some churl were making a move towards his girl's skirts) – at this time now, it wouldn't be fitting for a bell-ringer to rub it in . . .

Märten slapped some mortar onto the belly of the nun tile with his trowel and pressed the monk tile in place on top of it: ". . . To make sure you harlots'll stay up here for the next two hundred years despite winds and frosts and cannonballs . . ."

It was painful at times to watch this tough old fellow, Balthasar . . .

forging ahead, eyes wide open yet with blinkers on, like a dray horse turning a millstone, trudging along in single-minded pursuit of a bundle of oats dangling from a stick in front of its nose, on and on and on . . . except that Balthasar was himself both wielding the stick and dangling the oats . . . Alright . . . True, what was driving him seemed to be something of enormous importance . . . if a three-quarters bell-ringer were permitted to venture an opinion on the Herr Pastor's work (after merely glancing at parts of it).

To be sure, had Märten not chanced to see that one damnable kiss on the day the cannonball hit the roof, he would have had nothing to hold against Mihkel in the course of the year that followed. But it was apparent, if only to an eye more watchful since then, that young Herr Slahter looked flushed and animated whenever he encountered the lady of the house. And only the ear of one who knew could have detected the tremor of emotion in the man's voice each time he addressed Elsbet . . . And Elsbet? . . . Oh Beelzebub! . . . It would be easier to read Hebrew than determine from a woman's behaviour what is brewing within her. (Which is why a clever man will say, when he chances upon girls ready to play: Let's have our little frolic, let's have our little fun – but not pair up nor ask for more when the day is done . . . For anything more would involve such laborious calculations and such a bending and bowing to another's fancies, that it would simply not be worth it . . . A piece of wood, no matter how hard it is – and at times it is so full of knots and turns that it seems best not even to try carving it – still, the hardest, knottiest block of wood is not as difficult to handle as a woman. Not even if the grain twists and turns every which way . . . In the long run, you can shape a piece of wood the way you want. But dealing with womenfolk is futile from beginning to end.) True, plenty of men do get women to cater to them, but then they end up being duped into becoming their slaves . . . well, let them be slaves, then – his fellow countryman

Balthasar, included . . . He doesn't actually behave like a slave or servant. He's managed somehow to keep his neck stiff and head more or less high. But maybe that's why he himself is lately no longer catered to, either. For as far as Elsbet is concerned . . . goodness, as though a pastor's affairs are any business of a bell-ringer's . . . as far as Elsbet is concerned, if one were to judge by how fervently she's been praying on the benches of Holy Ghost lately, one might think she had reason to seek God's mercy . . . (As though that were really any business of his . . .)

But Märten had chanced to notice something on New Year's Day in 1578, something that was in itself odd . . . Unless it perhaps meant nothing after all? After midday on the first of January, following a festive morning service and a light meal, Balthasar and Elsbet had prepared to set out for the annual New Year's festivities at the Great Guild. Märten remembered it clearly: Balthasar was waiting for Elsbet in the great-room. He was wearing a somewhat shabby wool-and-calfskin coat and holding in one hand a furry earflap hat. He looked energetic and rough-hewn, restless and cheerful. Cheerful, perhaps, because in the midst of all his many duties and obligations, he had finally chosen to participate, at least partly, in a family event, by going to the guild's festivities. For no matter how distressing the previous year had been – with the siege and other misfortunes – it had turned out to be another year of victory. Even with the devastation of the surrounding countryside, the town had managed to survive. True, the omens for the coming year of 1578 were grim indeed: It was hardly possible that the gigantic sickly-yellow comet – even more frightening than the one twenty years earlier, which had foretold the start of a time of troubles – yes, hardly possible that it had hung in the north-east skies like the curved blade of a Tatar's sword, for several weeks before Christmas for no reason at all. Nevertheless, the year 1578 would most likely appear on the title page of Balthasar's opus, God willing

. . . And the arrival of such a year must by all means be celebrated.

So, Balthasar had been standing in the middle of the room, hat in hand, absentmindedly swatting his coat with it – he was eager to set out. Elsbet had arrived, wearing a splendid otter fur-coat and a mink muff dangling by a ribbon from her wrist. Serious as usual. Especially recently. With a slightly pained shadow darkening the soft corners of her mouth, perhaps a result of the passage of years (which leave their mark on us all), or of the most recent difficult times, or perhaps the result of a secret care, God knows. A faint fragrance of rosewater wafted from her, as it often did these days. And Märten noticed (for he had just then been lighting a fire in the fireplace of the great-room for the afternoon, lest the house become too chilly by evening, and had raised his head and seen . . .) how Balthasar's nostrils flared with pleasure at his wife's rose scent. Mihkel came downstairs just then, having lived in their home ever since the siege – and, frankly, Märten held that against him more than anything else. Even though he had heard Balthasar say to Mihkel: "You will remain under my roof. Why should you go elsewhere?"

And so Mihkel had come downstairs. Mihkel was Mihkel, the same as ever. Except that he too was dressed to go to the guild's festivities along with the others, for it was understood that they go together. Even though he was not a member of the Council of Clergy (there was still no adjunct position in the garrison church), he was among the invited guests. He was wearing his high boots and a short cloak edged with fox fur, and a comely stoat beret, which he had cheerfully pushed to the back of his head. Catching sight of the lady of the house below, he politely removed the beret. And then Märten chanced to see Elsbet's face – and Mihkel's as well. The way they gazed at each other in mutual admiration, as if spellbound. The way Mihkel came to a standstill for a moment on the stairs. The way Elsbet took a step back, unawares, towards Balthasar and tugged at his sleeve, saying: "Well . . . let's be on our way, Balthasar . . ." but for the duration of several heartbeats did not turn her eyes away from Mihkel . . .

Päärn, son of Traani-Andres, had just climbed up with ten roof tiles, and now, as his perspiring, bearded face rose cheerfully into view above the eaves, Märten swung his leg over the roof ridge he had been straddling and lowered himself down the ladder towards Päärn, to take the new tiles from him. Then the back door below creaked open and Epp's voice called from the courtyard:

"Hoo-hoo! Come on men! Come down! Herr Balthasar wants you!"

"Alright, right away!" Päärn answered genially. He heaved the tile rack onto Märten's shoulder and backed down the ladder. Märten muttered as he crawled up to the ridge with his burden:

"Well then, since he's summoning us, let's see what he wants . . . though I can't understand what could be so urgent in the middle of the day, while we're working . . ."

When they stepped into the great-room, Märten understood at a glance that something must indeed have occurred. The members of the household were sitting around the table as they did at mealtimes, but its scrubbed surface was bare, and neither the twin girls nor little Balthasar were present. The new ceiling above the table was in place, but the cracks between the boards had not yet been sealed. And Mihkel was sitting – look at that – to the right of Elsbet, but this was merely by chance, of course, and most likely not noticed by anyone except Märten. Nor did anyone else take note of old Jakob and Aunt Kati's brooding, worried expressions – Why were we, of all people, dragged here on this occasion? – nor of *köster* Meckius' unctuous, stammered remarks, nor of Mihkel's big, pale dog-eyes, darting towards Elsbet in spite of himself; nor of Elsbet's face, softening momentarily as she turned towards him, then stiffening again into the proper expression of the lady of the house as she stood up and left, returning to the table with goblets and a jug of wine.

But Märten did not have the opportunity to observe the assembled company at length – to read from their faces the recent strains and tensions within the household, nor to wonder about the reason for the present gathering. For just then Balthasar came down the stairs. His bronze beard, iron-grey near his ears, framed an especially gleefully grinning, defiant mouth. He was holding a book. Placing it on the table, he looked at each person in turn, and then spoke:

"My friends! Some of you have noticed for yourselves, and those who have not will now learn . . ." He began in country-tongue, the language he spoke in the pulpit and with members of the congregation (furthermore, over half the listeners present would not have understood him in German) – then, thinking it more appropriate to use German on account of Elsbet and Mihkel and Meckius, continued in both languages – until he finally decided that everyone at the table understood enough country-tongue and stopped translating his words.

"For several years now, I have been expending much effort here, under this, our common roof, on the difficult task of writing a major work . . ." And here he added, for the benefit of those who had no idea of this work: "A so-called 'chronicle', a book about things that have happened over the course of time here, in our beloved and sorely tried Livonia. Perhaps, during this period, I have overlooked some things that I should have attended to in my parish and my household." He did not apologise to them for his possibly insufficient attention. (It would be foolish for him to do that, thought Märten.) Balthasar picked up his book and said simply:

"I have finally finished this work. What happens to it now – well, we might say that that depends – first, on our own seamen and then on the German printers, and finally, God willing, on those who read the printed work. In a word, it will depend on so many, that we must consider its fate to be in God's hands. But I would like to invite you all to drink a goblet of wine with me, here, now, to celebrate its completion."

He placed a quarto volume with black covers on the table and filled eight goblets with pale Rhine wine. The sound of the wine pouring into goblets mingled with the sounds of heavily laden wagons rumbling over the cobblestones beyond the church, and of the weathervane atop the Almshouse, creaking in the spring wind.

"Well then . . ."

By the time the women had just managed to take a small sip of their wine, and Päärn, Jakob and Mihkel were still savouring their first draught, Märten and Balthasar had already emptied their goblets. Balthasar said:

"Märten, here's money. Go to Elken's. I ordered a juniper-wood box from him last week, made to specific measurements. Pay him and bring it here."

Cabinet-maker Elken brought out Herr Balthasar's box for Märten right away. It was a full span long, almost as wide, and half a span deep, made of thin juniper boards, with expertly dovetailed corners, and rubbed with fine sand to a silky smooth surface both inside and out, as though old seal-face Elken knew exactly just how precious a thing it would contain and what a long distance it would travel. Märten, the box under his arm, had already stepped out of the workshop, leaving behind its smell of bone glue and piles of wood-shavings. He was on the stoop, about to step onto Suurtüki Street, when Master Elken called after him:

"Hoy – bellman – just a minute!"

"Yes?"

"That fellow . . . um . . . Herr Slahter, from your household, ordered another box from me a couple of days ago, exactly the same as Herr Balthasar's. It's finished, too. Aren't you taking that one as well?"

"Another one, exactly the same . . . ?"

Why should Mihkel's box concern him, Märten? Balthasar had asked for this, the one he had under his arm. Let Mihkel fetch his own box . . . Why should he wait on that fellow? But why had Mihkel ordered it – another box, exactly the same as Balthasar's . . . ?

"No. I'm going to take only this box. I don't know anything about the other one."

Märten walked along Suurtüki Street, all the way to Lai Street, darted between grain wagons heading for the horse mill, strode for a stretch along Lai Street, towards the tower behind the Almshouse, with Toompea rising above it into the streaked grey sky – all the while thinking, barely noticing the houses, walls, doors, stoops, wagons and pedestrians coming towards him: What the devil . . . ? As if the affairs of pastors and would-be pastors were of any account to a bell-ringer . . . but still, what possible reason did Mihkel have for ordering an identical box . . . ? Had someone coming towards him chanced to look closely at him at that moment, he might have wondered why the scraggy bell-ringer from Holy Ghost was walking in this way . . . his upper body rushing on ahead, with his legs trying to hold him back . . .

At the corner of Pikk and Hobusepea streets, where the Scottish mercenaries' chapel had once stood, Märten froze suddenly in his tracks, gripped by an appalling thought. It was not the recollection of the sudden, bloody, inexplicable death of the Scotsmen, but a dismaying suspicion that unexpectedly – God knows where it came from – took root beneath his shock of pale hair . . . Yes, it can sometimes happen that one simply stumbles upon one's prey. A group of hunters sets out. The dog handlers surround a patch of woods with eighty underfed dogs and push on into the thicket. They shout, the hounds bay, horns blare. Crowds of people are on the move all at once. But the sly old wolf streaks like lightning past the dogs and vanishes like a mirage. As if it had never existed . . . But sometimes a man will go

373

alone into a vast forest. And walk along, following no trail in particular, somehow choosing the most direct path through the most dense growth of trees and shrubs (who knows how he finds his way – with his nostrils or the skin on his cheekbones or the hairs of his eyebrows). He stops under an oak, looks up, and sees, sitting directly above him, a little yellow lynx – and there is nothing to do but get out of its way before it pounces . . .

Märten pushed open the gate into the courtyard of the old prayer chapel. He looked around, stepped inside the gate, pulled a knife from his belt, and cut a tiny notch into the bottom edge of the box. Just in case. Big enough to make the box identifiable by touch even in the dark, among others no matter how similar.

When he arrived at the parsonage he asked casually for Mihkel. Epp replied that Herr Slahter had just hurried out somewhere.

"Aha," Balthasar said, standing at the small lectern in his study as he turned towards Märten. "Well, bring it here!"

He took the box, stroking it with a kind of wry satisfaction. He put it down on the broad slate windowsill, brought the bound manuscript from the lectern, and tested the size of the box.

"A perfect fit."

From behind the iron door of his wall-cupboard, he took out a letter secured by a wax seal.

"These are my instructions to the printer: That he select a beautiful font for the initial letters. And that he use red to embellish the title page. And that he keep a hundred and fifty copies for himself to cover his expenses."

Balthasar placed the letter and the manuscript between the black leather covers, and from a drawer in the lectern took out a hammer and eight thin nails. Once more he opened the volume to check that the letter was in place. Then he pressed the top of the box into position, held a nail against the corner of the lid, and picked up the hammer.

He looked at Märten with a curious smile, pleased yet apprehensive, and said:

"We'll see whether this box turns out to be a coffin or a cradle."

With brisk, firm blows, he nailed down each corner and the midpoints along the edges and pressed it into Märten's hands:

"Take it directly to the harbour and give it to the captain of the *Barbara*. You know him. He's about to weigh anchor."

Märten put the box under his coat and left. In the dim corridor behind the door, he stopped and squeezed his eyes shut and thought, clearly and quickly, that it would be wisest to do as he had been asked – go straight to the harbour and no more. Perhaps the apparition of the lynx was nothing more than the spectre of a fool's sudden fears. Yet if he took the box directly to the ship, no-one would ever know whether there had been plans hatched here, or of what kind . . . Which is why, even though he recalled Balthasar himself saying that sometimes nothing good comes of knowing, he went down the stairs.

"Epp – is Mihkel back?"

"Yes, he just came in. Went up to his room. That's where he'll be."

Märten went back upstairs. In the dim corridor, he felt as though he were forcing his way onto a fairground stage as a player in a silly farce with no participants other than himself, and this so angered him that he spat, the gob of spittle landing directly in front of his boots. But then he stepped quietly to Mihkel's door and stooped to peep through the keyhole. It was not the cool draught meeting his eye that made him blink. It was what he saw – which was, inexplicably, exactly what he had expected to see: Mihkel, in profile, sitting at his little desk under the window. The twin to Balthasar's box was on the desk. Mihkel was hurriedly cramming a book with black covers into it, and starting to nail down the lid.

Märten straightened himself up behind the door, feeling his head clear as it rose out of the haze of doubt, realising that his eyes were not playing tricks on him. He now saw the game – gleefully, defiantly, with utmost clarity. Should he summon Balthasar, knock on the door, step inside? No. Mihkel would immediately provide an explanation: My dear friends – what could be more self-evident than what you see here? I saw the box Herr Balthasar had ordered at Elken's . . . It was so beautiful! So perfect for my books. So I ordered the one you see on my desk. As a remembrance of Herr Balthasar's delightful house. Since I will perhaps soon be leaving to become pastor in Kullamaa or Kolovere . . . (There had recently been such talk) . . . Märten stepped back from the door and stood for a moment on the landing. He bit his upper lip, catching his moustache in his teeth, and said out loud:

"Why you little grubworm inside the cross of Jesus . . ."

He went down the stairs and whispered into Epp's ear, warm from the heat of the hearth and the steaming soup she had been stirring:

"Ask Mihkel to come down to help you. Take him outside into the yard, just for a moment. Tell him you'd wanted to get me to help but couldn't find me. And that there's no-one else at home. Tell him you want to bring up the vessel of meat from the cellar – tell him whatever you want!"

Märten stepped into the shadows behind the hearth. He could not hear what Epp told Mihkel, but a moment later they went out into the yard. Märten raced upstairs to Mihkel's room. There was no real hiding-place there, and he quickly found the box under the bed. It took but an instant to exchange the boxes . . . Actually, I wouldn't do this merely on account of Mihkel, the maggot! And the devil knows, maybe not even on account of Bal . . . but when something like this is at stake . . . So that when Mihkel and Epp came back into the house, carrying a heavy kneading trough between them, Märten was standing in the great-room with the box he had taken from Mihkel's room. He said in passing: "This is it . . . And now I have to take it to the ship setting sail for Rostock."

He darted a look at Mihkel and it seemed he caught the man's look of dismay. I'd like to know what he'll do next, Märten thought. Will he offer to take it to the harbour for me? Or come with me? But I won't give him the chance. Just this once I'm going to be more devilish than the Devil himself . . . He held out the box to Mihkel:

"Herr Mihkel, would you hold this for me for a moment? I'm going to put on my short sheepskin. There's likely to be a chill wind in the harbour."

He handed Mihkel the box, and again it seemed to him that he caught something in his expression, something in the way Mihkel moved as he reached for the box, as he seized it with the eagerness and excitement of one who has seen a priceless opportunity about to slip his grasp, and then finds that it is suddenly again within reach . . .

When Märten returned to the great-room, wearing his sheepskin coat and fur cap, Mihkel was standing exactly where he had been before, at the head of the table, smiling genially. And as Märten took the box into his hands, his fingers found the unmistakable notch in its bottom edge.

He did not have the chance just then to think more thoroughly about what it meant – that Mihkel had gone upstairs and exchanged the boxes again and had now given Märten what he thought was the wrong one, imagining the right one to be upstairs under his bed . . . Incidentally, the right one for whom? In effect, it did not matter. Märten tucked the box under his coat and glancing fleetingly at Mihkel, thought: Here we are, two sly rogues, face to face. Mihkel's smile was uncertain – perhaps forgiving, perhaps apologetic. Märten said:

"Well, now we'll see it go into print without a hitch, and it'll be beyond the clutches of any and all devils who might want to interfere."

Three hours later, as twilight began to fall, Mihkel entered the Pastor's house by way of the back door, without knocking. Taking advantage of the fact that both the kitchen and the great-room were dark and empty, he hunched his shoulders and crept up the stairs. For he had returned in order to collect his things and depart. After what had happened in this house earlier in the day, he had no choice but to disappear. And he wanted to make his escape without running into Herr Balthasar . . . For something fateful and wholly inexplicable had happened:

An hour after Märten had taken the replica of the box to the harbour (the replica ordered and constructed on the clever advice of Herr Maidel, to hold Mihkel's catechism instead of Balthasar's chronicle), Mihkel had delivered the correct box to Herr Maidel on Toompea.

O God in Heaven, You know that in the end Mihkel did it with a fairly easy conscience – after wrestling at length with You, that is. As Herr Maidel had once put it – Mihkel's conception of good and evil was still on the level of what he had been taught in confirmation class, and consequently, it had taken a long time for his decision to mature. Even though what he was expected to do was explained to him little by little – in view of the limited ideas and attitudes he had acquired in his burgher household. At first, Herr Maidel had shown great under-standing and patience with him and seemed interested only in finding out what Balthasar was writing, nothing more, since the Pastor was, in any case, sharing it with Mihkel. Only later, when Herr Maidel began to quiz him about the chronicle, did Mihkel sometimes feel odd answering his questions. But he had managed it nonetheless. For it was in the interests of the *fatherland* – as Herr Maidel had stressed – and with the goal of preventing possible future unpleasantness . . . Dear God, the interests of the fatherland are in themselves those that any subject is obliged to serve if he hopes to receive his daily bread and the respect of his superiors. And Herr Balthasar certainly did not need any future unpleasantness – that was true enough, Lord. Furthermore, he did not have to fear any unpleasantness at all on account of his writings (what was there, after all? A few pointed comments about the nobles, to be sure . . . but, in most instances, nothing personal, and all of it, in any event, served up in an honest Lutheran gravy). And was it not clear that there would be even less unpleasantness to fear if he, and especially he, provided a reliable account of Balthasar's work to Herr Maidel? . . . So that by undertaking this task, Mihkel had not served the interests of the crown alone: he had done something that would please not only the king but God as well. In effect, he had also defended his somewhat uncouth, yet estimable and worthy pastor – indeed, defended him better than anyone else could have done or would have dared . . . Herr Maidel had had confidence in his brief and laudatory accounts of the contents and nature of the chronicle, and had listened with sincere interest. Once, Herr Maidel had remarked with a smile, that a young man who had such high regard for his pastor, "even though he is in love with his wife" (Good God, he could have heard this embarrassing detail only from the prattling of Wolter Tisenhusen) – that a young man like that had truly proved himself and deserved a good position, which he, Herr Maidel would arrange for him nearby . . . For example, a position as Pastor of Kolovere castle . . . Since there was still no position for an adjunct at the Tallinn garrison, and Herr Maidel had been appointed by our Gracious Majesty as administrator of the royal fief of Kolovere . . . In spite of all this, the conversation on the preceding Thursday evening had alarmed Mihkel from the first moment.

He had set out for Wolter's house, as usual. Herr Maidel was there, sipping *klarett* with Wolter's papa.

"Well then, Mihkel – how far along is our chronicler with his work?"

"So far along that he's ordered a box to be made for it."

"What kind of box?"

"One for shipping the manuscript to Germany, to a printer."

Normally, when Herr Maidel spoke with Mihkel, he was seated

while Mihkel remained standing. But this time he had hastily asked Mihkel to take a seat, while he himself had stood up and started pacing. This is when he had laid out the scheme – so, so, and so – for switching the boxes:

"My dear young man . . . I have the utmost confidence in you. And in . . . *ahem* . . . Herr Balthasar as well. But I simply cannot say to those who ask me . . ." (and Mihkel could only assume that he was referring to the vicegerent or the district magistrates), "I cannot say to them, after all, that Herr Balthasar's book is, in spite of certain instances of coarseness, a good and fine and acceptable work – though I have not read it. You can, of course, understand that?"

"Of course, but . . ."

And in fact he did understand. Naturally. For he himself had – just recently – suffered the same embarrassment before Herr Maidel and Herr Tisenhusen. But even so, Herr Maidel's scheme seemed, at least at first, well, a little excessive . . . Good Lord . . . where did the meddling in another's affairs, the spying and snooping and prying, begin, if not in a scheme such as this one . . . ?!

Yet when he uttered his somewhat uncertain "but", it hung suspended between them for a mere instant before Herr Maidel quickly brushed it aside:

"Oh no! Because everything that you are doing is with the purest of motives – for the good of our Livonia and for the good of Herr Balthasar. Isn't that so? This is an extraordinary confluence of interests – the interests of our fatherland, the crown, that is, and your personal interests."

"Ye-es . . . That does seem to be the case . . ."

He could, of course, have posed a question: Fine, Herr Maidel. You will read the manuscript and we'll send it on to Rostock as if it had never taken this little detour to Toompea. But what if you find something there that . . . I don't know exactly what . . . but something that

380

you or the knighthood or the crown or all three find objectionable . . . What then?

Perhaps Mihkel would indeed have posed such a question had Herr Maidel not stopped in front of his chair, laid a friendly hand on his shoulder and said:

"Michel, if you manage to carry out this thing skilfully – and I will assume all responsibility for it as a matter of honour – you will become my pastor at the castle of Kolovere as of next month. To begin with."

And why should Mihkel's uneasy conscience not have been relieved when a man like Maidel – of noble ancestry (never mind if Herr Balthasar called him the great-great grandson of a peasant butcher), a royal admiral and feudal lord – absolved him of all responsibility, taking it wholly upon himself "as a matter of honour"? Especially as there was no violation of honour at all in this matter, for it was all done (even if in a slightly unorthodox manner) in the service of the fatherland and in order to protect Herr Balthasar from possible negative repercussions – and was in both respects thoroughly chivalrous – for by protecting Herr Balthasar was he not also protecting Elsbet . . . ?

Mihkel had found rather irritating the eagerness with which Herr Maidel – up there on Toompea, in his study with windows overlooking the sea – snatched the box from his hands and rummaged in his desk drawer for a knife with which to prise open the lid. (The western sky was clear of clouds and still so bright that candles had not been lit.) Yes, the man's impatience had discomfited him. But then, it merely indicated how greatly Herr Maidel prized getting hold of Balthasar's manuscript. Mihkel could see immediately what a great service he had performed for the admiral, which was of course a pleasant realisation; however, had he been given more time, he would have wished to minimise its importance. But Mihkel was not given more time. Herr Maidel had found a knife and, with the help of Herr Tisenhusen,

Senior, who had left his stool by the fireplace to offer assistance, prised the lid off the box. The gentlemen then learned what we already know: they were in possession not of Balthasar Russow's manuscript of the Livonian Chronicle but of Mihkel Slahter's Lutheran catechism.

Herr Maidel thundered: "What is the meaning of this?"

Mihkel stared as the catechism was lifted out of the box under his very eyes and did not know what to say. Just as he did not know why Herr Maidel was shouting at him – whether because it was a plan of his own devising that had gone awry in this stunning and inexplicable manner in Mihkel's hands, or because Herr Maidel was indeed not a real nobleman but hailed from peasant stock after all . . . For the gentlemen Tisenhusen (Wolter had suddenly appeared as well) did not shout at all. They merely burst out laughing . . .

"Why you . . . you unforgivable bungler!" Herr Maidel shouted – and something else, something else as well: "You're not fit for anything but baking buns, like your father! And for humping Russow's wife, maybe! But to manage affairs of state – never, never!" Something along those lines, which Mihkel, to spare himself, did not attempt to recall in detail . . .

"Herr Maidel, as God is my witness, I do not have the slightest idea . . ."

"He could see through your friendship from the outset! He was watching you the entire time! And at the decisive moment, he was able to trick you, make a fool of you!"

"Who?"

"Why that simpleton Russow, of course!" Herr Maidel bellowed, and then, smirking, lowered his voice: "This man – whom you once so insightfully described as 'quite obtuse with respect to the subtleties of real life' . . ."

"But my respect for him, my friendship for him, if I may say so, was utterly sincere! And only for that reason have I never taken his wife."

God, that should not have passed my lips, even if it is the truth . . .

"Oh, you haven't? . . . Really!?" The senior Herr Tisenhusen had asked between guffaws, as he rounded his fish eyes in theatrical disbelief. "Well, if indeed you haven't . . . then it's not out of respect for the husband. It can only be because it has not pleased the wife to . . . That's what usually lies behind a man's virtue – when a man like you is in a situation such as yours. *Ha-ha-ha-ha!*"

"My Lords!" Mihkel had cried in dismay. "I swear . . . it has to be the work of the Devil!" He crossed himself as he said this. "No-one else could have managed such a sleight of hand right under my nose!" Here it flashed into his head that perhaps it was the yokel villain, that cursed bell-ringer . . . though he could not imagine how in the world . . . But it was better to hold his tongue in this house, and elsewhere as well in fact, about the likelihood that the fellow had so outwitted him . . .

"It's all the same!" Herr Maidel cried, his voice still quavering with rage. "Whether they be devils or angels that serve your Russow – we shouldn't have sent an oaf like you to manage things with them! Just think, if there'd been a more competent man in your place – that confounded chronicle would never be published!"

So that's how it is, Mihkel thought, and realised that in a certain respect, this was a turn of events of the utmost significance, but he grasped it merely in passing, superficially and fleetingly . . . So, it meant that Herr Maidel's acknowledging remarks and nods and concurrence when he, Mihkel, had presented an overview to him of the chapters of the chronicle and described at length its tone and perspective – all of it had been mere pretence. Maidel had long ago made his decision. And a reading would only have confirmed him in that decision . . . Is that how it was? Perhaps he, Mihkel, should in fact thank God that the Devil had tricked him . . . ? Oh God, he didn't understand anything anymore . . .

In such confusion as this, and under such blows, it was not likely that Mihkel gave a thought to the way his prospects for the pulpit at Kolovere had crumbled. But who knows, perhaps it did fleetingly occur to him, and he thought it politic to hold his tongue about it, given the dim possibility of salvaging the situation once the admiral's rage had subsided somewhat . . . Unfortunately, the admiral himself had not held his tongue about it. From his place by the window at a distance from Mihkel, and with his back turned, he had declared with utmost scorn, landing hard on the consonants:

*"Se – to minem Slottpastor! Nymer in der Welt!"**

He had then turned towards the room and, with an especially piercing look at Mihkel, arms crossed on his chest, his right hand cupping his stony chin and covering the lower part of his scar, said:

"Gut. Ick nem se tom Lodeschen Scriba. Kenen dim mer. Und dat se sik propere ut der Stadt maken. Up alle Fall."†

And now Mihkel, fortunately undetected, hastily mounted the back hall stairs of the parsonage, to his room – still his room, for now. He shut the door behind him, quickly yet cautiously. In the semi-dark he flopped onto the stool in front of the organ, rested his elbows on the keyboard, his chin in his hands, and squeezed his eyes shut, trying to think. His mind was reeling – a tumult of thoughts and feelings. His ears rang with Herr Maidel's coarse insults and the two Herr Tisenhusens' laughter. A blur of white boxes and black-bound quartos whirled past his closed eyes, spinning like a squirrel in a cage . . . Finally, out of the chaos there arose slowly – no, not a face or even a form, but simply *a feeling* with a consoling, calming effect and a name that, in a sweet, secret way, gave everything purpose and meaning: Elsbet . . .

* You – as pastor in my castle – never, in this world! (Middle Low German).

† Alright, I'll take you on as scribe at Kolovere. Nothing more. And in any case, see that you disappear from this town as quietly as possible. Just in case (Middle Low German).

Elsbet was the one who had first told him about Balthasar's chronicle. And immediately, or shortly thereafter, he had realised that if he could find a way of helping with the manuscript (for Herr Balthasar had no secretary and would find no-one better) he would often be near Elsbet. And then Balthasar, by God's inscrutable will, had indeed proposed to him exactly what he had been hoping for. Out of love for Elsbet he had taken it upon himself to defend her husband's work and her husband himself before these lords. That was how it was. And also, out of love for Herr Balthasar himself, granted. But above all, out of love for Elsbet. This was also the reason he had arrived at the Pastor's house during the siege and let himself be invited to live here – not, as he had claimed, from a sense of embarrassment at burdening the Tisenhusens during a time of want. Love for Elsbet had made him stay here until now . . . but also, respect for Herr Balthasar, of course . . . Oh Lord, was he not permitted to ask how many others in his place would have retained their respect for Elsbet's husband, as he had done? How many would have refrained, in so exemplary a manner as he, from harbouring even in private a thought such as: What a boor this Balthasar is, this fellow who knows more about everything in the world than he knows about his own wife . . . !

But he, Mihkel, had entertained such thoughts only when he told himself that he actually did not think them at all . . . (Every such a refusal to think must surely weigh as pure virtue in the Heavenly Scales . . .) Yet now, in spite of everything, he was at this absurd impasse and about to flee the house where he had loved . . . Thank God, that he at least had his love . . . and Elsbet's face, so refined in its reserve, so gentle in its austerity, and the captivating, stubbornly girlish toss of her head as she shook away stray locks of hair from her brow, and the graceful, self-assured way she moved, and the longing for a better world in her dark eyes – all this, so dear, it made him feel weak in his loins . . . and last but not least in all these things: the look in Elsbet's eyes, which had become ever more alarmed and amazed and intense when she turned towards him . . .

Mihkel heard the organ creak under his elbows and then emit a low growl – he was caught up in his own thoughts:

And even if my love for her is not entirely free of sin – for I have sinfully kissed her and more than once lusted after her! – Yet I have no sinful intentions with regard to her. And even if such thoughts did enter my head, dear Lord, it happened in this last month, in anticipation of the position in Kolovere, at times before waking in the early morning, imagining myself in a short robe and high boots going to meet Elsbet at the gate of Kolovere castle and helping her down from her saddle – she's escaped from Tallinn and come to me and is breathing hard as she throws her arms around my neck . . . I blush even here in the dark, when I think about it – but can we not find, even in the lives of my fellow pastors, similar thoughts – human and pardonable – from the forty-year-old tales about Holy Ghost's own Wanradt, to the weaknesses of the departed Bishop Geldern . . . Almighty God, You see that it is my honourable love for Elsbet that has cast me where I now am . . . And thus I can say that my case is not the worst . . . And in Kolovere I will at least have my daily bread. Even though it be by the humiliations meted out to me by high and mighty gentlemen – but then, it is the privilege of the powerful to humiliate. And their might resides in this privilege. Indeed. Where else . . . ?

He carefully struck a spark with flint and steel to light a candle, placing the candlestick on the floor, under a corner of the table. He pulled out his chest from under the bed and opened it, squatting as he looked over his meagre belongings – an old woollen coat, a shirt, thick blue woollen socks riddled with moth-holes – looked them over without really seeing them. The only way to rise above them – it's not for nothing I studied theology at the university – is to surpass them in love . . . What was it that the chortling Tisenhusen said? – If you haven't . . . it's only because the lady did not invite you to – Pig! . . . But, by God, if she had invited me – I would of course have gone to her . . . for if she had offered me the bridge, I would not have been stepping on Herr Balthasar's honour by walking across it . . . Oooh . . . but she could indeed have made an overture – she could do it even now . . .

Mihkel heard a sound at the door. He considered blowing out the candle, but could not come to a decision. Jumping up from his open chest, he turned around – to come face to face with Elsbet. For one moment of inebriated triumph he thought: *Am I a magician?* But then he saw Elsbet's face – it frightened him. She shut the door behind her and leant against it. Almost whispering she said:

"Mihkel, I beg you, leave this house."

Mihkel knew he should tell her that that was why he was packing, preparing to leave immediately, and that he was sorry, but this was how it had to be. Instead, he said, in half-serious, half-feigned alarm:

"Leave?! But why . . . ?"

"I cannot bear it anymore . . . There are vile, base stories about Balthasar all over town, as it is. I must not, on my part, provide grist for the gossip mills. You understand, I'm sure . . ."

"You mean, that you too . . . that you, too . . ." (now using the familiar "you"). "Elsbet . . ." his voice was dull with disappointment and wounded pride. And then it became brittle, agitated . . .

"Does Herr Balthasar . . . also wish . . . that I leave . . . ?"

"No, I'm the one asking you to leave . . ."

Thank God, thought Mihkel – that meant that neither the Devil nor the bell-ringer had talked to him yet . . . He stepped closer to Elsbet and gripped her shoulders – and poured out what he felt – or had decided to feel.

"Elsbet, I love you. You know that. I've loved you for a long time. And you love me too. I know that. Why are you sending me away – instead of—?" He gripped her upper arms. They were supple and soft, and the realisation that they belonged to someone else, but might, possibly, be his, agitated him. He spoke fervently, ardently, voicing both a command and a plea:

"Elsbet, let us not deny, either to ourselves or before God, that we love each other!"

Elsbet was silent. Mihkel shook her and drew her into his arms, so that the shadow of the table leg wobbled on her face – a pale, greenish-grey in the candlelight. Just then the door behind her back flew open, to reveal Balthasar on the threshold.

Elsbet tore herself away from Mihkel. But she did not cry out. She covered her face with her hands, standing between them, silent.

For just an instant, Balthasar's eyes rested on her. He did not speak, murmuring merely a *Hmm*, the way one would respond to an incomprehensible and pointless problem. Or to a random, meaningless blow that upon occasion strikes a man as if out of nowhere. Then he turned towards Mihkel. In a voice so toneless as to seem merely a whisper, he said:

"Out of my house!"

He used his foot to push Mihkel's open chest to the threshold. As Mihkel bent over to close the lid (by bending over he was also able to avoid Balthasar's eyes) Elsbet rushed out of the room.

Mihkel knelt in front of the chest, his hands shaking as he attempted to turn the key in the lock. Balthasar, standing behind him, remained silent. A wide, warped floorboard creaked under his foot. Overwhelmed though he was by his distress, Mihkel tried to picture himself straightening up from the chest (after he had managed to turn the key in the lock), and saying with a smile that would overcome all misunderstandings: Herr Balthasar – God will be our judge . . . At the same time, he felt that he should not dare call upon God as his judge – even though Balthasar was, at the moment, banishing him only because of the declaration of love he had overheard, and did not yet know anything, thank heavens, about the matter of the manuscript box. No, no . . . He could explain everything – almost everything – to God! But not to this Herr Balthasar with his stony, peasant face – whose proximity he sensed on the back of his neck. Not at this unfortunate moment. And then he heard the rustle of skirts and knew that Elsbet had returned. That emboldened him. He managed to lock his chest. Gripping it under his arm, he stood up, his back to Balthasar.

"Here," said Elsbet, holding out a box decorated with painted flowers. "I know he still owes you five hundred marks. Take this. It is my mother's jewellery box. This should settle at least half the debt."

Mihkel, with his chest under his left arm, stepped over the threshold, out onto the landing. There was nothing for him to do but leave. He wanted to depart with dignity, for Elsbet's sake and his own. And to get away from Balthasar with no further delay, at least at this dreadful moment. He looked into Elsbet's pale face and dark eyes. Like a man caught in a rushing current, he shot a desperate look at the box in her outstretched hand. His right hand rose to receive it. It was his right to accept repayment of the debt, he felt, and at this time he had pressing need of it, since he was dependent on Herr Maidel's unreliable charity . . . and furthermore, these were Elsbet's jewels that would become his . . . But he let his hand hang motionless as another thought struck him. Might it not seem to Elsbet tomorrow that he had demeaned himself by accepting her jewels at such a moment . . . ? No-one knows which consideration would have triumphed in the end. For Balthasar interrupted Mihkel's deliberations. He strode precipitously past him. And God alone knows what spurred him on. For although the impulses behind Balthasar's action seem clear – blind jealousy, miserliness, a prideful need to settle scores – no-one, save God, can know in what proportion each was present. (Whether he thought: I cannot bear the prospect of my wife and that wretch touching the same object at the same time! Or: He will not get a crumb of what is mine! Or: Let him have her silver trinkets! But I want to see him on all fours, picking them up . . .) God knows just how these motives were intertwined in Balthasar's ignoble act. But they all played a part as he shot past Mihkel, grabbed Elsbet's jewel box, and hurled it down onto the top step. It landed with a crash. The lid flew open, the box twisted apart at the hinges, and several pounds of silver scattered over the stairs, the beads of Elsbet's broken necklaces clattering down the steps in a matter of a few heartbeats . . .

Shock and the sound of the rolling beads chained Mihkel momentarily to the spot. When the clatter came to an end, he looked back with the look of a man drowning, of a man fleeing. A long, pained gaze at Elsbet: Dear one – I know – you are not to blame for our immeasurable misfortune . . . I know that we love each other. Even though I do not know what will become of us . . . And a brief, pained look at Balthasar, a look in which the bitterness of one who has been humiliated was so intermingled with a victor's readiness to forgive, that it was impossible to guess which emotion would eventually overcome the other.

Then – his hat and chest under his arm – Mihkel raced down the stairs in the wake of Elsbet's beads and shut the door of the great-room behind him, surprisingly quietly, considering his haste.

CHAPTER TEN,

*which has been strung onto the thread of our narrative, first, because
it has become our practice to conclude the stages of our tale with a sea
voyage, although until now the departures alone have been depicted:
second, because we might be able to reduce Balthasar's indebtedness
to Märten Bergkam, and perhaps also because the story that is set
down in black and white in this chapter was of great import especially
for him, at least in Balthasar's opinion.*

The first month after that momentous and unhappy day at the
parsonage was no doubt the most oppressive. Because of the grey wall
of silence that had unexpectedly arisen between Balthasar and Elsbet.

The reason for Elsbet's silence was, above all, a sense of guilt, of
course. For she had permitted a young man, a stranger, to declare
his love for her – without crying out in protest: Be silent! Stop such
unseemly talk . . . ! She had even permitted him to claim that she loved
him too – without protesting: That's not true, not true, not true! . . .
Furthermore, during the time that this young man dwelt under their
roof, she had, at intimate moments with her lawful husband, permitted
her sinful imagination to substitute, for her husband's hot breath
above her, the breath of that young man, had permitted the Devil to
paint, behind her closed eyelids, his face radiant with love . . . Yet, had
it been only guilt that she felt, she would have gone to her husband
on the second or third day after Mihkel's departure and, kneeling
on the rough floor of his study, pressed her face to his knees and confessed – as an honest, chastened wife should certainly have done after

seeking God's guidance. But Elsbet had not done that. She recognised that sharp skewers of stubbornly perverse feelings protruded from the humble, upright pole of her sense of guilt. And every time that the pliant rod of her guilty conscience was about to bend submissively and accept punishment, she felt those needle-like skewers rising up inside her . . .

Had not Balthasar himself brought Mihkel into their house? Had not Mihkel been Balthasar's own ward and confidant? And creditor as well? And was not Balthasar himself – by virtue of who he was and such as he was (it made her wince) – one who still seemed foreign, who was still a *stranger* in her own beautiful German town of Tallinn . . . And it was Balthasar himself, after all, who, more than once, almost as if to provoke his wife, had left her in Mihkel's company or had asked him to accompany her . . . Wasn't that the case even on the fateful day that Mihkel had dared kiss her under the damaged ceiling of the great-room . . . ? And even though she remembered it in detail – it had been on that Thursday morning, after they had run home from St Nicholas' Church and Sunschein's sermon on the sin of self-righteousness – nevertheless (or perhaps because of it), Elsbet made no attempt to break through the wall of silence once it loomed between her and Balthasar. He, of course, did not take the initiative either. His stance on it was as inflexible as an anvil: If, in circumstances such as these, the wife remained silent, the husband must naturally do likewise. So each stood on his or her side of the wall and attempted as best as possible to come to terms with the heaviness of heart that had settled upon the parsonage like the ashen twilight of an eclipse.

In the presence of the other members of the household, little air holes and peepholes of various shapes opened here and there in the grey wall: a *yes* or *no*, a *thank-you* or *fine*. And once, when Papa Gandersen came to visit – as he did on occasion, to bring his grandchildren a little puppet made of a cat's pelt, or to cast an inquisitive eye on his daughter's life – Elsbet did something she had not done for several weeks. After dinner she stepped behind Balthasar's chair and, laying her hands on his shoulders, leant over nearly to his ear, to ask:

"Would you like me to serve the *klarett* in the sacristy or upstairs in your study?"

"*Hmm* . . . the sacristy would be fine," Balthasar said, feeling as if a millstone had slightly lifted from his heart, and rejoicing for a moment in a sense of relief, until he felt the weight of the stone settle back into place. For he sensed the tentativeness of his wife's hands and the effort at pretence in her voice and realised that there was nothing more behind her gesture than the desire to conceal from her father the change in their relationship.

Had Balthasar not finished his great work, he would have burrowed fiercely into it now. But unfortunately, the chronicle was completed and at the mercy of Neptune, riding the waves towards Rostock . . . Or perhaps it was already in Rostock, where the foremen at the printing press were taking it apart, word by word . . . Whenever Balthasar thought of his chronicle (which was several times a day and sometimes at night as he lay in his marriage bed, rigid in the dark, his back to Elsbet, who seemed to be breathing with irritating calm), he felt as though he were plunging into a void – realising, with a shock, that not the smallest detail in his work could now be altered. Whereas he knew it contained some serious errors. For example, in the sixth chapter of the first book, he had cited the date of the founding of Tallinn as 1223, even though, as he had discovered last week, his own notes gave the year as 1219 . . .

Sometimes, simply in order to be alone and to avoid brooding about his wife and Mihkel, he sat in his study, thumbing through his small grey manuscript pages, occasionally jolted by how brazenly self-confident some of his assertions were on the times and events of the distant past, and how uncertain the foundation upon which they rested . . . And how thin his descriptions were compared to the sounds and colours and smells of the living events, even those that he had actually witnessed. And how skewed his portrayal of some things – evidence of how he had permitted himself to be swayed. Yes, he reread his text, stunned and dismayed at how he had elevated that red-moustachioed boaster and braggart Ivo, son of Schenkenberg the minter, to the status of hero, along with his band of arsonists and plunderers . . . He bit his lip and squinted his eyes, and when, demanding of himself a mercilessly honest response, he posed to the white-washed walls of his study the question of *why* he had written as he had, the answer came to him. He had done it, above all, because it had given him enormous pleasure to include in his account something about the peasant population, wherever it seemed warranted. In depicting the turbulence in Tallinn and the surrounding countryside, he had, after all, wanted to show that in the chaotic mass of German and Swedish and Danish and Russian and Scottish fighters, there were also peasants who had banded together and played a role in determining the fate of their town and country . . . After all, the peasants were participating! But he had had a specific reason for singing the praises especially of Hannibal and his Greys: he had done so not only as an act of repentance with regard to Tiidrik, who had fallen while under Hannibal's command, but even more, as an act of spite. That was the truth. To nettle none other than Mihkel Slahter. For a year now, he had held a grudge against Mihkel for the derisory way in which he had spoken of his old schoolmate Ivo. These remarks should not have upset Balthasar at all – he could in fact have joined in the laughter, for there was a grain of truth in them. Ivo really was a loudmouth and braggart, who exaggerated threefold his own heroic deeds and those of his men. But when Balthasar had heard Mihkel, for the second or third time, say, guffawing: "That Ivo is still playing the role of

Bramarbas, the Miles Gloriosus that he played as a boy in our school play," something inside Balthasar rose up in protest . . . And when the talk turned to Ivo's background and that of his men – which happened several times during the course of the most recent siege – Balthasar had had to listen repeatedly to Mihkel's opinions, uttered in irritatingly low, confidential tones of unmistakable contempt: "It's true . . . that band of yokels is good at hauling in the booty – 'cause by their very nature they're closer to being robbers than the rest of the looters . . ." It was then that Balthasar decided: he would not argue with the dolt – because of Elsbet, because of Meckius, because of Mihkel himself, for the man did not acknowledge his own peasant blood, Heaven help him. And because of all those likely to be shocked or offended or dismissive of his arguments – whether by snorting or silence – he had merely smiled and pursed his lips, without uttering a word. But here in his study, on his grey sheets of paper (and also in his chronicle, confound it!) he had given full vent to his thoughts and had perhaps gone too far when he wrote:

> . . . in addition, the honourable Town Council had also hired a company of peasants from Harjumaa, over four hundred men. All proud, brave lads, nearly all of them trained in the crossbow, and their leader was Ivo Schenkenberg, the son of Tallinn's master minter, a stalwart, a courageous young man who trained his men so well, in accord with German standards of discipline and duty, that they wanted nothing more than to battle the Russians day and night, battles in which they were often victorious. For which reason others became resentful and started calling Ivo Schenkenberg "Hannibal" and referring to his men as "Hannibal's men" . . .

. . . and so forth. The account went on to describe how Hannibal's people were more skilful looters than the foreign forces, in part because they knew all the marsh paths and forest trails better than the strangers did . . . Yes indeed. But had he wanted to challenge and contradict Mihkel solely because of Mihkel's social aspirations (considering that he would not even be aware of Balthasar's argument until God knows when – not until he read them in the pages of the chronicle at some future time)? Or were there perhaps other reasons for wanting to contradict Mihkel – more specific, but deeper reasons? That was a question he did not pose to his shadow on the wall. God knows, perhaps he was avoiding asking it. Perhaps he suspected that whatever answer the shadow gave would be more than absurd. That if he, Balthasar, asked: Fine, I did it to vex him, but why would I keep vexing this knave who is in pursuit of a pulpit? – his shadow would whisper from the whitewashed wall: Because of jealousy! For you no doubt noticed right away, from Mihkel's first few visits to the parsonage, how very polite, like a popinjay, the rogue was towards Elsbet. And the admiration with which he soon began to look at her, and then, of course, the way Elsbet herself began to notice the attentions of the no-good dolt . . . But perhaps that had not happened, after all? Perhaps what he sometimes thought he heard when he pushed open Mihkel's door that time and saw the two of them spring apart was not, "We love each other", but something that merely sounded like that? Or perhaps it had never even happened . . . ? The Devil knows, the Devil knows . . .

To escape this uncertainty Balthasar plunged into – what else but his daily responsibilities? Suddenly it seemed there was no end to them: presiding at Sunday services, weddings, christenings, and funerals; praying at the bedside of the afflicted, listening to pleas for spiritual succour, providing confirmation instruction, inspecting the school, busying himself with money matters at the Collegium of the Church Treasury (even though responsibility for its finances had been shifted ten years ago to other shoulders), and advising, consoling, pardoning,

admonishing . . . At first he marvelled, wondering *where* he had managed to snatch the time, with all these obligations, to sit and work at
his chronicle. Until he suddenly noticed – it was probably no more
than a week later – that he seemed to have ever more time – empty,
grey, idle, oppressive time. So it was that he found himself, on several
occasions in the spring of 1578, squatting on a stool in the sauna of
the parsonage, his back against the sooty wall, among piles of wood-
shavings fragrant of maple, aspen and juniper – the leavings of Märten's
spoons and other carvings of his. Or perhaps in the Green Frog tavern,
on Nunnade Street, sitting at a table for the gentry; or looking across at
his old friend, Märten in either sauna or tavern, keen-eyed Märten, his
yellow beard pressed against his mug, grunting in response to
Balthasar's questions – for example, about what Märten's sea voyage
long ago had in fact been like.

Balthasar had included the following account in his chronicle:

In November of 1562, Duke Johan of Finland, brother of the
King of Sweden, travelled through Livonia to the town of Tallinn,
along with his royal consort, Lady Catharina, sister of the Polish
king, Sigismund Augustus, shortly after the Duke had wedded
that most illustrious maiden in Vilnius. And after resting a few
days in Tallinn, he and his spouse boarded a ship on the fourth
of December and sailed to Turku, Finland.

Yes, Balthasar had indeed included an account of the trip that "his"
duke had made to Tallinn. Although in general, his practice had been
to refrain from describing many of the events that had occurred during
his lifetime if he had not himself been witness to them. He had also
omitted events, as we know, with which he had been too intimately
involved.

The story of the trip, sixteen years earlier, of the then Duke of
Finland, currently our gracious King Johan III, was therefore somewhat

questionable in two respects. First, Balthasar himself had been in Germany at the time – in Lübeck, on the look out for a ship to Livonia. He had not arrived in Tallinn until a month after the duke's departure. The duke's trip, therefore, could clearly have been included with events that Balthasar had chosen to omit from his chronicle. Second, Märten, his stubborn old blood-brother, had been closely involved, "up to his eyes", as they say, in this trip of the duke's. In this respect as well, it would have been better to remain silent about the royal visit. Especially since the stories Balthasar had heard about it over the years were not suitable for inclusion in a chronicle – if for no other reason than that people of such prominence were involved.

Be that as it may, Balthasar was now seriously interested in the affair. God knows why. (Perhaps in part because the contrast between his bland, noncommittal account in the chronicle and the intriguing details of the actual event was dispiritingly apparent. And when he contemplated "what we have written and what we might have written", he could not refrain from reproaching himself from time to time.)

To be sure, whether they were in Märten's sauna or at the Green Frog tavern, convincing Märten to talk in any detail about this event of sixteen years earlier was in itself a laborious task. As he tried to drag words out of his friend, Balthasar felt like a bird-catcher attempting to free finches and wagtails from bird-limed branches that held them fast. (And what exactly does "to free" mean in this context . . . ? For in order to transform these little bundles of feathers into domestic creatures that provide delight and amusement by their flight and song and plumage, one has to soak them in ale and dry them in the sun and smooth them with a goldsmith's brush . . .)

To everything that Balthasar had heard over the years from the townspeople and from Märten's occasional remarks about the duke's much earlier visit, he added what he had recently learned by questioning his friend with renewed curiosity. This is the story, as put together piece by piece:

In the autumn of 1562, the town was buzzing with news about the imminent arrival from Riga of Duke Johan and his bride. He was said to be travelling with an enormous cargo of possessions and a large entourage, including our former vicegerent, Henrik Klausson (who had also been in Poland with the duke), and the current vicegerent, Count Svante Sture, among other dignitaries. A flurry of preparations was rumoured to be underway at the castle on Toompea as rooms were hastily readied for the eminent guests. For their lowlier attendants, the entrances and floors of Tallinn's taverns were swept clean. Amidst the swish of brooms, those claiming to know described the duke as a splendid young gentleman with upturned moustaches and declared his royal wife to be beautiful as a blooming lily. As Märten had remarked: "*Khm* . . . well, what would you expect such high-level persons to look like? The men are always like little Saint Georges and the women like rosebuds!"

Approaching by way of Pärnu Road, the entourage arrived. Those townsfolk with nothing better to do hurried past Vaestepatuste Road and Jerusalem Hill, some going as far as the Sandhills at the lake, to meet the visitors. At their head were Burgomasters Rotert and Pepersack and Councilman Beelholt and the leadership of the Blackheads' brotherhood. For them this show of zeal was, of course, a matter of honour, expected of them by virtue of their official position. Although their expressions were rather sour as they sat there on horseback, waiting, with the sleet raining down, they all broke into smiles – looking as genial and humble and eager to please as can be – upon catching sight of the retinue in the bend of the road between the wind-twisted pines. The mouths of the curious onlookers crowded behind them fell open in awe. Following upon the royals' carriage with its rounded top and golden tassels, and the coaches of the governors, came

– on wagons and horseback – at least a hundred and fifty people: lords and ladies, stewards and tutors, councillors, scribes, pages and young ladies-in-waiting, squires, servants, housemaids and cooks, three Catholic priests and four dwarfs in floor-length velvet cloaks, who were not the last by any means. But all their coats and tassels and armour and muffs, wet from the sleet that had been falling steadily, were dripping like crows' feathers, and their backs were both sodden and speckled with snow.

The procession came to a halt. The town dignitaries dismounted and hurried through the mud towards Duke Johan's carriage. The duke and a few lords leapt onto horses that had been walking alongside the carriages, to trot fifteen paces towards the Tallinners. At the duke's request, Count Sture introduced the town fathers to him. Having received their bows and words of greeting, he directed them to his carriage. Lady Catharina's hand, adorned with six gold rings and three gold bracelets, reached out from the carriage window, and the town worthies covered it with their wet beards and kisses . . .

Märten had somehow observed most of this for himself. Incidentally, he would not have raced out there on his own to gawp at the visitors, even though some of Balthasar's curiosity had rubbed off on him over time. But Hans, the skipper from Torstholm, aboard whose two-masted schooner Märten was earning his bread as helmsman, was in the harbour of Tallinn with his ship, awaiting his cargo, and he had said to Märten: "Why don't you go and look the worthies over. So's you can tell me and my men all about them later . . ."

And so Märten had trudged to the. But, in response to Balthasar's question as to what the duke looked like, Märten replied: "Why, you've had a much closer look at him than I have . . ."

And to the question about Frau Catharina, he merely said: "Hah! I didn't get near enough to see much of her. But later, well, later I saw her from pretty close up. *Hm*. Kind of yellowish eyes, like a wild goat's . . . looked like she had a cold. But a genteel lady, in any event."

As Märten told it, the entire entourage had continued on to the town and dispersed, going either up to Toompea or into the lower town, according to status and stature, and he had nothing more to do with the lot of them for a good week.

"But what stories did you hear about them in town?"

"And when is there ever a shortage of stories?"

"Well, true, but what did you hear that time?"

"Who could possibly remember?"

"Come on – don't tell me you don't remember!"

"Alright. All kinds of stories were going around then. He had just become duke then . . . But now . . ."

After a time Märten recalls something about which Balthasar too has a hazy recollection: In the autumn of 1562, the Duke and Duchess of Finland – now our gracious King Johan III of Sweden and his Queen – were not permitted to pass through the gates of Riga. This, of course, became common knowledge in Tallinn after the duke's arrival, and the ingratiating smiles of many of the councilmen froze on their worried faces at the news. It is true that Riga, unlike Tallinn, was not a town of His Majesty the King of Sweden. It was striving to remain independent and escape the notice of Poland and Moscow and Stockholm. And its rebuff of the duke and duchess could not be attributed to dislike, but to fear. However, if Riga denied entry to the brother of the Swedish king and the sister of the Polish king, even as town dignitaries directed them, bowing and scraping, to lodgings in a manor house outside the town walls, it followed that the town must have considered the enemies of the royal couple not only dangerously powerful but also exceedingly sensitive . . . Just who, in Riga's mind, were these enemies? Mere fear of Moscow would scarcely have made Riga behave with such extreme caution . . .

Riga, of course, had good reason to be worried about Moscow. The duke and duchess had even more to fear. A second story, which had spread immediately throughout Tallinn, was that the duke and his entourage had increased their speed considerably between Vigala and Märjamaa, and that at the Märjamaa parsonage, where they spent the night, some of the duke's guards had watched all night, fully clothed and armed, with their arquebuses and powder horns and bags of ammunition close at hand. All because a warning had been delivered to the duke as he travelled along the highway: From Viljandi, or somewhere, a force of several hundred Muscovites was moving west, intent on taking the duke and duchess and their retinue prisoner.

"Well, it's true enough – the Grand Duke did lament for years that the duke's wife, our queen that is, should by rights be handed over to him," Märten said.

But Balthasar would not have learned who it was, in addition to the Grand Duke, that the inhabitants of Riga feared in connection with Duke Johan – had it not been for something that, in accordance with God's inscrutable will, happened to Märten a week after the duke's arrival.

This is the story: The schooner belonging to Hans of Torstholm lay gently rocking at its berth off the timber wharf in the inner harbour. Every day, Hans went to Merchant Luhr's place or tried to intercept him right there, in the harbour, in an attempt to claim his cargo of roof tiles, so that he could set sail for home before the sea froze over. But the matter of the roof tiles dragged on from one day to the next. For although Merchant Luhr made daily visits to the harbour, he had much more important business on his mind.

The splendid vessel, *Ursus Finlandicus*,* property of Turku's gentry, in which the duke had sailed to Danzig to woo his bride, had for some reason been left behind in Poland. In Tallinn, Herr Horn had begun hurriedly to look for a new ship to transport the duke back

* The Finnish Bear (Latin).

home. Of the twelve or so ships already at their winter moorings, he had selected Herr Luhr's *Olaf*. It was a fairly roomy three-master that would easily accommodate the duke's retinue and all their belongings. The horses were to be shipped by schooner later. So Hans and his men, Märten among them, could do nothing but wait on their low deck, watching the painters painting and the carpenters hammering on the *Olaf*, and Herr Luhr making daily visits to the captain on the opposite side of the harbour.

In the evenings Hans left his yawl in Märten's care (there were only five men on board) and, skirting the long row of docked barges, walked to the custom house to play a game of dice and drink ale with the toll master and his men, for the toll-master also hailed from Torstholm. On occasion men from the *Olaf* stopped by at the custom house. The ship had been moored directly across from it for a week already, a fine ship, now spruced up to be even finer, just waiting for the duke and duchess and their retinue. And from time to time, when the players at the custom house looked out of their windows, as people with lanterns happened to be moving about on the deck or on the ladders of the *Olaf*, they would see the yellow balustrades of the railings and the stairways, freshly painted in honour of the duke, flare into view in the lantern light and gleam like gilded bottles in a row. And a man going out onto the pier to relieve himself between swigs of ale would hear, above the slap of the waves against the icy pilings, the flapping of the five-cubit sails against the *Olaf*'s masts rising high into the darkness.

On the afternoon of December 2, a boat from the custom house pulled up alongside Hans' schooner. Hans was told to put on a clean coat and to appear at the custom house.

"What the devil do they want with me all of a sudden . . . ? A 'clean coat' indeed . . ."

But when Hans was rowed back to his ship an hour later, his Sunday coat smelling slightly of tar was a bit snug, and he planted his feet in their sealskin boots wide apart, and a faint odour of juniper spirits wafted from him.

"Well, Märten, now I have sold my hide for thirty marks. And yours as well."

The duke and duchess, with their bags and baggage and all their retainers, would board the *Olaf* on the morrow and set sail the morning following. When Hans had entered the custom house, he found not only the captain of the *Olaf* but Herr Horn himself waiting for him. They had stressed that they did not want to risk sending the ship into unfamiliar waters on its own, considering how valuable a cargo it would be carrying. On the recommendation of the harbourmaster and the customs master, Herr Horn had summoned Hans. He had posed ten questions to Hans and was convinced, after their exchange, that this sturdy, red-bearded fellow with his wandering eye really had been riding the western waters of the Finnish Gulf for thirty years, from its northern to its southern ports and back again. And then Herr Horn had offered to pay Hans thirty marks if he would take the wheel of the *Olaf* into his hands and carry the burden of responsibility upon his shoulders.

"But what was it you said about my hide?" Märten asked.

"I told them I would take my helmsman along to assist me."

"I see. And what will the helmsman get for it?"

"Well, Herr Horn is paying me, for thirty years of sailing, a mark a year, but you haven't been on the sea for even four years yet, and that includes your time privateering with me. So, three marks is more than enough for you."

Märten had not related this detail to Balthasar earlier. And when now, sixteen years later, it came out, either in the sauna as he whittled his spoons or over an ale at the Green Frog, Balthasar remarked caustically:

"A real skinflint he was . . ."

But Märten replied: "Look, I've been going out to sea with the men of Kalamaja from the time I was still wetting my pants. He couldn't very well pay me a mark a year for all those years now, could he?"

In any event, Märten moved aboard the *Olaf* the next morning, along with his skipper, and watched from the high poop deck as the duke and his entourage boarded the ship.

The duke and his wife were dressed in Burgundian velvet of grass-hopper green and hooded cloaks of tightly woven grey silk, to shield them from the damp autumn wind. They trotted at the head of their courtiers, side by side on two grey-brown horses, down the long pier and all the way to the *Olaf*'s gangway. There the duke sprang nimbly out of his stirrups, helping the duchess down from her sidesaddle and accompanying her up the gangway. Upon closer view, it was clear that under her powdered face and rouged cheeks she was considerably older than her husband. Though shivering in the cold and the wind, she attempted a brief smile at their attendants and then quickly drew the duke into their cabin.

Herr Horn and the other worthies accompanied the couple aboard ship. The duchess' entourage followed in their wake: priests, ladies-in-waiting, dwarfs and Polish servants bearing the heavy dowry chests. When Märten mentioned the chests, Balthasar recalled the way he had once peered down from Doctor Friesner's window at the arrival of the coadjutor, and how the man's trunks had been carried into the house after him. The thought flashed into his mind, as it had at that distant time: It was as if great wealth had the magical power to transform prominent men into powerful men, even as it became a disfiguring hump so heavy that it could only be transported piecemeal by others following at their heels . . . He recalled something else: even twenty years ago, he had thought with wry amusement: didn't his image of wealth as a hump on a man's back come from the complete absence of any such hump on his own – since there was not the faintest sign of a protuberance on his flat shoulder blades . . . ? Lord, if there had ever been a time in his life when he might have felt the slightest prickling of an incipient wing, then perhaps twenty years ago, when he owed not a shilling to anyone, when he had a little money towards his studies jingling in his pocket and the muscles of his legs throbbed at the prospect of leaping into the halls of higher learning . . . But now, the tiles he had ordered for his roof were still not paid for; he was just about out of money, and his chronicle, if it did indeed ever appear in print, would probably bring him more problems than profit. Furthermore, he had debts amounting to about six hundred marks, five hundred of which were owed to *that one* . . . And the thought of Elsbet stung like the thorn of a sweetbrier bush inside him . . .

Following close upon the trunks came mercenary soldiers with halberds and swords, and behind them a group of Tallinn's merchants and their journeymen carrying lengths of fabric that flapped in the wind, rolls of tanned leather and bundles of pelts, and small chests with handles, containing silver dishes or even gold jewellery – all designed to tempt the royal couple into making a purchase. Until darkness fell, there was a steady back and forth of untold numbers of people on the pier. But at dawn the ship set sail.

The sunrise was ominously blood-red, and the south-west wind blew in such violent gusts that it would have been wiser to postpone the departure. But the duke had made his decision and announced it, and rulers must always appear to have a pact with the Almighty with regard to the weather and other such matters. Märten said:

"I don't know whether the captain of the *Olaf* even dared broach with the duke the subject of postponing the trip. But I heard Hans tell the captain that although the winds blowing from the direction of the islands of Paljassaare might not yet be considered a storm, as of midday he would advise against shitting into the wind."

"Why?" the captain asked.

"The turd will fly back in your face," Hans replied.

Then they cast off, the pilot boats guiding them out of the harbour. If the captain had more to say, no-one could hear it any longer, for the guns in the harbour and the cannons in the towers facing the sea joined in a salute in honour of the duke, adding such a thunderous roar to the roar of the wind that for some time nothing else could be heard.

Had they headed west between the islands of Suurup and Naissaare, they would have been sailing directly into a strong south-west wind. On Hans' advice, the captain of the *Olaf* decided to proceed north-northwest, keeping to the eastern shore of Naissaare for shelter, and to head north-west only after he had passed the island.

But before they could reach the protection of the island's south-eastern tip, the ship was caught up in a wild dance. On the other side of the islands of Paljassaare, the swells grew high enough to rise above the eyes of the ship's figurehead, washing over the portside with such force that at times the water was a foot deep on deck. But at first, everyone put on a good face, and the captain went into the duke's cabin to explain to him (for he realised that this was what the duke would want) that such weather was frequent in the Gulf of Finland – that it was but an everyday matter for the seamen.

"And it was true," said Märten. "It was not the storm of the century, not at first. It was the kind of storm that comes about every five years."

In the afternoon, the southern tip of the island began to provide some shelter from the elements. The wind had blown the sky clear of clouds. The sun shone. And the calm of the sea seemed so complete that the courtiers, their faces green, dragged themselves up onto the deck for a breath of fresh air.

Märten asked, as he smoothed the handle of a little wooden soup-spoon with a piece of glass: "Do you know who else was on board? I recognised him at the railing of the deck below."

"Who?"

"Doctor Friesner."

"Oh-ho!" cried Balthasar, standing up from his stool in surprise. "You never told me that before. What was he doing there?"

"He was doing what he does. The duke had met him in Riga and convinced him to come aboard. To minister to the high-born . . ."

But in the shelter of the island, the royal pair found the voyage so delightful that the duke led the duchess by the hand, out to the stern-castle, to gaze at the dark-purple sea with its bright, foaming white-caps. And it was more than a little odd to see him put his arm around his weak-kneed wife's waist and shoulders to support her, and whisper encouragement in her ear as her hair tickled his lips (she seemed to have a bad case of seasickness), and to see him kiss her earlobe, not seeming to care in the least that Hans of Torstholm was standing right there, near them, feet firmly planted on the deck, peering determinedly at the sea over the big wheel, yet aware of everything going on, of course. What was really odd was that she did not seem to mind the presence of strangers at all. Their attendants put two chairs for them next to the railing, side by side, and the duchess instructed that they be placed right up against each other, and then she sat down and actually laid her head on the duke's shoulder.

"*Hm*," said Balthasar, "so it wasn't merely a marriage of convenience for interests of state?"

"*Khm.* Guess it wasn't," Märten said, popping a salted bean into his mouth. "But I'm just describing what.I saw."

Balthasar drank some ale, aware of the bitter liquid slightly relieving the foolish dejection he felt, but without dispelling it entirely. Dejection – because he was trying to recall a time that Elsbet had rested her head on his shoulder in the presence of strangers, and he could not remember a single such instance in their eight years of marriage.

But the duke and duchess did not sit on the deck for long. The wind soon penetrated their fur coats. The waves gathered new force. They stood up, and their personal attendants – who were themselves struggling to keep their balance as the ship lurched and tossed – helped them across the wheelhouse gallery and to the ladder. At the top of the ladder, the duke handed his wife momentarily over to the care of the attendants, paused, planting his feet wide as he gripped the railing, and beckoned to Märten, who was standing next to Hans.

"What did he want with you?"

"Nothing much. He let go of the railing and rummaged in his pockets. Almost landed on all fours. And I didn't know whether to offer him support or not – whether it was permitted to touch him."

"Come now—"

"You never know – maybe some courtier would've raised an alarm and shouted at me to keep my hands to myself – I didn't need trouble like that. But the duke managed to grab the railing and keep himself upright. And he'd found a silver thaler in his pocket as well."

"For you?"

"Yes indeed. He put it into my hand and said: 'Drop this into the helmsman's pocket – that he remain vigilant.'"

"*Ha-ha-ha-haa*," Balthasar laughed, "you've never had much luck when it comes to money . . ."

The helmsman did indeed need to be vigilant, for no sooner had they passed the northern tip of Naissaare than the storm sank its teeth into their portside and the dance – much wilder than earlier that morning – started up again. Now they had to reef both the headsail and mainsail and, using the gaff sail on the mizzenmast, they tried to stay more or less on course by tacking. But Hans was seriously worried that the south-west storm might drive them onto Tallinn's notorious shoals. None of the duke's men ventured on deck in the turbulence, except when, to the delight of the seagulls, one or another of the braver lords lunged towards the railing, eyes bulging, as though he had swallowed a frog.

As twilight fell, the fury of the storm only grew. A dense winter darkness descended upon the sea, through air thick with spray from the roiling waves. It was most extraordinary, how, in the impenetrable darkness, one could sense with particular intensity the tempest raging around them and the ship creaking and rocking and floundering in its grip, without seeing a thing other than two swaying lanterns and two forecabin windows and occasional gleams of light on the creaking ropes and the wet boards of the deck.

At eleven that night, the captain and his helmsman were standing next to Hans, trying to determine how far to port they should keep in this storm. They had no other way of setting their course than by the force of the icy spray stinging the left side of their faces and the sound of the waves slamming against the ship's hull. The captain shouted above the storm into Märten's ear, to go below and bring up something warm to eat from the duke's cook for him and the skipper.

"And then what happened?" Balthasar asked.

"Nothing. I left them there at the wheel, with two lanterns, and went below."

"Did you see the duke and his wife there?"

"I did. I looked through the window of the stern cabin."

The innkeeper, bowing, put a goblet of Rhine wine on the table. Balthasar nudged it towards Märten.

"And?"

"There's not much to tell. They were sitting on a wooden bench in the cabin. The ship was lurching so hard that they had to hold on to the bench and each other. The duchess' priests were kneeling on the floor and with great difficulty holding a portable altar – or whatever it was – in place, as two of the ship's carpenters tried to nail it to the floor. It seemed they were planning to hold a service. And that's when the cracking sound came."

"What was that like?"

"First, it was a kind of swish and then a tremendous crack and a crash."

"And what had actually happened?"

"I didn't understand at first. But it came from above us, so I ran back up. One of the lanterns was shattered, but the other one was still lit. The railing of the wheelhouse gallery was broken, and the mizzenmast, with all its rigging and ropes, was hanging with one end over the side of the ship, as if it had been chopped down at the base and fallen over the edge of the gallery. And three men were lying on the sterncastle deck. Afterwards I learned that the helmsman of the *Olaf* had already gone to Our Lord, but the captain and my skipper regained consciousness by morning."

"So now you took the wheel?"

"Yes. Their other helmsman and I took turns at it."

"And that's when it happened?"

"Well, at first there was all kinds of confusion and activity as they chopped the mast loose from the shrouds and threw it overboard."

"But what happened after that?"

"Confound it, I already told you all about that once . . . Fool that I was. And you're the only one who knows about it . . ."

"Tell it to me again," Balthasar urged, looking at Märten with an oddly insistent look. "Just when did it actually happen?"

"Well, I guess it was about two hours later, when I was at the wheel by myself. The lookout was up on the foremast. If, that is, he was still there – after the mizzenmast cracked. And the deck officer was on the fo'c'sle."

"Yes, and then?"

"Then I saw a man creeping up the ladder to where I was. As I said, one of the lanterns there was still lit."

"And what did the man say?"

"What did he say? . . . You know what he said. He told me to change

411

course. To sail north-east, to run before the wind. That we'd be beyond the island of Keri by morning, where the Grand Duke's ships would be waiting, and they'd tow us in to Narva."

"And how much did he offer you?"

"He patted his trousers' pocket . . . you could hear the coins jingling . . . handed me a coin, so's I could test it with my teeth. Genuine silver marks, struck in Tallinn. I know coins. And like I said, one lantern was still lit."

"How much did he offer you?"

"Three hundred."

"Heavens! . . . And what else did he say?"

"Well, he said the Grand Duke had every reason to claim the duchess for himself. Said she'd been promised to him by her brother . . . and as soon as the Grand Duke had her, there would be peace forever in Livonia and in all of the eastern part of Europe. And all of Russia would become Christian through and through . . ."

"Indeed! And all of this could be brought about by you, for three hundred marks?"

"Right."

"And what about you?"

"I was wondering why he didn't just hit me on the head and take over the wheel."

"But what did you *say* to him?"

"That's what I said."

"You're mad . . . And then?"

"He started to laugh and told me he was, after all, a merchant."

"And that's when you recognised him?"

"Why no. I told you, there was a lantern still burning."

"And you're sure it really was Melchior Krumhusen?"

"Absolutely. I've known him ever since the time he came to Tallinn to have his father's storehouses set to rights. I spent a good amount of time cleaning out their grain sheds and cellars. You remember, in '57."

"Yes I do. But what did you say to him?"

"What did I say . . . ? I said I would have to think a bit about a stunt like that . . . Told him to come back after the three o'clock bell. I'd give him my answer then."

"And he came back?"

"*Khm*. Confound it! He did and he didn't . . ."

"What do you mean? You haven't told me this part of it, have you?"

"No, I haven't. *Khm*. It's such a stupid story that . . . Well there I was, standing up there, trying to stay on my feet, guessing which way to turn the wheel to keep more or less on course. The north-west course, that is. The ship creaked and groaned every time the waves slammed against the hull. The air was thick with sea spray. All the royal Poles were crowded below in the cabin, singing their *laudamuses*.* I caught only snatches of the singing above the roar of the sea. And then I saw Krumhusen clambering up the ladder again – what a fool. Couldn't manage to wait until three – and me with no answer whatever for 'im . . . And then Krumhusen was clutching the rope, pulling himself up to where I was – and you know what? It was your old friend, Friesner!"

"Damnation! . . . And what did *he* want?"

"*Khm*. The same thing."

"What do you mean?"

"Well . . . I was to change course. Wanted me to head west. In the interests of the duke. He claimed that King Erik wanted to talk to his brother. And that if he did not get the chance to talk to him immediately, disasters and wars aplenty would surely befall Sweden and Poland and Livonia . . ."

"And you were the one who could prevent them all?"

"U-huh."

"How much did he offer you?"

* Songs of praise to God, from *laudamus*: we praise (Latin).

413

"Also three hundred. As I'm sitting here."

"And you?"

"I told him to come back after the three o'clock bell. That I needed to think it over."

"What did you decide?"

"*Khm.* I thought about it for a long time. And then I somehow got hold of one end of a rope. I tied the wheel for a moment and grabbed an axe from the same box. And went and chopped through the tenons of the ladder leading up to the deck where I was standing."

"And?"

"And then I pulled the whole thing up to the railing and dumped it overboard. Neither one of those gents could get to me without the ladder – not with the sea heaving as it was."

Balthasar was silent for a long while. Finally he asked:

"But what happened the next morning?"

"In the morning, though we'd nearly sunk, we were already near Ekenäsi, near the islands of Jussarö and all the rest, and this was the duke's territory."

Balthasar was silent for another little while, and Märten continued eating the oniony codfish broth that Balthasar had ordered for him from the tavern-keeper. At last Balthasar asked:

"And what happened to the duke and his retinue?"

"You know that well enough . . . They were all taken ashore, where they rested awhile and then went on to Turku."

"But what about you and Hans?"

"Hans spent a week recuperating at the parsonage at Inkoo. Rubbing himself with Doctor Friesner's ointments. And then we sailed back aboard a sloop, from Roseborg to Tallinn."

"And you didn't see the Doctor or Krumhusen again?"

"No."

"And you got your three marks from Hans?"

"To the last shilling."

"But tell me – why did you twice refuse an offer of three hundred marks? I never realised that you were so attached to the duke."

"What do you mean, attached? Look, I'd been taken aboard ship and I'd gone with the understanding that I would help them get to Turku..."

"But what did you really think when they tried to recruit you? You must have had some thoughts on the matter."

"Well, when Herr Krumhusen spoke to me, I thought, alright, all well and good, but this Lady Catharina is not going to lay her head on the Grand Duke's shoulder the way she rested it on her Duke Johan's. And I realised that the Grand Duke would no doubt lock this duke up in a prison tower – if he didn't impale him, that is."

"And what about what Friesner said?"

"Then I thought – well, the king must be really desperate to get his hands on the duke if he's willing to spend so much money on it that Doctor Friesner can offer me three hundred marks for it . . . And of course, I realised as well that those poor wretches – harebrained though they were, billing and cooing like that in front o' the whole world – they couldn't expect to be getting a honeymoon cake from the king any tastier than what the Grand Duke would serve them . . . There were already stories floating about to that effect, and, as it turned out, the king put them behind bars before six months had passed . . . But my thought was that it was not up to me – deep as they were in their great love – even if it really was our Gracious Majesty's command . . ."

Balthasar pushed the empty mug away. In his voice there was an unexpected tone of disapproval, even a sharp note of reprimand:

"What you're saying is that it was because of their – how did you put it — their billing and cooing in public that you didn't have the heart to change course? That's what saved their skins?"

Märten's pale eyes looked at him and he said, in a manner confoundedly casual and evasive and discerning:

"That's it. Unless we want to believe it was the hand of God."

"Fine!" Balthasar grunted, dismissing further discussion with a wave of his hand. (What could he do with this fool of a bell-ringer?) "But did it never occur to you, as they were bargaining with you, that three hundred was perhaps too small a sum? Did you think about how much they should offer to get you to do their bidding?"

"*Khm*. Well, since I didn't do their bidding, I suppose three hundred was not enough. But whether I thought about how much – yes . . . I did think, in both cases – what would I do if the old devil offered me three thousand instead of three hundred . . . ? All of Estonian territory, after all, had been sold in one fell swoop for nineteen thousand (you yourself told me that), and if they were to offer me a sixth of that price simply for steering the ship off course – would I do the deed?"

"And?"

"You know, I decided I would not, 'cause it would have been all too nakedly apparent just how desperate the king and the Grand Duke were to get their hands on this ship, and too damned amusing to have left them to their plight and pictured their distress."

"*Ho-ho-ho-ho*," Balthasar laughed, raising his mug to his lips for another draught of ale, but the mug was empty and his laugh, loud and resonant. "But what about the fact that, as you said, you'd been taken on board and accepted the assignment to help deliver them to Turku – how large a part did that play in your decision?"

Märten looked over his empty soup bowl at his old pal and current boss with an odd, somewhat quizzical look of someone cornered:

"*Khmmm*." It was his most emphatic grunt of the afternoon, and he rasped: "Confound it! It's not as if I had an apothecary's scale here for weighing powdered rubies and mouse-droppings, so's I could tell you 'how large a part' it played!"

Balthasar gave Märten half a mark to pay for the codfish broth and wine and ale. "You'll have some left over from this. Buy yourself another mug of ale. To commemorate your turn at the helm. I'm going to take a little walk."

Balthasar pushed his black beret to the back of his head and went out into a vacant Nunnade Street, out from under the low, smoky vaulted ceilings of the Green Frog.

It was a windless afternoon in late May, but frigid. The copper sky behind the towers of the monastery presaged a cold night, cold enough for the water jugs near the wells to be covered by a glassy layer of ice by morning, cold enough to turn the apple blossoms brown by dawn and to frost the scraggy surface of the town walls.

Balthasar did not want to go home yet. At home there was Elsbet, whom he would either have to avoid or ignore. Neither was a pleasant prospect. True, he had his study at home as well, and in the drawer of his lectern, a few good volumes worth reading, especially the *Eis heauton** of Marcus Aurelius, in the famous Amsterdam edition. Though he had attempted to read it eighteen years ago, only recently had he read it several times, and with real enjoyment . . . But today he knew his study was unheated, and on an evening as cold as this, it would be unpleasant . . . Yes, at home there were also the children. But the Devil knows . . . recently he had been playing with the little ones in a somewhat odd way, he had to admit. The day before yesterday, for example, he had suddenly noticed that he was sitting on the floor of the sacristy on the dogskin rug, with a knife in one hand and an alderwood stick in the other, and Balzer and Anna and Elisabet were kneeling or on all fours on the floor near him, and he was showing them how to carve cows – not in the usual way, but cows with matchstick legs. And the entire herd, including a couple of handsome red–green bulls, were grazing on the dogskin rug under the gaze

* *Meditations* (Greek).

417

of their somewhat self-conscious creator and three delighted little cowherds...

Balthasar had stood up – he, the children's father, had suddenly risen to his feet in painful embarrassment, not only because both Epp and Elsbet had been watching him and the children through the partly open sacristy door, but also because he had been stung by the realisation that these three dear little snub-noses on the floor with him, whose chattering and warmth and lively delight had drawn him to enter their world of play, were exactly as much – confound it – to an even greater extent – yes, to an even greater extent Elsbet's flesh and blood than his own! . . . And getting close to the children was unavoidably a way of getting close to Elsbet, who, for her part, had not deigned to approach him at all, nor to encourage him, her husband, to do so . . . Naturally, Elsbet continued to instruct and coddle the children as before (perhaps even more often and more obviously than before, as it seemed to Balthasar from what he had chanced to see out of the corner of his eye), but that did not mean there was in any way an attempt on her part to narrow the gulf between herself and her husband. Not at all. First of all, it was a wife's place to be involved with the children. Secondly, children did, after all, belong more to the mother than the father . . . At least *in hac re.*[*] Unfortunately.

And so – no, Balthasar did not head for home. But neither did he want merely to wander about. And since it was his habit, even on walks that he undertook for the purpose of reflection – and he had the time for these now – to stride along as if towards a definite goal, he set out along Nunnade Street, in the direction of St Olaf's, as though he knew exactly just where he wanted to go to mull over Märten's story.

He passed the town wells on the corner of Aida and Suurtüki streets. Two or three people drawing water greeted him. He went on, the buildings on his left in a cold, blue-green shade; the tops of the

* In this case (Latin).

418

façades on his right illumined by a bleak and feverish evening light. Passing the door of St Olaf's (the door was open, and, deep inside the church, someone was playing the organ), he paused for a moment and looked up. It did not surprise him that the cold bronze sky around the steeple was vacant, but in one corner of his heart he felt a slight pang of disappointment that the magic rope of the flying acrobats was no longer there . . . Balthasar turned into Tolli Street and marched up to the corner of Pikk Street. The more uncertain he became about where he was heading, the more decisively he strode on. He even picked up his pace. And then he came to a sudden standstill. From the cellar door of the Three Sisters, a grey-striped tomcat shot out and streaked across the street and through the cat-door of merchant Reppelen's gate, into his courtyard. Balthasar had already decided, before he got here, that this was where he was going.

He pushed open the gate, marched through the passageway and across the echoing courtyard, ducking three times under the blue and grey and white underwear and skirts and sheets hung out to dry on lines stretched between the walls. The cat had disappeared, but Balthasar now knew exactly where he was going. He came out of Reppelen's back gate, crossed the street and stood outside the sturdy, riveted oak door of Stolting Tower.

He knew that no matter which of the junior officers of the town militia happened to be the head watchman tonight, he would gain entrance. At least at Stolting Tower there still was a guard. Even though the councilmen had once more, as was common in peacetime, returned their stores of grain and salt and seal oil to several of the other towers. And so it was. Balthasar did not know the watchman with the booming voice who opened the door for him, but the man recognised Balthasar immediately:

"Oh-ho! Is the Muscovite at the town walls again?! (We didn't know 'bout it!) Well, 'cause Herr Pastor is come again to climb the tower for

419

a look around. You just go up, high as your legs'll take you. All the way up t' the Almighty's toes!"

Balthasar hurried up the high, narrow stone steps of the spiral staircase, pushing against the rough walls for support as he went. He did want to look around up there. He wanted to take in the town. Perhaps he also wanted to think over Märten's peculiar sea voyage. But now, somewhat out of breath here, in the dimness of the twisting stairwell, in this bark-beetle burrow inside the town walls smelling of limestone dust and dove-droppings and gunpowder soot, he repeated to himself for the thousandth time: Am I now really a cuckolded husband? Am I now really a rider of the white mare . . . ?

Each time he asked himself the question, he felt as though an iron glove were rummaging around in his innards. But now, here, he asked himself for the first time, after posing the other question for a thousandth time: Or have I, out of spite and stubbornness, leapt into the saddle myself? Without Elsbet having given me cause?

On the fourth level of the tower, Balthasar saw the heavy rumps of four culverins resting on log-mounts, and on the fifth level, defensive guns on their stands, aimed at the loopholes. He climbed further and came out into the circular room under the log ceiling of the tower. Continuing up a ten-rung ladder, he pushed open a trapdoor with his back and stuck his head out.

No, by God, Elsbet has given me no reason whatsoever for it.

He jumped onto the flat limestone slabs and looked around. Most of the conical roofs of the towers had been hurriedly dismantled at the outset of the siege, to prevent the enemy from destroying them with firearms or flames, and to provide flat surfaces for mortars and catapults. The rebuilding of the roofs had barely begun since the end of the siege. Stolting Tower was also missing its roof, and so Balthasar stood there, under the open sky, in the centre of a stone circle two cubits high and three thick, and at least twelve cubits across. He rested his hands on the edge of the wall and hoisted himself up onto it. Now he could take a good look at what lay around him.

This was not, of course, the tower of the erstwhile magic rope, the tower of his first intimation of wingless flight. No, it was not. St Olaf's – it now seemed to him – had almost swayed, fragrant with resin, under the heavens. This tower was much lower, but still, with its strong, thick-set leg and upright chest, it rose straight up out of the stone wall itself. It was this tower, with its stone torso, that was part of the very body of the town. Part of this grey town in the evening light, under a frosty, pale-green sky . . .

But when he gets home, Balthasar will simply ask Elsbet:

Do you love him?

And he knows already what she will say. Just as he has, over time, begun to anticipate people's replies and questions and turns of thought, begun to know what they will say a moment before they say it, in the same way that he knows, an hour ahead of time, what his wife will say. He knows she will look at him with her unusual, dark, oval eyes and shake her head. And then he will ask her – probably for no other reason than to tease both himself and his wife: But why do you not love him?

And Elsbet will answer – as he knows ahead of time: Because I am your wife.

And he, Balthasar, will think – he knows already what he will think . . .

But now, up here on the tower, he is thinking: This grey town on this frosty evening . . . On the horizon behind Kakumäe Hill, a yellow sunset. Here and there, between the bluish courtyard walls and the reddish rooftops dark in the shadows and glowing in the sunlight, apple trees with their sparse green clusters of buds, cowering in the cold. And right here, at the town wall, the sea, with its streaks of iron-grey. The same sea that Märten sailed in that storm . . . And suddenly Balthasar realises something:

It is one and the same. Entirely one and the same: A ship sailing across the sea. A town or country sailing through Time . . . The Stolting Tower here, like a *dansker* on the starboard side of a giant stone ship. And the towers Rosenkrans or Paks Margareeta and the turrets of the Great Coast Gate here below: the bow and bowsprit. Toompea there on the left: the sterncastle. The church steeples: the masts. St Olaf's: the mainmast. (Actually, St Olaf's should be the foremast, and the mainmast should be Holy Ghost! But so be it . . .) On the shores beyond the sea, the dukes and grand dukes and kings. And on the deck, it is he – who has come on board in order to steer the ship through Time . . . Between the covers of his chronicle . . . not into the harbours of dukes, grand dukes, or kings . . . but into the harbour of Truth . . . (The co-ordinates of which the Saviour did not, in the end, reveal to Pilate . . .) Yes, he, Balthasar, is at the helm, gripping the wheel, and those many who strove to thwart his efforts are unrecognisable in the darkness . . . For Märten had told him, soon after Mihkel's expulsion, how that snake had tried to steal the chronicle, it was not difficult to work out at whose behest . . . And if there was, as of now, no-one offering to bribe him to change course, then it could only be because they did not yet know about his chronicle. Thank God! But truly – Märten's ship sailing across the sea, and this town, sailing through Time (in his book) . . . what a parable-like parallel! The only difference being that his old friend Märten had given his answer sixteen years ago, but he, Balthasar, had yet to give his . . .

But he does know, clearly, what he will think after his wife has replied. He will think: She could have said to me: Because I love you. But I have lived with her for eight years and she has never in that time laid her head on my shoulder in the presence of others. Why shouldn't I be able to continue as before, if she at least admits: I do not love him, because I am your wife. That is enough for me. Since I also have my chronicle.

I have to summon strength for my answer . . .

He jumped down from the edge of the wall and turned to look at the sea. With his palms resting on its damp, rough surface he leant so far over the edge that it hid the town gate and strip of shore and harbour from view. Between the wall and the sky there was only the grey sea with a streak of yellow where the sun was setting.

He thought – perhaps he spoke out loud, for there was no-one about but the seagulls and God: I must gather strength for my answer. But for now I will go home and sit down next to Elsbet on the edge of the bed in my old, playful manner, and I will look into her eyes and ask:

Do you love him?

And she will shake her head, and I will ask: And why not?

And she will say: Because I am your wife.

And I will say: Then be my wife.

And she will be.

APPENDIX ONE

Notes

21. The Beguines: "holy women", who at the beginning of the 13th century began to form communities in the cities of the Low Countries. A Christian lay religious order independent of Church hierarchy, they dedicated themselves to a life of poverty and prayer, and to caring for the poor and sick. The movement spread rapidly throughout the Low Countries and to several towns and cities in the rest of Europe.

23. *Trinummus* (Three Coins): A comedy by Plautus (c. 254–184 B.C.), Roman dramatist, considered the greatest of his time by his contemporaries.

26. "In the sweat of your brow shall you eat bread . . ." (Genesis 3:19).

34. Thaler: A silver coin that was used for almost four centuries throughout Europe.

38. Susi-Hans (died 1549): Estonian poet and translator, first to translate biblical verses into Estonian. Died of the plague as a very young man.

62. His Jagiellon: Catharina [Catherine], of the Jagiellonian Dynasty, a royal dynasty that included the kings of Poland, Hungary, Bohemia and the grand dukes of Lithuania, reigning in Europe from the 14th through the 16th centuries.

87. "Malyuta, the Persson of Muskovy": Malyuta Skuratov (died 1573). Tsar Ivan IV's most trusted counselor, a cold-blooded killer, ordered countless executions and the public torture of those suspected of disloyalty.

88. "Jöran Persson, the Swedish Malyuta" (1530–68): Most trusted counsellor of King Erik XIV. Ruthless and vindictive, responsible for countless executions, including of all aristocrats suspected of plotting against the king in 1567.

107. *Oprichniki* (Russian): Special forces or personal guard for Tsar Ivan IV, essentially the secret police of the *oprichnina*, a separate territory created in 1565 by Ivan the Terrible on lands seized from their owners, most of whom he condemned to death.

149. Draught of a ship: The distance between the waterline and the bottom of the keel.

161. Trinitarians: Catholic mendicant order founded in the twelfth century. Their mission was to free Christians held captive by non-believers.

161. The Rzeczpospolita: Polish for Commonwealth or Republic, referring to the union in 1569 of the Kingdom of Poland and the Grand Duchy of Lithuania as the Polish-Lithuanian Commonwealth.

168. Manormen: Term used for mounted troops in the service of the landed gentry, and for militias of the manor lords, which could include freemen as well as foreigners. In the novel, the manormen are depicted mostly as adventurers and mercenaries.

168. "I will make your seed as the sand of the sea, which cannot be numbered for multitude" (Genesis 32:12).

177. From Samuel 7:12: Samuel took a stone and set it between Mispeh and Shen and called it Ebenezer, saying, "Hitherto the Lord has helped us."

195. May Day revelries: Folk festivals in Northern Europe dating back to ancient times, in celebration of the newly awakened spring and of youth and fertility.

235. Hat of hope: A "hat of nails" (fingernails). It renders the wearer invisible. According to folk wisdom, cut fingernails should not be left lying about lest the Devil make a magic hat of invisibility for himself.

237. St Bartholomew's Night: The night of 23–4 August 1572, when hundreds of Huguenot Protestants were killed in Paris, apparently on the orders of the Catholic King Charles IX of France and his mother, Catherine de Medici. This set off a wave of killings all over France, resulting in the massacre of many thousands of Huguenots.

237. Milk-brothers: Boys who have been nursed by the same woman, but are not related to one another.

238. *Venusberg* (German: Venus mountain): Mythical mountain in Germany, which was said to contain in its hidden caverns the court of Venus, hidden from mortal men. According to legend, the knight Tannhäuser spent a year there worshipping the goddess.

238. A Dane at the Herrevad monastery: Tycho Brahe, who on 11 November 1572, recorded a new star as bright as Venus and visible even in daytime. Brahe's many observations surpassed in accuracy all others of his time.

248. Henricus de Lettis: Henry of Latvia: A priest and chronicler who wrote *Livonian Chronicle of Henry*, giving eyewitness accounts of events in Livonia from 1180 to 1227.

249. One-foot blacksmith: The term "one-foot peasant" refers to peasants with a small plot of land for which they owed the manor one day of work per week. The one-foot blacksmith has a similar arrangement with regard to land use.

250. Renner, Johannes (1525–c.1583): A chronicler, the author of *The Livonian Chronicle 1556–61*, which recounts the rise of Ivan IV. Balthasar encounters him in *The Ropewalker*.

257. Saunaman: A landless peasant who lived in a small hut or in the sauna on the landowner's property.

262. The viper-king: According to folklore, the king of snakes was the size of a horse, with a crown like a cock's red comb.

278. *Magdeburg Centuries* (published 1559–74): Compiled by several Lutheran scholars known as the Centuriators of Magdeburg, under the direction of Matthias Flacius. It traces the continuity of the Christian faith over thirteen centuries to 1298, focusing on one century at a time. (Centuriators: Historians who distinguish time by centuries – described as a "revolutionary method of presenting history".)

288. Carnival mask: Kross uses the Middle Low German word *Schoduvel* – mask here, meaning "scare-the-devil" mask, worn in order to scare off the evil spirits of cold, death and danger.

300. *Miles Gloriosus* (The Braggart Soldier) by Plautus. (See note to p.23.)

307. Lufft, Hans (1495–1584): Printed first complete edition of Luther's Bible in 1534, with illuminations in gold and colours by Lucas Cranach. In the forty years following, Lufft printed more than 100,000 copies of the German Bible.

326. Augsburg Confession: The primary confession of faith of the Lutheran Church, submitted at the Diet of Augsburg in 1530 to the Holy Roman Emperor Charles V. Considered to be one of the most important documents of the Reformation.

326. *Formula concordiae* (1577): Lutheran statement of faith, the work of a group of Lutheran theologians and churchmen. By addressing the quarrels that had arisen after the death of Luther between his disciples and the Melanchthonites, it was a major factor in the preservation of Lutheranism.

327. Buridan's ass: An ass between two identical stacks of hay starves to death because it cannot make a rational decision as to which one to eat. The story satirises the philosophy of moral determinism of the French philosopher Jean Buridan (1295–1363), and in illustrating the consequences of indecision, it had a strong influence on the Reformation.

368. "Gigantic, sickly-yellow comet": The Great Comet of 1577. It passed close to the Earth and was seen by people all over Europe.

422. *Dansker* (German): A toilet facility in medieval castles and fortresses. Often visible as a box-like protuberance on an outer wall.

APPENDIX TWO

Selected Historial Figures

Catharina Jagiellon: (1526–83) Sister of Sigismund II Augustus, married Duke Johan in 1562, becoming Duchess of Finland: 1562–83; and Queen of Sweden: 1569–83. She was talented and accomplished, spoke Latin and Italian and was wooed by Ivan IV of Russia, Duke Albert of Prussia, and Archduke Francis Ferdinand of Austria. When Erik XIV imprisoned his brother Johan in 1563 (on a charge of treason), Catharina chose to accompany her husband. She bore two children during their four-year confinement in Gripsholm Castle. The years of imprisonment forged a strong bond between them. She remained a devout Catholic, influencing Johan in politics and religious policy in favour of Catholicism. She also negotiated with the Pope regarding a counter-reformation in Sweden.

Erik XIV: (1533–77). King of Sweden from 1560 to 1568. Intelligent, artistic, well-educated, but mentally unstable. Half-brother of Duke Johan of Finland, whose political ambitions clashed with his own. After 1560, Erik became increasingly violent and paranoid, arresting and condemning to death may in his court. In 1563 he accused Duke Johan of high treason, declared war on him and subsequently imprisoned him. In 1568 the Swedish nobles rebelled and Erik was deposed. Duke Johan, who then became King Johan III of Sweden, had Eric imprisoned in various castles in Sweden and Finland until 1577, when he died after a meal of poisoned pea soup.

Horn, Henrik Klausson (Klausson is spelled Claesson in *The Ropewalker*): (1512–1595) Principal counsellor to Duke Johan, Horn was his closest adviser from 1558 to 1563. He subsequently served under Johan's half-brother, Erik XIV, King of Sweden, who in 1563 made him a colonel in the Livonian Wars, governor of Swedish Estonia and high military commander in the Baltic. When Erik was deposed and imprisoned in 1568, Horn lost his post. Under King Johan, during the Russian siege of Tallinn in 1577, Horn was in command of the forces defending the town, along with his son, Karl Henrikson. (Karl Henrikson visits Tõnis Maidel in Chapter 4 of this volume, to deliver to Maidel an offer from his father of an admiralship.)

Ivan IV, aka Ivan the Terrible, the Muscovite, the Grand Duke: (1530–84) Grand Duke of Muscovy from 1533 to 1547. The first to be crowned "Tsar of all the Russians": 1547–84. Created an empire from what had been a medieval state when he assumed power. Started the Livonian Wars, launching successful attacks against Tartu in 1558 and then Narva. For over two decades, Ivan battled varying coalitions of Denmark–Norway, Sweden, Lithuania, Poland, as he wreaked havoc in Livonia, until the wars finally ended with the Treaty of Plussa (Plyussa, Pljussa) signed by Russia and Sweden in 1583.

Johan III of Sweden: (1537–92) Ruled Finland as Duke from 1556 to 1563, and was King of Sweden from 1568 to 1592. A patron of arts and architecture, he married Catharina Jagiellon, sister of Sigismund II Augustus in 1562. She was Catholic, he Protestant. Together they attempted to close the rift between the Catholic Church and the Lutheran Church of Sweden. Johan was accused of treason by his brother, King Erik XIV, in 1563 and imprisoned with his wife Catharina. They were released by members of the high nobility in 1567. Johan was crowned King Johan III in 1568. He successfully fought Russia during the Livonian Wars, which ended with the signing of the Treaty of Plussa in 1583. (In *The Ropewalker*, Balthasar was sent by Dr Friesner across the frozen Gulf to take news of the outbreak of war with Ivan IV to the young Duke Johan in Turku, Finland. There Balthasar also met Henrik Horn, counsellor and adviser the duke.)

Kaiser Karl: (1500–1558) Holy Roman Emperor Charles V, reigning from 1519 to 1558. His domain, which included Spain, Germany, the Netherlands, most of Italy and much of Central and South America, was the first to be described as "the empire on which the sun never sets". In 1541 he embarked upon a disastrous expedition to recapture Algiers, which had been under the control of Ottoman Emperor Suleiman since 1529. (Kross describes the venture from the perspective of Tõnis Maidel, who recounts it to his sons, in Chapter 4 of this volume.)

Kruse, Elert (d. 1587) and Taube, Johann: Livonian noblemen. Shifted allegiances numerous times during the Livonian Wars, seeking to join whatever side offered the most in fame or fortune, whether it was the Order, Ivan IV, Magnus, or Poland. Kruse and Taube were captured by Ivan in the mid 1560s, kept prisoner for a time, and later served him in a diplomatic capacity. Their time in Muscovy (1564–71) overlapped with Ivan's *oprichnina* (1566–72), and their accounts of the tactics and horrors that characterised the *oprichnina* are among the original historical documents from that time. The two participated later with Magnus in the siege of Tallinn: 1570–71, after which they fled to Sigismund II Augustus in Poland. (In 1578 Kruse published a scathing condemnation of Russow's chronicle, entitled "A Forthright Rebuttal to the Livonian Chronicle".)

Magnus, Duke of Holstein: (1540–83) Prince of Denmark, younger brother of King Frederick II of Denmark, who bought the bishopric of Saaremaa–Läänemaa in 1559 and gave it to Magnus, on condition that he renounce rights to succession in Schleswig and Holstein. Magnus landed on the island of Saaremaa in 1560 and was immediately made bishop. (In Chapter 6 of this volume, the young Magnus, as a twenty-year-old, appears to Balthasar in a dream sequence.) In 1570 Magnus went to Moscow, where he took the oath of allegiance to Ivan IV, who pronounced him King of Livonia. In August of that year he set out from Moscow with 20,000 Russian soldiers, intending to conquer Tallinn, under Swedish control at the time. By March of the following year, he had abandoned the siege. (In Chapter 3, Magnus' siege is the reason that Balthasar's wedding to Elsbet is postponed for several months.) In 1577, having lost Ivan's favour the previous year, Magnus was taken prisoner by Ivan's forces at Wenden. Upon his release he renounced the royal title Ivan had conferred upon him.

Melanchthon, Philipp: (1497–1560) German theologian and reformer, friend of Martin Luther. He wrote the Augsburg Confession (*Confessio Augustana*), which became the official statement of faith of the Lutheran Church. A humanist and educator, he had an important role in founding and reforming public schools in Germany. (In Chapter 8, Balthasar describes disputes between the followers of Melanchthon and Flacius, and his own inability to determine "where the truth lies".)

Monninkhusen, Christopher/Christoph (aka Christoph von Münchhausen/Munchhausen: (d.1565) Declared himself Danish vicegerent in Livonia in 1558, announcing that Tallinn should become subject to the Danish crown. The citizens of Tallinn objected. Monninkhusen was ousted by Gotthart Kettler. (In *The Ropewalker*, he brutally put down the peasant rebellion of 1560. In Chapter 6 of this volume, he reappears as a figure in Balthasar's dream–memory–nightmare of the peasant uprising and the tortures inflicted upon the peasant king.)

Schenkenberg, Ivo, aka "The Livonian Hannibal" and "The Hannibal of the Greys": (c. 1548–79) Schenkenberg was encouraged by Sweden to organise the non-German peasants and train them as fighting troops against the Russians. In 1576 the Town Council designated him commander of a peasant fighting force, the members of which gained wide fame in Livonia as "the sons of Hannibal". They were active in 1577 in putting out fires started by the Russians' firebombing of Tallinn. (In Chapter 8 of this volume, Epp's son Tiidrik, who had joined Hannibal's forces, is reported to have been killed fighting those fires.) Ivo Schenkenberg and a unit of his men were captured in 1579 and subjected to a cruel death.

APPENDIX THREE

Archaic Units of Measurement

Cubit: length from fingertip to elbow: about 18 in./0.5 m.

Fathom: widest length between fingertips of outstretched arms: c. 2yd/1.8 m.

League: the distance a person could walk in an hour, commonly defined as 3 miles/4.8 k.m.

Span: width of palm plus length of thumb: c. 6 in./15 c.m.

Pood: c. 36–40 lbs/16–16. 38 k.g.

APPENDIX FOUR

Names of streets, gates, towers, villages and bridges

The words in parentheses in the translated names are not part of the Estonian names as listed, but are understood.

Aida: Storehouse (Street)

Apteegi: Apothecary (Street)

Härjapea: Oxhead (River)

Härmapõllu: Hoarfrost Field

Hobusepea: Horse's head (Street)

Hobuveski: Horsemill (Gate)

Hongasaare: Old-Pine Island

Hundimäe nukk: Wolf Hill Point

Jahuvärav: Flour Gate

Jänese küla: Rabbit Village

Kakumäe: Owl Hill

Kalamaja: Fish House (Village)

Kalarand: Fish Shore

Kannuvalajate: Pewterers' (Street)

Karja värav: Cattle Gate

Kellamäe: Bell Hill

Kiek in der Kök: Peek-into-the-Kitchen (Tower)

Kiriku: Church (Street)

Kivisild: Stone Bridge

Köismäe: Rope Hill

Kolmapäeva värav: Wednesday Gate

Kuldjala: Gold Foot (Tower)

Kuninga: King (Street)

Kureküla: Stork Village

Kuressaare: Stork Island

Läänemaa: Lääne County (lit. Western land)

Lai: Broad (Street)

Laitänav: Broad Street

Lasnamäe: Teal Hill

Lontmaaker: Ropemaker (Rise)

Lossi: Castle (Street)

Lossiplats: Castle Square

Lühike jalg: Short Leg (Street)

Mäealuse: Base-of-the-hill (Street)

Munkade: Monks' (Street)

Munkadevärav: Monks' Gate

Mustjõe: Black River

Mustkoopa: Black Inlet

Müürivahe: Between-the-Walls (Street)

Neitsimäe: Virgin's Hill

Nõelasilm: Needle's Eye (Passage)

Nunnade tänav: Nuns' Street

Nunnatorn: Nun's Tower

Nunnaväray: Nun's Gate

Paks Margareeta: Fat Margaret
(Tower)

Pikk: Long (Street)

Pikk Hermann: Tall Hermann
(Tower)

Pikkjalg: Long Leg (Street)

Pikksild: Long Bridge

Pirita: St Bridget's (Convent)

Pleekmäe: Bleaching Hill

Pühajõe: Holy River

Puusilla: Wooden Bridge

Rataskaevu: Wheel-well (Street)

Ristimäe: Hill of the Cross

Rüütli: Knight (Street)

Saiakang: White Bread Way

Seppade: Blacksmiths' (Street)

Soesoo: Warm Marsh

Suur karja: Big Cattle (Street)

Suur-Paljassaare: Big Barren Island

Suursaare: Big Island

Suurtüki: Cannon (Street)

Tollitänav: Customs Street

Tönismäe: St Anthony's Hill

Toomkirik: Dome Church, Cathedral

Toomkoppel: Dome Pasture
(Cathedral Hill Pasture)

Toompea: Cathedral Hill (the upper
town)

Vaestepatuste: Poor Sinners' (Road)

Väike Rannaväray: Small Coast Gate

Väike Rataskaevu: Small Wheel-well
(Street)

Väike-Toomi: Small Dome (Street)

Vanakuradi Vanaema: Devil's
Grandmother

Varessaare: Crow Island

Veskiväray: Mill Gate

Viru väray: Viru Gate

Newport Community
Learning & Libraries
2 4 MAR 2018